BITTERSWEET JUSTICE

BITTERSWEET JUSTICE

Victoria Burks

TATE PUBLISHING
AND ENTERPRISES, LLC

Bittersweet Justice
Copyright © 2011 by Victoria Burks. All rights reserved.

No part of this publication may be reproduced, stored in a retrieval system or transmitted in any way by any means, electronic, mechanical, photocopy, recording or otherwise without the prior permission of the author except as provided by USA copyright law.

Scripture quotations marked "NIV" are taken from the *Holy Bible, New International Version* ®, Copyright © 1973, 1978, 1984 by International Bible Society. Used by permission of Zondervan Publishing House. All rights reserved.

This novel is a work of fiction. Names, descriptions, entities, and incidents included in the story are products of the author's imagination. Any resemblance to actual persons, events, and entities is entirely coincidental.

The opinions expressed by the author are not necessarily those of Tate Publishing, LLC.

Published by Tate Publishing & Enterprises, LLC
127 E. Trade Center Terrace | Mustang, Oklahoma 73064 USA
1.888.361.9473 | www.tatepublishing.com

Tate Publishing is committed to excellence in the publishing industry. The company reflects the philosophy established by the founders, based on Psalm 68:11,
"The Lord gave the word and great was the company of those who published it."

Book design copyright © 2011 by Tate Publishing, LLC. All rights reserved.
Cover design by Sarah Kirchen
Interior design by Christina Hicks

Published in the United States of America
ISBN: 978-1-61346-729-9
1. Fiction / Christian / Suspense
2. Fiction / Christian / Romance
11.10.11

DEDICATION

I wish to dedicate this book to my friend of thirty-five years, Sue Taylor. In those years we've supported each other, encouraged each other, interceded in prayer for each other, laughed together, cried together, taken trips together, shopped together, drank tea together, watched old movies together, and hung out together—all the above, in my opinion, like no one else can but us.

ACKNOWLEDGMENTS

First, and always, I wish to thank my husband, William, and my family for your love and encouragement at all times. Thank you to all my friends—you know who you are—for all your supportive comments. God bless you, Pastor Darryl and Faith, for your faith in me to accomplish my dream. A special thanks to you, Kay, for your willingness to guide me in each project and your candidness when critiquing my work. And to my friends Jan and Kyle Willaford, Jim Jenkins, and Craig Wyant, thank you for sharing information I needed to advance the plot of *Bittersweet Justice*. Also, I wish to express my gratitude to those in my church family who pray for me, support me, and encourage me in this call God has placed on my life. And, as ever and always—to God be the ultimate glory.

"The Lord has done this, and it is marvelous in our eyes" (Psalm 118:23).

WINDS OF CHANGE

Into your presence, dear Father, we go.
It's you, oh Lord, we desire to know,
Ever ready to learn and do your will,
Watching your everlasting Word fulfill
Signs, wonders, and miracles from above,
Demonstrations of your unfailing love,
Only your salvation setting captives free,
The Holy Spirit—Comforter, Teacher, and Friend
Guiding wayward sons and daughters to Thee.

Roberta Palmer
Victoria Burks

CHAPTER 1

"Son, listen to me! Haven't you suffered enough from the past? How can you consider returning to that horrid place? You're just asking for more heartbreak."

Colin Lambert darted a glance toward his upper arm, his mother's touch like the singe of a hot iron. He pulled away from her grip. "Mother, you may have forgotten Dad's words after the trial, but I haven't. He said he didn't kill Grandfather Lambert. I've never known him to lie."

Eileen Lambert Hemphill stood motionless, her crisp blue eyes wide with shock and disbelief at her son's reaction. Regaining her composure, she glanced at her arm, which she held suspended in the air. Straightening, Elaine rested both hands on her hips, digging her heels into the carpet, like a soldier settling into a trench armed and ready for battle.

"Fairy tales are for children."

Pulling himself to his full height of six feet, two inches, Colin's eyes narrowed. "Yes, I was only a boy at the time. But I remember how truth blazed in Dad's eyes. I vowed to find Grandfather's killer someday." Colin shook his head. "I can't believe the jury convicted Dad. No one will ever convince me that Dad murdered his own father. I've always believed the true assassin is stashed away in Oklahoma's 'black gold' country.

Although his identity has remained anonymous for more than a quarter of a century, I'm determined to unearth the scoundrel."

Colin turned aside to stare into the fireplace. The flames that licked at the sides of the brick seemed to part like curtains on a stage, the final act of his father's trial playing in his mind.

Sitting on the edge of the wooden bench in the musty courtroom beside his mother, twelve-year-old Colin's flesh prickled when the bailiff handed the stern, wizened-faced judge a folded paper. Feeling the touch of a hand on his shoulder from someone in the row behind him, Colin turned briefly to smile at his great-aunt Beatrice and great-uncle Maxwell, siblings of his murdered grandfather, Braxton Lambert. With a trembling hand Colin smoothed the lock of his dark brown hair inching upward from the crown of his head, the rebellious strand curling upward in spite of his attempt to keep it in place.

Judge Quail laid aside his reading glasses and turned to the left. "Has the jury reached a verdict?"

His heart pounding, young Colin eyed the jury foreman's slow rise to his feet. A deeper hush settled over the room—the silence clanging in Colin's ear like the sound of cymbals played at a Fourth of July parade. He wiped away the beads of perspiration on his upper lip with the back of his hand.

"Yes, we have, Your Honor."

The judge turned his attention on Stuart. "Will the defendant rise?"

Colin darted his eyes back and forth between the jury and his father. Again, the judge addressed the foreman. "And what say you?"

"We the jury, find the defendant, Stuart Lambert, guilty in the first degree for the murder of his father, Braxton Lambert." The gasps from the courtroom spectators sounded like an off-tune musical note sung in unison by a choir.

Closing his eyes, Colin flattened his palms against his ears. The pent-up air he'd held captive in his lungs rushed from his lips. No! It couldn't be true. Brushing away tears, he turned toward his father. Stuart stared back at him, his expression a sea of anguish. "I didn't kill your grandfather, Son. You must believe me." Neither Colin nor his father noticed the flash of the camera when a tall brawny newspaper reporter snapped their picture, his expression a mask of compassion.

Before Colin could respond, his mother had ushered him from the courtroom, parting the crowd of shocked onlookers uttering their disbelief of the jury's decision. Outside the Osage County Courthouse, a throng of press had greeted the Lamberts, each reporter hoping to be the first to interview a member of the prestigious family. When a television newsman thrust a microphone into Eileen's face, Colin had watched his mother shove it away with such intensity the man had lost his balance and fell onto the concrete steps. Noting his father's exit from the building, Colin had run and clasped his arms about Stuart, unleashed tears staining his suit. It had taken two deputies to pry Colin from his dad.

Within moments Eileen had her son in tow, pulling him toward their car. Just before they'd reached the automobile, Colin had turned to see the county sheriff escort his dad to a waiting vehicle for transport to the county jail to await his day of sentence. A few days later, his mother moved them to St. Louis, Missouri, to begin a new life.

Eileen's resounding expletive jolted Colin back to the present. His lips thinned. "Mother, can't you see returning for Uncle Max's funeral is an ideal time to put in motion a plan to clear Father's name? I should have started the quest to find Grandfather's killer before now, but George needed me at the agency."

Eileen backed away from Colin's entreating gaze, her complexion so flushed her shoulder-length, platinum-blond hair clasped

BITTERSWEET JUSTICE 11

stylishly at the back of her neck paled to the shade of unbleached flour. "You're living in a fantasy world. Stuart Lambert was a brutal man," she said, her mouth pinched with disgust.

Colin stared at his mother, shaking his head. "I don't recall Dad that way at all, just the opposite, in fact."

"With you, yes. But I suffered numerous times from his outbursts of temper."

Wincing, Colin recalled his parents' many heated discussions. Eileen couldn't understand why her husband preferred to sit on a hillside attempting to capture the beauty of the landscape on canvas when he could take his place as heir apparent in the family enterprise, the sale of his artwork not supporting her in the fashion she desired. Often Colin saw Stuart emerge from his bedroom, shoulders slumped, his ebony eyes shimmering with hurt and regret—whether he despised the quarreling, his marriage, or both, Colin never knew.

For that matter, Colin remembered, neither did Braxton comprehend his son's lack of ambition in the oil firm. The two had quarreled over the issue the morning Braxton had been found slumped over his desk, Stuart standing next to the murdered body, his own firearm, a .38-caliber handgun, gripped in the palm of his hand.

At the trial Stuart had testified he'd come in from the stables and had just reached the upper level of the house when he'd heard the shot, running back down the servants' stairs to check on his father. Stuart said he didn't remember picking up the gun but did recall the sound of a car racing away from the estate through the open window across from his father's desk.

Grayson, Braxton's manservant, had appeared in the office doorway, later testifying at the trial that the look on Stuart's face had been one of astonishment, not that of a cold-bloodied killer.

Stuart's attorney had argued that someone outside the open window could have fired the shot. During his cross examination, Sheriff Tucker had grudgingly agreed with the defense, counsel's premise based on the angle of the bullet found lodged in Braxton's chest, the coroner's report validating the theory. However, Stuart hadn't been able to explain how the firearm, which he'd kept in his bedroom had become the murder weapon, or why his were the only fingerprints found on the gun. The prosecutor charged that Stuart had returned from his ride that morning, taken the gun from his room, returned downstairs, found his father alone and murdered him, Stuart's motive—anger against Braxton because he'd threatened his son with disinheritance if he didn't give up the foolish notion to become an artist and return to Lambert Oil.

In his efforts to establish reasonable doubt, Stuart's attorney had stated the real killer had stolen Stuart's gun, donned the pair of gloves found near the window to conceal his fingerprints, and then fired the weapon from outside the office, killing his victim, rushing from the scene as Stuart entered the office. And in a state of shock at finding Braxton dead, Stuart had unconsciously picked up the gun from the floor, thus the reason for his having the gun in his hand when Grayson had discovered him at the scene of the murder. But, with no evidence to prove another individual had motive or cause to kill his grandfather, the defense attorney's argument had been in vain.

Drawing a long, deep sigh, his eyes speckled with remorse, Colin bent his solidly built body forward to give Eileen a hug, kissing her cheek. The color of the chic, ice-blue satin robe hugging her pixie frame seemed to merge with the expression on her face. The image of a snow-covered Rocky Mountain lake flashed before Colin. "If it's the agency you're concerned about, don't be. George's sudden death took its toll, but business is back to normal now, everything running smoothly. Tom Thorpe is a great assistant. He's more than capable of handling the agency until I return."

Eileen stretched her lips so thin they seemed to disappear into her heart-shaped face. "How can you consider leaving me, knowing that I'm still in mourning for George?"

A snort of disbelief flew from Colin's mouth before he could prevent it. "I thought you discarded your widow's weeds the day you deposited the life insurance check in the bank."

Eileen flung away from her son, a look of haughty denial on her face. "Colin, how can you be so cruel?"

"Mother, you don't have to play the role of grieving widow with me. We both know you and George hardly spoke to one another."

Eileen tightened the belt on her robe, a guilty flush staining her cheeks. "I-I did care for my husband. And you know how much your stepfather loved you. He proved that by leaving you the advertising agency."

"For which I'll always be grateful. I loved and respected him too." Colin strode toward the door of his mother's home, contrition biting at his thoughts. Why did he allow his mother to goad him into saying things he regretted? *Forgive me, Father God.* He paused then turned to face her. "I'm sorry, Mother. I wish we could agree about this trip. But nothing you can say will convince me otherwise. I promised Father just last week during our visit that as soon as I could manage some time off from work, I intended to keep my promise to see justice done in his behalf."

Eileen seemed to wilt before his eyes. "Colin, you were just a boy. You're father would never hold you to that oath."

"That's what he said when he tried to talk me out of it. But I don't want Dad to die in prison. The doctor said the cancer has spread throughout his body, his prognosis less than six months of life. You know how hard I've tried to get the state to consider parole for health reasons, but the governor of Oklahoma won't budge. A life sentence is a life sentence to him. I think politics is the motive behind his decision. A hard business man,

VICTORIA BURKS

Grandfather's influence in the state and the generosity to his political party has yet to be forgotten."

Eileen's lips curled into a sneer. "You don't have to tell me how arduous he was. If you crossed him in any way, you could count on nothing from him. And he hated me ... tried his best to keep Stuart from marrying me—treated me like I was dirt under his feet. If your aunt Mary hadn't taken us in, we'd have been subjected to living on the street."

"But, Mother, you met George soon after your divorce from Dad. He took great care of us."

Eileen shrugged her shoulders. "Yes, you're right. It could have been much worse. I wanted us to have a decent life. And George did grant that."

Colin turned to leave and then did an about-face, his eyes glaring. "One more thing, Mother. When did you intend to tell me about Uncle Max's death? After I'd read his obituary in the *St. Louis Post Dispatch*? I'm sure by now every top newspaper in the country has printed at least a few lines about the late heir of Warren Delaney Lambert, one of Oklahoma's famous deceased oil barons."

At Eileen's guilty start, a half smile appeared on Colin's face, smoothing the cleft in his chin. "When Nicholas Girard phoned the office this afternoon concerned he hadn't heard from me, he indicated he'd telephoned you two days ago, moments after he'd been told Uncle Max had died."

Eileen lifted her chin into the air. "He did, but I thought it best to spare you the news"—she appealed to him with softened eyes—"so you wouldn't have to endure any grief from seeing Briarwood or any of the Lamberts again, dead or alive."

Sighing, Colin ran a hand through his hair. "I guess I can understand that. You could go with me, you know, if nothing else, to show respect for my family."

BITTERSWEET JUSTICE 15

Her chest swelled, indignation boiling in her eyes. "It will be raining ice in Hades before I ever plant my feet on Briarwood soil again."

He shrugged his shoulders then opened the door. "I'll phone to let you know where I'm staying."

Eileen, having followed him into the entryway, grabbed his arm. "Colin, please don't go. I beg you."

Colin drew back, startled by what he read in her eyes. "What is it, Mother? Why are you afraid?"

She lowered her gaze toward the floor. "I-I'm not frightened. I just don't want you to get hurt again." At the look of determination on his face, she stepped backward. "You're as Lambert as they come. I can see my words are futile. Nothing I say or do will deter you. Pardon me if I don't wish you luck. And don't say I didn't warn you when you return with an empty bag for all your hunting."

Sighing, Colin kissed his mother good-bye, pulling at his tie the moment he stepped outside, the day promising to be another scorcher. Why hadn't his mother been able to lay aside the bitterness she'd held toward the Lamberts? And what accounted for her fear of his return to Briarwood, the Lambert estate? She could deny it all day long, but he'd seen it, stark and brash in her expression.

About to enter his car, Colin stopped cold, his knuckles whitening as he gripped the door latch tighter than necessary. Could she be frightened he'd discover something that would implicate her in his grandfather's death? Releasing the tension from his body, he smiled. Eileen wasn't the warmest person on the globe, but she valued social standing far too much to mar her reputation with murder. Colin sobered. Or did she? Would he regret the promise he'd made all those years ago? *God, please don't let Father die until I uncover the truth.*

·····

The next morning, Colin drove into Haven, Oklahoma, situated on the southern edge of the Tall Grass Prairie in Osage County. He glanced at the deteriorated buildings. Not much, if anything had changed since he'd moved away. Located near the place known as Lambert Pool where his great-grandfather, Walter Lambert, a young wildcatter, had discovered oil in the late twenties, Haven had shot up practically overnight like similar towns during the "oil boom" era in the state. But Haven had outranked its sister towns by a wide margin in the collection of the four *B*s—Baptists, bootleggers, bordellos, and bandits. Not even the so-called lawmen could be trusted in this haven for every sin known to mankind, thus the reason for the town's name.

Colin smiled, recalling the old timers who'd congregate on the benches outside the town meeting hall to whittle on pieces of wood, have tobacco-spitting contests, and spin yarns about outlaws such as Henry Wells, Henry Starr, and Pretty Boy Floyd, who the elderly citizens claimed frequented Haven in the early days.

Colin felt sadness rush over him. All that remained of the oil town was a few businesses sprinkled in between boarded up windows along each side of a brick-paved street three blocks long. Outside the perimeters of Main Street, a few side streets yielded a crop of residences that had seen better days. If not for the many ranches surrounding the town, he guessed, the place would have become another ghost town, like so many other boom towns all across the state.

Colin slowed at the sight of the two-room houses just past the railroad tracks, the homes just a notch or two above what most people would call shacks. He eyed his mother's meager beginnings. He'd never met his maternal grandparents but had seen them from a distance one time, thanks to his overhearing a bystander in town mention their identity to Colin. His mother

BITTERSWEET JUSTICE   17

later told him her parents had moved to California to become itinerant farmers.

Suddenly, as memories flooded his soul, Colin felt twelve again as time and space seemed to migrate backwards. Before the death of Braxton, he'd been content in Haven, the status that accompanied his name meaning little to him as he played with friends and discovered the world about him. Spending time with his father had been a favorite pastime. He'd taught Colin so many important things about life—how to ride and care for his horse, how to shoot rifles and hand guns, how to hook the biggest fish in the creek, how to be a good sport, how to respect his elders, even when they didn't deserve it, but most importantly, how to reverence and love his Creator.

Colin sighed. All that had been lost when they'd moved to St. Louis. When his mother remarried, he'd resented the marriage at first, but as the years passed, Colin had grown to love his hardworking stepfather and appreciate his efforts to provide for them. But, Colin thought, their relationship never compared to the bond he shared with his father.

A few moments later, Colin drove onto the grass-littered gravel parking lot of Grace Missionary Church, his place of worship as a child. The funeral about to commence, he slipped inside and took a seat on a pew at the back of the sanctuary. He loosened his tie to ease his breathing then smoothed the back of his hair. The air conditioner wedged into the back wall of the 1940s building did little to cool the intense heat of the sweltering Oklahoma summer.

A grin touched his lips at the sight of the initials CDL carved into the varnished wood of the pew in front of him, his smile fading as a lump formed in his throat. The pearl-handled knife he'd used to etch the letters in the wood had been the last Christmas gift he'd received from his father. He pressed his hand against the pocket of his trousers, curling his fingers around the small Case pocketknife still in his possession after all these years.

An hour later, Colin made his way to the front of the church to view the corpse inside the burnished silver coffin. The last person in the line of mourners, Colin stood eyeing the man he could barely remember, trying to find at least one feature about him that seemed familiar. Uncle Max hadn't frequented Briarwood too often while Colin had lived there, preferring to reside in Tulsa, Oklahoma, the headquarters of Lambert Oil. When his wife died from an illness in the early nineties, Maxwell, well past retirement age, had opted to sell the business to a competitive petroleum company and return to Haven to live with his sister at the family estate.

Standing near the gravesite in the cemetery next to the church a few moments later, Colin scanned the crowd, seeking the person he longed to see. However, none of the elderly females listening to the tall, gaunt preacher reciting his final remarks before the burial came close to resembling the memory of his beloved "Duchess." Colin glanced up at the black jack oaks hovering near the church. Not a single leaf moved, uncommon for the windy Oklahoma plains.

All at once a horrible thought struck him. Did her death precede Uncle Max's? Had Eileen kept her death from him as well? With a slight shake of his head, he dismissed the idea. She knew how much he'd loved his great-aunt, Beatrice. But his mother's awareness of the love he held for his father hadn't persuaded her to allow Colin to visit Stuart in prison, regardless of Colin's numerous requests when he was young. On his eighteenth birthday, however, without his mother's consent, Colin had driven to McAlester, Oklahoma, to see his father, visiting him often since that day.

Glancing toward the string of reporters stationed nearby, his gaze settled on the only woman among them. Fascinated by her beauty, Colin had trouble concentrating on the minister's soft-spoken words recounting the virtues of a heavenly afterlife. Seeming to sense his eyes upon her, she glanced toward him, lowering her lashes when he smiled at her. Drawn to the forlorn expression in her almond-shaped, dark-brown eyes, he made a mental note to exchange introductions just as soon as the funeral ended.

Colin marveled at the warmth spreading through him. He hadn't felt attraction toward anyone for months, not since his relationship with Allison Moore had diminished. They still saw each other on occasion, but they had outgrown their college relationship, friendly affection evolving from their initial romance. Their interests changing, she'd decided to pursue a modeling career in New York, while his destiny seemed designed for marketing in the St. Louis metropolitan area.

Ignoring the half-concealed glances thrown his way by the dispersing crowd, Colin started toward the raven-haired woman he desired to meet. He'd taken but a few steps when he felt a tug on his arm. He turned to see a hefty, well-dressed gentleman stretching out his arm to shake hands, a friendly, yet guarded smile smoothing the vivid blue veins in his ruddy complexion.

"You have to be Colin Lambert. Were I not aware of your father's … ah … unfortunate circumstances, I could have mistaken you for Stuart three decades ago. Oh, sorry, son. I'm Nicholas Girard, attorney for the Lambert estate. We spoke on the phone yesterday."

Colin's smile wiped the confusion from his brow. "Of course. Please forgive my lack of recognition. I've been away from Haven a long time." He discreetly brushed his hand against his trouser leg to remove the moisture lingering from the lawyer's sweaty palm.

"Yes, you were just a lad when your mother whisked you away to Missouri. How is she? She told me of her recent widowhood when we conversed on the phone a few days ago."

Colin noticed how the man's features softened at the mention of Eileen, his gaze becoming distant as though his thoughts wandered to a different time, different place. "She's well." Colin glanced away to hide the cynicism creeping onto his face. "We both were shocked by George's untimely death, but we're holding our own."

"There are folks in these parts who still speak of her beauty... We were engaged once, you know. It didn't matter to Stuart or me that she didn't have an affluent background; we were crazy about her. But Stuart's father never accepted her, said she wasn't the potential wife he had in mind for his son. When Eileen broke off her engagement with me to marry Stuart, Braxton refused to give them a wedding. Her parents couldn't finance the event, so they eloped." Girard smiled but not in time to hide the look of resentment that flashed in his eyes. "I guess she felt life with a struggling young attorney couldn't compare with marriage to a Lambert."

Colin's spine stiffened. "I wouldn't know." He glanced toward the reporters. "Say, Mr. Girard, do you know the lady reporter over there?"

The lawyer turned in the direction Colin indicated by the nod of his head. "No, I've never seen her before. Attractive, though, isn't she?"

Colin lowered his gaze to hide the stab of irritation that leaped into his eyes. He decided to change the subject. "Were any of my other relatives present at the funeral?"

Girard shook his head then looked toward an elderly woman observing their conversation near the church steps. Colin glanced in the same direction, his brow creasing. Something seemed familiar about her. Colin abandoned his interest in the woman at the sound of Girard's voice. "I-I don't think so. Maxwell and his late wife bore no children and... of course, Beatrice never married."

Colin flicked a twig across the thirsty grass with the toe of his shoe hesitant to inquire about the person he'd longed to see among the crowd. "Is the Duc—I mean Aunt Beatrice still alive?" He watched the young woman reporter drive away from the church.

Girard nodded. "Yes, but she's much too frail to stand these temperatures." He pulled a handkerchief from his suit pocket to mop away the perspiration oozing from his hairline onto his face, the effort rumpling his few strands of gray-brown hair styled to hide semi-baldness. "Mrs. Frakes—I'm sure you remember her—an adequate nurse and housekeeper for Beatrice, is expecting you to drop by Briarwood before you leave town."

Colin stifled a grin. He could never forget Briarwood's dour Korean housekeeper "Mrs. Freaks," the name he'd dubbed her in boyhood. He'd thought it creepy the way she'd padded about the house in her sandals and colorful kimonos, her sudden appearance at the onset of one of his mischievous escapades, unnerving him. The penetrating look of disapproval in those black slanted eyes had never failed to discourage his momentary whim. Now that he thought about it, she'd probably saved him many a reprimand from his parents and grandfather. The Lamberts had doted on the woman, his mother the exception, however. Eileen had felt she didn't receive proper respect from the housekeeper.

Colin reigned in his reverie. "Thank God Aunt Beatrice is still alive. I'll go see her now."

Girard paused in their stride to the two remaining cars in the parking lot. "If you don't mind, I'd like you to stop by my office first. I'm sure you're eager to return to Missouri, and I need you sign some papers…"

Colin held up his hand. "Pardon me, but I'd really like to visit my aunt before I travel to Pawhuska."

The lawyer smiled. "I'm sorry. I should have mentioned that I maintain a small office in Haven as well. Although most of my clientele live in the Pawhuska area, Haven folk seem to prefer to have a lawyer within easy reach, so to speak. I'm usually in town one or two days a week. As I started to say a moment ago, I need your signature on the deed to Briarwood. Have you decided what you will do with the place?" Girard smiled at the surprised look on Colin's face. "I see Eileen didn't discuss your inheritance with you, either."

"I just assumed Aunt Beatrice would inherit Uncle Max's share of Briarwood along with his other assets."

The lawyer shook his head. "Your uncle wasn't the shrewd businessman Braxton became. With a major portion of his stock lost in the collapse of Enron, the blight on the economy, other unwise stock market investments, and his love of the horses, I'm afraid there's not much left of the Lambert fortune. It's my understanding Max even lost Stuart's inheritance in high-risk commodities.

"What Beatrice did with her legacy from Warren is still a mystery. She just stares at me with a blank expression in her eyes each time I mention the matter." Girard paused, noting Colin's baffled expression. "She's suffering from early stages of dementia, according to her doctor. A shame, I might add. I can remember how her presence seemed to light up a room when she entered it."

"Yes, I've often recalled her vibrant personality." Colin shook his head. "I'm sorry to hear that. I've heard about the disease, but my knowledge of it is limited."

"Well, let's hope a cure will be found soon. Back to the matter of Beatrice's estate, if Mrs. Frakes knows about Beatrice's monetary situation, she's not talking."

Colin smiled. "That doesn't surprise me. I don't think I heard our housekeeper say a dozen words when I lived at Briarwood. She didn't need to. Her eyes spoke volumes."

BITTERSWEET JUSTICE 23

Girard nodded then grew thoughtful. "I'm sorry about the meager inheritance left to you."

Colin shrugged his shoulders. "My father told me about the loss of his bequest. It grieved him to know he had nothing to leave me after his death. I assured him it didn't matter to me." Colin's eyes glinted with merriment. "Not that additional assets to my personal portfolio wouldn't have been appreciated, of course."

Girard stared off into space, seeming not to grasp Colin's remark. "Your father has suffered many disappointments."

His smile fading, Colin nodded. "But he's made a life for himself that yields some happiness in spite of the incarceration. He studies art, conducts a Bible study for the inmates on Sunday with the aid of outside ministers, and is respected by most of the other prisoners. But, of course, it doesn't make up for the freedom stolen from him. To this day, I believe him innocent of his conviction."

Girard looked stunned momentarily before a look of wariness stole across his features. "Do you have any proof of his innocence?"

"No, but as a lawyer, I'm sure you know of cases where the wrong man paid the price in lieu of the guilty. I was too young at the time to do anything about the situation, but I'm grown now. I guess Mother told you he's dying."

Girard studied Colin a moment then nodded. "Again, you have my sympathy."

"Thanks." Colin watched the attorney's eyes dance back and forth as he glanced around the church lot, a sudden tic appearing in his jaw. What had brought on his sudden nervousness? Colin looked around but saw nothing unusual.

When they reached their respective vehicles, the lawyer clapped Colin on the shoulder, his air of confidence restored. He glanced at his watch. "Why don't you grab a quick lunch, then we'll tend to business. You can't miss my office. It's on Main Street across from Taylor Drug."

"Right. And if we don't finish our business today, you'll be able to reach me at Briarwood. I've decided to stay in Haven a few days to become reacquainted with my aunt."

Girard seemed taken aback at Colin's announcement. "Yes … well … that's understandable," he said, unlocking his late-model sedan. With a smile that didn't penetrate his eyes, Girard lifted his hand in farewell. "See you soon."

Before he entered his car, Colin watched the attorney drive onto the steaming, ill-paved road of motley asphalt, wondering about the man who'd handled the Lamberts' affairs for decades, the family his first clients following graduation from law school. According to Eileen, Stuart, and Girard had been both friends and roommates at Oklahoma University, the friendship accounting for the attorney's lucrative business so soon into his new law practice.

The man's puffy red eyes and bloated features told of alcohol abuse, but that didn't explain his wariness when Colin had voiced his intention to prolong his visit. Did his mother's trepidation and Girard's anxiety have anything in common? If so, did it have something to do with the murder? What else would account for their misgiving about his sojourn in Haven?

Colin's lips tightened. Mysteries were made to be solved, and he would do his best to unravel this one. He had to expose the truth … *had* to … as a last gift to his dad.

CHAPTER 2

Feeling the weight of the July sun on his head, Colin glanced back at the weather-beaten, clapboard house of worship nestled within the rolling, craggy Oklahoma plains, the place where he'd accepted Christ as his personal Savior at nine years of age. The memory had been tucked away in his heart like a lost first love—the experience shadowed by maturity in life but never forgotten. He hadn't been allowed to attend church while living with his mother and George, the two refusing to speak of religion. But when he'd reached his teens, he frequented the youth services at a church close to his house, renewing his salvation experience. A surge of guilt ripped through his thoughts; during college, he'd drifted away from God, remaining so until a couple weeks ago.

His visits with his father of late had spurred a desire to rekindle the youthful experience. Colin had rededicated his life to Christ during his drive back to St. Louis from McAlester after a soul-searching discussion with his father on spiritual matters. The joy and peace he'd known early in life was restored in a matter of moments.

Colin blinked back the tears gathering at the corners of his eyes. The hours he spent at the prison on visiting day always seemed too short. Stuart wanted to know everything about his son's life and vice-versa. On one visit Stuart had given Colin a portrait of the horse he'd received for his tenth birthday. Colin had been amazed that his father had remembered the horse well enough to paint a near-perfect likeness of the animal. Colin sighed. He just had to find his grandfather's killer. It would be only a minute token of repayment for the love he'd received from his father.

Colin fixed his gaze toward the rising and falling countryside. The parched willowy reeds of the blue stem grass in the distance bowed to the sudden balmy breeze lifting the lapel on Colin's suit jacket. "I will lift up my eyes to the hills—Where does my help come from? My help comes from the Lord the Maker of heaven and earth." Colin jolted at his sudden recollection of the scripture found in the Psalms. He closed his eyes. *God, I've read in your Word that there is no truth hidden that won't be revealed, so I'm asking for your help to offset what law enforcement failed to do for Dad. Please give me the grace I need to solve this crime. To God be the glory! Amen.*

Wiping away the sheen of moisture from his brow, Colin shed his sports coat. Yes, his father had been a great Christian example to follow. However, another individual had played a major role in his spiritual education as well. He smiled at the thought of the Duchess. His smile faded at how upset she would be should she learn that he hadn't attended church in several years. Once he returned to St. Louis, finding a church home would be a priority.

Colin took one last look at the building, thinking it looked diminutive in comparison to the majestic bell tower and sharp-pointed steeple rising, it seemed, to immeasurable height in the cloudless sky. In spite of the peaceful setting in the flaming temperature, a sudden chill raced down his spine as a sense of foreboding crept into his mind. Could it be a premonition of danger? Rejecting the notion with a shake of his head, Colin entered the midsized car he'd rented at the airport early that morning in Tulsa.

BITTERSWEET JUSTICE

However, the impression hung over him like a sudden menacing storm about to shatter the stillness of a spring dawn.

· · · · ·

A few minutes later, Colin sat on a stool at the soda fountain in Taylor Drugstore and Pharmacy ordering a tuna salad sandwich on toast and chocolate malt. A gentleman, his features crusted with age, seated a couple of stools down from Colin studied him a moment then broke into conversation.

"Howdy, mister. Strangers in Haven are a rarity. Just passing through?" He thrust out a hand toward Colin. "Jonathan Baker, at your service."

Colin wiped the toast crumbs from his fingers with a paper napkin then accepted the friendly handshake with a smile. "Hello. I'm Colin Lambert," he said, at once noticing how Baker's large protruding ears seemed to diminish as his wrinkled face smoothed beneath a wide smile.

The man cupped his hand around his right ear. "Lambert, you say? Came to Haven for Maxwell's last rites, I suppose." Mr. Baker pushed back a lock of thick white hair that loped onto his forehead when he leaned forward to better catch the stranger's response.

Colin nodded. "Yes, I did."

Mr. Baker eyed his new acquaintance, a thoughtful expression capturing his features. His green eyes widened. "Why, blast it all, you can't be none other than the late Braxton's grandson all grown up now. My, my… Has it really been that long since the tragedy? I tell you it was a black day in Haven when we heard your grandfather had been murdered. I remember the day like it was yesterday. No one in this town believed Stuart Lambert, God-fearing man that he was, pulled that trigger. If it's any consolation to you, young man, the jury deliberated several days before they brought in a guilty verdict. A crime of passion they called it in the newspapers."

Colin looked down at his half-eaten lunch. He pushed the plate aside, deciding it would be hard to swallow past the tightness in his throat. "Did you know the Lamberts well, Mr. Baker?"

"Not personal like, mind you, but I did work for Braxton in my younger days. If the plumbing didn't work, I fixed it. If one of their cars wouldn't go, I made it run. If the grass needed mowing or the flowers needed watering..." Mr. Baker smiled, his eyes twinkling with mirth.

Colin grinned. "I guess you're what people call a jack of all trades."

Mr. Baker laughed. "And master of none."

All at once Colin sobered. "It's all coming back to me now. Didn't you have a son that came with you on occasion to Briarwood? I'm sorry; I can't remember his name."

"Yes. Sometimes I would need Alfred's help in doing a job there."

Colin grew thoughtful, his face brightening after a moment. "Alfred Baker... of course... *Alfie*. How could I forget? Dad and I often took him fishing with us at Sand Creek."

Mr. Baker nodded. "Yes, my son thought Stuart could do no wrong, his feelings almost to the point of worship for your father."

Colin's thoughts wandered. Alfie had been a teenager then but still a child in so many ways. The boy, born late in his mother's childbearing years, had been born with Down syndrome. Although mentally incapacitated to a large degree, the young man knew how to love his friends and enjoy life. Nature and animals appealed to him. Colin never knew him to be angry except one time... when he saw a visitor to Briarwood kick Sparky, Colin's dog. Stuart had had to calm Alfie when he'd started toward the man, aiming to club him with a baseball bat.

BITTERSWEET JUSTICE 29

"I'm sorry, Mr. Baker. What did you say?"

"I asked if you intended to stay awhile at Briarwood."

"Yes, a few days, anyway. Mr. Baker, you mentioned earlier that no one in town believed my father guilty of murder. It's good to know others share my sentiment. Can you think of anything that might prove his innocence?"

The old man rode the swiveling stool to a more comfortable position. "Well, there was some talk around that time..."

An elderly woman, her spine bent, entered the drugstore. The girl behind the counter turned from wiping a spill to call out a cheerful greeting. "Good afternoon, Mrs. Baker. Mr. Baker is up to his old trick of entertaining the customers." The attendant winked at Colin then patted the older man on the shoulder.

Mrs. Baker guffawed. "Doesn't surprise me in the least." She rolled her eyes toward the ceiling. "And they say women were born with the gift of communication."

Mr. Baker smiled at his wife. "Just listen at you, Nellie. What other time can a man speak his piece without interruption except when his wife is off getting herself all fancied up?"

Mrs. Baker patted her fresh coif. "Tell me, old man, where else would you have me go to find a few moments of peace and quiet?"

Colin, chuckling beneath his breath at the lighthearted banter, watched the slender man slide off the counter stool. "Glad to have seen you again, Mr. Baker. Maybe we'll get a chance to talk before I return to St. Louis."

"Likewise, Colin, my boy. Land sakes, I must have left my manners at home. Nellie, this is Colin Lambert, Mr. Braxton's grandson, Stuart's boy... came back for Maxwell's funeral."

Nellie pushed her glasses upward, moving closer to Colin to get a better look at him. "Well, of all things, I never thought we'd see you again, not after the way your mother hightailed it out of these parts all those years ago. My goodness, you sure

VICTORIA BURKS

grew into a handsome young man. I hope you took after your father in mind as well as looks.

"After your mother married your father, you'd have thought she became a queen, all of a sudden too good to associate with the rest of us country folks. Her high mindedness didn't set too well with the town, especially since she came from below the railroad tracks."

Eyeing the strained expression on Colin's face, Mr. Baker put his arm around his wife's shoulder. "Nellie, we best be on our way. We can't leave Alfie too long, you know. He might wander off somewhere." Mr. Baker opened the door and guided her onto the sidewalk. Turning, he saluted Colin. "We'll get together again before you leave. We can speak more about your father then."

"Yes, I'd like that. Good day to you both." More than anything Colin wished he could have heard what Mr. Baker had started to say before his wife had entered the drugstore. Just before the door closed, Colin heard the woman question her husband.

"Just what did you say to Mr. Lambert about his father? You weren't spreading old wives' tales, were you? No need to stir up trouble after all these years."

Colin frowned. What did she mean? He would make it a point to converse with Mr. Baker soon. But right now he must keep his appointment with Girard.

Leaving the fountain girl a large tip, Colin hurried across the street. Once inside the attorney's outer office, Colin couldn't squelch a look of surprise as he glimpsed his surroundings, the plush contemporary décor quite a contrast from the exterior. Smoothing his expression, he informed the secretary of his appointment, the woman announcing Colin's arrival to Girard immediately. Within moments the phone on her desk rang.

"You may go in now, Mr. Lambert," she said, smiling.

BITTERSWEET JUSTICE

Colin didn't miss the woman's "I'd like to get to know you better" look in her eyes as she stood to open the door to her employer's office. With a curt nod, Colin ignored the silent plea. Bold, flirtatious women had never appealed to him. The image of the petite, dark-haired girl with the woebegone expression flashed in his mind, compassion for her overwhelming him. What had caused her sadness? He hoped their paths would cross again.

"Come in, Colin." Girard said, standing from behind his desk. "I can't begin to tell you how many memories your presence here today has stirred in me."

Colin forced a smile. "Good ones, I hope." He resisted the urge to refuse the lawyer's handshake. Twice he had seen Girard and had yet to find something he liked about the too-friendly man.

"Yes … and some … " Girard waved away his secretary then offered Colin a seat with his outstretched hand. "But, of course, you know all about that."

Not desiring to discuss what he assumed to be on the attorney's mind, Colin didn't comment, glad that Girard's effort to distribute his excessive weight into his chair drew attention away from the unresponsiveness. However, a sideways glance from the attorney made Colin's pulse quicken, his neck muscles straining against the starched collar of his shirt. He pulled at the knot in his Christian Dior necktie. Why did he all of a sudden feel threatened? Or had he just imagined a look of menace in the lawyer's eyes. Was the desire to free his father from prison causing mental delusions?

While Colin settled into a chair, Girard studied the papers in the file laid out across his desk. If he noticed Colin's discomfort, he gave no sign of it. "I gathered from Eileen you are well established in the advertising business you inherited from your stepfather."

"Yes. I'm proud to say we employ some of the best graphic artists in the field. When technology began its heyday, George recognized what the computer age could do for marketing and built the agency into a first-class and profitable entity."

"It's too bad your uncle Maxwell didn't possess like tendencies. Braxton inherited his father's business finesse and doubled the fortune Warren made, but Max didn't inherit their business savvy."

Colin nodded. "Unwise investments, I believe you said. But if my memory serves me well, Briarwood should be worth a small fortune."

"Yes, if there had been enough cash flow to keep up the place. Braxton set up a trust fund to do just that ... however, inflation and low interest rates have reduced the original amount significantly as you'll discover in a moment. That, along with time and inattention has dealt a severe blow to the place."

"I see."

Girard pushed a sheaf of papers toward Colin. "I took it upon myself to have Max's CPA, Mark Kellar, put together an accounting of Lambert worth. I hope you're not too disappointed with the final analysis."

Colin studied the report with a critical eye, noting the attorney's pessimistic summation had merit. Once the outstanding debt had been satisfied, all that would remain of Lambert's assets would be a few thousand in cash, some measly dividends from assorted company stock and Briarwood itself. Colin couldn't help surmise what Warren Lambert might say about the status of his empire if he could view this testimonial. No doubt he would be outraged, his multi-million dollar fortune acquired by hard work and ingenuity reduced to a pittance.

Sighing, Colin closed the file. "I'll tidy my uncle's affairs before I leave town. Also, I want to make arrangements for my aunt's care. But I need to speak with her before I start pulling options out of a hat."

"Should she understand, I'm sure she'll be pleased by your concern for her welfare," Girard said, pausing to extract another document from his desk. "Here's the deed to the estate. Please sign where I've indicated. I'll see that it's recorded this afternoon. Have you entertained any more thought about Briarwood?"

Colin penned his name and handed the deed back to the attorney. "No. But I still don't comprehend why the Duc... I mean Aunt Beatrice didn't inherit the estate."

"More than likely Warren thought she'd marry well because his will stated that firstborn Braxton would inherit the family home and likewise for other firstborn male heirs on down the line. However, since your father wouldn't be able to maintain the estate, he authorized Maxwell as his power of attorney until his death knowing you were the next heir apparent. As I declared earlier, the whereabouts of Beatrice's share of old Warren's holdings are yet to be discovered. And believe me, as the family attorney, I've tried for years to get the information out of her, but she wouldn't budge, and now it's too late."

Taking the deed from Colin, Girard stood to his feet, retrieving a business card from a holder on his desk and extending it toward Colin. "The death of Maxwell terminates my position as the Lamberts' attorney... unless, of course, you wish to retain my services. Beatrice stated years ago she would handle her own affairs."

Colin laughed. "That sounds like her. Now that I think of it, even Grandfather wouldn't interfere with her decisions. And as for the other, I have my own attorney in St. Louis, but thanks for the offer.

Girard nodded, a half smile lifting the corners of his mouth. "Braxton's love for his little half sister was legend in these parts. Born to Warren's much younger second wife, Beatrice took a liking to her oldest brother when only a babe, reveling in the attention he bestowed on her. According to the local historians, she was never far out of his sight except when he was away on business." Girard's smile widened. "If I can be of any assistance while you're in town, don't hesitate to give me a call."

"Sure thing," Colin replied, rising from the chair. "And now, I must not keep my aunt waiting any longer."

After a quick handshake, Colin hurried from the building. As he stepped into his car, a sudden notion struck him. Not a word of interest in his father's well-being had crossed Girard's lips. Strange, Colin decided, since at one time they'd been the best of friends.

A short time later, Colin drove the road that followed the winding contour of Sand Creek, the years falling away with each passing mile like sand trickling through a child's fingers. The road had been built during the Great Depression in the 1930s by men employed by the Work Projects Administration, commonly known as the WPA, Colin recalled, just after his great-grandfather had brought in the last oil well in Lambert field. "It could sure use some help now," he muttered after swerving the car to miss a deep pothole.

Glancing at the trees lining the roadway, he noticed a frazzled piece of rope tied to a branch overhanging the creek. Smiling, he recalled Ray Trent, his best childhood friend. Ray, his honey-blond hair plastered against his head and dripping water, had stood on the opposite bank. With arms waving, he'd urged Colin to take the rope tied to the branch in hand, swing out over the creek, and then let go. But Colin had hesitated, fear keeping his feet glued to the ground.

"Come on, old buddy, you can do it!" Ray had yelled. "Don't listen to those other guys. You're not chicken."

Colin had glanced toward the other two boys, Petey and Kyle, who strutted in a circle like yard fowl, clucking their tongues and flapping their elbows like wings in the summer breeze. Lifting his chin into the air, Colin's lips straightened with determina-

BITTERSWEET JUSTICE 35

tion, courage he hadn't known he possessed taking hold of him. He grabbed the rope. Backing up as far as he could, he closed his eyes for a moment then grinned. His best Rebel yell shooting out his mouth, he ran forward and leaped into midair. A rush of excitement gripped him so tight he thought his lungs would burst in his chest. A moment later, pulling his body from the water, the boys congratulated Colin with much clapping on his shoulders at his bravery.

A squirrel leaped from the road to a nearby tree erasing Colin's recollection. At the next sharp bend, the road began to climb away from the creek. Stands of blackjack oak dotted the landscape atop the large slabs of red and yellow sandstone jutting from the ridge to shield clumps of weeds and grass from the sun. He smiled at the efforts of a scissor-tailed flycatcher to balance itself on the twig of a bush. At the top of the next hill, he slowed the car. Feasting on the view to his left, his heartbeat quickened.

Briarwood Valley stretched out before him, the fields of blue stem grass swaying like harp strings at the touch of a harpist. In his mind's eye he could visualize roaming buffalo feeding on the ensilage in past centuries. A thrust of pain gripped Colin as he recalled the many hours he and his father had ridden their horses throughout the countryside. He swallowed hard, forcing back tears.

His emotions in control, Colin took in the sight of the sprawling mansion built in 1928 by his great-grandfather when oil gushes were at their peak. His heart swelled with anticipation. He couldn't wait to step inside his boyhood home once more. Gunning the engine, Colin steered the car onto the road that plunged into the valley, each dip and turn beckoning him closer to his past.

As he neared the rock wall surrounding the entire spacious lawn, he came upon a familiar red sports car parked near the entry to the circle drive. His breath caught in his throat when he recognized the woman emerging from the car. Pulling to a quick stop, Colin swiftly unfastened his seatbelt and lifted his long legs from his car. Determined not to miss another opportunity to meet the woman who'd so intrigued him at Uncle Max's graveside service, he hurried toward her.

"Good afternoon, I'm Colin Lambert. I believe I saw you at my uncle's funeral this morning. May I help you?"

At the sound of his voice, she turned to stare at him, recognition of him showing in her eyes. She held out her hand. "Hello, Mr. Lambert. I'm Julie Lonetree with the *Tulsa World*. I hope you don't mind. I just want to get a few shots of Briarwood for the story I'm working on for our newspaper." Julie retrieved a camera bag from her car.

Colin shrugged his shoulders then backed up to lean against her car, folding his arms across his chest. "I guess it would depend on what kind of story you're writing," he ventured, wariness filling his eyes.

A smile touched her lips. "Nothing harmful, I assure you," she said after noting his expression. "Just items of Lambert history tucked in with the story of the last rites for the son of an infamous oil baron … a human interest story I believe the public would like to read." She grinned. "A story that won't make front page headlines, I'm afraid, but a good read."

Colin relaxed. "I see no damage in your intentions, Miss … or is it Mrs. Lonetree?" Colin glanced toward her left hand, breathing easier when he saw no wedding ring.

Following the direction of his gaze, she winced, her eyes hazing over with unshed tears. She lowered her head. "Actually, neither. Ms. Lonetree spends most of her day writing ads for classified. I've wanted to break into reporting for some time. When I saw Maxwell Lambert's name in the obituary column a few days ago, the idea to do a story on the Lambert family came to mind, so here I am."

Colin wanted to ask if she'd lost a companion to death, but afraid she would bolt, he put off the question. He didn't want anything to endanger his chance to become better acquainted with this Native American whose beauty brought such havoc to his senses. "Well, Ms. Lonetree, I wish you luck."

Again, she smiled. "Thanks. Now if you'll excuse me, I'll get to work. By the way..." Julie looked at Colin as though she just remembered his name. "I don't suppose you'd be interested in giving me an interview. You are Stuart Lambert's son, right?"

Colin straightened, rising to his full height, a reddish hue deepening his deeply tanned complexion. His eyes sparked with irritation. "No. I would not."

"Look, don't get mad. I just thought I'd ask. In case you're wondering, I've done my homework." Julie laid her hand on his arm. "However, I understand. The thought of your grandfather murdered by your father must be tough. I wouldn't want to talk about that either." She hesitated then continued. "I understand your father is dying with cancer."

"Ms. Lonetree, it's obvious you've researched your project. I'm sure I couldn't tell you any more about the family than you already know. I'm sorry I snapped at you. I just don't relish the thought of my family's misdeeds publicized once again to be melodramatically clucked over some morning then thrown in the trash later that day. The past is best forgotten, don't you think?"

"Unless a mistake can be made right." Colin eyed her with suspicion. "What do you mean?"

Julie toyed with her camera. "Mr. Lambert, I don't mean to drag up any more painful memories for you. But after researching the trial records at the Osage County Courthouse and old newspaper accounts, I came across something that disturbed me—a picture in the *Tulsa World* of you hanging onto your father with the caption that read: 'Father Denies Guilt to Son.' It was the look in your father's eyes that got to me.

"Checking the byline of the reporter who did that story, I realized he still worked for our newspaper, so I asked him about that day. He shares my opinion that your father is innocent, having heard your father's words to you in the courtroom moments before he snapped that photograph, he'd wanted to do some investigative work on the case, but the editor of the newspaper at the time refused to accept the idea."

Julie pulled a pen and notebook from the outside pocket of her camera bag, scribbling something on the pad before she tore off the top sheet and handed it to Colin. "Mr. Lambert, should you ever want to reopen the case, I'd like to help you with it." She pointed to the paper. "That's my office number and e-mail address if you decide you'd like my assistance in locating the real killer. Call it woman's intuition, a hunch, or whatever, but somehow I know you desire to clear your father's name."

Sighing, Colin smoothed the back of his hair as he lowered his head, denying her the privilege of seeing the shock her words had created in him. He forced calmness into his expression. He lifted his eyes, the look of compassion on her face almost his undoing. "Ms. Lonetree, what would you gain should you prove the justice system convicted the wrong man? Are you really interested in setting the record straight, or is it just notoriety and a pay raise you seek?"

"Neither. Let's just say the agony of a little boy's heartbreak through the eyes of a young reporter twenty-five years ago is my motivation."

Colin's anger vanished. "I believe you said you needed to get back to your photo shoot. Good day, Ms. Lonetree. Perhaps we'll see each other again, the next time in less stressful circumstances."

"Good-bye, Mr. Lambert. I wish you well. By the way, if you want a copy of these pictures, just let me know."

A moment later, Colin drove through the open wrought iron gate, which had in the past shielded Briarwood from the outside world, now a rusty assemblage hanging limply on its hinges. Eying Julie through the side mirror of the car, he wondered if his earlier inclination about her had merit. Had she lost a loved one to death in a wrongful action? Is that what accounted for her sadness and her willingness to assist him in his venture? Had he said something to make her suspect his intention to find the true killer? Colin thought over their conversation, soon concluding he hadn't.

Catching his eye in the mirror, she smiled at him then waved. He marveled at his intense desire to alleviate the unhappiness he'd read in her eyes. "And there will be a next time, Little One," he said under his breath.

CHAPTER 3

Colin parked on the circle drive in front of the stately mansion. Emerging from the car, he scanned his surroundings. Girard hadn't exaggerated in his description of Briarwood. The yard was overgrown with weeds, the bushes lining the portico hidden behind untamed vines that grew spasmodically and clung to the eaves of the stucco-finished home. It wasn't anything like he remembered, the landscape always manicured to perfection by Mr. Baker and Alfie. Colin eyed the peeling paint and broken roof tiles, shaking his head. Could this dilapidating structure be the home he'd cherished as a child? If the inside compared to this, it would cost thousands of dollars to refurbish Briarwood estate.

Perspiration trickling down his neck, Colin started to climb the chipped concrete steps onto the front porch that stretched the full length of the house. All at once sensing that someone observed him from the balcony, he glanced upward. Half hidden behind a curtain, an old woman stared down at him from the glass door that opened onto the lanai. Realizing she'd been caught spying, she dropped the curtain. As he watched, the calendar in Colin's mind turned backward.

A boy again, he'd run outside not bothering to close the door. In a hurry to catch up with his father, who'd promised Colin he could ride the new thoroughbred stallion, he'd stopped short at the voice calling to him from overhead.

"Colin, a gentleman would never exit the house in such a manner. Please return and close the door the proper way."

A sheepish grin on his face, he'd turned and smiled at his aunt awed by the beauty of her shiny natural blond hair falling in waves to below her shoulders, giving her the look of an angel. Not wanting to disappoint the Duchess, he'd hurried to obey the soft-spoken command, knowing a plate of cookies and milk would be waiting for him when he returned from the stables. The memory fading, Colin made his way toward the entry and reached to ring the doorbell, the large door creaking open before he could press the button.

Colin stared at Mrs. Frakes. Her coal black, straight hair now tinged with silver streaks was held together in a chignon, the way she'd always styled it. Although her face didn't break into a smile, he saw a look of pleasure in her eyes.

"Hello, Mrs. Frakes. It's been a long time. How are you?"

The woman bowed low. "Welcome home, Master Colin. I tell Miss Lambert you would pay us a visit, but I'm not sure she understand. Mr. Girard stop by this morning, just after other townsfolk bring us food, to let me know you were on your way to Haven."

Colin nodded, smiling inwardly. The housekeeper still spoke in the present tense as she had in his childhood, although her Korean accent wasn't as pronounced as in the past. "I spoke with Girard earlier. He explained about her illness."

Once inside the foyer, he glanced around. As far as he could tell, nothing had changed since he'd been away from Briarwood. The same flocked wallpaper donned the entryway, although now faded in spots and beginning to peel. Following the housekeeper's steady gait up the stairs, he paused to observe one of the paintings hanging on the wall above the staircase, a family portrait of Erin and Braxton Lambert. Colin marveled at the beauty of his grandmother. Her flaming red hair framed lovely features. Her heavily lashed green eyes sparkled with mirth.

Braxton had met her in Lubbock, Texas, while on a business trip there. Several years after their marriage and pregnant with their first child, Erin and Beatrice took an extended vacation in Europe. A few months later, Erin, overcome with an illness she contracted in Naples, died giving premature birth, the child hospitalized for several weeks. Braxton had flown to Italy to bring his wife's remains home, the Duchess remaining by her nephew's side. When Stuart was released from medical care, Braxton had returned to Naples to escort his son and sister home to Briarwood, Colin recalled, his visits to the prison often rewarded with bits and pieces of his family heritage when the talks with his father took that route.

Colin glanced at his grandfather's image. Unlike his wife, his countenance revealed an austere expression, the look in his blue eyes reminding Colin of the feel of steel, cold and unrelenting to pressure.-Although not affectionate in an outward manner, his grandfather had shown his love for his grandson in other ways, often allowing Colin to travel with him to Tulsa, first to the office to take care of business, then the two spending the rest of the day at Bell's Amusement Park. Only on those days or when the Duchess was nearby did he see his grandfather's expression soften and laughter spill from his lips. In those moments Braxton became a different person from the tyrannical businessman he projected to others in his world.

Another painting drew his attention. It was a portrait of his father commissioned soon after his graduation from college, if Colin remembered correctly. Stuart's long black hair style, so popular in the early seventies, made his eyes appear even darker. Colin recalled his father's testimony of when he'd made Christ, the Lord of his life.

It was during the spiritual awakening known as the Jesus Movement. Coffee houses had sprung up on college campuses all over the country with live Christian music and speakers as the entertainment. That night Stuart listened to a young man share his experience of how God had changed his life from that of a drug addict to a youth minister. The testimony inspired Stuart to accept the plan of salvation at a campus church the following week, serving Christ to this day.

Colin's thoughts returned to the painting. As he studied the portrait, he frowned. *Odd*, he thought, wondering why he'd never noticed it as a boy. His father's dark eyes and deeper skin tones were in direct contrast to those of his parents. Was it possible his father had been adopted? Colin squinted to get a closer view of his relatives' likenesses. No... his father and grandfather bore the same prominent, aristocratic nose, same high cheekbones and cleft in their chins. However, after careful inspection, Colin couldn't find any feature of his grandmother in her son. Colin smiled. God must have traveled far into former generations to collect his father's DNA.

A sound above him startled Colin. He glanced up to see Mrs. Frakes staring at him from the landing, a ghost of a smile on her lips. "If you're ready, I'll take you to see your aunt now."

"Yes, of course. I'm sorry. I can reminisce later." With that Colin caught up with her, the swish of her kimono the only sound as she led him to his beloved Duchess.

A moment later, Mrs. Frakes opened the door he remembered so well. Stepping over the threshold, Colin glanced around the room, memories of his childhood sailing across his mind. The Austrian drapes he'd often hid behind when in trouble with his mother now hung limp against the window, the nap worn in spots and their once deep color faded to various shades of red and pink. Within the niche of the bay window, his aunt sat in a Queen Anne wing-back chair gazing out the window, a Bible in her lap. Colin gasped. Could this shriveled, wrinkled old woman clothed in black be the lively, witty, slightly eccentric aunt he'd adored as a boy?

He recalled the day he'd nicknamed her the "Duchess." His aunt Mary from St. Louis and her son, Robert, were at Briarwood visiting Eileen. Beatrice had gently chastised Robert at the dinner table for his lack of manners. Robert, later making some snide remarks about her refined traits to Colin, asked him, Who did she think she was, a duchess? Colin had promptly kicked his cousin in the shins and ran to hide in her room, later deciding the word a perfect title for his beloved aunt. From that moment forward, she'd been so named in his vocabulary.

As she turned toward them, Colin smiled at her, his voice too constricted with emotion to utter a sound.

Mrs. Frakes stepped toward her charge. "Miss Lambert, your nephew, Colin, is here to see you."

Beatrice looked up, her eyes growing wide as she clasped her hands close to her heart. "My baby, my baby," she said softly.

Mrs. Frakes moved closer to Beatrice. "Miss Lambert, it's your nephew, *Colin*." Again the housekeeper spoke, this time her voice louder. "It's Master Colin. He's come home."

At last seeming to understand the housekeeper, Beatrice started to rise from the chair. Colin rushed forward, lifting his aunt into his arms, her Bible falling to the worn carpet beneath her feet.

Colin pulled her against him. "Hello, Duchess."

She gazed at him, her eyes seeming to brighten with recognition. Placing her long fingers on each side of his face, she spoke, her voice raspy and weak. "Oh, Stuart, how I've missed you." All of a sudden fear filled her eyes. "You must leave quickly. Danger lurks inside the walls of Briarwood. He may kill you too. I saw him, heard them, but the sheriff believed him, not me."

"Duchess, what are you saying?" As he waited for her response, he soon realized there would be none. Her blue eyes so bright a moment before grew dull, as she faded into a world Colin couldn't enter. He glanced at Mrs. Frakes, her hand poised to offer him a comforting touch. Instead of following her intention, she dropped her arm, shaking her head instead, sorrow filling her eyes.

Lifting his aunt, Colin carried her to the daybed on the far side of the sitting room and laid her down. Within moments she fell asleep. Removing his arms from around her as gently as possible, he tiptoed away from the bed, pausing to retrieve the Duchess's Bible from the floor.

As he gazed at the faded cover cracked from age and use, tender memories caressed his thoughts. Often he had sat at her feet, his aunt's melodious voice recounting the stories from its pages, his favorite the saga of David and Goliath. He smiled as he recalled the sword, shield, and slingshot she had fashioned from sticks, cardboard, and string to make the story more vivid.

Colin's lips straightened. How he'd missed those times with the Duchess after his mother had moved them to Missouri. But a large portion of all those scriptures he'd memorized as a child had never left his mind, even sustaining his Christianity during his youth in a home devoid of theological training.

Turning, he closed the Bible and placed it on the table next to Beatrice's chair. Lifting his eyes, he noted the wisp of a smile on Mrs. Frakes's face. Returning her smile, he slipped out the bedroom door, the housekeeper close behind him.

Once in the hall, he turned to Mrs. Frakes. "She thinks I'm my father."

The housekeeper nodded. "I'm sorry. I hoped she recognize you. But you look much like your father. The mistake is understandable. And in her mind today, you still boy. Been long time since she see you."

Colin nodded. "What do you suppose she meant by her statement that danger lurked here?"

Mrs. Frakes averted her eyes then stepped toward the stairway, avoiding his direct gaze. "Who knows what in her thoughts? I'm sure she confused about lots of things."

"I don't think so. I believe the Duchess was referring to my grandfather's death. Who does she think killed my grandfather?"

Mrs. Frakes laid her hand on Colin's arm. "She could never bring herself to believe your father capable of the crime. She had hard time adjusting to her brother's death, imagined all kinds of theories how it might have happened, the sheriff at the time not considering any of her speculations plausible enough to investigate. Seeing you must have triggered one of them."

Colin shrugged his shoulder. "Perhaps. I wonder what she saw and heard that makes her think my life is in danger, or as she believes, my father's?"

Mrs. Frakes started down the stairs. "Will you be staying for dinner?"

"Yes, in fact, I'll be bunking at Briarwood for a few days. I need to settle Uncle Max's affairs before I leave and make arrangements for the Duchess's care."

Mrs. Frakes straightened. "I see. Dinner will be served promptly at seven."

Colin frowned. What had caused the housekeeper's sudden drop in friendliness—the fact that he would be around awhile or his plan to provide other care for his aunt? He watched her exit from the foyer, the only sound her sandals sliding along the marred wooden floor.

His suitcase and laptop collected from the car, he climbed to the upper level, knowing Mrs. Frakes would settle for nothing less than him taking his rightful place at the ancestral mansion. He stopped at the door of his old room and peeked inside but decided the twin bed he'd slept in as a child would not give him the rest he desired, thus giving in to the stalwart precedence the housekeeper had always commanded when the situation called for it. Smiling, he proceeded onward to the other wing of the house. A few minutes later, his clothes hanging in the closet and his toiletries arranged in the master bathroom, he reached for the suit coat he'd tossed on the bed earlier. However, his hand fell to his side as he centered his attention on the oval-shaped, dark-framed images of his great-grandfather and great-grandmother, Warren and Loretta Lambert, hanging above the four-poster king-sized bed.

Colin eyed the portraits, his great-grandfather's bushy handlebar mustache adding appeal to his strong features. In contrast, his great-grandmother's dainty features might fool a casual viewer, but a closer look above the Victorian lace shrouding her neck would reveal the depth of inward strength and determination the artist had captured in her dark eyes.

According to Dad, Warren's parents, Scottish immigrants, had migrated to Indian Territory to participate in the Great Land Rush in April of 1889, homesteading their 160 acres located northeast of Oklahoma City. Their son, newly grown and an adventurer at heart, began to hear about the discovery of oil in the Bartlesville area, arriving in the town on March 25, 1897, the day the first commercial oil well, the Nellie Johnstone Number One, blew in. Rushing to the sight of the gusher, he immediately hired on as a roustabout, learning as much about the industry over the next few years as he could.

With his thirst for knowledge, his willingness to work long hours and his winning personality, he soon caught the eye of some local businessmen who financed his desire to prospect for oil in Osage County along with other wildcatters in the region. His hunch soon became "pay dirt" for his benefactors, his talent for "smelling out a rich pool of oil" spreading throughout the territory. His greatest accomplishment, Lambert Field, with its production of hundreds of barrels of oil per day, not only gained him notoriety among his peers, but the reputation of the youngest wildcatter in history to start his own oil entity, thus the beginning of Lambert Oil Company.

Once his business became established, Colin recalled, Warren had married Loretta Marks, the granddaughter of an Osage Indian chief. When a plague of typhoid fever swept through the territory, Loretta died of the disease after spending hours nursing her husband and sons, Braxton and Maxwell back to health. Surviving both his wife's death and the Great Depression, Warren turned his thoughts to the wartime demand for oil, the company prospering in both crude oil and natural gas, his "nose for the black gold" again his ticket to success.

A few years later, Warren married the daughter of a New York philanthropist. However, the young socialite, unable to adapt to a life on the Oklahoma Plains, had deserted her husband and infant daughter to return to New York, divorcing Warren soon afterwards, giving custody of Beatrice to her father. Grabbing up his coat, Colin shrugged into the garment as he hurried downstairs, the desire to reacquaint himself with Briarwood a priority until the dinner hour, his first stop the living room.

Glancing around the large room a moment later, he realized nothing had changed in the years he'd been away. The sofa and love seat, the contrasting occasional chairs, the side tables, and the lamps occupied the same space as on the day he and his mother had left the estate. The outdated dark-green shag carpet, its pile tucked around the bottom of the furniture legs, was faded where the sun had shed its rays through the windows onto the floor. Colin frowned. What had been the name used to describe this particular color of green? He smiled as his memory returned. Ah, yes, avocado. The multicolor fabric covering the furniture ranged in earth tones to shades of avocado green and that deep brick-like color that reminded Colin of rusted steel pipe.

BITTERSWEET JUSTICE

The living room had been his least favorite room in the house, the place where he'd endured wet kisses and cheek tweaks from distinguished guests. The only exception to his dislike, the Christmas holidays when his aunt would go all out to celebrate the season, the giant Christmas tree towering over the room, its festive decorations as well as the outdoor holiday décor lit up for all to see from the road along the ridge.

Colin turned from the doorway startled to see Mrs. Frakes hovering nearby. *Amazing*, he thought. She still had that uncanny way of just appearing without a sound.

"Mr. Lambert, dinner will be served in fifteen minutes." She bowed and walked toward the kitchen.

Colin glanced at his watch. He had just enough time to check out the combination library/den where the Lamberts had enjoyed numerous evenings together, the Duchess's incessant rule of no conflicting conversation while the family congregated in this room keeping disagreements at bay until a later time and place. Entering the room, he studied every nook and cranny that had monitored some of his happiest moments as a child.

His gaze fell on the oak library table where he'd done his homework, his father close by in case Colin needed help with his studies; the scene in his mind so strong he could almost visualize and feel the movements of each family member as they discussed the events of the day or watched a television show on the console in the corner of the room. When Colin had closed his textbooks, often the family would pull out a game, such as Clue, Monopoly, or others that would guarantee a few challenges and laughs before bedtime.

As Colin ran his hand along the back of the sofa, he had a sudden realization. It was as though life at Briarwood had ceased to exist the day his grandfather died. He felt a shiver race down his spine at the sudden chill engulfing the room. Did danger truly exist within the walls of his beloved home as his aunt had stated? Colin jumped at the sound of the housekeeper's voice.

"Master Colin, dinner is ready."

"Thank you, Mrs. Frakes." Colin made his way to the formal dining room. Entering the room, he noted that tableware occupied only one spot atop the lace tablecloth, the place where his grandfather had sat, his commanding aura at once felt by family and guests alike when he had occupied that chair. Colin hesitated before he took the seat. Aware that Mrs. Frakes expected it, he sat down, unsure that he deserved the honor. Could he fulfill the role of family patriarch? Although able to provide care for his aunt, he knew the responsibility to live up to the Lambert name required much more—possibly more than he was equipped to give.

Earlier that afternoon, he had detected Mr. Baker's initial respect for the family in his words and actions. How could he restore the nobility of the Lambert name in the community—that which Girard had insinuated his uncle had failed to do? What did he have in his hand to achieve the task?

You have me.

Colin started at the sound of the still small voice inside him. One of his aunt's favorite scriptures filled his thoughts. *"I can do all things through Christ which strengthens me." But where do I start?* He lifted his eyes to scan the horizon through the windows, which stretched across the west end of the dining room, the rolling hills in the distance reminding him of his thoughts late that morning before he'd left the church grounds. "I will look to you, God, for your guidance in this situation as well," he said softly.

When Mrs. Frakes had collected the last of the dishes from the table, Colin followed her to the kitchen, offering to help with the cleanup. Receiving a look that would turn a fresh-baked slice of bread into stone, he backed away, settling into a chair next to the table across the room.

"Mrs. Frakes, please tell me about Uncle Max and the Duchess. The years since I left are a loss to me. I don't think Mother kept in touch with anyone here." Colin swung his arm outward. "I am saddened by what I see. Mr. Girard explained some of the financial distress, but after reviewing the financial statement, there would have been money available for maintenance and"—he glanced at the outdated appliances—"some updating."

While Mrs. Frakes took in Colin's words, he tried to remember how long the woman had served the Lambert family; before he'd been born, he was sure. He did recall someone mentioning that she'd been a war bride, her husband dying from injuries he'd received in battle soon after he'd returned home from the Korean War, bringing his child bride with him. She must have become part of Briarwood staff soon after his death. What had prompted her to remain here all this time? It couldn't have been the salary; the financial statement had revealed the disgrace of her wages when compared to incomes today, the fact of which he intended to change immediately.

Mrs. Frakes turned to face her new employer. "Where would you like me to begin, Master Colin?"

"Why did Uncle Max sell Lambert Oil? I have Girard's version of the story, but I'd like to hear it from you."

Mrs. Frakes studied Colin. "I afraid my perspective will not be pretty story. First of all, I don't trust Mr. Nicholas Girard. Always, when I see him, I think of the weasel."

Colin couldn't stop the grin that spread across his face. "I'm inclined to agree with you, although I can't say he's given me reason to be suspicious of any wrongdoing. Now, you were about to tell me about the sale of the company."

"Yes. Mr. Maxwell not confide in me about his state of affairs, but often I overhear conversation between your uncle and aunt or guests at Briarwood and sometimes when Mr. Maxwell talk on phone."

Colin nodded. "I understand. Please continue."

"After Mr. Braxton was mur… died, Mr. Maxwell seem to manage company fine, but from what I understand, he not like drop in price of oil, company investment losses and takeover attempts by large stockholders; he not want to risk more financial loss. And too, Mr. Maxwell's wife terminally ill at same time. He tell Miss Beatrice his intention to sell the business, claiming he not feel capable of dealing with both issues. A few weeks later, on a weekend visit to Briarwood, he tell your aunt he sell Lambert Oil to a competitive petroleum company for hundred million dollars."

Colin released a long whistle. Doing some fast calculations in his head, he realized once the stockholders had received their dividends, there still should have been a tidy sum left for Uncle Max and the Duchess to live in style for the rest of their lives, if invested properly. Yet according to Girard that had been the problem.

Mrs. Frakes put some dishes away in a cabinet then continued. "After Miss Agatha pass away, Mr. Maxwell sell his home in Tulsa and move to Briarwood. He change much then, drink heavy and, according to Miss Beatrice, lose lots of money betting on horse races at Oklahoma City. When he no longer seem interested in horses, he become like recluse, never leaving house and would fall asleep in den most nights in drunken state. Not even your aunt could pull him out of misery from losing his beloved wife. The drinking make his health worse and worse. I'm surprised he live as long as he did, although he seem better two weeks before he die."

Colin drew a long sigh. "That explains a lot, at least in respect to the condition of the house. When did my aunt begin to show signs of Alzheimer's?"

"About three years ago. Not too bad at first, just forgetting where she put things or not recalling day of week. Just recently I notice she begin to fade more often into that mindless stage of disease. I have studied much about dementia so as to better care for her. Please excuse now, I must see to her dinner. I'm sure she awake."

"By all means. I appreciate all you have done for the Duchess. I need to make a phone call anyway. I'll check on her when I've completed my call." Returning Mrs. Frakes's bow, Colin climbed to his room to phone his mother, hoping she would keep her thoughts of his journey muted during their conversation.

Once seated in the overstuffed chair in his suite, he pulled his cell phone from inside his coat and pressed the speed dial key connecting him to his mother's phone. "Hello, Mother. I just wanted to let you know I'm at Briarwood instead of a hotel."

"I'm not surprised."

Colin chose to ignore the sarcasm in her tone. "I need to clear up Uncle Max's affairs, and staying here will make the task easier."

"Why can't Nicholas or Beatrice handle that? I need you at home."

Colin sighed. "In case you've forgotten, Briarwood is mine now. It's my responsibility to see to my family. And don't act surprised. Girard told me this afternoon he'd made you aware of the situation when he phoned you about Uncle Max's death."

"Yes, he told me, also informing me of its rundown condition. You have a good income, but not the kind of money needed to refurbish an eighty-year-old estate. You surely can't be thinking of that, no matter how much you love that place."

"Thanks for the idea."

"Colin, you can't be serious."

"No, not at the present time anyway."

Colin heard Eileen's sign of relief. "I need to ring off now. I want to visit with the Duchess awhile before I turn in for the night. I'll phone you in a day or two."

"As you wish, Colin. Just don't stay away too long."

"Good-bye, Mother. Take care." He pushed the end button on his Blackberry and hurried toward his aunt's suite, praying she would distinguish him from his father.

Mrs. Frakes bowed Colin into the sitting room. The Duchess sat at a small table in the corner of the room eating her dinner, the finesse in her demeanor and movements a familiar sight to him. He had never known anyone else who could turn a simple meal into pomp and circumstance. He pulled out the additional chair and sat down, smiling at his aunt.

"It's so good to see you again, Duchess."

Beatrice glanced up, placing her hands, gnarled with age, into her lap. She studied her visitor then spoke. "Why, Stuart, how nice of you to stop in for a visit. You've been away a long time. Did you bring Colin with you? I haven't seen him for quite some time. I miss him."

Colin reached forward and placed his hand over hers, pleading with his eyes for her to comprehend his identity. "Duchess, I am Colin. I'm grown now. Dad is still in prison; but don't you worry, I'm going to take care of you."

After several long moments, a tear trickled down her cheek. "Colin," she gasped. "You are really here."

"Yes, Duchess, I'm here," he said, joy filling his heart that at last she recognized him.

She reached out and placed her hand on his cheek. "I wrote you so many times, but the letters were returned to me unopened."

Colin held her fingers against his lips, afraid if he spoke the anger he felt for his mother would gush from his mouth. How could she have withheld those letters from him? He breathed deep exhaling slowly. "I'm sorry, Duchess. I never saw them."

Colin saw similar indignation flash in Beatrice's eyes. "Your mother...your mother..." Beatrice seemed to think twice about what she intended to say. "How is your mother?" she said, her voice growing shaky and faint.

Mrs. Frakes stepped forward. "Miss Beatrice, perhaps tomorrow would be a better time for you and your nephew to visit."

"But, Mrs. Frakes, she knows..." Colin silenced his protest at the stern look on the housekeeper's face. He stood then bent over to give his aunt a hug.

"Duchess, we'll visit tomorrow after you get a night of rest."

She grabbed his arm with a strength that surprised Colin. "You won't leave me, will you?"

Startled by the same look of fear he'd read in her eyes earlier, Colin hugged her once more. "No, Duchess, I'm not leaving. I'll see you in the morning."

Leaving his aunt in Mrs. Frakes's care, Colin started toward his room then decided to get a breath of fresh air, hoping the nightfall had cooled the brazen temperature of the day. He pulled the tie from around his neck and unbuttoned a couple of buttons on his shirt. His first duty as owner of Briarwood would be to have someone check out the cooling system as soon as possible. *Maybe Mr. Baker would be the person to call*, he thought, smiling.

Once outside, Colin realized the heat was as stifling on the portico as it had been inside the house. He seated himself in one of the wicker chairs, his thoughts returning to the dismay he'd noted in the Duchess. What did she have to fear? Was she concerned about her well-being now that Uncle Max had passed away, or did her alarm stem from something else altogether? Now that he was responsible for her, he must discover the cause. And he guessed the best place to start his investigation would be to ask her about it. But would tomorrow find her able to answer him in a coherent manner?

Aware the heat would prevent sleep until later that night Colin decided this would be a good time to begin sorting through his uncle's papers. Stepping back into the house, he passed the dining room on his way to his grandfather's office. He thought it remarkable that within a few hours of his presence at Briarwood, it seemed he'd never been away.

When he stepped into the alcove leading to the office, he was surprised to see Mrs. Frakes standing with her hand on the doorknob of the office door.

"Oh," she said her eyes wide with fright. "You startled me. I-I thought you might like set of keys to house. I was about to retrieve them from your uncle's desk where I placed them after he die."

"Thank you, I'll find them. By the way, how is the Duchess? I hope my coming here hasn't been too unsettling for her."

"On the contrary, Mr. Colin, I believe she more at peace tonight than for some time."

"I'm so glad she realized I'm Colin and not my father."

"Yes. But who know about tomorrow? Good night, Mr. Colin. If you need anything, you know where my room is."

Colin nodded. "Good night." He watched her retreat from the area, wondering what she would do or where she would go when he moved his aunt to St. Louis. A moment later, he opened the office door and stepped inside, his mouth falling open in surprise at what greeted him.

CHAPTER 4

Colin stared at the chaos surrounding him—file drawers open and pillaged, papers and books scattered on the floor, the drawers of his grandfather's desk ransacked. He picked up one of the books strewn near his feet and started to place it on the bookshelf but realized he probably shouldn't touch anything else until the authorities had investigated the crime.

His initial shock abated, the image of Mrs. Frakes standing outside the office door a few minutes before entered his mind, her eyes fearful of his approach. Had she just left the room instead of about to enter it as she'd stated? Colin frowned, his initial thought of wrongdoing on her part scurrying away. The woman had access to the office 24/7. She could seek at will with no need to leave a mess behind her. He glanced around, at once noticing the open window across from the desk. Who had entered the house? What did he hope to discover, and did he find it?

Colin shook his head as though to clear his thinking, pulling his phone from his pocket seconds later. Scrolling down his list of phone numbers, he entered the Google search listing, speaking to an officer at the Osage County Sheriff's Office within moments. The deputy promised to notify Sheriff Kinney right away, explaining he'd be at Briarwood within the hour to survey the damages. Ending the call, Colin spied a set of keys in the open top middle drawer of the desk. Assuming them to be the ones Mrs. Frakes had mentioned, he pocketed the keys and then went in search of the housekeeper.

A few minutes later, Mrs. Frakes, her expression full of confusion, stood just inside the office door taking in the condition of the room, not uttering a sound. She looked at Colin, her eyes questioning.

"My thoughts exactly, Mrs. Frakes. Who is responsible? And why? Did you open the window earlier in the day?"

"No. I had intended to air out the office after Mr. Girard said you would be using it but was unable to perform the duty with so many visitors arriving this morning before the funeral. Later, the task slipped my mind. I'm sorry."

"Don't worry about it. When was the last time you were in the office?"

"The morning I discovered Mr. Maxwell had passed away in his sleep. After the coroner removed his body from the premises, I cleaned and aired his suite, deciding I should place the keys to Briarwood in his desk, as I explain earlier."

"Did you notice if any of the visitors this morning or anyone else since his death came near the office?"

"No…however, Mr. Girard asked to wash his hands to rid them of the juice that had dribbled from the pie his wife baked for us." Mrs. Frakes pointed toward the bathroom located between the kitchen and the office. "But he return from restroom soon afterward. He not have time to do the damage I see."

Colin frowned. He may not have rummaged the office, but it would have taken only a few seconds to enter the room and unlock the window as a means of entrance and escape from the house later.

The doorbell pealed, the sound startling them both. "Excuse me, Mr. Colin. I must answer door."

"I'll get it, Mrs. Frakes. Maybe you should go and check on the Duchess, in case she noticed the arrival of the sheriff. We don't want to frighten her."

Colin escorted the housekeeper to the front entryway of the house, disturbed at the notion nettling his thoughts. Could his aunt have been responsible for the disarray of the office files? Had she at some point in the previous days entered the room without Mrs. Frakes's knowledge, searching for something only she could reveal? Or had cash or other valuables been the target of the intruder? Did the person plan to ravage the rest of the house?

Colin rubbed the creases from his brow. Best to let the sheriff find the answers. Still, he couldn't conqueror the impression that it hadn't been a common burglary, but a pursuit of something connected to his grandfather's murder.

He waited until Mrs. Frakes had reached the upper level before he answered the door. The stench of evil in the air hung over him like a black cloud reminding Colin of an occasion in St. Louis when he'd stopped by a funeral home to pick up a contract for the agency, the odor of embalming fluid in the place, overwhelming. Colin opened the door, and following introductions, he led Sheriff Kinney to the back of the house.

The sheriff finished with his report within a few minutes, motioned Colin toward the window. "You can see by these scratches on the windowsill the intruder entered through here. However, there are no fingerprints on either side or top of the window where he would have gripped the casing to enter the house, making it obvious he wore gloves." Sheriff Kinney scanned the room again. "I wonder if his search proved successful."

Colin shrugged his shoulders. "I have no idea what he hoped to find. To be candid, since my arrival this afternoon, I haven't seen anything in the house worth stealing."

Bidding the officer good-bye a short time later, Colin climbed to his room, sudden emotional exhaustion overtaking him.

Having sensed the danger that could accompany his delving into the past, Colin had started to mention his mission in Haven to the sheriff but had remained silent, aware he had nothing at this moment to offer that might alter his father's conviction.

Following a cool shower, he started to place his soiled clothing into a bag when the bright-colored notepaper Julie Lonetree had given him caught his eye. He extracted it from his shirt pocket and read what she'd jotted on the paper. A moment later he opened his laptop and waited patiently until he could send her an e-mail.

> Ms. Lonetree, I've considered what you said about aiding my endeavor to search for Braxton Lambert's killer and would like to speak with you regarding this matter. My cell number is 555-283-5757. Respectfully, Colin Lambert

His electronic correspondence read and answered several minutes later, he shut down his computer and crawled into bed. Uttering a prayer of thankfulness and a request for direction in the days ahead, he closed his eyes, the day sinking into oblivion.

· · · · ·

Something dragged Colin out of a deep sleep. He glanced at the clock on the bedside table. Three a.m. He felt someone sit down on the side of his bed, the moonlight streaming through the windows capturing the silhouette of a woman. Startled, he switched on the table lamp. The Duchess leaned forward and placed her hand on his cheek.

"Stuart, you must listen to me. I know you didn't kill Braxton. I think it was Nicholas. I heard an argument between Braxton and another individual in the office. Your father said if the money wasn't back in the accounts within the week, he would turn it over to the sheriff.

"Standing in the hall near the restroom, I listened closely, but couldn't identify the other person, his voice too muffled. Then Braxton yelled again. He said he didn't have to prove the money had been stolen; it was in black and white for the auditors to see. And then your father asked the man how he could do such a thing? Had he not treated him more than fair, giving him an excellent-paying position in the company?

"I stood stark still, hoping to learn the identity of the man, but Braxton opened the office door. He told the individual he didn't want to hear any more excuses for his behavior, assuring the individual the matter would be taken to court if not rectified, the situation crucial should the stockholders of Lambert Oil discover the fraud.

"Afraid I'd be seen, I slipped into the bathroom, purposing to speak to Braxton about the matter as soon as possible. Less than an hour later, Agatha and I heard the shot, soon discovering my beloved brother was dead. Stuart, it must have been Nicholas. Don't you remember? Braxton hired him fresh out of law school, and he came that morning to see Braxton.

"I'm frightened, Stuart. I told the sheriff about the argument, but Nicholas told them I made it up to save you. And he said if I ever told the story to anyone else, he'd sue me for defamation of character. I know he's your friend, but I don't like him, never have. I'm afraid he'll try to kill you too."

Colin sat up in bed and placed his arm around his trembling aunt, the tears streaming down her cheeks dampening his pajama shirt. "Shh... Duchess, it's okay. Let's just pray like we used to when I was a boy. Father God, I ask you for peace. Please take away my aunt's fears and let her rest in your love. In the precious name of your Son, amen."

Drying her eyes on the corner of the sheet, Beatrice smiled. "Oh, Stuart, it's so good to have you home again."

Sadness filled Colin's eyes. "Duchess, I'm Colin."

She laughed. "That's silly. Colin is just a boy. He's fast asleep. I checked on him before I came to see you."

Colin sighed. "Duchess, we need to get you back to bed. Mrs. Frakes will skin me alive if she discovers I'm keeping you awake." He arose from the bed and led his aunt back to her bedroom, his arms holding her close to him. Once he awoke later in the day, he decided, he would ask the housekeeper to move upstairs in the suite next to his aunt's rooms at the first opportunity. Settling her into bed, he waited until she'd fallen asleep before he retreated to his side of the house.

The sun high in the sky, its heat saturating his room, Colin awoke at the sound of his cell phone alerting him to respond to an e-mail message. Too tired to analyze the Duchess's words in the wee hours of the day, he knew he couldn't ignore them now. But first things first. He had to talk to Mrs. Frakes about his aunt's early morning trek to his room. What if she'd fallen and injured herself, or worse taken a tumble down the stairs? Colin swallowed hard. They had to come up with a plan to prevent such an accident.

As soon as he'd eaten his breakfast, he didn't wait for Mrs. Frakes to clear the dishes from the dining room table but gathered them up and made his way to the kitchen. Just back from taking his aunt her meal, the housekeeper lifted an eyebrow at the sight of dishes in Colin's hand.

He smiled at the look on her face. "Mrs. Frakes, I'm used to taking care of myself. However, I want to thank you for the meal last night and this morning. I'd forgotten what a wonderful cook you are.

Mrs. Frakes smiled. "Thank you, Master Colin."

Colin stood stunned. He couldn't remember seeing her face light up like that.

She laughed as though she read his mind. "Let me have china before it fall from your fingers."

"I'm sorry, Mrs. Frakes. I just don't recall you smiling in that way. You're beautiful."

"Thank you. You're grown now. Children need discipline. You plenty mischievous when a boy."

He laughed. "You're right." Colin grew serious. "Mrs. Frakes, I need to speak with you about the Duchess."

Several hours later, the chore of moving Mrs. Frakes into the rooms next to his aunt's suite complete, he thanked the housekeeper for her willingness to abide by his request. His previous observance of her gentle handling of his aunt proved how much Mrs. Frakes cared for the Duchess.

Finished with hanging the last of her clothes, Mrs. Frakes turned to Colin. "I had thought of doing this a few weeks ago, but wasn't sure Mr. Maxwell would approve. I will rest better now that I can keep a closer eye on Miss Beatrice."

"The same here. I'm glad there's a connecting door so you can leave it open at night."

Later, in the kitchen, Colin accepted the fresh cup of coffee from the housekeeper. "Just as soon as I finish lunch, I'll straighten Uncle Max's office."

"Would you like help?"

"Thanks, but I have to sort through the papers so I'll know what to keep or throw away. If I have any questions, I'll ring for you."

Mrs. Frakes bowed then left the kitchen to organize her new quarters, leaving Colin to munch on the sandwich she'd made for him. Taking a last drink of coffee, he hurried upstairs to fetch his laptop, taking a few minutes to phone Tom at the agency and schedule a conference call for later in the day before proceeding to the office to begin the cleanup. About to begin the task, his cell phone beeped announcing an incoming e-mail. Opening the message on his Blackberry, he read:

Mr. Lambert, I'm available this evening after five. If you can meet with me, let me know. Julie Lonetree

Smiling, Colin replied, requesting they discuss the matter over dinner in Tulsa, suggesting she choose the restaurant. Within a few minutes he received an answer giving him the address of the Olive Garden restaurant in the Utica Square Shopping Center. That settled, Colin began his mission, the Duchess's accusations against Nicholas Girard a deepening concern in his thoughts.

If what his aunt had stated was true, his grandfather had discovered some form of embezzlement. Colin's jaw tightened. Had the attorney been the man his grandfather confronted that morning? Taking in the scattered debris, Colin sighed. He didn't have time to ponder that now, restoring the office to order his priority at the moment.

A few hours later, he placed the last of the files to sort on his desk, deciding the job could wait until tomorrow, along with the clearing of the desk as well. Not much to entice a thief, he thought, taking in the pile of old bills, receipts, equestrian magazines, outdated household management records, etc., the whole of which he tossed into a large trash bag. Any current bills he found he placed in new files, making a mental note to ask Mrs. Frakes for an updated list of accounts payable. He glanced at his watch, realizing the afternoon had gotten away from him. He had just enough time to check in on his aunt, shower, and then drive to Tulsa to meet Julie.

Closing the office door, he ran up the back stairs, skipping every other step. Finding the Duchess asleep, he knocked on the door of the adjacent suite, Mrs. Frakes peeking around the door a moment later. Informing her of his appointment in Tulsa and the time he expected to return, he avoided the curiosity written in her eyes, rushing to his rooms to prepare for his dinner date. His electric shaver in hand moments later, he smiled, his heartbeat accelerating at the thought of seeing Ms. Lonetree this soon.

• • • • •

Colin stood in the crowded foyer of the Olive Garden waiting for the arrival of Ms. Lonetree. He checked the time on his watch. Fifteen minutes late. He smiled to himself. It seemed the meaning of on time and deadline in the eyes of this reporter bore no resemblance to each other. He eyed her entrance into the building, his eyebrows lifting at the sight of the gentleman about fifteen years Colin's senior holding the door open for her. Colin felt disappointment sweep over him as he stared at the tall, broad-shouldered man, his grey-speckled haircut in the cropped style worn by preppies in the fifties.

"Good evening, Mr. Lambert. I hope you don't mind, I... Oh, sorry. Mr. Lambert, Jack Granger. Jack, Colin Lambert." She watched the two men shake hands amidst their polite pleasantries then led them aside to a less crowded section of the waiting area. "I asked Jack to come along since he was the reporter from the *Tulsa World* who covered your grandfather's murder. I told you about him yesterday."

Colin nodded. "Yes, I remember," he said, his earlier apprehension ebbing away. The two reporters were just coworkers.

She held up a bulging file folder. "These are copies of newspaper accounts, court documents, and photos connected to the murder and trial. Don't worry about getting it back to me. I have a file as well; Jack the originals. Also, I've asked my brother, Clay, who's an Osage County deputy to help with the investigation, all incognito of course, unless we find something the authorities can use to reopen the case. Of course, the three of us will only be able to help you in our spare time, but at least you can begin your search with these. "

Colin handed her the hostess pager in exchange for the file. "Thanks. I'm indebted to you. This will save me a lot of time and legwork." The pager began flashing, the three following the hostess to their table.

"I want to thank you both for your faith in my father's innocence," Colin said once the waiter had taken their order.

Julie smiled at him and then looked at Jack. "The only thanks we need is...to see your father's conviction exonerated"—her smile widened—"and a good story for the newspaper wouldn't be bad either, a reward in itself."

Colin returned their smiles. "Nothing I can say or do would compete with that." He grew serious. "I just hope we discover the truth before it's too late." He turned his eyes toward Jack. "I suppose Ms. Lonetree told you my father is terminally ill."

Jack nodded. "Yes. I'm sorry. As Julie probably explained, I heard your father make his declaration of innocence to you after the trial, and I believed him. The next day I talked with both the editor in chief and your uncle Maxwell about further investigation into the murder, but neither believed it worth the while. The chief thought it an open and shut case."

Colin's eyes widened. "Uncle Max refused your offer to try to prove his nephew innocent?"

Jack nodded. "He said it would be a misuse of time. Too much evidence against Stuart."

"Well, it's not a waste of effort or time for me," Colin retorted, clenching his fists. "Somehow, someway, with God's help we're going to discover the truth."

"I agree," Julie said, holding up her water glass, the men following suit until all three glasses clinked together.

Colin felt a jolt of electricity as his hand brushed Julie's fingers during the toast. He watched her grow rigid then relax. He smiled inwardly, sure that she'd felt the attraction also. Lowering her eyelashes, she turned to Jack.

"Once we wade through the material we've collected with a critical eye, let's meet again and compare notes. Maybe something will catch our attention and put us on the track of the real murderer."

Colin nodded. "Sounds good. Oh, I almost forgot. I met a man yesterday at the drugstore in Haven who may have something significant to contribute as well. His name is Jonathan Baker. He was groundskeeper and maintenance man at Briarwood when I lived there. He stated that no one in town at that time believed my father guilty of the crime. He was about to convey some information which might have bearing on our case when we were interrupted. I plan to visit him tomorrow in hopes he'll share what he had on his mind."

"Good," Julie said as the waiter approached the table with their meal. "We need all the help we can get."

Each enjoying the first bites of their meal, Colin pondered the rejection he'd felt from Ms. Lonetree. No doubt remained in his mind that she'd suffered from a recent adversity. Sure, it wasn't any of his business, but something told him the road of his immediate future pointed in her direction. He couldn't explain it, but in his heart he knew she would share his destiny. *This might be a tough one, God. But I know that "in all things you work for the good of those who love you and have been called according to your purpose."* Realizing Jack had spoken his name, Colin gave him his full attention.

"What did your mother tell you about the day Braxton died?"

"She refuses to talk about it. Anytime I've mentioned the murder, she's adamant about her opinion—that I should forget it and concentrate on the present not the past."

"According to her testimony, she'd left the estate that morning to go shopping in Bartlesville and wasn't at home when it happened, her alibi substantiated of course."

"I don't recall my mother's testimony. I wasn't allowed to attend every session of the trial, both school and the Duchess keeping me away."

Julie leaned forward. "The who?"

Colin smiled. "My great-aunt, Beatrice Lambert. I've referred to her as the 'Duchess' since I was a child." He pulled a long breath. "My aunt suffers from dementia. I awoke last night and found her sitting on my bed. Believing me to be my father, she voiced her fear for my safety, explaining she'd overheard an argument between Braxton and another man she presumes to be Nicholas Girard, the confrontation due to some missing funds from Lambert Oil."

Jack nodded. "Yes, that's what Miss Lambert told the sheriff at that time." He pointed to the file. "The account is in Sheriff Tucker's report. But after speaking with Girard, the authorities came to the conclusion Miss Lambert lied to save her nephew."

Colin nodded. "Mrs. Frakes told me the same thing. However, I've never known the Duchess to lie and Girard was on the property close to the time of the murder. Also, as the attorney for Lambert Oil, he may have had access to company assets."

Julie smiled. "Well, it's a place to start anyway. I'll do what I can to run a thorough check on the distinguished attorney." She winked at Jack. "I bet it's not the first time you've encountered a crooked lawyer in your years as an investigative reporter, huh?"

Jack laughed. "More than one or two, I'm afraid." He turned his attention to Colin. "We'll get started on this lead ASAP. In the meantime, find out as much as you can from the housekeeper and Mr. Baker." Jack looked at his watch. "Today is Friday. Let's meet Sunday afternoon, say at my place, and mull over all the information we've collected. Okay with you, Julie?"

"Yes, sir. Will that work for you, Mr. Lambert?"

He smiled. "Yes, and please call me, Colin. Since we'll be spending a considerable amount of time together in the coming days, don't you think first names are in order?"

"Yes," they said in unison, returning Colin's smile. Colin's heart raced at his minor victory, insisting a moment later he would pay the check. "The least I could do," he said.

Once Jack had given Colin directions to his house, they left the restaurant. "Till Sunday, Julie, Jack," Colin called as they made their way to their respective cars. Returning their waves, Colin looked forward to seeing them again. Opening his car door, he grinned. *Especially the intriguing Ms. Lonetree.*

Driving away from the restaurant, Colin thought over the evening. He'd arrived in Haven determined to find a killer on his own, but God had provided assistance in an unexpected manner. "Thank you, God, for your faithfulness."

Once on the road leading from Haven to Briarwood an hour and a half later, Colin heard the sound of a car approaching from the rear. He glanced into his rearview mirror. Drawing close to Colin's rental car, the driver slowed the vehicle, keeping pace with Colin. Colin adjusted the mirror, the bright lights of the vehicle blinding his vision. He drove close to the edge of the road so the other driver could pass him. However, the car moved closer, bumping into the rental car. Backing off, the driver again gathered speed to rear end Colin's car a second time before bypassing him at a speed too fast for Colin to distinguish whether the driver had been male or female.

Shaking with anger, Colin slowed his car to a stop. "The intoxicated fool," he muttered. All at once a feeling of uneasiness crept over him. Had the incident been intentional? The memory of Girard's wariness of Colin's decision to remain in Haven flashed in his mind. Had he been followed tonight by someone intending harm? Could his growing suspicion about Girard have merit? If not the lawyer, who? Colin grimaced at the insight flooding his thoughts. *No one, except a person or persons unknown who didn't want Braxton Lambert's grandson to get any ideas about warming up a cold case of murder.* Were the ransacked office and attempted accident related as means to frighten him away from Briarwood?

Calm once again, he decided to forego the option of phoning the sheriff. After all, he hadn't been injured, just intimidated.

Nevertheless, the events in the past twenty-four hours gave considerable credence to the theory of his father's innocence, if gut feelings were valued.

A short time later, Colin drove onto the circle drive in front of Briarwood, glad to see Mrs. Frakes had left on the porch light. Too dark to assess the damage on the rental until morning, he unlocked the door of the house, making sure all doors and windows in the house were secure before he retired to his suite.

As he prepared for bed, Colin tightened his jaw. Not a person alive would keep him from acquiring the justice his father deserved, no matter who or what he had to face down to bring it to pass.

CHAPTER 5

The next morning, Colin entered the kitchen yawning, rubbing at what seemed like sand in his eyes, the long night perusing the file Julie had given him now taking its toll. The disappointment he'd felt the night before still plagued him. He'd found nothing that would abate his father's guilt.

He watched Mrs. Frakes put the final touches on his breakfast as he poured himself a large cup of coffee into a mug he saw sitting next to the coffee urn. When he saw that she intended to tote his breakfast to the dining room on a tray, Colin held up his hand. "Mrs. Frakes, if you don't mind, I'd like to eat in the kitchen this morning. I have something to discuss with you."

Sadness filled her eyes. "Oh. When will you take Miss Beatrice away?"

Colin stood open mouthed watching silent tears roll down her cheeks. He stepped toward the housekeeper placing his hand on her arm. "Please, Mrs. Frakes, that's not what I meant. I've something else on my mind."

Mrs. Frakes pulled her hand from Colin's palm to rip a paper towel from a holder near the sink, dabbing the corners of her eyes. "I'm sorry. My impression you want other care for her."

Colin smoothed the back of his hair, his hand coming to rest on the side of his neck. Although her surmise was true, he'd discuss that issue later, he thought, observing the grief on her face. He waited until she seemed composed before taking his seat at the kitchen table, holding his words until she'd served his breakfast.

"Mrs. Frakes," he said after he'd blessed his food. "Do you believe Dad murdered Grandfather?" He watched her expression grow thoughtful.

She lifted her eyes to stare at her employer. "Why do you ask?"

"Because it's imperative to what I wish to share with you." Colin held his breath, waiting for her response.

"No, I do not think Mr. Stuart kill his father. But I know of no one else."

Colin felt the air rush from his lungs. "That's wonderful news. Neither do I believe it nor, like you, know of anyone capable of the crime." Colin hesitated, rubbing his fingers across his brow. "One of the reasons I've extended my stay in Haven is to search for the true murderer. It may be he's long gone from this area, but a hunch I've had for years tells me otherwise.

"Since my arrival in Haven, I've become acquainted with a couple of people who share our feelings and want to help in my investigation, Julie Lonetree and Jack Granger, both writers for the *Tulsa World* newspaper." Colin buttered a slice of toast. "And what I need from you is an account of all the events you witnessed that terrible morning. As you might recall, I didn't learn about Grandfather's death until that afternoon when Mother took me out of school early to tell me the news.

Mrs. Frakes nodded then tapped her finger against her lips, her brow creasing in thought. "But if you do this, it could be dangerous for you"—her eyes filled with fright—"and…perhaps Miss Beatrice."

"Yes, I'm aware of that. In fact, a car tried to run me off the road last night not far from the entrance to Briarwood. It may have been just an intoxicated driver succumbing to a fit of road rage, but with the break-in the night before, I don't think so. In my opinion my presence in Haven is making someone nervous. But, if they think I'm going to be frightened away like a scared rabbit, they are wrong."

The housekeeper gasped. "But, Mr. Colin, what good would you accomplish by your efforts? You can't bring back the dead, your grandfather or your father." She averted her eyes from his face.

Abandoning his breakfast, Colin stood from the table to pace back and forth across the worn tile. "I see you already know about Dad's prognosis."

"Yes, your aunt tell me after receiving letter from Mr. Stuart."

He halted his steps. "I have to do this for Dad. He has six months at most to live, and if I can acquire freedom for him, even if only for a few days, whatever I suffer will be worth it." Colin sat down again, lowering his face in his hands.

Mrs. Frakes came to his side, laying her arm across his shoulders, speaking to him as though he were still a lad. "Master Colin, I remember how you love your father. However, I do not think Mr. Stuart would want freedom at risk of your life." She paused momentarily. "Nevertheless, I do what I can to help you."

Colin raised his head. "Thank you, Mrs. Frakes. Please tell me what you recall about the day Grandfather died. Something you consider inconsequential could be of vital importance toward discovering the real killer." While Mrs. Frakes settled into a chair across from Colin, he took a portable dictating machine out of his shirt pocket and placed it on the table. "I hope you don't mind the recorder. Julie and Jack will want to listen to your statement."

She shook her head then turned her eyes toward the window. "It was warm spring morning, chirping birds loud in my ears. Mr. Braxton rise early, eat breakfast about six thirty, just have toast with marmalade and drink several cups of coffee, looking over papers he brought to dining room with him. He seemed worried and sad at same time. He say he plan to work here a few hours then go to Tulsa office, tell me he didn't want to be disturbed except when Mr. Girard arrive. A few minutes after Mr. Braxton go to office, rest of household come to dining room for breakfast, along with your uncle Max and his wife. They arrive night before, Miss Agatha desiring to spend few days at Briarwood with Miss Beatrice.

"Following breakfast, family parted company, your mother hurrying you to get ready for school, your two aunts retiring to library to 'catch up' as I hear them say. Mr. Maxwell return to room to get ready to go to Tulsa office, but your father remain a few minutes to drink more coffee and finish reading newspaper before he go for his ride." Mrs. Frakes paused to take a breath.

Colin cleared his throat. "About what time was this?"

Mrs. Frakes glanced upward. "About seven thirty or so."

"Then what happened?"

"While Grayson and I clean up kitchen, your father come in and ask if your grandfather still at Briarwood. I say yes, he in office but doesn't want to be disturbed. Your father laugh, then say he wouldn't disturb him, just talk to him. But pretty soon Grayson and I hear loud voices from office. A few minutes later, the doorbell ring. Mr. Girard arrive early for his appointment with Mr. Braxton. When I take him to office, we hear your grandfather yelling at Mr. Stuart. Your father come out of office, turn down hall, and go out backdoor, your grandfather standing beside his desk, a look of anger mixed with sadness on his face. I motion for Mr. Girard to enter office then I go to kitchen where I see Mr. Stuart walk toward stables through kitchen window."

Sheriff Tucker say at trial your father murder Mr. Braxton when he return from his ride."

Colin nodded. "Yes, I remember. Continue, please."

"After that Grayson and I go upstairs to straighten rooms. A little over an hour later...about nine, I think, I step from

BITTERSWEET JUSTICE

patio door onto the lanai outside Miss Beatrice's sitting room to shake a rug. I see your uncle Max walk toward his car, his briefcase in hand ready to leave for Tulsa. He move slow, his shoulders slumped, like he got lot on his mind. He turn and look toward house a few minutes then wave at me. He look like he not feel well and maybe trying to decide to go to work or stay at Briarwood. As he open his car door, we both notice arrival of Mr. Baker, the back of his pickup loaded with landscaping plants and materials. Your uncle Max waits for Mr. Baker and his son, Alfred, to get out of the truck then walks over to shake their hands, taking time to visit with them. I return to Miss Beatrice's rooms to complete my work there." Mrs. Frakes stood to refresh their coffee and then repositioned herself at the table.

"Leaving Miss Beatrice's suite a few moments later, our tasks complete, Grayson and I return to kitchen to begin preparations for lunch. Within a short time, your mother enters the kitchen on her way to get her car from garage. She tell me should she not be back from shopping in time to meet school bus, I must pick you up at bus stop. Mr. Girard come out of office. He exchange a few words with your mother and then leave through back door to go to his car, which he always park at back of house. Miss Eileen check contents of her purse before she go to garage a few minutes later.

"After they gone, I go to den to see if Miss Beatrice and Miss Agatha need anything, your aunt requesting I serve them lemonade in the sunroom where they would resume their visit. Returning to the kitchen to squeeze the lemons, I see Mr. Girard through window above sink having heavy conversation with your mother in the flower garden."

Colin sat upright, holding up his hand. "What do you mean 'heavy conversation'?"

"They both seem upset, your mother shaking her head, her face picture of anger. Then Mr. Girard say something that make her go quiet. She stood a moment frozen-like then stepped away from him and come inside house. I hear her run up back stairs. When I return from serving lemonade to your aunts, I start to peel potatoes for lunch and again notice your mother and Mr. Girard in the garden. Miss Eileen looks around as though to see if anyone else is in sight, pushing a small shopping bag into his hands before she hurries into garage. A few minutes later, when I step outside to dispose of trash, I see your mother in her car talking to Mr. Stuart, who'd just returned from his morning ride."

Colin waited patiently while the housekeeper sipped her coffee. "Then what transpired, Mrs. Frakes?"

"When Grayson offer to check on your aunts, I say I will set dining room table for lunch. While gathering the plates from the china hutch, I hear sound like a car backfiring on road. I look out dining room window, but not see car. Shortly thereafter, Grayson rushes into dining room to tell me to phone the sheriff because Mr. Braxton has been shot dead by your father.

"While Grayson comforted your aunts, I phone sheriff and then page Ms. Eileen. After speaking to her, I phone Mr. Maxwell at Lambert Oil, thinking he should have arrived to office by then. When they say he not there, I call his car phone. He say he return as fast as he can, your uncle arriving at Briarwood a few minutes after your mother walk in house, the sheriff and coroner a few minutes later."

"And where was Dad?"

"After I finish my phone calls, I go to office and peek inside. So tragic… your grandfather lying across his desk facedown, your father sitting in the middle of the sofa, sobbing in his hands, a gun near his feet." Mrs. Frakes pulled a deep breath, exhaling little by little. "So sad. Sheriff Tucker tell everyone to congregate in living room when he arrive, so he can take our statements one at a time. We all in shock, Miss Beatrice crying the whole time, hardly able to speak when questioned by sheriff.

Colin ran his tongue over his lips. "And how did my mother react to Grandfather's death?"

Mrs. Frakes hesitated a moment before she spoke. "Like stone carved out of marble. I overhear sheriff tell his deputy when they returned next day to look at office again, that had her alibi not been ironclad, he could have easily believed Ms. Eileen the murderer rather than her husband." The housekeeper took note of Colin's features, stretching out her hand to cover his. "I'm sorry. But you and I know no love between Ms. Eileen and Mr. Braxton."

Colin nodded. "Or anyone else in my family for that matter."

"Miss Beatrice did not like how her brothers treat Ms. Eileen, showing much kindness to your mother, but she rejected the efforts. So much hate in one so young."

"He sighed. "Well, score a thousand for the Duchess, anyway." All of a sudden, Colin's eyes brightened with perception. "Did Girard seem upset when he came out of the office?"

She frowned. "No. I don't think he upset."

Colin stood and walked over to the coffee pot, pouring himself a third cup of coffee, taking a few sips before returning to the table. *Could Girard have been the person Dad heard leaving the estate that morning, racing away from the scene of murder? But how did he get hold of Dad's handgun?* Colin stared into space, a moment later his heart racing. *Oh, merciful heavens! The shopping bag.* What had it contained? *No, God, please, not Mother!*

"Master Colin, what is it?"

Colin turned to the housekeeper, her face ashen with concern. "I-I was just wondering if Girard had been Grandfather's murderer. Did you hear a car rush away from the house as my father testified?"

The housekeeper stood to stack the dishes on the table. "No, but I pay no attention to vehicles…so many come and go at

Briarwood. Please excuse, Mr. Colin. Miss Beatrice awake by now. I must take breakfast to her."

"Sure, Mrs. Frakes. Just one more thing, though. Sheriff Tucker's report stated the Duchess had overheard a heated discussion about midmorning between Grandfather and another individual over stolen company funds. Did Grandfather have a meeting scheduled with someone other than Girard?"

She paused in her work. "I not think so. Mr. Braxton always tell me who he expect for appointments. But he not his usual self at breakfast. Maybe he forget to say about other meeting."

Colin's thoughts swirled. *So the confrontation the Duchess heard must have occurred after Mrs. Frakes and Grayson went upstairs. Girard would have been in Grandfather's office near the same time. Was he the embezzler his Grandfather had been shouting at when the Duchess overheard his heated words? If so, had Girard encountered his mother upon leaving the house and forced her to bring him Dad's gun, returned to the office, shot Grandfather, and then sped from the scene in his car, leaving behind the gun to implicate Dad in the murder? Arriving for his appointment, Girard had, after all, been witness to the argument between Dad and Grandfather. Had Girard thought this his opportunity to get away with embezzlement of Lambert Oil assets? But if not Girard, then who?*

"By the way, is Grayson still in the area?"

"No, he go back to England where Mr. Braxton find him."

So much for that possible source of information. "Thank you, Mrs. Frakes, you've been a great help. If you think of anything else, I'll be in the office. Then I plan to look up an old acquaintance after lunch."

When Mrs. Frakes turned away to prepare the meal for his aunt, Colin had trouble enduring the sadness in the housekeeper's eyes wondering if she was still concerned about the future care of his aunt. Was it possible he could work out something for all concerned? He strode toward the office, his lips softly echoing the words in his heart. *"What's your plan, God?"*

• • • • •

Close to the noon hour, Colin had his uncle's office in tip-top condition. Now ready to begin preparation to settle Uncle Max's affairs, he drew the accountant's reports from the top drawer of the file cabinet, adding the financial report documenting the status of the estate Mark Kellar had prepared for Colin. After studying the reports for the past year, he decided everything seemed to be in order. Although not an accountant per se, he did have at least an apprentice's knowledge of the subject, the CPA for his advertising agency keeping him abreast of the company's financial structure.

Colin frowned. These reports only verified the income and expenses for the estate. What about Uncle Max's personal bank account? Colin stood from the desk and marched over to the file cabinet. Not recalling whether he'd come across any of Uncle Max's personal bank statements the day before, he searched each drawer again. He returned to the desk shaking his head. Odd, he thought. Maybe he'd missed them when cleaning out the desk.

Mrs. Frakes knocked on the door, entering the room at his call. Paying little attention to her query as to where he would like to dine, kitchen or dining room, he stood in the middle of the office smoothing the back of his hair, frustrated by his fruitless search—neither a bank statement or checkbook in Uncle Max's name anywhere in the room. All at once Colin grew still. Had the intruder stolen those items when he'd plundered the office?

Between bites of a chef salad and refreshing glasses of iced tea a few minutes later, Colin quizzed the housekeeper. "Mrs. Frakes, I found the accountant's financial reports for Briarwood. And, from Mr. Kellar's notations, it looks as though he had access to the bank account to pay the bills for Briarwood. Is that correct?"

"Yes, that is true. All statements for house bills were mailed to Mr. Kellar to pay, and then he send monthly report to Mr. Maxwell."

"Did Uncle Max have a personal account as well? I didn't find any bank statements for him."

The housekeeper frowned. "I believe so. I see checkbook on desk many times when I dust office, his name engraved on cover."

"Have you cleared his rooms of his personal things?"

"No. Wasn't sure if you want me to go through his rooms. Should I do it while Miss Beatrice nap?"

"If you don't mind, we'll take a look at his suite later," Colin said, swallowing the last of his tea. "Right now, I'll look in on the Duchess before I drive into town." He smiled as he stood from the table, sliding his hand inside his trouser pocket to make sure he had the slip of paper on which he'd recorded the Bakers' phone number and address. "Thanks for lunch." He pulled at the collar on his sports shirt, hoping he wouldn't forget to ask Mr. Baker if he knew anyone in the air cooling business. Taking the front stairs two at a time, he reached his aunt's sitting room in less than a minute. *God, please let her know me today.*

A little out of breath, he knocked on the door then peeked around it. "Hi, Duchess, may I come in?"

Beatrice, reclining on her day bed, pillows perched behind her back, seemed startled momentarily and then smiled. "Why, of course. My, my, I can't believe how much you look like your father. The accident took him, you know, the burning timbers from the oil well falling on him, his death occurring moments after they pulled his charred body from the debris. I wish he could have seen you. He would have adored you. Such a gorgeous baby you were, those dark eyes just like your father's not missing a movement around you. And such a gorgeous smile, melting everyone's heart when they saw it, especially your father's. Braxton loved you so much."

Colin cringed, each step into the room keeping rhythm with his thudding heart. What did she mean? Is she referring to me or my father? Did the passing thought he'd had when he first arrived about his father's possible adoption true? With a slight shake of his head, he decided she must have him mixed up with two different people. How could Dad's father be alive and dead at the same time? Maybe she had another relative in mind.

Colin sat down on the bed, leaning over to give his aunt a gentle hug. "How are you today, Duchess?"

She tilted her head to the side, her eyes narrowing with confusion. "Duchess, you called me Duchess. Only young Colin calls me by that name."

Colin smiled. "That's because I am Colin. But I'm not a boy anymore; I'm all grown up."

All of a sudden Beatrice's eyes grew bright with recognition. "Colin, oh Colin." She looked around him at the door. "Is your mother with you? We haven't seen you for years. How long do you get to stay?" The Duchess reached up to caress his face.

Colin held her hand against his cheek. "I'm here for several days, anyway." Colin hesitated, his words softening. "I arrived a couple days ago for Uncle Max's funeral. However, Mother didn't feel like she could attend the memorial."

Beatrice grew sad. "Yes, I remember now. Max was a tormented man, could never get over Agatha's death. Nonetheless, Mrs. Frakes said he died peacefully in his sleep. I-I guess I wasn't able to go to his funeral. I ... I forget things sometimes. But they have a new medicine out now the doctor seems to think will help my memory. When did you say he was buried?"

"Two days ago. Did you know I own Briarwood now? Duchess, I'm going to make sure you have the best of care."

She looked out the window next to her daybed, her expression a mirror of concern. "I beg you, Colin, please don't take me away from Briarwood. I was born in this house over seventy years ago this September, and I want to die here. In all my travels, this is the one place I've loved the most." She gazed at him, the plea in her eyes too hard to resist.

"Duchess, if that's what you want, I'll see to it you have your desire." Hearing a sound, he looked toward the door, the housekeeper entering the room with a tray in her hands, her face bright with delight.

"Miss Beatrice, it's good to see you so perky. I hope your appetite just as ... how they say ... upbeat?

Colin laughed, the smile on his aunt's face a pleasure to behold, her beauty shining through the dust of age. "Well, if you ladies will excuse me, I need to drive into town for a visit with Mr. Baker. Do you remember him, Duchess?"

"Why certainly. He used to do odd jobs around the estate, quite apt in his work. Had a child born with Down syndrome, I believe, a likeable child, really."

"Yes. Dad and I took him fishing with us several times."

All of a sudden Beatrice eyes filled with tears. "Your father ... Stuart ... have you seen him?"

Colin nodded. "Many times since I turned eighteen."

Beatrice folded her hands across her chest. "I'm so glad." All of a sudden, tears flowed unchecked onto the bodice of her day dress.

"My poor baby. How I wish I could see him." All at once she straightened. "I-I was the only mother he had. And I want you to know, just in case the next time I see you and don't know you, your father did not murder Braxton. He could never do anything so vile."

"Duchess, I never believed he did."

Mrs. Frakes stepped forward. Miss Beatrice, why don't you eat your lunch now? Master Colin will return later to visit you."

At the look in the housekeeper's eyes, Colin stood then made his way toward the door.

"Yes, Duchess, I'll look in on you this evening."

He blew her a kiss from the doorway, his head reeling with myriad thoughts. Standing on the porch steps a few minutes later, he watched a flurry of small white butterflies dance the minuet in and out, around and through the thirsty, jewel-toned flowers bordering the walkway. The sight which seemed to reflect his soul, held him captive against yet another sun-drenched day. He shook his head trying to make sense of the Duchess's earlier statements. *Must be a characteristic of the dementia,* he decided, *her confusion about people, places, and situations.*

Satisfied he'd found the answer to her prattle, he turned his thoughts to his plan for the afternoon as he stepped toward the rental car. Eying the rear of the vehicle, he exhaled a sigh of relief, thankful the damage from the hit-and-run the night before was less than he'd imagined. He scrutinized the broken taillight and the small dent in the bumper. Should be no problem for his insurance to cover, he decided.

Driving from the estate toward town for his visit with the Bakers, Colin recalled his encounter with Jonathan Baker. Did he know vital facts that would speed up the investigation? The image of Stuart's face appeared in Colin's mind. He hoped so. Not a moment could be wasted in his war against time to win his father's freedom.

CHAPTER 6

Colin pressed the doorbell on the small, sandstone-rocked house, again checking the number on the house against the address the young attendant at the drugstore had given him two days earlier, just before his appointment with Girard. While he waited, he made sure the battery on his dictation device still showed an adequate level of usage, switching to the on position before he inserted the apparatus back into his shirt pocket. A moment later, a man a few years older than Colin, whom he believed to be Alfie Baker, stood speechless in the open door, his eyes wide with shock.

"Mama, Mama, Mr. Stuart. It's Mr. Stuart. He's come to see us."

Mrs. Baker walked up behind her son, wiping her hands on the apron protecting the front of her dress. "No, Alfred, it's Colin, Mr. Colin Lambert. Step back and let the gentleman come into the house."

Alfie shook his head. "No. Mr. Stuart." Alfie's eyes brightened. "Are we going fishin,' Mr. Stuart?"

Mrs. Baker took hold of her son's arm, pulling him inward from the doorway. "Come in, Mr. Lambert, before you cook like a turkey. Alfred, go get your father. He's in his workshop."

Alfie turned toward the back of the house, looking over his shoulder. Mr. Stuart good. Mr. Stuart not shoot father. Mr. Stuart good man."

Mrs. Baker threw Colin an apologetic look. "I'm sorry. I'll try to explain things to him when he returns with his father." She looked away then straightened as much as her spine would allow. "Mr. Lambert, I'm sorry about the other day at the drugstore. I had no right to say those things about your mother. My only excuse is the surprise of seeing you in Haven." She smiled. "Alfred's mistake has merit. You're a reflection of your father."

Colin waved away her contrition. "Since I arrived in town, Alfie's not the only person who's mistaken me for my dad." Mr. Baker and his son entered the room from the kitchen area, Jonathan extending his arm to shake Colin's hand.

Mr. Baker waved his visitor toward a chair next to the sofa. "Welcome, my boy, please have a seat."

Colin settled into the chair accepting Mrs. Baker's offer for a glass of iced tea. She spoke to Alfie, motioning him toward the kitchen. When they'd left the room, Colin turned to Jonathan, who'd sat down on the sofa. "I'm sorry to intrude on your day, Mr. Baker, but I'd like to ask you some questions about the day my grandfather died. In our conversation at the drugstore, I got the impression you may know something that might help me reopen my father's case."

Looking toward the doorway his wife had walked through moments ago, he leaned toward Colin. "I'm not one to take much stock in wives' tales, but if you stay in town long enough, no doubt someone will tell you those long ago rumors anyway. I don't mean to hurt you. However, if the information will bring justice to an innocent man, then so be it. As I started to tell you the other day—"

"Well, now, Mr. Lambert, this should cool your throat," Mrs. Baker said, striding into the room carrying a tray filled with iced tea glasses. "I sure hope we get rain soon. The garden is just about dried up. I'd hoped to can a lot of vegetables this summer; they look mighty fine in the pantry when the snow is flying."

"Thanks, Mrs. Baker," Colin said after taking a long drink. "Yes, we could sure use the rain. I noticed on my way into town that Sand Creek is lower than usual."

Mrs. Baker looked toward Alfie, who'd taken a seat in the far corner of the room, muttering to himself. "I tried to explain to him you were Colin, not Mr. Stuart, but I'm not sure he understood."

"That's okay. After I'm finished with my business, I'll talk to him. Maybe I can help." Colin sighed. "Mrs. Baker, I'm here seeking answers. I know Dad didn't kill my grandfather. And I've now the opportunity to prove it. My father is dying from cancer, and I'd like to give him a few months, a few days of freedom, whatever I can before he meets his Maker."

Mrs. Baker nodded, her hazel eyes filling with sadness as she gazed at Colin. "So much grief you've endured in your short lifetime." She glanced at her husband, a look of warning crossing her features. "I'm not sure we can tell you anything that will aid your cause, but ask your questions."

Colin turned to Mr. Baker, who stared at the floor. "Mrs. Frakes recalled that you and Alfie"—Colin glanced at their son, who toyed with the tail of his shirt, seeming to pay them no mind—"were at Briarwood on the morning of the murder. Can you tell me if you noticed anything unusual or saw any strangers about the place?"

Mr. Baker glanced at his wife. "It's been a long time, and my memory isn't as good now as then. Let me think… No, just the same as other days, the usual comings and goings of the family. Like I told Sheriff Tucker, Mr. Maxwell, about to enter his car when we drove onto the estate, stopped his departure to visit a spell with us. Ready to leave again, he glanced toward the house as he'd done a number of times while we talked then mumbled something about a forgotten briefcase, turning to wave goodbye to us just before he entered the house.

"Glancing around, I knew Mr. Girard was on the place because I recognized his car parked at the garage end of the house. Not wanting to delay my work any longer, I reached for the gloves I kept in my toolbox but couldn't find them. A moment later I remembered I'd left them at the back of the house the previous day, where I'd started to plant a row of boxwood. Deciding I didn't want to unload the truck without gloves, I sent Alfred to the back of the house to find them…"

Alfie stood from his chair and came toward Colin. "Stuart not bad man. Stuart not kill father. Bad man shoot gun." Alfie started trembling, tears rolling down his cheeks. "Hurt Mama, hurt Daddy. Stuart went away."

Mrs. Baker arose from the sofa, placing her arm around her son. "Alfred, it's okay. Yes, like you, we hurt when Mr. Stuart had to go away." She shook her head back and forth, a plea for understanding in her eyes as she glanced toward her guest. "Sheriff Tucker questioned everyone on the property that day, and Alfred has since suffered a great deal of trauma from that experience. He recalls it often." She patted Alfie's shoulder. "This is Colin, Stuart's son. Don't you remember playing with Colin?"

Alfie pointed toward Colin. "He Stuart. Colin boy like me. Colin my friend."

Mrs. Baker sighed. "I'm sorry, Mr. Lambert."

Colin glanced upward. Noting the mirror above the sofa, an idea struck him. Rising from his chair, he stood beside the man-child. "Alfie, look in the mirror." Alfred looked in the direction Colin indicated. "I'm Colin, Alfie. See, we're both grown up now. Do you remember Sparky, my dog? He always came with us when Dad took us fishing at the creek."

VICTORIA BURKS

Alfie looked confused momentarily then reached out and touched Colin's image in the mirror. "Colin Stuart. Stuart Colin."

"Yes, I look like Stuart, but I'm Colin."

Alfie smiled then hugged Colin, glancing once again at their images. "We not boys. We man, like Father. Colin my friend."

Colin laughed, embracing Alfie in return. "Yes, Alfie, I'll always be your friend."

Mrs. Baker took her son's arm, leading him back to his chair, picking up a magazine from a stack on the floor. "Look at your animal friends, now, Alfred, while Dad and I visit with Mr. Lambert."

Returning to her place on the sofa, she turned to her husband. "Now where were we?"

Mr. Baker cleared his throat. "While I waited for Alfred to return with my gloves, I noticed Mrs. Lambert drive from the rear of the manor, stopping a moment to chat with her husband, who was walking toward the house from the stables, but I wasn't close enough to them to hear what they said. Then she drove away.

"I realized after a few minutes something must have distracted my boy, he not returning right away... that often happened, a colorful butterfly, a spider building a web..." Jonathan smiled at Colin. "Boys you know... so I unloaded my things from the truck barehanded. A moment or two later, I pushed my wheelbarrow piled with tools, plants, and supplies toward the rear of the mansion, pausing to check the roses that grew on the north side of the house. Noticing that aphids had attacked the leaves, I returned to the truck to get some insecticide to rid the bushes of the insects. That's where I was, spraying the plants, when Mrs. Frakes came to tell me Mr. Braxton had been shot, the sheriff notified and on his way to Briarwood.

"I hurried to find Alfred, locating him in the garden sitting on one of the concrete benches crying as though his heart would break, his hands covering his ears. After questioning him, all he would say was 'Mr. Stuart sad, Mr. Stuart sad.' I tried to pull his hands away from his ears, but he wouldn't budge. Noticing the window to the office open, I wondered at the time if Alfred had heard the shot. He's always been scared of loud noises. He went deer hunting with me once as a lad, but the sound of the gun upset him so much, I never took him again."

"Mr. Baker, at the trial my father stated that he'd heard a vehicle speed away from the estate when he returned to my grandfather's office after hearing the shot. Did you by chance notice the sound of a car leaving Briarwood at a high rate of speed?"

Mr. Baker shook his head. "'Fraid not, Son." He pointed to the hearing aids attached to his ears. "I lost most of my hearing when I was in my forties. I don't wear hearing aids when I work outside. The wind noise bothers me. That's probably the reason I didn't hear the gunshot that day. And when I'm working, I tend to shut out the world around me."

The three adults grew quiet. A few minutes later, Colin spoke. "Mr. Baker, pardon me, but I feel as though you've something else you'd like to share with me."

Mr. Baker glanced at his wife, whose eyes held the same look of warning Colin had noticed earlier. Jonathan straightened, a look of determination settling in his eyes. "Now, Nellie, blast it all, you can see the boy is desperate. He's a grown man. I'm sure he realizes that all people make mistakes. More than likely it was just speculation among the townsfolk, anyway."

Mrs. Baker frowned. "Gossip never benefits anyone, only causes harm."

"Yes, but it could be more than rumor in this case, dear."

She nodded, a sigh of affirmation escaping her lips. "Whatever you think best, Jon."

Colin moved to the edge of his chair, his attention peaked. "Please, I need to know…if what you have to say will help my father."

Mr. Baker looked away. "Well…it seems a few days before the murder a waitress at Chloe's Diner overheard…ah…your mother tell Mr. Girard if he didn't convince Mr. Braxton to allow Stuart a bigger allowance, she'd get more money one way or another, even if she had to 'kill the old skinflint so her husband could become the head of Lambert Oil.'"

Colin snorted, his eyes narrowing. "I'm sure that news traveled like wildfire through the town." He noted his hosts' expressions of pain. "I'm sorry. I know you want to help." Colin breathed deep. "So you're saying the town believed my mother murdered my grandfather. But you said yourself, you saw her leave the estate."

"Yes, but she could have returned and left again while I worked. The driveway on the other end of the house isn't visible from where I tended the roses. Also, the townsfolk were aware of the bad blood between your mother and grandfather. It's not surprising they drew that conclusion, especially when she left town so sudden after the trial, not even showing up at the jail to tell her husband good-bye."

Sadness mingling with regret crisscrossed Colin's features. "Yes, I know. Is there anything other than the waitress's report that might have supported this incredulous talk?"

Mr. Baker glanced at his wife. "Now, Nellie, don't look at me like that. Remember, we witnessed the possibility ourselves at that restaurant, you know, when we had taken Alfred into Bartlesville for one of his doctor appointments." Mrs. Baker turned away from her husband's probing eyes then hung her head, Mr. Baker centering his attention on Colin.

"Eileen broke her engagement to Nicholas Girard to marry your father. However, during that time, people believed the relationship never ended between your mother and Girard, some even swearing they'd seen them together at different times. Since Mrs. Frakes had witnessed the two in conversation shortly before the murder, the town adopted the theory that Eileen and Girard had overheard the argument between father and son, seized the moment to kill Mr. Braxton and then live a life of ease on Stuart's inheritance once he'd been executed for the crime. However, if that were the case, justice in one sense outwitted them... Mr. Stuart receiving life in prison rather than a death sentence."

Colin shook his head, the bewilderment he felt clothing his expression. "That's ridiculous. Like a plot in a B movie."

Mrs. Baker leaned toward Colin. "Please understand, Mr. Lambert, the people of Haven liked your father. Don't be too hard on us. Whether the stories were based on fact, who knows? But the town had good in mind, similar to your cause now, exploring options, seeking out truth, and hoping against hope to free a man they respected." She gazed at his battle for self-control. "I wanted to spare you this additional sorrow." She threw a look of anger toward her husband. "But now you know."

Noting the look of strife between the couple, a wry smile clipped the corners of Colin's mouth. "Don't be upset. I probed you for answers, and you gave them to me. Truth can often be unpleasant." He turned to Mr. Baker. "Thank you for your candor. I suppose time will indicate whether the rumors were false or accurate. Now I must be going."

Colin stood from the chair and walked toward Alfred. "Alfie, if I have time while in Haven, I'll take you fishing." Colin threw Mr. Baker a glance over his shoulder. "Maybe your dad would like to join us."

Alfie closed his magazine and jumped up from his chair. He touched Colin's face. "Colin, not Stuart. Yes, go fishin.' Sparky too?"

"No, Alfie. I'm sorry. Sparky can't come along this time," Colin said.

Mrs. Baker crossed the room to open the door for Colin, Mr. Baker close behind her. "Please, Mr. Lambert," she said. "You're welcome anytime. If we can be of further help, just let us know."

Colin smiled at them. "Thank you." He glanced toward her husband. "By the way, do you still do repair work?"

He nodded. "Some."

"Would you mind coming out to Briarwood on Monday to check the cooling system. It doesn't seem to be working properly."

"Be glad to do it."

"Great. I'll see you then." He smiled at Alfie watching them from his chair. "Bring Alfie with you. Good-bye and have a good day."

Shutting off the dictation machine, Colin backed the rental out of the Baker's driveway. The driver of a black sports car parked a short distance from the Baker residence glanced toward Colin when he drove by and then turned away to speak into a cell phone. Suspicion deepened the lines in Colin's brow. He eyed the vehicle in his rearview mirror, noting that the right headlight had been shattered. The memory of the hit and run incident the night before flashed in his mind.

Was this the car and driver? If so, had he followed him to the Baker's house? Stopping at the intersection, Colin tried to recall the driver's features semi-hidden beneath his cap, however, nothing concrete came to mind other than someone young and of medium build. *Would now be a good time to brush up his early skills in marksmanship?* he thought, wondering if any firearms could be found at Briarwood.

A portion of scripture from the Psalms he'd read that morning came to mind. "Blessed is the man who fears the Lord ... his heart is secure, he will have no fear, in the end he will look in triumph on his foes."

Turning onto the road leading to Briarwood, Colin glanced over his shoulder to see if the black car tailed him. The vehicle not in sight, his heartbeat slowed. "Thank you, God, that I can trust in you; that I can count on you for direction in this situation. Don't let Julie, Jack, or I miss anything that will bring true closure to this case."

As he drove toward Briarwood, Colin's thoughts turned to his conversation with the Bakers. Could the rumors they voiced be true? Had this been the motive for Eileen's discouragement of his trip to Haven—the fear he'd discover she'd been a co-conspirator in murder? Colin smoothed the back of his hair. Should he confront her about the rumors? Colin rubbed his chin, the feel of his face as prickly as the idea. It might be easier to tangle with a mother bear that had lost her cubs to a poacher.

Okay, so his mother might have had an affair. But murder? Inconceivable! Yes, she was stubborn and ruthless about many things, but a murderess? Colin shook his head. No, that idea would never fly with him, no matter what the waitress at Chloe's Dinner had overheard. People often said things they didn't mean when angry. Colin's heart lurched. But … what if he found the talk to be true? How could he learn to live with that knowledge? Or forgive?

• • • • •

Later, following his arrival at Briarwood, Colin looked in on the Duchess but found her napping. He motioned to Mrs. Frakes, who sat in a nearby rocking chair, reading. She followed him into the hall. "Yes, Master Colin, what is it?"

Colin smiled. So many people in these parts had never allowed him to grow to manhood. "I thought this might be a good time to go through Uncle Maxwell's things, if you're available. I need to find his checkbook. And I can help you pack up his clothes. I suppose there's a charitable organization in town that can distribute them."

Mrs. Frakes nodded. "Yes. It's called The Agape House and is an outreach of our church. Come, I have boxes in the pantry I've collected for this purpose."

He nodded and followed her down the stairs. A short time later, they stood in his uncle's suite. Glimpsing the contents of the room, Colin sighed. "Where do you think we should start?" When Mrs. Frakes didn't respond, he stepped toward the dresser. "I guess we can begin here."

Colin felt strange filtering through his uncle's possessions, a sort of déjà vu feeling. It had only been a few weeks since he'd helped his mother with a similar project. Concentrating on the chore, his thoughts turned to his uncle. Although not sharing a close relationship with him, there had been some good times spent with Uncle Max, Colin recalled, especially at holidays.

He smiled, remembering the Christmas Uncle Max had given him a new train set, helping him assemble the track and village that had come with the gift. His uncle, grandfather, and father had spent the entire Christmas afternoon playing with the set, to Colin's delight. But Uncle Max had been a quiet man, spending hours in the den reading when at Briarwood, seeming to fall beneath his brother's shadow when around family or guests in the home. Grandfather, the more ostentatious of the two, was always the center of attention, his presence in the home much like a king commandeering his court.

When they'd completed their task of emptying the dresser and not finding the item he hoped to discover, Colin turned toward the chest of drawers, frowning, his thoughts taking a different road. "Mrs. Frakes, I need to ask you something."

"Yes?"

He paused a moment before speaking. "I had a visit with Mr. and Mrs. Baker this afternoon, you know, Jonathan Baker who used to do odd jobs here on the estate…"

She nodded. "I remember."

"During the course of our conversation, Mr. Baker told me some of the rumors that circulated in town at the time of Grandfather's death…quite disturbing to me, I must admit. And I thought you might be able to either validate or refute them."

"Master Colin, I not like gossip."

Colin appealed to her with his eyes. "Please, I have to know."

She sighed, Colin aware of the look of annoyance that crept onto her face. "What stories you hear?"

"It seems the people think my mother and Nicholas Girard were involved and plotted to kill Grandfather, frame Father, and then together enjoy my father's inheritance once he'd been executed for the crime."

Her face pinched with thought, Mrs. Frakes pulled open the top drawer of the chest. "I know no such plot." She began to take out garments and place them in a box on the floor.

Colin watched her movements momentarily then asked, "And the other?"

Mrs. Frakes turned toward him her expression stolid. "Perhaps you should speak to your mother."

Swallowing hard, he reached to aid the housekeeper with her chore then dropped his arm. "Yes. Perhaps I should. Excuse me. I'll be back to help you in a few minutes." Colin slipped out of the room, not stopping until the sun burned hot on his head in the flower garden at the back of the house.

Sitting down on one of the concrete benches in the garden, he hung his head in his hands. No need to ask his mother anything. Mrs. Frakes had said it all without uttering a word against his mother. "Oh God. My mother, an adulterous wife. And her lover"—Colin recalled his previous encounter with Girard, cringing—"of all men, the sleazy lawyer. How could she do that to Father—a man loved and respected by so many others?" Colin shook his head.

Girard's statement on the day of the funeral implying Eileen had married into the Lambert family for money and prestige hadn't been lost on Colin, but he'd tossed the notion to the wind. Sure his mother and father had had their problems, but didn't most couples have disagreements at times? But to deliberately forsake her marriage vows! He felt anger grip his soul.

There is no one without sin, no not one. Colin lifted his head. All of a sudden, he heard in his mind the Duchess reading that scripture to him along with yet another Bible story as he listened to her mellow voice so long ago, this one about the woman found in an adulterous act. When her plaintiffs had thrown the woman at the Master's feet, voicing their accusations, He'd picked up a stick and wrote in the sand. When He'd raised his head a few minutes later and saw no one but the woman, He'd asked her, "Where are your accusers now?"

Colin recalled how he'd questioned his aunt about the writings. "Well, no one on this earth knows for sure," she'd said, "but it's my guess Jesus had these in mind." Then she'd read the Ten Commandments to him. His assignment from her that day had been to memorize the commandments, the reward, once he'd quoted each commandment to her, a trip to the Omniplex in Oklahoma City for a day of education and fun.

He took in the flowers blooming nearby, staring at the pure white lilies in the center of the patch. He smiled in spite of his feelings. "You're right, God. Who am I to judge? My life hasn't been lily white either." Colin glanced upward, eyeing the windows bordering one side of his uncle's suite. He'd been away long enough. He still had to locate Uncle's Max's checkbook and wallet.

BITTERSWEET JUSTICE

Once again in his uncle's room, he realized Mrs. Frakes had finished clearing out the chest of drawers. At his questioning glance, she shook her head. "No checkbook."

"Okay, you do one nightstand, and I'll take the other." He looked across the room. "There's also a drawer in that table over there." After careful search of the nightstands, the two had uncovered only a few prescription bottles, a couple of books, a notepad, and some coins. However, when he pulled open the drawer on the writing table, Colin had some luck, Uncle Max's wallet lying on top of his personalized stationery.

Realizing the letterhead no longer usable, he tossed the stationery into a trashcan beside the table, handing the stamps to Mrs. Frakes, suggesting she keep them for her personal use. He then proceeded to look through the wallet, the usual items inside, credit cards, driver's license, a picture of his wife, a couple hundred dollars, which he also gave to the housekeeper. At her questioning gaze, he smiled. "Buy yourself something nice. You deserve it." At her look of protest, he held up his hand. "Just call it a token of appreciation for all you do at Briarwood." Colin bowed in response to her like expression of gratitude, restoring his attention to the wallet.

Colin tugged a picture from another holder in the billfold, realizing it was a photograph of himself, his father, grandfather, and Sparky taken on the porch of the estate, all three of them smiling at the camera while the dog gazed up at Colin. He tried to recall the event, but nothing came to mind. He set the picture aside to place in his own wallet later, beholden to the individual who'd snapped the photo, his uncle, no doubt.

The wallet empty, he stared at it. Should he keep it for sentimental reasons? No, he decided. He and his uncle hadn't been that close. Starting to toss it into the trashcan, he noticed something white on the bottom of the lengthwise section reserved for monetary bills. Realizing the wallet had a hidden slot, he pulled the flap upward, exposing a scrap piece of notepaper on which the number 685 had been written. He started to throw the paper away with the wallet, but something stayed his hand, the feeling the number might be important arresting his thoughts. Placing the note into the pocket of his jeans, he turned to the housekeeper, glimpsing the filled cartons on the floor.

"We're about done. Just the closet left."

"Mr. Colin, I should see about your aunt. And I need to begin dinner."

He glanced at his watch. "Sorry, I didn't realize the time. You go ahead." He smiled. "We'll complete this task after dinner, if you're up to it."

Mrs. Frakes bowed. "Yes, as soon as I settle Miss Beatrice for the evening."

"When I finish answering my e-mails, I'll sit with her while you cook dinner."

"As you wish, Master Colin," she said, turning to leave the room.

• • • • •

When Colin entered Beatrice's sitting room an hour later, she sat in her chair staring out the window, her shoulders sheathed in a crocheted shawl, her Bible in her lap. Good evening, Duchess. Did your day go well?"

She turned to him, her lips tilted upward in a smile. "Good evening, Colin. Yes, it was a good day, even better now that I know you've come home. Did you enjoy your afternoon at the Bakers?"

Colin's face lit up, his smile brilliant. The new medicine seemed to be working already. "Yes," he said, giving his aunt a hug. He glanced out the window understanding her fascination with the view, the magnificence of the approaching sunset breath-taking. "It was great to see Alfie again." Colin laughed.

"Although it did take us a while to convince him I was Colin and not Dad."

Beatrice extended her arm to take Colin's hand in hers. He gazed at her gnarled fingers, smiling to hide the sadness that overwhelmed him. How long before Reverend Smith would read her last rites? *I see you still like that bright red polish. Now, what is the name of that nail color? Scarlett Thread?"*

She pulled her fingers away from his, resting her hands on her open Bible. "Oh, Colin, how you love to tease me."

He laughed. "Only because you enjoy it."

She grinned. "That I do." She pointed to the occasional chair across from her. "Please, sit down. You must tell me about your life in St. Louis."

"Once in Missouri, I missed you, Dad, and Briarwood so much, I threatened many times to run away, but soon after starting school I found new friends. Mother married a few months after her divorce from Dad. Mr. Hemphill was good to me, and I grew to love him, not like Dad, of course, but genuine respect. When I graduated from high school, I went off to college, graduating with a master's degree in commercial marketing, soon afterwards beginning my employment on the ground floor of my stepfather's advertising agency." When my stepfather died a few months ago, I inherited the business."

She leaned forward. "When did you last see your father?"

"A few days prior to Uncle Max's death, I drove to McAlester for a visit with him."

"We keep in touch by mail. He's not expected to live long, I guess you know. The cancer is widespread now."

Colin nodded, allowing her a moment to deal with the sadness that etched its way across her porcelain features. Should he tell her about his intent to free his father? Would the news be too much for her delicate condition?

She looked deep into his eyes. "Colin, something is troubling you. What is it?"

He hesitated, not sure if he should answer. "In addition to closing out Uncle Max's affairs, I've decided to reside at Briarwood in hopes of—" Colin darted his eyes toward the sound at the door.

Mrs. Frakes entered the room, toting a large, heavy-laden tray. She glanced at Colin. He winced at the look of disapproval in her eyes. Maybe he shouldn't mention his pursuit of a killer to the Duchess after all. He glanced at the housekeeper. How does she do it? Had she saved him yet again from another grave mistake like so many times in his childhood? He stood to take the tray from her hands. Avoiding her eyes, he placed it on the table.

Mrs. Frakes helped his aunt to her feet. "Miss Beatrice, I thought you might enjoy dinner with Master Colin this evening."

"Why, thank you, Hanako." The Duchess smiled at her nephew. "I can't think of anything more pleasant at this moment."

Later, when Mrs. Frakes returned to take away their dinner service, Colin noticed that his aunt had begun to tire. Escorting her to a more comfortable chair, he leaned over to take her into his embrace. "I love you, Duchess. Please forgive me for not visiting you all these years. I have no real excuse. And I know nothing will make up for it now; however, I must say, although you were out of my sight, you were never out of my heart or mind."

"Colin, please don't berate yourself for decisions you regret. Everyone makes mistakes. It's the nature of mankind to fall short of God's best for us. Remember, the Apostle Paul said in Romans, chapter seven, 'Those things I desire to do, I do not, but the things I desire not to do, I do.' But it's a person's willingness to learn and grow from those blunders in life that counts."

She took hold of his hand. "I know how much you loved Briarwood, the family, and how difficult it would have been to return to the scene of your grief. Just remember, God works his will for his pleasure. Besides, you're here now." Sorrow flashed in her eyes. "And, just in case I don't remember who you are tomorrow, don't forget, God has a plan and purpose for your life. In fact, I believe at this moment you're in his perfect will."

Colin took her face in his hands. "Thank you for all your prayers for me." He laughed. "And all those scripture verses you made me memorize." He kissed her cheek. "Now, I must attend to some other things. I'll see you in the morning."

She raised her hand to his cheek. "Good night, dear boy. And may the Lord bless you and keep you. May His face shine upon you and be gracious to you. May He turn his face toward you and give you peace."

"Same to you, Duchess."

As he walked out of the sitting room, he wiped away his tears with the back of his hand. The dialogue just spoken between them had been routine when he was a boy. As soon as his parents had tucked him in for the night, the Duchess would venture into his room for a final story and then speak over him the blessing she'd just recited taken from the biblical book of Numbers. The nightly visits had been their special secret.

A short time later, after he entered Uncle Max's rooms, Mrs. Frakes appeared in the doorway. "Your aunt is settled and already asleep. Do you still intend to finish this tonight?"

"Yes, if you don't mind. Shall we take care of the rest of his clothes before we tackle the sitting room?" At her nod of approval, Colin opened the double doors of the closet, which stretched across the entire length of one wall, revealing a large number of suits, sports jackets, shirts, and several built-in drawers. He looked over his shoulder to eye the empty boxes on the bedroom floor, hoping there would be enough cartons to hold all the clothing.

As he handed the garments to Mrs. Frakes one by one, he noticed she checked each pocket on the items before she folded and placed them into a container. He grinned. "If you keep that up, this will be an all-night chore."

She returned his smile. "Always before I send Mr. Max's suits and coats to cleaners, I search pockets. He sometimes forget to take out money and lottery tickets from his pockets."

His smile widened. "Maybe we might get lucky and find a winning ticket." He looked around him at the faded, although clean, room. "It would be nice to restore the old place."

A couple of hours later, while the housekeeper put the last article of clothing into a box, Colin scanned the closet once more in case they'd missed an item, opening the doors as far as possible. He spied a man's suit hanging in the darkest part of the closet. He stepped inside the area and took it off the rack, noting the garment seemed larger in size than his uncle's clothing.

He held it up for Mrs. Frakes' inspection. She eyed the navy suit then gasped, her eyes widening in alarm. Surprised by her reaction, Colin turned the front of the suit toward him, his chin dropping in disbelief as a groan escaped his lips.

CHAPTER 7

Colin stood immobile staring at the suit, his grip on the hanger so tight he could feel the wire cutting into his hand. He looked at Mrs. Frakes, her Asian complexion opaque around the edges. "Is this what I think it is?" he asked, his gaze glued to the small, round hole on the upper left side of the coat. He gulped back the nausea that surged to his throat. He felt sure the large brown stains around the hole and down the length of the jacket had been made by his grandfather's blood.

Mrs. Frakes pulled her gaze from the garment to look at Colin, the expression in her darker than usual eyes matching his own. "Yes. That is suit Mr. Braxton wear the day he die. I remember he spill coffee on his suit during breakfast. I tell he should go change, but he say he must get to office right then but would change before he go to Tulsa." She stepped close to Colin, to peer at the coat then pointed to a lighter brown spot on the right lower pocket. "Not blood, coffee stain."

Colin ran his free hand over the back of his hair. "Why in heaven's name do you suppose it was hanging in the closet?"

"I do not know unless..."

Colin darted his gaze from the coat to the housekeeper. "Unless what?"

"When funeral home employee arrive from Bartlesville to take Mr. Braxton from house, Mr. Maxwell follow hearse in his car to accompany body to mortuary. Mr. Maxwell must have brought suit back to Briarwood that afternoon or ... maybe, next day when he and Miss Beatrice go to make arrangements for funeral."

"I can't imagine him doing such a thing." Colin's eyes brightened as he studied the clothing. "As gruesome as it sounds, this might be a good thing. I've a meeting scheduled for tomorrow afternoon with Ms. Lonetree and Mr. Granger. I can take this with me to give to Mr. Granger. Perhaps he knows the location of a police lab where he can get the suit analyzed. I don't recall reading a lab report about the coat in the file Ms. Lonetree gave me, which surprises me." Colin shrugged his shoulders. "All else aside, this"—he held up the hanger—"may give us the break we need to find the real killer or a step in the right direction anyway."

Mrs. Frakes nodded. "We shall hope so. Now I go find bag for clothes." She shuddered. "I beg you, Mr. Colin, *please* do not bring it back into house."

A grimace cloaked his features. "No need to worry. After tomorrow, I hope I never see it again."

When Mrs. Frakes left the room to carry out her errand, Colin hung the suit back in the closet, the hanger not leaving his hands fast enough. What possessed his uncle to do this? Had he loved his brother so much, he'd enshrined the clothes he'd last worn? But that hardly made sense. If Colin's memory served him well, the brothers didn't seem that close. But of course, his father and the Duchess had been the affectionate ones in the family.

When Mrs. Frakes had returned and his grandfather's suit packaged for the trip to Tulsa the following afternoon, Colin observed the movements of the housekeeper, noting the pallor of her skin. "Mrs. Frakes, why don't you call it a day, our experience tonight harrowing to say the least? As soon as I check Uncle Max's sitting room for his checkbook, I'm going to bed also." Colin crossed the room and drew the housekeeper into a quick embrace, her eyes widening in surprise. "Rest well, Mrs. Frakes."

The housekeeper bowed, a slight smile touching her lips. "Good night, Master Colin. I'll fix you special breakfast in the morning. Will make you feel better."

Switching on the light to the adjoining room a moment later, he stood in the doorway to take in the sitting room, the masculine décor and furnishings like the rest of the house, needing an update. He sat down in the large recliner next to the window facing the front lawn to contemplate the days since his arrival in Haven. Had it really been less than three days? Colin leaned back against the cool leather, his thoughts weighing heavy on his body, the time in his boyhood turf seeming like years—too much information, too many events, in too short a time to comprehend and absorb. He reached for his cell phone inside his trouser pocket.

About to phone his mother, he pressed the speed dial number then pushed the end button, deciding to postpone the call. He couldn't talk to her right now. Maybe in the morning. He needed to give his faith in God's policy to forgive and forget more of a chance to become reality. Didn't someone once say, "Time heals all wounds"? Colin sighed. But didn't that occupation belong to God?

Yes, Son, I am Jehovah-rapha, God your healer. As Colin acknowledged the still small voice in his heart, he lifted his eyes toward the ceiling, his voice full of irony as he spoke. "Before all this is over, God, you may have quite a job on your hands."

Nothing is impossible for me. Colin's lips tilted into a slight smile. "Thanks, Father God, I'll remember that." He pulled the handle on the chair to bring it back to a sitting position, adamant that considerable divine intervention would be necessary for the days ahead.

The sound of a car motor pricking his ears, Colin glanced out the window, the lamps on the gate posts revealing a slow-moving vehicle on the gravel road bordering the west side of the estate. He squinted to get a better view of the car. Yes, it was the same automobile he'd seen parked near the Baker's house. A moment later the car gathered speed and drove out of sight. Had the driver seen Colin standing at the window? He stepped backward, a touch of alarm crowding into his thoughts. *Dear God, please protect the Duchess and Mrs. Frakes.*

Should he phone the sheriff and tell him someone seemed to be watching the house? He reached for his cell phone but drew back his hand. A bypassing car in front of Briarwood hardly classified as criminal activity. Didn't Julie say her brother was an Osage County deputy? Perhaps he'd be willing to be a source of advice in the matter. Julie's image in his mind, Colin felt his heart skip a beat. He looked at his watch, smiling, thankful his opportunity to see her again would occur in less than twenty-four hours.

He crossed the room to the bookshelves, moving aside books, décor items, and magazines. No checkbook. He glanced around the room. Only one place left to search. A moment later, he pulled open the drawer to the side table next to the recliner. He withdrew the remote control, a television program guide, and a box of cough drops. He sighed. Maybe the theory of his uncle's checks stolen by the interloper had been correct. Hopefully he would discover the whereabouts of the account in time to prevent a loss of funds from forged checks.

Opening the drawer to its full length, his eyes fell on a book at the back of the drawer. He removed it from the space, realizing it was a journal. Flipping through the pages, Colin discovered the diary held letters his uncle had written to his wife after she'd passed away. Not wanting to intrude on his uncle's private thoughts, he started to replace the journal then reversed his plan, curiosity overriding his initial intention. Seated in the recliner once more, Colin began to read, hoping for a glimpse into his uncle's life. His missives each basically the same, Uncle Max had articulated his grief, loneliness, and love for Aunt Agatha. Colin started to lay the book aside when one of the letters toward the end of the journal caught and held his attention.

>*My dear Agatha,*
>
>*Weeks have passed since you were taken to your final resting place. You're gone, but you're not away from me. It's as though your presence is still by my side. But when I turn to speak to you, only space greets me. My darling, how can I continue to live without you?*
>
>*Beatrice tried to comfort me by explaining that in time the pain would diminish and I'd be able to remember you with more joy than sadness. Such thoughts are inconceivable to me. You were my life, the breath I breathed, my reason to exist.*
>
>*I went to the churchyard again today to visit you, the ache for you so strong, I felt sure I'd die any moment. Aggie, we were going to live out our twilight years together, remember? But the demon of cancer took you from me.*
>
>*So many things I wanted to say to you, but I couldn't get the words past my lips. I'm so sorry... I just couldn't tell you the truth. I would have lost you forever. You were so good, so kind to everyone and... I... I... wanted to give you everything. Please forgive me, darling.*
>
>*Before I left the grounds, I went inside the church and sat in the back staring at the cross in front of the church. I soon departed, knowing I had no right to expect forgiveness... not from God, not from you—for all those nights I left you alone, the drinking, gambling and... and for... oh God in heaven, I can't abide the thought... I didn't deserve*

you, Aggie. I suppose that's why God took you from me, my just punishment for now, and later? Only God knows.

Your Max

Colin reread the letter. What could Uncle Max have done to his wife? A liaison with another woman, a string of women? A myriad of feelings flooded his mind—sadness, disenchantment, resentment. After all, his mother had proved the Lambert family wasn't immune to infidelity. Frowning at his attitude, he placed the journal inside the drawer. *It would sure be nice if a person could forget when he forgives.* Best not to think about Eileen now or he might find his phone in hand, the words in his mouth prompted by disapproval and disillusionment rather than love and forgiveness.

He studied a photograph of his aunt and uncle sitting on top of the side table. Funny, he'd have never classed Uncle Max as a womanizer. Maybe it had been an isolated situation and the thought of the pain his wife would suffer should he disclose the affair had restricted his confession. His letters proved how much he'd adored Aunt Agatha. *Oh, well, I've more to be concerned with than the revelation of Uncle Max's great sin. It's probably best the secret expired with him,* Colin thought, hoping his uncle had been able to settle the matter with God.

Colin lifted the cushions on the sofa, thinking the checkbook might have slipped from his uncle's pocket into the cracks between the cushions. Disappointed by his lack of success, he took a last look at each of his uncle's rooms then exited into the hallway, pulling back the covers from his bed a short time later.

His prayers said, he thought over the events of the day, the absence of a paper trail to his uncle's bank account befuddling. Of course, he might not have had an account, but Mrs. Frakes had been certain she'd seen a checkbook with his name on it. All at once he brightened. Scrambling to his feet, Colin threw on his robe and within moments stood outside Mrs. Frakes's room. Seeing the light beneath her door, he knocked.

"Yes?"

"Mrs. Frakes, may I come in? I have a question."

"Come in."

Colin entered the room to find Mrs. Frakes sitting upright on the bed, her elbows propped on the sheet covering her body, a book in her hands. "I'm sorry to intrude, but the financial statements for the estate noted Bank of Oklahoma as the location for the house checking account. Did Uncle Max have his personal account there as well?

"I not sure. Maybe you ask bank people."

He smiled. "That's my objective, first thing Monday morning just as soon as they open for business. And now, I won't bother you anymore this evening. Good night."

"I'll see you at church in the morning. I must go early. I teach children about Jesus. But like I promise, I will make you breakfast and leave it in the warmer. Mrs. Johnson will be here to sit with Miss Beatrice. Her friends take turns each Sunday because your aunt too weak to attend church."

"I see. And yes, you will see me at church. Please don't worry about lunch or dinner for me. I intend to leave for Tulsa at the end of the service, and I'm not sure when I will return."

"Very well. Good night, Master Colin."

· · · · ·

Following his Sunday lunch at Monterey's Little Mexico restaurant in Bartlesville, Colin stepped into his car and switched on the ignition. While he waited for the car to cool, he punched the familiar speed dial number on his Blackberry. "Good afternoon, Mother," he said a couple of minutes later, forcing cheerfulness into his voice.

"Hello, Colin. Are you ready to give up your little fiasco and come home?"

"Not at all. I've learned a few facts that might connect me to a killer. The town had an interesting theory about Grandfather's murder. Care to hear it?" Colin heard his mother's sharp intake of breath. Had she guessed what he intended to say?

"Not really. It doesn't peak my curiosity in the least."

"Actually, I think you might find the story interesting."

"Colin, stop talking in riddles."

It's now or never, he thought. "Mother, what kind of relationship did you have with Nicholas Girard?"

"What do you mean?"

"Just what I said. Explain your relationship with your friend, the lawyer."

She grew silent, her pause long enough for Colin to know he'd hit on a truth. "Mother, are you there?"

"Uh, yes. Nicholas was a good friend to your father and me."

"How good? Good enough to forsake your marriage vows, plot with him to murder Grandfather then frame Father for the crime?"

Her gasp echoed in Colin's ear. "You can't believe that horrible tale."

Colin sighed his hopes of his mother's ignorance of the rumor vanishing. "I don't want to," he said, softening his voice. "But can you deny you hated grandfather or your lack of love for Dad?"

She took another long pause. "No, I can't deny that, but I didn't murder your Grandfather. Son, you *can't* think that of me."

"Even though a waitress overheard you threaten Grandfather's life?"

"Colin, no! I may have said something like that in protest against Braxton, but I *would not, did not* kill him."

"Mother, did you have an affair with Girard?"

Colin closed his eyes when he heard his mother's sigh of relinquishment.

"I wish I could tell you different, but yes, Colin, I did. I'm sorry."

A slow burn began inside his chest and worked its way upward, the same experience he often experienced when confronting issues that related to his past. He wanted to drown out her voice, the acknowledgment like the sound of a sharp instrument scraping dross from metal. "Girard told me you two were engaged before you married Father. If you cared that much about your attorney, why didn't you marry him when you divorced Dad?"

"Because he'd married a woman from Pawhuska by then. Colin, I made bad choices in those days, but I always loved you. You were mine. That's why I rushed our move to Missouri. I wanted you away from Briarwood before the Lamberts had a chance to seek custody of you. Thank goodness they didn't try. I could never have fought their influence and power." Eileen inhaled deeply. "I'm sorry, Colin, for your sake that I didn't love Stuart."

"Why did you marry him?"

"I came from the poorest of poor families. Stuart came home from college and fell in love with me. The thought of living in that fine house and having all the things that money could buy appealed to me. So I broke my engagement with Nicholas and married your father."

"I'm sorry also, Mother, that you couldn't love Dad. Did you ever try?" Not giving her a chance to reply, he pushed the end key. His phone rang a moment later, but he ignored his mother's return call.

Putting the car into gear, Colin drove out of the restaurant parking lot, turning south onto Highway 75. Hostility swelled in his mind like the building force of a volcano just prior to eruption. He slammed his fist against the steering wheel, the taste of bile in his throat.

"Lambert, you just had to open your mouth," Colin said, his lips twisted with self-loathing. "Doesn't the Bible say something about 'ask and you shall receive'? Well you heard your answer. Now deal with it."

A few moments later, his ire against Eileen submerged beneath compassion for Stuart. How could she have not loved his father—a man so loving, kind, gentle—yet strong and audacious, enduring his life sentence with aplomb and fortitude in spite of his innocence. Momentarily, another thought forced his lips to curve upward. *Of course, it didn't hurt to have Shem, a three-hundred-pound, six-foot-five African American prison mate as your best friend, either.* On his first visit to see his father, Colin had met Shem. "My guardian angel," his dad had joked. Colin sighed. Life in prison could be disastrous for an inmate should he get crossways of a fellow prisoner.

Colin shook his head, his grin fading. To choose a man like Girard over his father, how could she? Colin gritted his teeth, the ache in his heart pressing on his chest.

Honor thy father and mother.

Colin glanced toward the sky. "That's easy for you to say. You didn't have a mother who married your father for money, cheated on him who knows how long, and then turned her back on him in his darkest hour."

No, but I have a Son who came to earth to proclaim my love so that no man should perish but have everlasting life. And those I loved rejected my Son; those he loved deserted him in his darkest hour. Do you remember what he said when he was nailed to the cross at Golgotha?

Colin winced at the inner voice. "Yes. 'Father, forgive them for they know not what they do.' But, Father God, He walked on this earth as both God and man. I'm just a man."

Approaching Jack Granger's house, Colin subdued his woes to focus on his expectations for the forthcoming afternoon, the meeting with his friends taking precedence over his mother's sins for the moment.

"Come in, Colin," Jack said, a smile of welcome on his face as he introduced the woman standing just inside the door. "This is my wife, Michele."

"Glad to meet you, Mrs. Granger."

She smiled. "Likewise."

Jack took his arm. "Come on. Julie's in the dining room. She arrived just ahead of you. He glanced at the file and bag in Colin's hand. Our work will be easier if we sit at the table. Michele made a fresh pitcher of lemonade. Boy, this heat is unreal, isn't it?"

Once seated in the spacious room, Colin accepted the cold beverage from Michele. "Thank you." He took a drink. "Mm, this is good." Michele smiled her appreciation and then returned to the kitchen.

Colin turned his eyes toward Julie. She looked gorgeous in her hot pink sundress and sandals to match. "Hello. How's it going?"

She laughed. "If we don't get some rain soon, I may become like the wicked witch in the *Wizard of Oz*, all spread out on the yellow brick road from a meltdown. Otherwise, I'm great. And you?"

Colin smiled wanly. "I have to say the eye-opening experiences of the last few days have me on edge, but I can't complain otherwise."

Jack sat down beside Julie across from Colin, reaching for the sheaf of papers on the table in front of him. "Sounds interesting. Why don't we begin with all the information you've gathered so far about your grandfather's murder?" Jack said, pulling a lined tablet from among his paperwork toward him. "Then Julie and I will tell you what we've accomplished."

Colin nodded, taking his recorder from his pocket.

The three grew quiet as they listened and took notes while the machine spilled forth Colin's conversations with the Bakers and Mrs. Frakes. The words spent a few moments later, Colin switched off the recorder.

Jack pointed to his stack of papers. "Most of what we heard is already in the reports, with the exception of an item or two. I don't remember reading anything about your mother giving Girard a shopping bag. Did the housekeeper know what it contained?"

Colin shook his head. "It could be the sheriff discovered the contents in the bag didn't having any bearing on the case. I'll make it a point to question Mother and Girard about it, though. Then we'll know for sure."

"Good idea," Julie interjected. "Anything else you can think of that might be significant?"

"Yes. I know someone in Osage County is not happy with my prolonged stay at Briarwood." At their startled looks, Colin explained about the break-in, the hit-and-run driver, and his conviction that his comings and goings were now monitored.

Julie's eyes filled with concern. "I'll talk to Clay about it and see what he thinks you should do. He wanted to be here today, but he had duty."

Colin leaned over to pick up the bag that held his Grandfather's clothes. "And I have this. Mrs. Frakes is sure this is the suit my grandfather wore the day he died." Colin handed the bag to Jack. "We found it hanging in my uncle's closet last night when we were packing away his clothes. However, she can't explain for certain why it was there."

Jack pulled the clothes from the bag, spreading the coat in front of him. "Wow. This is some piece of evidence." He frowned. "These weren't mentioned in any of the documents either. I wonder why."

Colin glanced at Julie, her face pale. He smiled. "Maybe a drink of lemonade will help."

"I don't think so. How could anyone keep that? Good grief, bullet hole and all."

"Yeah, I know. I thought maybe your brother or Jack could take this to a lab for analysis. And too, when I read the reports, I didn't see a ballistics report on the bullet fired from the gun. Why do you suppose not?"

Jack grew thoughtful. "That *is* odd. Unless the sheriff, thinking he had an airtight case, decided not to waste the taxpayer's money on a lab report. Who knows? But I have a friend in the forensic lab at the Tulsa Police Department who might be willing to check out the suit for us"—Jack grinned—"incognito, of course." He turned to Julie. "Might be faster than the red tape in Osage County."

She nodded, her face lighting up. "Jack, do you suppose the evidence from the trial would still be stored somewhere?"

"Usually evidence is stored indefinitely. Since the murder happened in Osage County, there should be a storage facility at the sheriff's office. Why don't you ask Clay to look for the evidence from the Lambert trial when he has the opportunity?"

She smiled. "Good as done. I'll phone him this evening when he gets home from work. Colin, how long do you plan to stay in the area?"

"I've taken a few weeks leave from work. My top assistant at the agency is efficient, and with daily input from me, he'll be able to handle the work until I return home."

"Sounds good. In relation to the incidents you spoke of earlier, like you, I think someone wants you back in St Louis pronto. All we have to do is find out who and why."

Colin nodded an agreement. "So what did you guys discover about Girard?"

Julie pulled some paperwork from a tote bag sitting on the table. "Born and raised in Haven, Oklahoma, by poor, but hard-working parents, good student, graduated from college and law school on scholarships, grants, and odd jobs. Best friend, Stuart Lambert, employed by Lambert Oil upon graduation where he worked his way up in the company ranks to become senior corporate attorney for firm." Julie lifted her head to look at Colin. "I assume you knew he and your mother planned to marry after he'd graduated from Oklahoma University."

"Yes, but my mother broke off the engagement to marry my father."

Julie nodded. "And the three of them still remained friends according to my research. Is that true?"

"So I understand." Colin lowered his head, pretending to study his notes, gritting his teeth against the surge of bile that attacked his throat. Finally, he looked up. "And his life today?"

A puzzled frown on each of their faces, Julie and Jack stared at him. Julie looked down, continuing to read. "Still practices law in Haven and in Pawhuska, the bulk of his clients from that area. He's married yet has a reputation for involvements with other women, no children, but helped raise his wife's nephew and niece. Nephew, Keith, a troublemaker, is in and out of jail. Niece, Maria, is employed as Girard's secretary and is married to a truck driver who's on the road most of the time."

Colin nodded. "Yes. I met her the day of Uncle Max's funeral just before my meeting with Girard that afternoon." Colin scowled within. *Like uncle, like niece?*

Julie looked over at Jack. "But this is the interesting part. He lives well above his income, his debt ratio blown off the chart. His income tax records reveal he should be at the courthouse tomorrow filing bankruptcy. According to my source in Pawhuska, he doesn't have enough clientele to finance his lifestyle. I drove by his house southeast of Pawhuska this morning, five hundred thousand-dollar home at least, plus acreage."

Colin recalled the expensive furnishings in Girard's office in Haven and the designer suit the secretary wore. She must earn a good salary. He wasn't positive, but he didn't think truck drivers earned that kind of money.

Jack interrupted Colin's thoughts. "So where do you suppose he gets his extra cash? On the take maybe? Drug sales?"

Julie smiled. "I believe that type of investigating is your expertise."

Jack grinned, shrugging his shoulders. "Maybe."

Colin cleared his throat. "Girard's bio is interesting, but did you find anything that might associate him with my grandfather's murder? Colin looked down at the file. We know he was at Briarwood that morning."

Julie's eyes filled with sadness as she eyed the desperate look on Colin's face. "Colin, we've just begun. If he's guilty, with time we'll prove it."

Colin slammed his palm down on the stack of papers in front of him. "That's just it. Time is the adversary," Colin declared. Taking in his companions' expressions, Colin lowered his eyes. "Sorry. Please forgive the impatience."

Jack waved away his apology. "We understand. It's too bad more investigation into your father's plea of innocence was sacrificed for a speedy trial and conviction." He thumbed through his copy of the court documents until he found the file he wanted, scanning it momentarily before he spoke. "At least the jury took some time to debate the issue. But you have to understand, the panel consisted of hometown country folk unfamiliar with official proceedings. They probably never considered the importance of lab reports, a ballistic report and the like, if they thought of them at all. Too much circumstantial evidence was stacked against Stuart. However"—Jack held up the sack containing Braxton's clothes—"even the most country of sheriffs should have known to have these analyzed."

A wry smile touched Colin's lips. "I guess this case is going to take a bit longer than an hour Whodunit." Colin's new friends laughed, dissolving the tension in the air.

"Look, Colin," Julie said after a moment. "We'll keep digging. If your father is innocent as we all believe, we'll find something that will lead to the killer eventually."

Jack agreed, giving Colin a look of encouragement. "You keep asking questions around Haven, and we'll go over the records again. I just have this feeling we're missing something." He gazed at the ceiling, smiling. "As you stated the other night, Providence may be the one who solves this case." Jack stood from the table, the others following his lead. "I have to be out of town this next week on assignment for the newspaper. Perhaps you and Julie can get together, say on Wednesday, to compare notes. I should be back on Saturday. Let's plan on meeting here again on Sunday afternoon. Same time. Is that okay by you?" The two nodded. "Good. We'll see you then."

After expressing their thanks to Jack's wife for her hospitality, Julie and Colin walked out the door. "Say, Julie. I was wondering. Would you like to come to Briarwood on Wednesday evening? Mrs. Frakes is a marvelous cook. I would love for you to meet the Duchess. Even if she thinks I'm my father, she will be her usual gracious self." He laughed. "Think of it as a chance to further your newspaper story on the Lamberts."

Julie smiled. "I would like that. Thank you. What time?"

"Six thirty?"

"Perfect. I'll come straight from work."

"Good." Colin opened the door of her car. Once she was seated, he gave her a wave. "See you Wednesday." Returning his gesture, she backed out of the driveway.

Colin stood looking after her until she drove out of sight, his heart swelling with joy. At last, his chance to be alone with her, a break to find out more about this lovely individual who'd tilted his world, causing his insides to dance the tango and the rumba in simultaneous motion at just the thought of her.

His thoughts still on Julie an hour later when he turned onto the road leading to Briarwood, all at once Colin straightened, his nerves growing tense as he scanned the scene in the valley below, his heart racing at the sight of the flashing red and blue lights outside his house. He pressed the gas pedal, driving as fast as the road would allow. "Oh, God, please let them be okay!"

CHAPTER 8

Colin whipped the rental car onto the circle drive and screeched to a stop behind the patrol car, entering the house in record time. Voices from the living room catching his attention, he rushed into the room where Mrs. Frakes sat in a chair conversing with Sheriff Kinney seated across from her, another officer standing nearby.

At the sound of Colin's entrance into the room, the three looked up, the deputy's hand clasping the gun strapped to the side of his hip a second later. Seeing the reaction, the housekeeper stood and hurried toward her employer. "Master Colin, thank goodness you home."

Colin put his hands on her shoulders. "What is it? Where's the Duchess? Is she okay?"

Mrs. Frakes raised her hand to silence Colin. "Yes, she's fine. Asleep upstairs."

Colin leaned forward releasing air from his lungs. "Thank God." He turned toward the officers, Sheriff Kinney standing from the sofa to shake Colin's hand. "Hello, again, Mr. Lambert." The sheriff glanced at his deputy. "This is Deputy Clay Walsh."

Colin stepped forward to shake the deputy's hand. Could this man be the brother Julie had mentioned? "Nice to meet you."

Colin directed his next words to the sheriff. "What happened here?"

The sheriff arched his hand toward Mrs. Frakes. "Perhaps you should hear the details from your housekeeper."

She sat down again, keeping her gaze on Colin. "I upstairs straightening Miss Beatrice's sitting room after she fall asleep when I hear car on driveway. At first I think it probably you returning from Tulsa, but then I hear noise on front porch, like a loud thump followed by sound of doorbell. I assume you forget your key, but then I realize you probably phone if that happen, so I come downstairs to see who call at house late.

"I switched on porch light, but looking out of side window next to door, I see no one. When I open door a car speed away on road, but too dark to see kind of car. I start to close the door. Then I notice big rock on porch with paper tied around it." She pointed toward a sandstone rock measuring approximately eight inches by eight inches by six inches in height occupying the floor near her chair.

Colin noticed her hands were trembling. He crossed the room to stand beside her, patting her shoulder. "It's okay, Mrs. Frakes; just relax. Then what did you do?"

She shaped her hands as though holding the rock. "I carry it inside and remove long paper from stone." Tears formed in her eyes. "Then I read."

The sheriff stood and eased across the room, holding up a plastic bag containing what looked like to Colin several sheets of wrinkled copy paper. "This is what she found on the rock, a banner"—Sheriff Kinney reached for a notebook inside his shirt pocket—"IF YOU LADIES VALUE YOUR LIFE YOU'D BEST TELL LAMBERT TO HIGHTAIL IT BACK TO MISSOURI WHERE HE BELONGS."

Colin strode to the sofa and sat down. *Holding the world on one's shoulder couldn't feel any heavier*, he thought. He lowered his head into his hands. What should he do now? Obey the instruction and avoid the perilous situation he'd created for the women of his household? Or continue his journey for truth at their risk? He breathed deep. Whatever his decision, it would be a Catch 22 for all parties involved.

Sheriff Kinney sat next to Colin. "Mr. Lambert, Earlier I asked Mrs. Frakes if she knew a motive behind the threat and she said I should speak to you. Would you care to clarify what she had in mind?" The sheriff reached for the pen in his shirt pocket while the deputy took a seat across from them.

Drawing a deep breath, Colin lifted his head. "Sheriff, are you familiar with the Lambert family history?"

"You can't be born in Osage County and not have some knowledge of your family."

"Do you remember my grandfather Braxton Lambert's murder?"

The sheriff nodded. "I had just come home from a stint in the army when it happened. I sure hated to hear that your father had been convicted for the murder. He used to come into the farm co-op store in Haven where I worked to buy oats for his horses, always friendly, taking the time to ask how my folks, kid brother and sisters were doing. Seemed more like the common folk around here."

Colin nodded. "Yes. That sounds like him. Anyway, to make a long story short, when the jury convicted Dad for my grandfather's murder, my father swore to me he was innocent. Aware even then of his honesty and integrity, I purposed at twelve years of age I would someday prove his innocence."

Colin stood, his face bathed with scorn. "After reading an account of the trial and the events leading up to it, the whole situation was a fiasco—my father convicted on circumstantial evidence alone, rotting in prison in place of the real murderer."

Colin clenched his jaw. "And I intend to find that infidel if it's the last deed I do on this earth."

Colin sat down again beside the sheriff. "When I heard my great-uncle Maxwell Lambert had died, I made plans to remain in Haven following the funeral and do whatever necessary to achieve my resolve."

The sheriff looked startled. "But I thought it was a cut and dried case. The individual who found the body also saw your father standing over your deceased grandfather, the gun that killed him in your father's hand."

"That would be Grayson, my grandfather's valet. That is true, but my father testified he, having heard the shot from upstairs ran into the room after the fact and didn't recall how the gun came to be in his hand."

"Have you discovered any evidence thus far that would indicate a wrong conviction?"

Colin shook his head. "Nothing yet. But you see, Sheriff Kinney, the break-in, the event tonight and the fact that someone is dogging my steps…" Colin enlightened the officers about the hit and run driver of the previous night. "All which proves to me the true felon is still in the area and my pursuit is not in vain."

Colin darted a glance toward Mrs. Frakes. "But now, I question my wisdom in continuing the project. I would never forgive myself should my aunt or Mrs. Frakes be harmed in any way."

"Don't you think the task should be left up to trained professionals?"

Colin's eyes narrowed. "You mean like those in charge twenty-five years ago? In my opinion a lot more could have been done in my father's defense."

Sheriff Kinney averted his gaze. "Well, I can't stop you, but if tonight is any indication, you might have a dangerous road to travel."

Deputy Walsh leaned forward in his chair. "Mr. Lambert, my sister, Julie Lonetree, phoned me a couple days ago to explain her new self-appointed assignment—to aide your endeavor to seek out your grandfather's murderer, stating that Big Jack Granger, as he's known at the *Tulsa World*, would be assisting as well. Then she asked if I could help to which I agreed as long as it didn't interfere with my job."

The deputy turned to the sheriff. "Since you were acquainted with Mr. Lambert's father, perhaps you might want to lend a hand as well. My sister, along with Jack, who covered both the murder and trial, share Mr. Lambert's feelings that the system convicted the wrong man."

Sheriff Kinney seemed to be intrigued momentarily with the carpet. Lifting his head, he spoke to Colin. "I believed the break-in the other night to be an isolated event, but now after your explanation and Deputy Walsh's comments, perhaps I should rethink the situation. My hands are tied unless I have tangible evidence to reopen the case." He cupped his chin, rubbing his fingers across the end of day stubble on his face. "Tell you what." He glanced at his deputy. "Clay and I will do what we can to help you."

"Thanks. I really appreciate it."

Deputy Walsh stood to his feet grinning. "However, my sister made me promise when the story breaks, she gets first crack at it."

All four occupants in the room laughed. Standing from the sofa, Sheriff Kinney's smile faded. "Now as far as the situation tonight, I'll order an extra patrol for this area. If someone is watching the house, we might be able to catch them. Meanwhile, keep everything locked up tight." He turned his attention to Mrs. Frakes. "Can you think of anything else you might have forgotten?"

She shook her head. "May I please be excused? Sometimes Miss Beatrice wake up and need drink of water."

"Sure, you go right ahead. We're through here anyway." He slipped the pen and notepad back into his pocket then extended his arm for a handshake, Deputy Walsh following suit.

"Good night, Mr. Lambert. If you need us, you have our number." The sheriff picked up the plastic bag, eyeing Clay's effort to thread his fingers into a pair of workman's gloves the deputy had pulled from a back pocket of his uniform before bending to retrieve the rock from the floor.

Sheriff Kinney scrutinized the paper in the plastic bag. "It looks like some type of poster or acrylic paint was used for the lettering. You can buy that kind of paint at most one-stop shopping marts and hobby stores. It would be a waste of time to try to find the person that bought the paint." He grinned as he pulled his Stetson into place on his head. "The clerks would probably laugh us out of their stores."

When the officers had driven away, Colin spent the biggest part of the next hour making sure every door and window in the manor had been secured, making his way to Mrs. Frakes's room soon afterward, desiring to know if his aunt had been disturbed by the events of the evening. Breathing a sigh of relief after Mrs. Frakes assured him all was well, he strolled toward his suite heavy of heart. He had a lot of thinking to do. But first he had to e-mail Julie to apprise her of the episode.

• • • • •

The next morning Colin parked his car near the Bank of Oklahoma on the east side of Bartlesville at straight-up nine o'clock. Reaching for his briefcase, he made his way toward the entrance to the bank. Smiling at the lady who had just unlocked the doors, he stepped toward the nearest clerk, who directed him to customer service. Colin entered one of the offices adjacent to the teller windows, returning the smile of the woman behind the desk on which sat a nameplate that read Cara Williams.

"Good morning, sir. How may I help you?" she said, motioning for him to take a seat.

"Hello, Ms. Williams. I'm Colin Lambert. My great-uncle Maxwell Lambert, passed away a few days ago, and as executor of his estate and his heir, I need some information about his accounts here at the bank." Colin opened his briefcase and handed her the file Nicholas Girard had given him to prove his statement. "I have records for the trust my grandfather established for the upkeep of Briarwood Estate years ago. However, while the housekeeper and I were packing up my uncle's belongings, we could not find his personal checkbook or bank statements anywhere in the house. In order to settle his affairs, I need to locate his personal account, and since the estate account is with this bank, I thought I'd start my search here."

Ms. Williams looked over the documents. "I will need to let my supervisor take a look at this file. Also, a couple items of identification, please."

"Sure," he said, reaching for his billfold. He watched while she made photocopies of his driver's license and Social Security card.

Ms. Williams stood from her desk. "Would you like some coffee?"

"No thanks. I'm good."

She smiled. "Very well then. I'll return shortly."

His phone signaled an e-mail.

> *Colin, got your e-mail this morning. Glad to know your aunt and Mrs. Frakes are okay. It's obvious we're on the right path. I'll try my best to come up with something that will help us by Wednesday. See you then. Julie*

Colin smiled as joy welled up inside him. Wednesday seemed more like two years instead of just two days away. Within a few minutes Ms. Williams returned to her office. Smiling, she relinquished the file to Colin.

"The vice-president of the bank assures me everything is in order. Now, let's see if we can come up with an account." She sat down behind her desk, placed her fingers on the computer keyboard, and began to type. "You're in luck, Mr. Lambert," she said a moment later. Your uncle did indeed have a personal account with us. I can give you a copy of his bank statements for the past twelve months. However, to go back farther, we'd have to send a request to research."

"I think the year of statements will do for now."

"Okay. I'll have those statements printed off in just a few minutes." She handed him the first copy shortly thereafter.

Glancing over the current month's activities, Colin noted that only two transactions showed on the account, one the deposit of his uncle's monthly Social Security check and... Colin sucked in his breath... a check written for cash close to ten thousand dollars a few days before his death, the remaining balance in the account a few hundred dollars. *How strange*, he thought. *Why would Uncle Max need so much currency?* Mrs. Frakes had implied he'd seldom been out of the house in months.

"Thanks," Colin said when Ms. Williams handed him the remainder of the statements. "If I need other years, I'll be back. Also, we had an intruder at Briarwood the other night; and in case the checkbook was stolen, I would like to close out this account and transfer the funds to my personal banking account in St. Louis, Missouri."

"Absolutely." Ms. Williams began extracting forms from a drawer. When she had taken all the information, she handed Colin the papers that required his signature, a few minutes later fitting his copies into an envelope. "Can I assist you with anything else today?"

Colin stood from his chair. "I don't think so. You've been a great help. Thanks again."

"You're welcome. If you think of something, just give me a call." She handed him a business card.

"I will. Good-bye."

Following brunch, Colin drove toward Haven, troubled by the discovery on his uncle's bank statement. Had Uncle Max still been involved with gambling close to his dying day? Colin frowned. Surely, his uncle didn't need that much money for alcohol.

Colin did a few calculations in his head. The estate funds handled the costs of the food, utilities, Mrs. Frakes's salary, and general upkeep of the house. And according to Girard, the Duchess had her own funds. So why write a check for that amount? Colin flinched. Had he kept cash in large amounts in his office? Did the intruder know that? Colin applied more pressure on the gas. He needed answers. He'd start with Mrs. Frakes then drive into Haven to see if Girard was in town and had time for an impromptu appointment.

Arriving at the house a short time later, Colin went straight to his office. He sat down at the desk, opening the file he'd taken with him to the bank, withdrawing the bank statements Ms. Williams had provided for him, laying them out in order by month. Colin's chin dropped in amazement, his eyes narrowing as he perused the data. Every statement revealed a monthly cash withdrawal, each amount just under the federal limit of ten thousand dollars. Quarterly deposits from dividend checks from a brokerage firm in New York City had covered the cash withdrawals. Colin lifted his gaze to stare out the window, questions drifting into his mind like the white feathery swirls of clouds wafting across the marine blue sky.

Didn't Girard state that Uncle Max had lost all his investments? Colin raised an eyebrow. Evidently his uncle had stock and/or other investments the lawyer didn't know existed. But that didn't explain the reason for the withdrawals. What had Uncle Max done with all that money? Colin straightened. Perhaps the money had been given to a church or some other charity. He sighed. But most people wrote checks for charitable gifts. Colin made his way over to the file cabinet in the corner of the room.

Sometime later, he climbed the stairs, disappointed. He'd found nothing to account for the cash withdrawals. He hoped the Duchess felt up to a visit. If she were coherent today, maybe she could solve the dilemma. He hadn't spoken with her since yesterday morning when he'd checked on her before leaving the house, her friend Mrs. Johnson stationed across the room ready to tend to her needs. Assured his aunt was in good care, he'd driven to church, looking forward to an hour or so of calm diversion.

Peeking around the door, he noticed his aunt partaking of her lunch. She looked up. "Hello, Stuart. Glad you're home. I have the most wonderful news. Braxton has decided to take Colin with him to Europe this summer when he goes to Norway on business. Wants to 'beef up his education,' he said … thinks you might want to tag along, father, son, father, son, that sort of thing. What do you think?"

Colin paused just inside the door. *Should I play along, or let her know I'm Colin?* He groaned inside. As soon as he returned to St. Louis, he'd do some research on dementia or, better yet, schedule a conference with her physician to probe his expertise for ways to better care for the Duchess.

All of a sudden, her fork clattered onto the table. She lifted her face to stare at him, recognition lighting up the dullness that had clouded her eyes a moment ago. "But that trip never took place did it? Your grandfather was murdered and your father sent away from me forever. I used to visit him every week until the doctor forbade me to travel. He said my heart can't withstand the stress associated with the trip."

Colin took her into his arms, holding her close, unable to look upon her grief-stricken countenance. "I know, Duchess. If only I could undo that horrible day."

She drew back from him, sliding her hands up his shirt until they rested on his cheeks, her fingers smoothing away the moisture from the corners of his eyes. "Dear Colin, we all have our burdens and afflictions to bear, but remember, God said he would deliver us out of all of them."

Colin sighed. "Yes, Duchess." *Too bad some deliverances take longer than others*, he thought, the ache in his heart like the Rock of Gibraltar each time his antagonism toward his mother surfaced. He groaned inwardly. He could seldom recall a time when he *wasn't* upset with her, the undercurrent of ire rising and falling to different levels or lying in wait for the next opportunity to drown his love for her in a sea of anger. And *opportunity* always seemed to present itself.

Son, love covers a multitude of sin.

Yes, I'm aware of that. But surely You understand my mother isn't the most loveable creature in the world.

Love thinks no evil. I didn't realize you had become the poster child for love.

Colin lifted his eyes toward the ceiling. *That's just a little below the belt, don't you think, Father?*

Just making a point.

Got it loud and clear.

Shaking off his frustration, Colin aided his aunt's movements to her chair by the window. He pulled a long breath. He'd try harder in the future to show more love to his mother. Still, what he'd give to have just one inclination about her that wasn't tied to annoyance or infuriation.

He waited until his aunt seemed comfortable then asked, "Duchess, do you feel up to a few questions about Uncle Max?"

She leaned forward. "Such as?"

"Did Uncle Max have a habit of keeping a lot of cash on hand?"

Her eyebrows drew together in thought. "I don't think so, not since his gambling days. Even then he was notorious for banking his winnings. Why do you ask?"

"I couldn't find his bank records, so I drove to Bartlesville this morning to see if he had a personal checking account at Bank of Oklahoma as well as the one for the estate, and he did. In looking over copies of his statements, I noticed large cash withdrawals at the first of each month. However, when Mrs. Frakes and I packed up his things; I only found a few hundred dollars in his billfold. I didn't find any money in the office, either. What do you suppose he would have done with that much cash each month?"

Her eye grew wide. "I can't imagine. He rarely ventured away from Briarwood." She hung her head. "Poor soul. Just couldn't come to terms with Agatha's passing, didn't want to live without her. Drank himself to death." Beatrice raised her eyes. "Why don't you ask Hanako? She might be able to tell you."

"Yes. I will."

As though on cue, Mrs. Frakes swished into the room. "Master Colin, you return already. Would you like lunch?"

"No, thanks, nevertheless, you might be a source of help in another matter. Did Uncle Max keep large amounts of cash here at Briarwood?"

She paused in removing his aunt's dishes from the table onto a tray. "I do not see lot of money, maybe two or three hundred on his nightstand sometimes when I clean his room."

VICTORIA BURKS

"When was the last time he left Briarwood?"

"A few days before his death. He asked me to drive him to bank in Bartlesville. Say he need to clear up something about the estate. I worry. He pretty weak but had not been drinking for several days, which surprise me. I offer to do his errand, but he say no, must do it alone. When we arrive at bank, he ask me to stay in car. He return to car in about twenty minutes, put his briefcase in back seat, and we drive home. I can tell the trip exhaust him. But he seem at peace, more so than in a long time."

Colin glanced at his aunt who dabbed at her eyes with a lace handkerchief, her hands trembling. Deciding to squelch his inquiry for now, he hugged his aunt, informing the ladies he had business in Pawhuska but would return by dinner time.

Returning to the office, he looked up the financial statements Mark Kellar had issued to Colin, via Girard, removing the business card stapled to the report. Colin glanced at the accountant's Pawhuska address. If anyone knew about Uncle Max's financial affairs, it should be his CPA. Also, he jotted down Girard's Pawhuska office address as well in case he wasn't in Haven. He placed the information in his billfold.

Colin reached for his phone. "On second thought, I'll take my chances," he muttered, deciding to bet on a marketing strategy. A surprise sale sometimes generated more customer purchases than normal advertising in businesses. Maybe the same technique would work in his favor today in regards to information.

As Colin drove from the estate, he met a county patrol car. He waved to the officer. If he had time, he'd stop by the sheriff's office for a quick chat, just to keep in touch. Driving down Haven's main street a few minutes later, he didn't see the attorney's car parked outside his office. Just as well. He preferred to meet with the CPA first anyway. Settling back into the car seat, he looked forward to the trip. It had been many years since he'd visited the unique historical town.

Entering Mr. Kellar's office less than an hour later, he was greeted with a friendly smile from the receptionist. Taking a seat after the young lady informed him the CPA would see Colin, he glanced around the conservative office, his attention drawn to the ceiling of the old building.

"Quite fascinating, isn't it?" the young lady said, following his gaze. "It's a metal ceiling made with tin. The motifs are hand sculpted. I've worked here for several years and have never grown tired of looking at them."

"It's good that someone took the initiative to preserve them."

The receptionist nodded and then returned to her work. In the meantime, Colin scanned the historical prints of people and places associated with the area decorating the walls, recalling times his father had taken him to visit some of the places, one of his favorite, the site where negotiations to buy oil leases from the Osage Indians had taken place. He gazed at the photograph of the famous "Million-Dollar Elm," still able after all these years to pick out his great-grandfather, Walter D. Lambert, from among the crowd of famous oil entrepreneurs of that day conversing with the Indians. He was glad the Lambert copy of the same photograph still occupied its place on the library wall at Briarwood.

Shortly thereafter, the receptionist's phone buzzed. "You may go in now, Mr. Lambert," she said, rising from her desk to escort him to the accountant's office.

Following introductions a moment later, Colin opened his briefcase, removing Uncle Max's bank records to show the accountant. "Mr. Kellar, since you handled my uncle's finances, I wonder if you could explain these cash transactions shown on these statements?"

Mr. Kellar pulled his glasses from the top of his head and settled them on the bridge of his nose, scrutinizing the documents one by one, a frown etched between his eyebrows and balding head. He looked up a few moments later. "I'm sorry, Mr. Lambert, I can't help you. Your uncle never divulged these transactions to me. Sorry I can't help you."

Colin retrieved the paperwork from Mr. Kellar and returned it to his case, sighing. "Thank you for seeing me today." Colin shrugged. "Well, I guess the next step is to go over Briarwood with a fine-toothed comb in case my uncle had eccentric tendencies to hide money inside the house." Colin grinned. "I have a friend who found fifteen thousand dollars cash in his grandmother's freezer some time back. I suppose one could refer to it as 'cold cash.'"

The accountant laughed. You have a point there. Mr. Kellar extended his hand. "Perhaps your uncle's former attorney, Nicholas Girard, could answer your inquiry."

"My thoughts as well. In fact, his office is my next stop. Good day, Mr. Kellar. Glad to have made your acquaintance."

Once outside, Colin glanced at the paper on which he'd written the attorney's office address. Only two blocks from where he stood. Brushing the perspiration from his brow, he made his way down the sidewalk, pausing to admire a small city park in between two buildings near his destination. The painted mural of a cowboy rounding up stray cattle had caught his eye. Aware that Pawhuska was the capital of the Osage Indian Nation, Colin became engrossed in the sculpture of an Osage Warrior on his horse at the entrance to the park. It was entitled "Osage in the Enemy Camp," sculpted by John D. Free, Sr. Colin read the inscription on the bronze plaque below the sculpture. "Seeking to obtain his tribe's highest war honor by touching his enemy."

As Colin studied the engraving, all of a sudden he felt he could identify with the words. According to his father, while some of the biggest names in the early years of black gold history had been rumored to do otherwise, his great-grandfather, Walter, had had the reputation of fairness and honesty in his dealings, thus gaining his wealth in a respected manner, his son, Braxton, following in his footsteps, his grandson, Stuart, an upright pillar in his community. To Colin, honor of his heritage stood in the balance. To "touch the enemy"—to strike his grandfather's killer with exposure and conviction—would restore Lambert integrity to its original veracity.

Colin turned away from the scene, his heart heavy, hoping against hope he had the grit to endure to the end for his father's sake.

CHAPTER 9

Stepping through the doorway to Girard's office, Colin forced a friendly greeting to the secretary, tolerating once again her sweltering gaze upon him.

"How nice to see you again, Mr. Lambert. Excuse me while I notify Mr. Girard you're here." After a moment she returned to her desk. "He'll be with you momentarily."

"Thank you." Colin sat down in the overstuffed sofa and picked up a magazine from the expensive-looking walnut table beside him. Before he opened the periodical, he took in the outer office. Like its counterpart in Haven, the furnishings spoke of quality. He recalled Julie's report on Girard. If the attorney didn't sport the necessary clientele for his good taste, then how could he afford this luxurious setting? Colin thumbed through the magazine. *Another business or stock in prospering companies?* But wouldn't Julie have dug up that information? Maybe she hadn't had time to research his investments.

A moment later, the man in question emerged from his office. "Good afternoon. I hope things are faring well at Briarwood." Without giving Colin a chance to answer, he turned to his niece. "Hold all my calls for now." He threw his arm around Colin's shoulder. Colin cringed.

"Come on in," Girard said, ushering Colin into a leather chair. "What can I do for you today?"

Colin removed his uncle's bank statements from his briefcase, offering them to the lawyer. "I thought you might be able clear up an interesting situation. Please note the checks for cash withdrawn each month on my uncle's account."

Girard studied each statement. After several moments, he focused his gaze on Colin, a hint of wariness in his eyes. "It looks as if Max never kicked his gambling habit."

Colin shook his head. "According to Mrs. Frakes, Uncle Max gave up that vice years ago. As his attorney, I thought he might have mentioned his use of the money to you."

"Maxwell was a studious and private individual. Our dealings were business related only."

"Of course he may have deposited the funds in another bank or invested it, but so far I've found nothing that would confirm either deed." Colin frowned. "To be honest, it's not any of my business how he allocated the funds…but my aunt is determined to remain at Briarwood until she dies and this money, if available, would pay for a major part of the reconstruction needed at the estate to ensure her comfort."

Girard drummed his stubby fingers on his desk, averting his glance toward the statements. "I often stopped by Briarwood to see your aunt and uncle. In fact, I visited them the evening Max passed away. As the Lambert attorney for decades, I felt it my duty to check on them now and then." Nicholas paused, his lips pursing in thought. "But I can't give you any information about this. Max seldom discussed his financial affairs with me. Say, how is Miss Beatrice getting along?"

"Some days good; others…well…those days could be better."

"I understand." Girard glanced at the clock on the wall. "I'd like to talk longer, but I have an appointment in ten minutes. Wish I could have been more obliging."

Colin nodded. "So do I." He stood and offered his hand to Girard in spite of the fleeting inclination to withhold the courtesy. "Oh, by the way, someone told me they witnessed an argument between you and my mother in the garden at the estate the morning of Grandfather's murder. It seems she came back inside the house for a few minutes and then returned to the garden to give you a package of some sort. Do you remember what was inside the bag?"

Colin watched the man's Adam's apple bob up and down, his complexion paling. Taking a deep breath, Girard leaned back in his chair and placed his hands behind his head, his gaze reaching toward the ceiling.

"I don't recall a dispute with Eileen that day nor a gift of any kind," he said, seeming to choose his words carefully. "But your mother and I didn't agree on several issues, so it's possible we had words." A vague smile touched his lips as he turned his eyes on Colin once again. "One thing about getting older, memory isn't what it should be."

Colin swallowed a retort of disgust. The nerve of the guy! But he had to hand it to him—anyone who could tell such a blatant lie and remain so calm deserved a Golden Globe. "Well, it must not have been too important, if you can't recall the meeting." Colin turned to leave. "Should you think of anything that would solve the money issue, please let me know."

Girard nodded and then walked Colin to the front entrance of the building, speaking to a gentleman approaching the doorway. "Hello, George, just go straight to my office. I'll be with you shortly." With a wave Nicholas Girard dismissed Colin and closed the door.

A strange feeling overcoming him, Colin settled into his car. Why did he feel like he'd just shot himself in the foot, unable now to walk in any direction? He looked at his watch. Three o'clock. Perhaps he'd have better luck gathering information at the sheriff's office. *Can't get any worse than the two strikes and four balls against me now,* he thought.

Colin lifted his Blackberry from inside his pocket, scrolling to the sheriff's phone number he'd logged in a few days ago. Seconds later, he heard his voice. "Hello, Sheriff, Colin Lambert. Yes, I'm fine. I'm in Pawhuska and thought if you could spare a few minutes, I'd like to stop by for a chat. Great. I just need directions to your office."

Ending the call, he placed his phone on the console, tugging the gearshift into reverse. Eyeing the historic triangle building that bordered Main Street and stood at the end of Kihekah Street, he backed the car away from the curb, deciding to do a quick tour of the town before heading south to see Sheriff Kinney.

Circling the building, he drove north toward the curved sign perched above the road that designated the entrance to the famous Tall Grass Prairie, realizing the only thing that had changed since he was a boy in the close-to-century-old town was the name above the doors of most of the buildings. Just before he turned left on Grand Street to view the Osage Tribal Museum and tribal offices, he glanced in his rearview mirror, and noting no traffic behind him, he slowed to take in the four-story building that sat on his right, next to the road, just as he started up the hill. The outside of the structure rocked with native stone had in its day been a lodging accommodation named the Virginia.

Wondering if the place was now occupied, he drove past the historic setting, making the turn that would take him to the place he both desired and dreaded to see. Parking the car in front of the massive building, known as the Osage County Courthouse he eyed the "at least a thousand steps to the front doors" he'd thought as a child, which actually were closer to fifty. Alighting from the car, he walked over to stand near the first step. He stared upward at the marbled hall of justice. Did its domineering presence cause

140   VICTORIA BURKS

a shudder of fear to streak down the spine of every criminal forced to enter its domain? During his father's trial, he'd been so sure justice would prevail and obtain his father's freedom. He glanced at the American flag flying next to the building. "Liberty and justice for all." Wasn't that what our country stood for? A mirthless laugh spilled from his lips. He guessed his father's case must have been an exception to the rule.

All at once he remembered something a Haven old-timer, who'd informed young Colin that one of the Dalton brothers had been a lawman in the county at one time, had made the remark…"If you want to kill someone and get away with it, just make sure it happens in Osage County." Colin pulled himself to his full height. "Well, Dad, you may not have gotten justice then, but if it takes my last breath to procure it, you'll get it now," he said as he returned to his car, praying the flame of justice burned brighter in the county's law enforcement today than in its history.

Later, standing in front of the Osage County Sheriff's Department, he eyed the structure built in recent years. Stepping inside the building, he noticed a female deputy in a cubicle adjacent to the room. Stepping up to the window, he gave his name, the officer directing him down the hall, first door on the right.

"Greetings, Sheriff," Colin said, taking a chair.

"What's happening," the sheriff asked, leaning back in his chair as he stretched his arms to place his entwined fingers behind his head.

Colin opened his briefcase. "I came to Pawhuska today to talk to Mark Kellar and Nicholas Girard, Uncle Max's accountant and lawyer, respectively, about some large withdrawals on my uncle's bank statements. But no luck." Colin handed the statements to the sheriff.

After taking a few moments to examine them, Sheriff Kinney picked up the phone and dialed an extension. "Clay, could you step into my office, please?"

"What's up, Sheriff?" Clay said, nodding a greeting to Colin as he entered the room.

"Mr. Lambert has discovered something curious about his uncle's finances." Sheriff Kinney passed the paperwork to his deputy who sat in the chair next to Colin. Clay examined the statements, a low whistle escaping his lips shortly thereafter. "That's a lot of money."

Colin nodded. "If Uncle Max kept this kind of cash on hand, it might not have been a secret, thus the reason for the break-in at Briarwood."

The sheriff looked at the ceiling. "It's possible... Mr. Lambert..."

"Please, sir, call me Colin. Mr. Lambert makes me feel middle aged."

The two officers laughed. "I started to ask... how well do you know the housekeeper, Mrs. Frakes?"

Colin's eyes widened. "Since I was born. You don't think... I mean... you're not suggesting, she would take my uncle's money?"

Sheriff Kinney shrugged his shoulders. "It's been known to happen. And you did say, your uncle had a serious drinking problem. She had every opportunity."

"Yes, I know. But you needn't worry. Mrs. Frakes has been a trusted employee of the Lambert family for decades. She's very devoted to my aunt."

Clay turned to Colin. "I'm glad you stopped in the office. I've got something to show you. I'll be right back."

The deputy returned within a few minutes, a cardboard carton in his hands. "I found this in our evidence storage room." Taking off the dust-covered lid, Clay extended the box toward

Colin and the sheriff for them to view the contents inside the container.

"The state determined the gun to be the weapon that killed your grandfather, and in here"—Clay withdrew a brown envelope from the box—"is the bullet taken from his body." Colin started to reach inside the box, but Deputy Walsh held up his hand. "Sorry, can't contaminate the evidence." He replaced the lid and set the carton on the sheriff's desk.

"But, if it's okay with the sheriff, I propose we send these to OSBI..." Clay paused to smile at the blank look on Colin's face. "The Oklahoma State Bureau of Investigation at Tahlequah so the gun and bullet can be analyzed."

Colin looked at the sheriff who nodded his approval. "Of course. Can you send them right away?"

Clay nodded. "I'll put them in the mail this afternoon for overnight delivery."

"Great."

"Don't set your hopes too high, Colin," the sheriff said, lowering his eyes toward the container. "The tests may do nothing more than tell us what we know already." A grin eased across his face as he winked at Colin. "But it's worth a shot."

Colin smiled. "This is the best news I've heard all day." He stood from his chair. "But now, I need to get back to Briarwood. I plan to do a thorough search of the premises just in case my theory about hidden money is correct. The officers nodded their understanding. "Let us know if your exploration proves successful."

A few moments later, Colin turned onto Highway 99. As he neared the convenience store located at the Highway 60 turnoff, he noticed a car that looked familiar. The driver eased the vehicle onto the highway, soon coming close to Colin's car. Colin slowed, hoping to get a good look at the driver in the rearview mirror. But the car whipped to the left, passing Colin at a high rate of speed, the driver barely able to get back in the right lane without colliding with an oncoming vehicle.

Glancing over at the driver as he passed by, Colin couldn't distinguish the man's features, but his average build and the baseball cap covering his hair were enough to convince Colin the man was indeed the same person he'd seen near the Bakers' residence. Colin snapped his fingers, frowning. His eyes on the near collision, he'd forgotten to get the license number of the sports car. *Some amateur detective I am,* he thought. *What's the guy up to anyway? He acts as though he wants me to know I'm being followed. Was it just another attempt to hurry my departure to St. Louis?* Colin gripped the steering wheel harder than usual. "It won't happen, not in a million years."

· · · · ·

As Colin drove onto the grounds of the estate late that afternoon, he met a pickup truck coming toward him. Recognizing the driver, Colin slowed to a stop, rolling down his window at the same time. "Hello, Mr. Baker. I assume you've been at Briarwood to take a look at the cooling system."

"Yes, and I'm sorry to say the compressors are on their last leg. They could go out any day. My suggestion would be to install a whole new system."

"I see. Can you give me an estimate of the cost involved?"

Mr. Baker rubbed his chin. "Probably about fifteen thousand dollars. You've got a lot of space to cool. Want me to check on some prices?"

Colin swallowed his surprise. Where could he come up with that kind of money? He had some savings, but not that much. Mother? He almost choked on his attempt to smother a laugh. He could hear her now. *I'll be happy to do it, just as soon as Hades is covered with a thick coat of ice.* "That would be great. And thanks."

"Glad to do it. I'll get back with you in a day or two."

"Good." Colin eased the car into gear. "Talk to you then."

As he pulled to a stop in front of the house, his cell phone rang. Glancing at the number, he frowned. For a day and a half he'd pressed the ignore button. He sighed. Guess he couldn't disregard her calls forever. Throwing the gearshift into park, he held the phone to his ear, wondering which side of his ongoing battle would win this time… honor or frustration. "Hello, Mother."

"Colin, are you okay? Why haven't you answered my phone calls? I guess I could just die up here and you'd never know it… or want to, now that you're living on that God-forsaken patch of earth. And what's this I hear about you taking a leave of absence from the agency? Don't you think it's a little soon for Tom to wing it on his own? No, don't bother to answer. I phoned Tom for information since you wouldn't answer my messages."

Colin felt his face grow warm. "Mother, slow down. To answer your questions, one by one… I'm fine. I've been busy. Aunt Mary has my number and would call me if anything was wrong. The Duchess needs me right now more than the agency, and Tom is very efficient. Also, he and I converse every day by e-mail and by phone, if necessary."

Colin heard Eileen's sigh of frustration. "I spoke with Nicholas yesterday, and he said you've been asking questions around town. I warned you to not get in over your head. If perchance Stuart didn't kill Braxton, you could be in real danger. You know how talk spreads in a small town." Her bitter laugh filled Colin's ear. "I should know."

Colin swallowed hard to keep his opinion of Girard's phone call from rising to his lips. "And how did *Mr.* Girard learn about my inquiries?"

"Said he ran into the handyman who used to work at Briarwood, what was his name?

"Baker. Jonathan Baker."

"Yes, that's it." She grew silent, softening the tone of her next words. "Colin, I'm worried about you. Please come home."

"Sorry, Mother. Can't do that right now. But, thanks for your concern. Will you at least try to understand, why I have to do this?"

He heard a snort on the other end of the line. "Why risk your life for someone who's going to die soon, anyway. You're wasting your time."

Colin pressed his lips together hard, the whole conversation with his mother like the sound of a ticking time bomb, the moment of the explosion seconds away. He took a long deep breath, exhaling as slow as possible. "Mother, can we please change the subject. There's something I need to ask you."

"What is it?" she said, exasperation apparent in her words.

"I've been told you had a heated discussion with Girard a short time before Grandfather was shot. And during that meeting you handed him a bag or package of some kind. Do you remember what you gave him?"

Eileen gasped. "Uh...no." Her breath quickened. "I don't remember any such conversation. It...it's possible we talked, of course. Nicholas came to Briarwood quite often. Why do you ask?"

Colin could sense his mother's effort to calm her nerves. "Just curious. Trying to discover as much as possible about that morning." Should he say her evasiveness didn't fool him for one second—that she knew exactly what had been in that sack? The Lamberts weren't the only side of his family who had strong wills. Why was she afraid to disclose the information?

Colin straightened. Had it held the murder weapon as Julie and Jack had suggested? Fear crushed his chest. Did his earlier supposition have merit? Had his mother and Girard indeed overheard the argument between father and son and then manipulated the situation into a murder to be laid at his father's feet?

As Colin recalled, storage areas for weapons in the house hadn't been a secret among family members. Even as a boy he had known where they were. She could have laid hold of his father's gun quickly. Colin lowered his face into his hand, his expression a portrait of agony. *Oh, God, how can I have such horrible thoughts about my own mother?* The sound of Eileen's voice startled him.

"Colin, it's dangerous for you to be there."

He felt a chill race down his spine. "Mother, you keep saying that. Do you know something about that day you're hiding? If so, I think you'd better tell me." He felt the familiar gnawing in his stomach.

"No … no … no! I'm just worried about you."

Colin closed his eyes, clenching his teeth, determined to fight off the storm brewing between his ribs. "I need to ring off, Mother, have to see about the Duchess. Good-bye for now." He pushed the end button before Eileen had a chance to say another word, hating his abruptness, yet knowing if he didn't end the conversation, his next words might prove hard to forgive.

Colin bit his lips. Did the trepidation that had coated her every word hold concern for him as she implied … or … her? He ran his hand down the back of his head. Why did he feel his life had begun to spin out of control? Was he as his mother had proclaimed "in over his head"? Perhaps his decision to keep from her the news of the happenings since his arrival in Briarwood had been a wise choice after all.

Colin's shoulders slumped. How could he love his mother and still harbor ferocity toward her at the same time? He lowered the sun visor until he could see his image in the mirror on the other side of the shade, positive the smidgeon of gray at his temples had increased a hundredfold in the last five days. The scar over his right eye from a wound he'd received playing football in high school seemed to stand out more than usual.

A moment later, Colin stepped from the car and leaned against it, crossing his arms over his chest. *Girard.* Colin spit on the driveway, watching as the hot cement dried the saliva within a few seconds. How he wished he could erase his mother's involvement with the lawyer just as fast. He looked up at the sky, noting the gray clouds peeking over the horizon. He pulled at his tie. Was there a chance of rain after all?

He glimpsed the fields in the valley, the grass bent and drawn, choking from lack of water. A good soaking rainstorm would solve the earth's problem, but what would douse this anger inside him once and for all?

Cast all your care on me for I care for you.

"So, God, are you saying, that I can just turn all this anger and bitterness over to you and I'll be free once and for all?"

Yes.

"Okay, God. It's yours."

Just remember, Son, patience is a virtue.

"I suppose you're telling me the journey won't be an overnight trip, but more like an expedition before victory becomes a reality." A portion of Hebrews, chapter eleven, verse one leaped into his mind. "Now faith is being sure of what we hope for and certain of what we do not see...." *Time and patience*, he thought. What priceless resources they'd become recently.

The temperature too high to remain in the sun any longer, Colin walked around his car glancing upward. He eyed the austere design of his new home. Rectangular in shape, it had been built more for versatility than beauty; although the Grecian columns supporting the balcony which stretched across the width of the house above the portico gave the home grace and elegance. He eyed the balustrade, which doubled as protection and ornamentation for the balcony. Like the rest of the house, the stucco exterior needed a couple coats of paint to restore its original beauty. He breathed deep. At the rate he could pay for the renovation, it would take years to complete the project. But he could start with small undertakings—maybe do some of the work himself on weekends. And, Mr. Baker might be interested in making a few extra dollars. Colin hit the roof of his car with his fist. If only he could find that money...

Taking the stairs two at a time a moment later, he started to cross the threshold to his aunt's sitting room when he heard her voice. Pausing just inside the door, he listened, realizing she was reciting a scripture found in Isaiah.

"'But they that wait upon the Lord shall renew their strength, they shall mount up with wings as eagles; they shall run, and not be weary; and they shall walk, and not faint...' Oh, hello, boy, come in. I've been admiring one of your father's works. It's one of my favorites. He gave it to me the last time I visited him at the prison." She nodded toward the framed painting above her daybed.

Colin studied the depiction of an eagle soaring above a gorgeous sunset splayed across the canvas. He stepped closer to the painting. *I think I understand, God. If I'm patient and let you have control, you will work it out for both of us. My victory depends on my trust in you. But my greatest desire is to see Mother accept you as her personal Savior. I know I haven't been the greatest witness of your love in the past, but by your grace, I'll do better in the future. Please work the power of forgiveness in my heart and let me see her through your eyes.*

At the sound of his name, he turned to his aunt, striding across the room and taking a seat in the chair facing her. "Did you have a good day, Duchess?" As he observed her countenance, his heart uttered a prayer of thanksgiving for God's intervention in scientific research and medicinal advancement.

"Yes. In fact, Hanako and I enjoyed a short time on the balcony this morning. It was good to breathe in some fresh air." She pointed to the television in the corner of the room. "And, this afternoon, following a nap, I listened to Christian television for a while. What about your day? Hanako told me you had business in Pawhuska."

"Yes. I wanted to talk to Uncle Max's accountant and attorney. I thought one or the other might know where Uncle Max disbursed the cash he took out of his account. But neither one knew the answer. After dinner I plan to search the house for the missing money."

Beatrice's eyebrows drew together as she contemplated her nephew's words. "That doesn't sound like Max. I know my memory isn't what it used to be, but he usually wrote a check for every purchase. He kept impeccable records for all his dealings. He would have never considered a cash purchase without a valid receipt."

Colin nodded. "I realized his organizational skills when I cleaned out his office." Colin watched his aunt fold and refold a lace hankie. He smiled. He couldn't remember a day in the time he lived at Briarwood that she hadn't had a dainty handkerchief either in her hand or lying within easy reach.

"Your grandfather's death was hard on him, but Agatha's death just about killed your uncle." She paused. "I suppose it did in the end. I tried to get him to stop drinking, but he wouldn't listen to me."

"Duchess, on my way home this afternoon, I remembered something that Girard mentioned about Uncle Max the day of his funeral. From what he said, I got the impression that Uncle Max had lost a lot of money in the stock market. But according to his financial records, he received generous dividends quarterly. Do you suppose he reinvested his money?"

"If he did, I don't recall his saying so." She smiled. "But of course, he didn't keep me informed about his financial affairs. But I do know he loved everything about the stock market, always wheeling and dealing on Wall Street when he was younger. Braxton counted on his brother's awareness of the latest tips in buying and selling stock." Beatrice raised her head her eyes sad. "I wish I could be of more help to you."

Colin moved his head back and forth. "If I don't find the money here, I'm lost as to what happened to it. If he did reinvest the funds, why cash and not a check?"

Beatrice closed her Bible and held it up for Colin to see. "'Ask and ye shall receive, seek and ye shall find, knock and it shall be opened.' Remember, Colin, the answers of life are found in God's Word and in prayer."

"Thanks, Duchess, I appreciate your encouragement."

· · · · ·

As he'd resolved to do earlier, following the evening meal, Colin began his search for hidden money. But after covering every inch of the upstairs with Mrs. Frakes's help, not a dime was uncovered. Once Beatrice had fallen asleep, the two made their way down the stairs to continue their mission, but as before, no cash was found.

Colin sent Mrs. Frakes to her room while he made his way to the office. Sitting down at his desk, he noted the brightness of the full moon spilling into the room, the radiance bright enough to see into the garden. Tired and disgruntled by their lack of success, he opened his laptop, opting to answer his e-mails before retiring.

He was starting to type a correspondence to Julie to share his recent discovery when the sound of a knock on the office door interrupted him. He stood to answer the knock, but before he could walk to the door, Mrs. Frakes entered the room with a tray bearing a tall glass of milk and cookies, the odor drifting toward Colin's nose affirming the pastry had just came out of the oven.

"How nice, Mrs. Frakes, but you should be upstairs resting."

"I remember how much you like milk and cookies. Thought they would cheer you up."

About to set the tray on the desk, something seemed to draw her attention toward the window. Noting the alarm that widened her eyes, Colin followed her gaze, his eyes widening in like manner. As a cry of terror gushed from the housekeeper's lips, Colin grabbed her arm, dragging them both to the floor behind the desk, the tray with its contents crashing onto the floor.

CHAPTER 10

With one arm slung across her shoulders, Colin held Mrs. Frakes tight against the floor as a volley of gunfire shattered the stillness of the night; the sound of splintering glass and bullets slamming into the wall above them suffocating the housekeeper's muffled cries. Then just as quickly, the gunshots ceased, the silence broken by the noise from a car motor revved for a quick escape moments later.

Fear clutched Colin's chest, the scene in the moonlight a few moments past still visible in his mind. A man of medium height and build, his features hidden beneath a ski mask had stood outside the window, the gun in his hand aimed toward the occupants inside the room. Something he couldn't explain had pushed him to react instantly. Or maybe an angel had knocked them to the floor. All he knew, they were safe for the moment. The prayer in his heart kept rolling over and over in his mind. *Thank you, God. Thank you, God.* His heart beat faster. *Oh, dear Lord. What about the Duchess?* Had she been awakened by the gunfire? Could he get to her? Had the intruder left in the car, or was he still lurking near the house?

He eased his arm from across Mrs. Frakes to reach for his cell phone. Alarm seized him. It wasn't in his pocket. He searched with his eyes, breathing a sigh of relief when he located the device under the desk. Moving so as not to frighten the housekeeper further, he slid his body toward his phone, grabbing it from the carpet. He punched in the speed dial number for Sheriff Kinney. A moment later, Colin's breathing slowed at the sound of the sheriff's sleepy voice. "Sheriff, this is Colin Lambert. We've just been attacked with gunfire from a trespasser on the property." Colin felt the officer grow alert.

"Be there in thirty minutes. Clay's on patrol in that area. I'll radio him. Hopefully he's nearby." The sheriff slammed down the phone, Colin deciding at the same time he had to find out how his aunt fared no matter what. Instructing the housekeeper to stay behind the desk, he lifted himself slowly from the floor, making ready to bolt for the door, praying that no one had entered the house from the broken window.

No one in sight, he stood, rushing through the door into the hall, turning toward the back stairs. On the landing he felt the presence of someone behind him. He whipped around drawing back his arm, ready to strike with his fist. To his amazement, Mrs. Frakes stood on the step below. She brushed past him, streaking across the width of the house, reaching his aunt's bedroom just ahead of Colin.

Easing the door open, the housekeeper peeked into the room. Colin heard his aunt's voice as she spoke to Mrs. Frakes. Noting Colin's presence, she smiled at him. "I thought I heard thunder. Is it going to rain? I told the Lord just this morning how nice it would be if he sent a good downpour."

Colin and Mrs. Frakes looked at each other, their expressions glowing with thankful relief. He strode to his aunt's side, sitting down on the edge of the bed. "I did see some thunderheads on the horizon late this afternoon. Maybe God will answer your prayer soon. But right now you need to go back to sleep. Can I or Mrs. Frakes get you anything?"

"Just some water, please." All of a sudden Beatrice frowned. "Is something wrong?"

Mrs. Frakes moved forward to fluff the pillows on the bed. "Just want to make sure you okay. I get your water now." She glanced at Colin, a warning in her eyes to not say anything disturbing to his aunt.

Seeing his aunt's efforts to cool herself with a Japanese fan, Colin placed his aunt's other hand between his palms. "Duchess, I'm having a new cooling system installed. Mr. Baker came by today to see if the one we have now could be fixed, but he advised against it. The system is too old to repair. Maybe you'll rest better then, not wake up so much."

"That's so kind of you, Colin. I had noticed my rooms were not as cool this summer. I'm sure Hanako will enjoy it too. She's so good to me. I wish I could do more to care for myself. But God tells us to be content wherever we are in life." The housekeeper returned with a glass of water in her hand.

Colin stood, the sound of an approaching car alerting him to his need to answer the door before someone rang the doorbell. "Good night, Duchess. I'll see you in the morning."

"Good night, boy. Sleep well."

Hurrying down the stairs, he opened the door just enough to distinguish whether the car pulling onto the drive was indeed a county car, stepping onto the porch a moment later where he informed Deputy Walsh about the heart-stopping incident less than a half-hour prior to his arrival. Just as he finished with the details, Sheriff Kinney drove onto the estate, Colin relating the incident a second time. The officers followed him to the back of the house to examine the office where the shooting took place.

After surveying the damage from the broken window, the sheriff and his deputy spent several minutes carefully digging the bullets out of the wall, six in all. "Considering the location of the bullet holes, I would say the trespasser intended nothing more than a scare tactic, since your statement indicated he could have easily killed both you and the housekeeper from his position," the sheriff said. "Who knows how long he'd been standing outside the window." He surveyed the bag of bullets taken from the wall and the casings he'd found on the ground outside the window. We'll get these off to the lab tomorrow. My guess is the gunman used a small automatic handgun."

Clay nodded. "Probably one that's been stolen or tampered with hoping to prevent a trace."

"I wouldn't be surprised." Sheriff Kinney took his hat off to wipe his brow with his handkerchief.

Colin smiled. "I apologize for the temperature in here. Someone is in the process of selecting a new cooling system for the house. You might know him, Jonathan Baker. He used to be employed as the maintenance man for the estate years ago." Neither officer alluding to an acquaintance with Mr. Baker, Colin continued. "I'll call him first thing in the morning about getting this window repaired."

Mrs. Frakes entered the room, pushing an electric sweeper with one hand and carrying a basket of cleaning supplies with the other. Getting permission from the sheriff, she tackled the cleanup while Colin saw the men to the door. Sheriff Kinney turned to Colin before he stepped off the porch.

"It's now obvious you're on to something where your dad is concerned. We'll check out the local mechanics to see if they've worked on the front of any cars in the last day or two. Maybe we can narrow the search for the hit and run suspect that way." He paused, his expression changing from thought to worry. "Be careful, Colin. Your night caller's aim might be lower next time."

"Yes, sir, I will." Colin grew thoughtful. "Sheriff, what's the procedure for purchasing a hand gun in Oklahoma? I felt so useless this evening, nothing but my fists as a means of protection for my aunt and Mrs. Frakes."

"Do you know how to use a gun?"

"My father taught me as a boy, but I'll need to practice up a bit."

The sheriff cleared his throat. "The first thing you have to do is attend an eight-hour class to qualify for a permit to carry a concealed weapon. Deputy Walsh has a class scheduled this Friday at our office. You'll be in the classroom for half the day, then at the firing range that afternoon. If you're serious, I have a friend in Bartlesville who owns a gun shop. If he has them in stock, I recommend a Glock automatic 9-mm model 19. Of course, you'll need to pass a background check before you can purchase a gun."

Colin nodded. "Do I need to sign up for the class before Friday?"

"No. Just show up about eight thirty. You can register then. In the meantime I'll work on your background profile."

"Perfect," Colin said, bidding the officers farewell a moment later. He watched them drive away then hurried to the office to help Mrs. Frakes with her task. The cleanup soon finished, the two hung a large quilt over the window to keep in a measure of cool and discourage the entrance of insects at the same time. Deciding to call it a night, they climbed the stairs, each to his own thoughts regarding the events of the evening, Colin weighing the risk against the fulfillment of his dream.

・・・・・

The next day close to noon, Colin returned from Bartlesville, his mission to pick up groceries and supplies for Mrs. Frakes complete. Driving onto the estate, he spied Mr. Baker's pickup in the driveway, soon discovering Mr. Baker and his son hard at work repairing the office window. "Good morning, Mr. Baker, Alfie. Thanks for responding so quickly to my call."

Mr. Baker looked up at the sky. "Wanted to get the window fixed before it rained. The weatherman has predicted a heavy rain storm for tonight or early morning."

Colin followed his gaze. "Looks like it, if those clouds rolling in are any indication. Do you have everything you need to do the job?"

"Yes. We're just about finished."

Colin turned his attention to Alfie. "Great to see you. Have you been taking good care of your mom and dad?"

Alfie's face brightened with pleasure. "Yes, Mr. Stuart...I mean, Mr. Colin. Bad man no hurt Mom, no hurt Dad. Bad man shoot Mr. Braxton, not Mr. Stuart."

Mr. Baker looked apologetic. "Sorry, Mr. Lambert."

"It's okay, Mr. Baker, I understand." All at once a thought struck Colin. "Alfie, Mrs. Frakes is in the kitchen. Why don't we go ask her for some cookies and milk?"

Alfie's eyes brightened. "Cookies. I like cookies. Colin motioned for the man-boy to follow him. Opening the back door, Colin called to the housekeeper. Stepping into the back foyer in answer to his summons, she smiled, taking Alfie by the arm to do as Colin directed.

Returning to Mr. Baker's side, Colin observed the man's work momentarily then spoke his thoughts. "Mr. Baker, do you recall what Alfie said a moment ago about "bad man no hurt Mom, no hurt Dad"? When I heard Alfie mention this at your house, I believed he referred to emotions. But from his words a moment ago, do you think it's possible he witnessed the murder? You even alluded to the fact he may have heard the gunshot. If the killer knew he'd been caught, he might have threatened to harm you and Mrs. Baker should Alfie tell what he'd seen?"

Mr. Baker looked shocked. "My word, I never even considered the possibility. If the killer shot Braxton from outside the window as your father's attorney speculated at the trial, then

VICTORIA BURKS

Alfred may … oh, Lord, why didn't I think of that then? What do you think we should do, Mr. Lambert?"

"Let's not say anything to the sheriff just yet. I want to discuss the possibility with some friends who also believe my father was framed. But if he knows who the murderer is, we must get him to tell us."

Mr. Baker nodded. "I'll talk to Nellie. If anyone can pry the information from him, it will be his mother." Jonathan watched Colin wipe perspiration from his brow. "Oh, by the way, your new air cooling system will arrive in the morning. I'll be here to make sure the installers do it right."

"Thank you, Mr. Baker. I really appreciate your assistance." Colin glanced off into the distance. He would have to trim his budget when he returned to St. Louis to compensate for the extra payment on his credit card, but no sacrifice was too great for the Duchess.

Alfie returned to his father's side, grinning, handing his father and Colin a couple of cookies. "Mrs. Frakes good cookie maker."

Colin laughed. "She is at that."

Alfie's eyes brightened. "We go fishin' now, Mr. Colin?"

Colin laughed. "Tell you what, if it's okay with your parents, we'll go tomorrow morning while your father is busy with the air conditioning people."

Alfie turned to Jonathon. "Papa, Papa, go fishin'?"

"Yes, Alfred. You may go fishing with Mr. Colin. In fact, I'll bring the poles and bait along in the morning too." Mr. Baker turned to Colin. "It's been a while since you were in the area, so I'll draw a map to the best location for fishing along the creek road."

"Thanks. It's amazing how time changes places, distorting one's memories.

·····

The cooler temperatures from the rain the night before a welcome relief, Colin and Alfie returned from their fishing trip, relinquishing one-half their cleaned catch to Mr. Baker. Seeing that the crew from the air and heating company were almost finished with their work, Colin dropped off his portion of fish to Mrs. Frakes and soon stood once again at Mr. Baker's side. Reaching for his wallet he'd collected from his room, Colin asked for the invoice from the person who seemed to be in charge of the project.

The man shook his head. "Already taken care of, sir."

Colin's jaw dropped. "Excuse me?"

Mr. Baker stepped forward. "Miss Lambert took care of the bill earlier by way of Mrs. Frakes while you and Alfie were at the creek, my wages too."

"I see. Well, I guess I'll go express my gratitude to my aunt." Colin gave Alfie a hug. "Thanks for helping me bait the hooks. You did a good job. And what about that whopper of a fish you caught. Maybe we'll get to go again sometime."

Alfie smiled. "Yes, go fishin' again."

Following lunch and a quick shower, Colin popped into his aunt's room for a visit, expressing his thanks for the redemption of the expenditure, the Duchess assuring him the amount wasn't a problem for her. Later, while the Duchess took her usual afternoon siesta, Colin checked on the preparations for dinner, the odors in the kitchen an assurance he and Julie would be served a delicious meal.

Shooing Colin away from the bowl of boiled shrimp cooling for the shrimp cocktail she planned to serve as the appetizer, Mrs. Frakes laughed at his attempt to grab another shrimp. "You not change. Just like when you a boy, always swiping food before a meal."

Colin leaned over to give the housekeeper a quick kiss on the cheek. "You're the best cook I've ever known." Colin sat down at the kitchen table. "Mrs. Frakes, upstairs with the Duchess a while ago, I had an idea. She seems so perky today; I thought she might like to have dinner with Ms. Lonetree and me. I wanted to discuss it with you before I said anything to her."

"Master Colin, I'm sure that would please her much, but doctor say she can't do stairs."

"No problem. I'll carry her down. And, if she's up to it on Saturday, I'd like to take both of you for a drive. Maybe to Bartlesville. How long has it been since either of you have spent any time away from Briarwood?"

"Long time. But I not sure drive would be good idea. She can't get too excited. We see how she is then. As for tonight, I believe it be okay."

Colin smiled. "When she wakes up from her nap, I'll break the news to her."

Mrs. Frakes smiled, the approval in her expression causing Colin to sit up straighter. "No, I tell her. She will need my help to get dressed for dinner. Master Colin, you so kind to Miss Beatrice, love her just like your father. Please excuse now, must set dining room table." She glanced at her watch. "You go get ready. Dinner, seven sharp.

On his way to obey the command of his solicitous housekeeper, the sound of his cell phone broke his stride. Pausing, his eyes lit up with surprise when he noted the name of the caller. "Hello, Jack, back from your assignment already?"

"No, still in DC, but couldn't wait to tell you about the call I received from my friend at the lab who offered to analyze your grandfather's suit."

Colin held his breath. "Good news, I hope."

"Pretty much what we expected, the blood type on the coat matched the one listed in the reports following the murder, proving the clothes belonged to Mr. Lambert. However, Lucas, my friend, said there were no powder burns on the coat, which means the gun was fired from more than a few feet away. Also, he found a note from your grandfather's personal memo pad in a pocket of the suit."

"Really? What did it say?"

"Just a minute. Now where did I put that piece of paper? Oh, here it is … it seems Mr. Lambert had written a reminder to himself, the date of the murder on top of the note. It reads, 'Meeting with Girard, nine thirty at Briarwood. Also, must speak with Tipper about the illegitimate company stock sales. Will ask him to come to Briarwood to meet with me privately.'"

Colin released a sigh of expectation. "So there was another person at Briarwood that morning. And no powder burns could mean the shot was fired from the window."

"Looks like it. Do you know of anyone whom your grandfather referred to as 'Tipper'?"

Colin thought long and hard. "No one that I can recall."

"Perhaps Girard would know."

"Much as I dislike speaking with the man, I'll give him a call."

"Good. I spoke with Julie earlier about this, and she informed me of her dinner engagement with you, so I asked her to stop by and pick up a copy of the report and note from Lucas to bring to you. He'll package the originals along with the suit and mail them to Sheriff Kinney to hold as evidence when the case is reopened, which I believe will be soon."

"Thanks. Julie should be here within the next hour. I assume we'll still meet on Sunday afternoon at your house."

"Right. But for now I gotta go. I've a dinner meeting I must attend. Have a good evening."

"Thanks. You too."

162 VICTORIA BURKS

Climbing the stairs, Colin shook his head. If only someone had been more attentive to his father's case in the beginning. What had his attorney been thinking? It seemed obvious to Colin now, the man must have believed his client guilty of the crime. Colin's lips tightened. Nothing more than a kangaroo court with the best of performers acting out the roles of injustice.

• • • • •

Later, the Duchess's eyes glowing with excitement, Colin eased her from his arms onto the living room sofa, stuffing pillows behind her back to ensure her comfort. "How's that, Duchess? You look absolutely stunning tonight." Although the dress Mrs. Frakes had chosen for her mistress seemed to swallow his diminutive aunt, it accentuated her beauty of years past.

"Thank you, Colin." She looked around like a child in a candy store for the first time. "This is wonderful. I can't remember the last occasion I was in this room." She gazed at her nephew, a look of longing on her face. "I know you have obligations in St. Louis, but I can't help wish you didn't have to return. You belong here, Colin. Briarwood is your destiny."

"I do love it here. But as you mentioned, obligations often keep us from following our heart." He smiled. "But at least I can enjoy you and Briarwood for a little while and then return as often as my schedule will permit."

The doorbell drew their attention. It was all Colin could do to keep his emotions from betraying him when he opened the door. Propelling his thoughts to a professional level, he greeted his guest, trying not to think about how beautiful she looked in her simple sleeveless black dress, her only jewelry dainty pearls clasped around her neck and short dangling earrings to match. With difficulty he squelched his desire to kiss her soft-looking, full lips.

Escorting Julie into the living room, he introduced her to his aunt, Mrs. Frakes announcing dinner shortly thereafter. Walking slowly to aid his aunt's journey across the wide foyer to the dining room, the three soon enjoyed the sumptuous meal spread among the beautiful china and centerpiece of fresh wildflowers created by the housekeeper's own hand.

As Colin observed the Duchess's regal demeanor interspersed with her friendliness throughout the meal, he felt as though he sat in the midst of royalty, his aunt living up to her nickname in the highest regard. Listening to Julie tell a humorous story, he noticed the Duchess's earlier animated manner wane. Mrs. Frakes entered the dining room. "Mr. Lambert, would you like your dessert and coffee here or in the living room?"

Colin smiled within. Mr. Lambert tonight, Master Colin tomorrow. Vacillating between boy and man might make a person dizzy after a while. He glanced at his aunt. "Perhaps the living room would be more comfortable."

Beatrice directed her gaze to Colin. "If you two children don't mind, I think I'll skip dessert. Colin, would you mind escorting me to my room?" Excusing himself to Julie and promising to return shortly, he helped his aunt from the chair and walked her to the bottom of the stairs, gently picking her up to carry her to her suite.

She giggled. "I guess this is what it means for a woman to be swept off her feet."

Colin laughed, his expression growing pensive. "Duchess, I've always wondered. Why did you never marry?"

Sadness filled her eyes. "I was engaged once in my early twenties, but my fiancé was killed in an accident. I just never found anyone else I wanted to take his place." She put her hand to his face. "Besides, I had to take care of your father, and then God sent you along to fill my heart too." She studied his expression.

"Please don't be concerned for me. I've had a wonderful fulfilled life. I wouldn't trade it for anything in this world."

Mrs. Frakes entered the sitting room just as Colin settled his aunt into her favorite chair.

"Ms. Lonetree and your dessert are waiting. I stay with Miss Beatrice." The housekeeper waved him toward the door.

Rushing down the stairs, Colin smiled at Julie, taking the time to refresh her coffee before he sank into a chair across from her seat on the sofa. "Sorry. I hope I didn't keep you waiting too long."

She shook her head. "I can see you're devoted to your aunt."

"Yes. She's been more like a grandmother than an aunt to me." Slicing a piece of Mrs. Frakes's Italian crème cake for each of them, he passed a plate to Julie then waited until she tasted the confection, smiling at her expression a moment later. "I see you share my opinion, a little bit of heaven on earth."

She laughed. "This is delicious. I can't decide which of the courses I liked the best. Don't let her secret get out or every famous eating establishment in the US will be vying to employ her as their top chef."

Colin looked toward the entryway, his finger to his lips. "Shh… don't talk so loud. Mrs. Frakes might hear you and ideas of that nature enter her mind. I need her here."

Finished with their dessert a few moments later, he set their plates aside, pouring them each another cup of coffee from the silver urn on the tray. "I guess we should get to business. Jack phoned me today about the note in grandfather's coat."

"Yes. I stopped by the lab to pick up a copy for you." The lab tech will send the originals to Sheriff Kinney along with the suit as evidence for a new trial.

Colin nodded. "Yeah, Jack mentioned that as well."

She picked up her purse and pulled two sheets of paper from it, extending them toward Colin.

After reading the lab copies, one a report on the suit jacket, the other his copy of the memo, he folded the papers and put them inside his pocket. "Now all we have to do is figure out the identity of Tipper. Sounds like a nickname. And it seems probable he or she was an employee of Lambert Oil. I have to wonder how he arrived and left the house without anyone noting his presence. Must have been when Mrs. Frakes and Grayson were upstairs and Girard was in the garden with my mother. By the way, do you remember me telling you and Jack about the Down syndrome child of Jonathan Baker and how his father had sent him to look for the gloves found beneath the office window the day of the murder?"

"Yes."

"Well, I asked Mr. Baker if he thought Alfie, his son, might have witnessed the murder. He keeps saying, 'Hurt Mama, hurt Daddy. Bad man shoot Braxton.' At first I thought he was talking about the Bakers' being upset over the murder. But, now, I think it's possible he saw the murderer. Mr. Baker said he and his wife would talk to Alfie about it."

"That's interesting. Let's hope they're successful. With all that's happened since your arrival, everything seems to point to the fact that I'd bet the killer is still in the area."

"I'll phone Girard tomorrow. He may know the individual named Tipper. I can't prove anything, but I've a feeling the lawyer is involved up to his ears, if not the actual perpetrator of the crime, then aware of something he hasn't disclosed. He tries to disguise it, but he gets edgy when I mention the murder. You got any suggestions where we might look, otherwise?"

Julie's eyebrows drew together as she gazed across the room. "I can surf the Internet again. Also another trip to the Tulsa Library might be worthwhile. I've researched the Lambert family there but not past employees of Lambert Oil. I might get lucky and find the name of one of their previous accountants still living in the Tulsa area. Since we know there was some kind of discrepancy in the company books, it's possible he may remember the situation."

Colin nodded then sighed. "I suppose I could ask Mother if she knows anything about the illegitimate stock." He noted the puzzled look on Julie's face as she gazed at his expression. "I'm having issues with my mother right now. She doesn't want me anywhere near Briarwood."

Julie looked away. "I see."

Colin smiled. "Why don't we discuss something else? You know a lot about me, but I'd like to know you better. Is Oklahoma your home state?"

"Yes, born and raised in Tahlequah, just east of Tulsa. Got my degree at Northeastern University in journalism then moved to Tulsa to work at the *Tulsa World*." Married after a year of college, but that ended in divorce a few years later. Now it's just me and my dog, Bandit."

Colin smiled. "And what kind of dog is Bandit?"

"A black Lab. He's a loveable animal but protective also." Her eyes filled with pain. "It's comforting to have him nearby."

The look on her face caused Colin's heart to lurch with compassion. It took his last ounce of restraint to keep his hands at his side, wanting to hold her in his arms, offering comfort the best way he knew how.

Instead, he leaned forward, his gaze searching for answers. "Julie, I don't mean to pry or be offensive, but since the first day I met you, I've sensed you're suffering from some kind of tragedy. And I'd like to help, if I can."

She looked away, sighing. "I'm not very good at hiding my feelings. Thank you for your concern, but it's not something I'd care to discuss right now." She stood from the sofa. "I should be on my way. I have to be at the paper early tomorrow. If you think of anything I don't already know about your father's case, just e-mail me."

Colin followed his guest's lead, giving himself a mental kick in the rear. *Lambert, you just couldn't keep your thoughts to yourself. You've probably lost your chance with her now.* Her reaction made him think of a bird with a broken wing doing its best to flee from the person trying to care for the injury. "Look, Julie, I'm sorry I upset you. Please, I'd like to make it up to you. What about a casual dinner and movie this Friday night?"

He didn't dare breathe while she pondered his request, her rigid stance a sight he'd seen in his mother's stature many times. Did Eileen agonize over a heartbreak of the past? Was that why she sometimes reacted in cold, cruel ways to negative situations in her life? Were those reactions merely a wall of defense to disguise pain? Colin, surprised at his inclinations, frowned. *Now where did those thoughts come from?* With a mental shake of his head, he turned his attention back to his guest.

Julie paused at the entryway to the hall. Turning, she smiled. "Colin, it's not anything you've done. There are some things I won't allow myself to think about much less discuss. But, yes, dinner and a movie sound like fun. What time?"

"Six okay?"

"Yes, I'll e-mail you directions to my house when I get home tonight."

"Great. I'll see you in a couple of days."

A short time later, Colin stood on the veranda watching Julie's car until she turned on the road leading to Highway 60, her taillights soon out of sight. *God, I know, you're aware of my attraction to Julie, but more than anything, I want to see the pain in her heart disappear. Please help her.*

Entering the house, he smiled, lifting his shoulders a little higher. At least she hadn't turned him down. Could her interest in him have traveled beyond their mutual desire to locate a killer?

CHAPTER 11

Lingering over a third cup of coffee following his breakfast the next morning, Colin watched Mrs. Frakes's ritualistic cleanup, aware his hesitation to leave the kitchen was nothing more than procrastination against the phone call to Girard to see if he knew who Tipper might be. "Thank you, Mrs. Frakes, for the great breakfast." He pulled at the waistband on his trousers. "If you don't stop feeding me so well, I'll have to buy new clothes when I go back to St. Louis."

She laughed then sobered. "When must you leave? Miss Beatrice will suffer much disappointment."

"I'll miss her too. Mrs. Frakes, speaking of clothes, I assume you recall Grandfather's suit we found in Uncle's Max's closet."

The housekeeper shuddered. "How can I forget it?"

"When I took it to Tulsa last Sunday, Mr. Granger offered to take it to a friend of his at the police lab in Tulsa for examination. Jack phoned me yesterday to let me know the blood type on the suit matched Grandfather's blood type listed in the court documents. But more interesting, his friend found a memo in a pocket with the date of the murder on it. Grandfather had listed a couple of a.m. appointments on the note, one his meeting with Girard and the other, a conference with someone named Tipper to discuss some fraudulent stock found on the company books. Do you perchance know the identity of this particular person?"

Creases formed in the housekeeper's brow. "Tipper. Name sound familiar, but I don't know when or where I hear it." She shook her head. "So many people come to Briarwood in those days. So sorry. Maybe I remember later."

Colin stood from the table. "I think I'll look in on the Duchess."

Mrs. Frakes sighed. "She had a bad night, tossed and turned, talked in her sleep. Not herself this morning."

Colin grew alarmed. "Is it her heart?"

Mrs. Frakes held up her hand, her eyes full of sadness. "No. She not know me this morning."

Without another word, Colin left the kitchen, running up the back stairs. A couple minutes later, he stood inside his aunt's sitting room observing the Duchess as she gazed out the window from her chair. She didn't seem to hear his approach. "Good morning, Duchess."

Beatrice turned at the sound of his voice. Colin felt a stab of pain in his chest as he beheld the dullness in her eyes. He knelt beside her chair, laying his head in her lap. "Oh, Duchess, you were doing so well." He lifted his eyes to gaze at her face, hoping if he looked at her long enough, he could pull her back to reality.

All at once a spark of recognition showed on her face. She glanced above his head at the door to her room then held his face in her hands. "Ethan, you shouldn't have come here. You know Braxton has forbid me to see you." She smiled. "But I'm so glad you did. We must find a way to convince my brother we love each other and want to get married. He's so stubborn sometimes. He won't listen to me. Oh, Ethan, I love you so much. You'd better go now before Braxton learns you are at Briarwood."

Colin took her hands from his face. "Duchess, I'm your nephew, Colin."

She stared at him. "Colin … who's Colin?"

Mrs. Frakes entered the room. He turned to her, the agony in his heart etched in his face. He stood and stumbled toward the door unable to stop the tears blurring his vision. The housekeeper held out her hand as though to comfort him. But he ignored the gesture, shortly thereafter closing the door to his suite just before he collapsed into the easy chair. His fists beating a resounding rhythm on its overstuffed arms, Colin lifted his face toward the ceiling. "Why, God, why? She's done nothing to deserve that horrible disease."

He dropped his face into his hands. If only he'd come to Briarwood sooner. But he'd put off the trip with one excuse after another, his desire to return to his roots warring against the displeasure he would endure from his mother, escaping the issue by focusing on his own dreams and ambitions in the advertising world. His lips curled with disgust.

And now he could think of no way to right the wrong. His family had needed him, and he'd shuffled them to the wayside. If he'd been here for them, maybe he could have helped his uncle cope with the loss of his wife, perhaps even steering him away from the demon of alcohol. Maybe he could have found better care and medicine for the Duchess, if unable to prevent the disease then slow its progress. *God, please forgive my selfishness.*

Colin raised his head at the sound of a knock on the door, swiping at the tears that lingered at the corners of his eyes with the back of his hand. "Come in."

Mrs. Frakes entered the sitting room and sat down on the ottoman opposite Colin's chair, placing the papers in her hand onto her lap. "Master Colin, you must not be angry with yourself. Miss Beatrice would not wish it. You can't stop or undo what is happening to her. The doctor say nothing can be done to stop the disease. Medicine only slow it down.

"I don't want to hurt you, but I feel I should tell you these things. The most critical is her heart. Doctor say she have genetic problem since she was born and as years have passed it has gotten worse. It is bad now. We could lose her any day. But please don't be so sad. She is ready to go, even prays that it be soon since God answer her longtime prayer—to see you again before she die. She so happy you here."

Moisture began to rebuild in his eyes. "I want to do so much for her, but I feel so helpless. I should have come back to Briarwood years ago."

Mrs. Frakes leaned forward her eyes searching his face. "Master Colin, the past is the past. You can't change it with feelings of guilt or shame. You must live for today and press toward the future. Not like the world say but like God say in Bible. 'Today is the day of salvation.' You here now; that what is important. God know best how to orchestrate our lives. He knew Miss Beatrice would need you now more than at any other time."

Mrs. Frakes picked up the papers in her lap and presented them to Colin. "These say you are your aunt's durable power of attorney. She called her lawyer in Bartlesville after you arrive, and he brought these to her while you at Pawhuska the other day. She at peace knowing you will take care of her now. If you have any questions, Mr. Jordan say call him."

Colin stared at the documents. Everyone seemed to have more confidence in him that he did. He drew a shaky breath. "I'll look these over and phone him if necessary. Thank you, Mrs. Frakes. I would not be able to do this without your help, nor would I desire it any other way now. You're a blessing both to the Duchess and me."

The housekeeper stood and bowed. "You are most kind, Master Colin. Please excuse now. I must see to lunch."

The odor of the tropical floral scent she'd always worn in the air, she exited the room. He marveled at the uncanny way she could still read his mind, even after all the years he'd been away, saying just what he needed to hear from as far back as he could remember. This caring woman who'd given up everything she held dear—country and family to follow her spouse to America; and at his death had transferred her love to the Lamberts, adopting them into her heart and soul. *How could one not adore her?* Colin thought, his sadness laced with a smile.

Laying the attorney's papers aside for now, he pulled his cell phone from his pocket. Time to get back to the business at hand. Dialing Girard's number, Colin waited while the secretary announced the call, the lawyer's smooth-as-silk voice humming in Colin's ears a moment later.

"Colin, my boy. I thought you might have returned to Missouri by now."

"No. Still taking care of things at Briarwood. Say, Mr. Girard, I've come across the name, or rather a nickname, I think, of another individual who had a meeting with my grandfather the morning of his death. Do you know anyone referred to as Tipper?"

Colin heard Braddock's sharp intake of breath. After a pause longer than necessary, he spoke. "No, can't say that I do. I don't recall anyone else at the estate that day. I would have informed Sheriff Tucker had I seen or known of any other appointee that morning."

Colin squeezed his lips together trying to keep his thoughts in check. He knew just as sure as he breathed that the lawyer had lied again. But why? What would it benefit him?

"Too bad you can't remember. The individual's presence at Briarwood makes him a suspect for murder."

"Where did you come up with this information?"

"I'm afraid that's confidential right now. But as I told you the day of Uncle Max's funeral, I've never believed my father committed the crime. And, one way or another, I plan to prove it. Once I discover the identity of this Tipper, my goal may be obtained sooner than I anticipated."

Silence struck the airwaves momentarily. "Well, good luck. If I can be of assistance, just let me know."

You'll help me, all right, straight back to Missouri as fast as you can or drag me to the bottom of Sand Creek. Colin shuddered at the thought. "Right. I'm sure I'll be talking to you soon. Have a good day." He felt like the worst kind of hypocrite. What he wanted to do was—Mrs. Frakes's name for the man suited him to a tee—grab the weasel by the throat and squeeze the truth out of him. Colin punched in his mother's dial code none too gently. Would she be just as elusive with the truth? He put the phone to his ear waiting for her to answer his ring, his mouth set like flint.

"Good morning, Mother. Having a good day, I hope."

"It would be better if you were here."

Colin rolled his eyes. "I have a question for you."

She sighed. "What is it this time?"

"Do you know anyone Braxton referred to as 'Tipper'?"

"Now, why do you suppose I would know that? He never confided his business to me or anything else, hardly spoke to me when I entered the room. Why do you ask? Not that it's any of my concern."

Colin ignored the sarcasm in her tone. "Mother, I know you hate it that I'm at Briarwood, but could you please try to cooperate with me? I've discovered another individual was at Briarwood the morning Grandfather died. You know how important it is to me to find the real killer." Several moments passed before he heard her speak.

"I'm sorry, Colin," she said resignation in her voice. "Yes, I know how bad you want to free your father. You can't blame me, however, for worrying about you. You are my son too. I don't want you involved in something that might harm you…"

"Please don't worry, Mother. I've got friends and even law enforcement in my court now. I'll be careful, I promise."

"See that you do." She paused, her voice breaking when she spoke again. "Colin, you're all I have."

He swallowed the lump rising to his throat. "I know." Colin turned at the light tap on the door, Mrs. Frakes's face appearing from behind the entrance. She motioned toward the clock, making Colin aware that his lunch had been prepared. "Mother, I'll talk to you another time. Mrs. Frakes just informed me that lunch is ready to be served."

"Okay, Colin, call me soon. I miss you."

A moment later, he descended the back stairs, amazed that the phone call with his mother, for the most part, had been pleasant. Could it be she had at last resolved herself to his presence in Oklahoma? About to enter the kitchen, a niggling of alarm broke into his thoughts. Since when had she ever given up on her agendas? And her scheme at this moment was to see her son back in Missouri as quickly as the plane could fly.

Munching on a watercress salad a few moments later, Colin, about to take another bite, held his fork in midair, startled by Mrs. Frakes' question. "See who?"

Mrs. Frakes continued to place sliced strawberries atop a fresh angel food cake she'd baked that morning, the sight of the fresh whipped cream in a bowl nearby, causing Colin's mouth to water with expectation. "I asked if you intended to see your grandmother while you are in Haven."

"Wh-what do you mean?"

Mrs. Frakes turned around to stare at him as though he'd suddenly grown another head.

"Do you plan to visit Mrs. Kirby, Eileen's mother, while here?"

Laying down his fork, Colin took several sips of iced tea, then a larger drink, his eyebrows knitted close together. "But I thought Mother's parents moved to California years ago."

BITTERSWEET JUSTICE 175

"They did, but Mrs. Kirby moved back here when her husband die with heart attack."

His shock abated somewhat, Colin continued to eat. "I wonder why Mother never mentioned it."

Mrs. Frakes turned her attention back to the dessert. "I don't think your mother know about it. She and your aunt Mary don't talk to their mother. I see Mrs. Kirby in town sometimes when I pick up Miss Beatrice's medicine at Taylor Drugstore. Mrs. Kirby lonely, sad about daughters."

"I'd like very much to see her. I always wondered about Mother's parents, but she refused to talk about them. I don't recall meeting them, either. Do you suppose I could see her today?"

Mrs. Frakes set his dessert before him, smiling. "I see Mrs. Kirby this morning and tell her she could probably expect you this afternoon. I think you will like your grandmother. She go to different church, but good Christian."

Colin studied the plate for quite some time after he'd taken the last bite of his shortcake, wondering if the housekeeper had any more surprises to throw his way. He gave his mouth one last quick swipe with his napkin then stood from the table.

"Does my grandmother still reside where she did when I lived at Briarwood?" How strange, now that he thought about it, how he could live in the same small town for twelve-plus years and never have a conversation with his mother's parents.

"Yes. Turn off Main Street onto Spring Avenue. Third bungalow on left."

Colin nodded. "I know which one it is. I often thought of sneaking over to see them when we were in town, but Mother kept too close an eye on me. And I suppose Dad just never thought to take me there."

"Thanks again for that wonderful meal. I'll see you and the Duchess when I return from town." Colin bowed in response to a like gesture from Mrs. Frakes, leaving less than a half hour later for Haven.

·····

Colin parked his car on the street in front of his grandmother's house, hesitant to alight from the car. What does one say to a grandmother he's never met? Scenarios raced across Colin's mind, none of them seeming appropriate. He pulled on the car door handle. *Looks like I'll just have to wing it,* he thought. He recalled the time he'd spent the night at his friend Ray's house and had learned the art of milking a cow. He'd kept squeezing, but no milk splashed into his bucket. At last he'd conquered the feat, a stream of white flowing from each of his hands. Maybe the words would be in his mind and mouth by the time he knocked on her door.

Taking a deep breath, he climbed out of his car and tapped on the door to his grandmother's house a moment later. Soon it opened, and he stared at the woman, a living portrait of his mother as she might appear twenty years from now. "Mrs. Kirby?" Colin felt like he had several cotton balls stuck in his throat. He moistened his lips. "Hello, I'm Colin Lambert, and I believe you are my grandmother." She smiled then nodded, widening the entryway so he could come inside her home.

"Won't you please sit down?" She pointed to a worn loveseat in the combination living room/bedroom, the space at the far end of the room occupied by a twin-sized bed adjacent to a small dresser. "Could I offer you a glass of lemonade? I made it fresh this morning."

He nodded. "Thank you. Sounds good."

While she emptied ice cubes taken from the small refrigerator into their glasses, Colin scrutinized his surroundings. Although clean, the house held few possessions, the furniture worn so much he doubted even Goodwill or the Salvation Army would accept it as a donation. A slow burn began in the pit of his stomach and inched to his throat as anger lifted its ugly head. How could his mother allow his grandmother to live in such meager conditions while she enjoyed a comfortable lifestyle? And what about Aunt Mary? Last he heard, her husband's salary was well over six digits.

"Here you go. I hope I got it sweet enough," Mrs. Kirby said, wiping the condensation off the glass with a napkin before she handed it to Colin."

He took a sip. "Perfect." He placed the glass on the less than sturdy-looking table, lifting his eyes to take in this relative he'd never known. "I'm sorry. I don't mean to stare, but I didn't realize you had returned to Haven until Mrs. Frakes told me about it during lunch today. I do wish I'd known sooner that you were in Haven. It's my understanding you lived in California until recently?"

She nodded. "We did until my husband…your grandfather died a few months ago. I didn't have any place else to go, so with the small amount of money we'd earned in the orchards, I bought a bus ticket and came back to Oklahoma, phoning a friend in Haven before I left California, asking her to meet me at the bus station in Bartlesville and drive me here.

"Since I owned this house, I thought I could get by on my Social Security check. I also earn extra money by making homemade pies for Chloe's Diner up the street. I've managed with God's help. As you can see…" Colin glanced toward the stack of books on the nearby shelf she indicated with her hand. "I like to read. Each time my friend takes me to the grocery store in Bartlesville, we stop by the library so I can stock up on reading material for a couple of weeks at a time. And, of course, I enjoy my church. So, all in all, it's not a bad life."

Colin felt the heat inside him rise to his cheeks. Even the deteriorating state of Briarwood would be a mansion compared to this. What had happened between his grandmother and her daughters, that they had cast her from their lives? "I assume you don't have a car. Do you drive?"

"No, Hector didn't see the need for me to know how." She laughed. "Now I'm too old to learn."

Colin watched his grandmother thread and rethread her hands she held on her lap. "Did Mrs. Frakes tell you I was staying at Briarwood?

"Not until this morning. But I was at Maxwell Lambert's funeral and saw you there. You wouldn't have known me. I started to come over and introduce myself, but Nicholas Girard led you away before I could say anything. Never did like that man. He had a mean streak down his spine when he dated your mother, always demanding Eileen to look a certain way, dress in clothes she couldn't afford. Slapped her around a few times too. I was glad she didn't marry him."

Mrs. Kirby eyed Colin, smiling. "You're the spittin' image of Stuart." She looked away her expression thoughtful. "Before…" She set her gaze on Colin then averted her eyes. "Before we moved to California, Stuart would sometimes come to our house and give me money when … when your grandfather used all his wages for whiskey. I suppose your mother told you how he used to beat her and your aunt Mary each time he came home drunk. He called them vile, ugly names, almost killed me a few times when I interfered with his 'gettin' them into shape' as he called it. I tried to divorce him once, but he found me and threatened to hurt the girls really bad if I didn't come back to him." Sadness filled her eyes. "After Eileen married your father, he beat Mary so hard one night, she ran away, and I've not seen or heard from her since then.

"Hector hated the Lamberts and wouldn't let me come near you. Just as well, maybe. Your mother feared he would hurt you. And the truth of the matter is he might have tried. Hector did a lot of bad things when he drank. But he was afraid of them also. Oh, he'd never have said so, but I knew. It had to do with the occasion Braxton Lambert worked my husband over good one night in a fistfight after he'd made an insulting remark to Braxton's wife earlier that day in town.

"One time Hector got drunk and drove to Briarwood, causing trouble for Eileen. The next morning, Stuart came here to have a talk with my husband, the two taking their conversation outside to the porch. A few days later, Hector decided to move to California. I'm sure the money we used for the trip came from your father."

Colin sat mesmerized by her words, details he'd never fathomed or been told. What a horrible life this woman had experienced. Did his mother know that her father had died? Would she contact her mother if told of her circumstances? Colin felt a twinge of guilt at his treatment toward her of late as the tide of anger in his soul began to ebb from his mind. Was Mr. Kirby's cruel treatment of his daughters the reason his father and stepfather had endured the sting of cruelty from his mother's lips?

Colin's thoughts were stilled by the sound of his grandmother's voice. "I'm sorry. What did you say?"

"I asked if you have a good life in St. Louis. And how are your mother and Aunt Mary? I think about them a lot. Would love to see them."

"They're both doing fine. Mother married again after she divorced my father, but he passed away recently, leaving me his advertising business. So, yes, I'm happy for the most part. Would like to find a wife and have children at some point, but I'm in no hurry. Just waiting for God to bring the right person into my life." An image of Julie barreled into his mind. *Is she the one you have in mind, Father?*

His grandmother nodded. "Always best to wait. I should never have married Hector, knew in my heart I'd made a mistake. Stayed with him out of obligation, not love." She sighed. Would have been better if I'd left him at the altar." She looked long and deep into Colin's eyes. "Just watch your step, Son, and wait until you know for sure. Don't mess up like I did."

"Yes, ma'am. I'll do my best." Colin waited for his grandmother's reply, but she seemed to have run out of words. When the silence grew heavier, he stood to his feet. "I guess I'll go now." He glanced toward the kitchen, where he scanned the pie-making paraphernalia she'd set on the table before his arrival. "I don't want to keep you from your work."

She nodded. "I do need to get those pies baked." She stood, clasping his hands in her palms. "It's been wonderful to meet you at last. Please tell your mother and her sister hello for me, that I still love them and my happiness would be complete if I could see their faces again. And, if you have time before you return to Missouri, I'd like you to drop by and pay me another visit."

Colin drew her to him for a quick embrace. "Good-bye, Grandmother. I'll pass your message along to Mother."

"Take care, Colin. Be good to your mother."

Nodding, he closed the door and returned to his car. All of a sudden he felt as though the world had dumped all its problems on his back: his mother, his father, the Duchess, Mrs. Frakes, and now a grandmother he'd hardly known existed, the responsibility for each of them now leaning toward him. Driving to the drugstore to get a drink to soothe his parched throat, he muttered his thoughts. "God, you said in your Word, you didn't give your children more than they can handle, but I'm starting to wonder about that." A stanza from an old hymn he'd sung as a child rolled into his mind from his heart. *Oh, what peace we often forfeit, oh, what needless pain we bear. All because we do not carry everything to God in prayer.* "You're right, Father. This is something you and I will have to work out together."

Driving onto Main Street a couple of minutes later, Colin braked in the middle of the street, his gaze glued to the front of Nicholas Girard's office. A smile touched Colin's lips. Could this be the break he'd been waiting to discover?

CHAPTER 12

Colin swung wide his car and parked next to the sports car alongside Braddock's automobile. Gazing at the obvious recent repair work on the fender and the new headlamp, he smiled. When the hit and run driver had struck the rental car from behind, Colin had heard glass shatter. He looked heavenward, muttering a prayer of thanks as he circled the car, jotting down the license plate number on the back of a business card he retrieved from his wallet. A smile of triumph on his lips, he opened the door to the attorney's office.

He eyed the man standing next to the secretary seated at her desk. "Good afternoon, Mr. Lambert," she said in a voice like syrup dripping from a fork. "Can I help you?"

"Just stopped by to chat with Mr. Girard a moment, if he's available."

She smiled, the look in her eyes sensual enough to scorch the tail feathers off a peacock. "Have a seat while I check." She picked up the phone, replacing the receiver momentarily. "He'll be out shortly."

While the man conversed with the secretary, Colin picked up a magazine and made a pretense of reading it, all the while scrutinizing the gentleman from beneath his lashes. His build and baseball cap on his head matched Colin's glimpse of the driver tailing him in Pawhuska as well as the physique of the man outside the office window at Briarwood.

Girard opened the door to his office and strode toward Colin. "Hello." He turned to his secretary, his eyes widening then darkening with anger as he took in the person next to her. Always the professional, the attorney turned his attention to Colin. "Mr. Lambert, you've met my secretary and niece, Maria, and this is her brother, Keith."

Standing, Colin forced a smile but didn't offer his hand. "Glad to make your acquaintance." *Am I ever!*

Nicholas motioned for Colin to follow him. "Come on back to my office."

"Thanks. I won't keep you long."

Once the two men were seated, Girard looked at Colin with interest, the anger toward the nephew still visible in the attorney's eyes. "Were you able to identify the elusive Tipper?" he asked, his manner reserved.

"Not yet, but soon I hope. Just thought I'd drop in to let you know I didn't find any large amounts of cash lying around Briarwood and was curious to learn if you'd remembered any remarks Uncle Max might have made regarding the matter."

Girard shook his head. "Sorry, haven't thought of a thing. But if I do, you can bet I'll phone you right away."

Sure you will. Colin's smile traveled no further than his mouth. "Thanks. Say, I met my maternal grandmother for the first time this afternoon."

"Interesting. And how is Mrs. Kirby faring?"

"Fine, it seems. She told me she'd attended Uncle Max's funeral. I'm surprised you didn't mention her presence there."

"I apologize. I did notice her at the church, but knowing your mother's feelings regarding her family, I thought it best not to say anything about the woman."

Colin uncrossed his legs and stood from the chair. "Yes, well, Mother's inclinations aren't always my own. Sorry I took up your time." Colin motioned for Girard to stay seated. "Don't bother getting up from your chair. I'll see myself to the door." Once in the outer office, Colin noticed that the nephew had left the building.

Once inside his car, Colin phoned the sheriff to relay the information about Keith.

"We'll get right on it, Colin. I'll have Clay pick him up for questioning. Glad you called. I was about to phone to tell you Marty who owns Marty's Repair Service in Pawhuska just returned my call, informing me he'd fixed Keith's car a couple days ago, Nicholas Girard paying the bill. If your suspicions about the lawyer are right, he may have ordered Keith to pull the shenanigans you've endured this past week. He's not above those stunts and will do most anything to support his drug habit… been in trouble with the law numerous times since he was a kid. As far as Girard is concerned, I've often said, 'give a suspect rope and if he's guilty he'll strangle himself with it.' If he is connected with the murder of your grandfather, it will be exposed sooner or later."

"For my dad's sake, I hope it's soon. Did you get my message this morning about the guy named Tipper?"

"Yes. Just haven't had time to get back with you. I've been busy with a report of possible cattle rustling. Seems the economy of late has produced a number of complaints from farmers and ranchers about stolen cattle. We have a lot of people out of work in the county. Stealing a few cows not only provides a way to supply meat for hunger but an opportunity to put some cash in one's pocket."

"I understand."

"Do you suppose your aunt would know this fellow called Tipper?"

"I intended to ask her this morning, but she doesn't recognize me today."

"Sorry to hear that. I know her condition must be hard for you. But, hey, if I discover anything worthwhile in my session with Keith, I'll give you a call."

"Thanks. Talk to you later."

Swigging a drink of his cola, Colin drove toward Briarwood, his thoughts on Girard. *If he did commit the crime, how can I prove it? And where do I begin? God, please show me what to do. And what about all that missing cash?*

Turning into his driveway, Colin's lips thinned to a straight line. One thing was certain. His uncle's money had benefited something or someone. All of a sudden a thought occurred to him. When did the monthly repetition begin? Entering the house, he strode toward the office, enjoying the coolness in the house. Quite a difference from the first day he'd entered the manor. Inside the office, he opened the drawer of the desk where he'd stored the business card from Ms. Williams, the cordial and helpful assistant at Bank of Oklahoma. Giving her his credit card number over his phone a few moments later to pay for the research of Uncle Max's account since its inception, he extended his gratitude for her help. Assured by her he would receive the information within a few days, Colin answered his e-mails then entered the kitchen to tell Mrs. Frakes about the visit with his grandmother Kirby while the housekeeper prepared their dinner.

· · · · ·

Returning to Briarwood the next afternoon following his training class for a permit to carry a concealed weapon, Colin glanced at the certificate of completion he'd laid on the passenger seat of the car, grinning. His natural ability as a young man to handle firearms hadn't been lost in the shuffle of time. He glanced at his watch. The purchase of a gun would have to wait until tomorrow. Tonight was his date with Julie. Colin put a little more pressure on the gas pedal. He couldn't waste any time if he were to arrive at her house by six o'clock.

Early that evening, seated in a well-known Tulsa eating establishment that specialized in Greek hors d'oeuvres and grilled steaks, Colin placed their orders, smiling at Julie as he gave the menus back to the waiter. "Did your day go well?"

"Yes, thank you. We may have another break in our case. While in the employee lounge this afternoon, I spoke to my friend Sarah about my search for Lambert Oil info and one of the editor assistants overheard our conversation. She told us about her brother, a CPA in a neighboring state, who'd started his career at Lambert Oil in the early eighties. She gave me his home number, and I plan to phone him in the morning. She said she'd call him tonight to give advance notice of my call."

Colin dipped a radish in the Greek vegetable dip, his smile widening. "Wonderful. Maybe he'll know about the bogus stock issue my grandfather referred to in his memo that day."

"That's what I'm counting on. What about you? Did you get your permit?"

"Yes. I plan to drive into Bartlesville tomorrow to purchase a gun. I just hope and pray nothing happens that will force the use of it. Did you get my e-mail about Girard's nephew?"

"Yes. It will be interesting to hear how his interview with the sheriff goes."

"For sure. Maybe we'll know something by the time of our meeting with Jack on Sunday. At least we're further along in our campaign than last week. With all that's happened, I know the puzzle is starting to take shape."

"I agree. And, after I speak with that accountant, we might be able to connect a few more pieces."

Conversation ceased momentarily while the waiter placed their order on the table. When Colin saw the food had been prepared as each of them desired, he bowed his head. When he finished blessing the food, he grew puzzled at the expression in Julie's eyes, a look of wariness entangled with remorse and pain.

"I'm sorry, Julie. Did I offend you by praying over the food?"

"No, not at all. I-I... Look, I want to apologize for my reaction to your kindness the other night at Briarwood. I was rude. I tend to be defensive about my life. I'm really sorry. I do appreciate your concern for me... and you were right. About a tragic event, I mean. Not only that, but I've been through a long, drawn out divorce suit that finalized just last month."

"I see. Please don't feel like you have to explain any of it to me. However, I can relate to grief, not in your specific circumstances, but heart-wrenching agony nonetheless, every time I visit my father in prison. Although the quote 'Life is not always fair' has been often regarded as a mere pun, my father has made me realize the saying can be a foundation on which a healing process can begin.

"When we talk about his inequitable imprisonment, he encourages me not to concentrate on the injustice of the past but rather live for today in anticipation of an abundant future, grasping every opportunity available to make changes in my life for the betterment of others. One of Dad's favorite scriptures is 'It is not I that lives, but Christ who lives in me.'" Colin smiled. "Not to discount Dad's frequent reminder that Christ came to serve others. That's how my father perceives his life—a chance to serve his Savior by being an example of Christ's love among the prisoners."

Colin observed the look of astonishment on Julie's face. "Oh, sorry, didn't mean to sound so philosophical."

"No... no... I mean, that's okay." She looked down at her plate. "I-I'm a Christian too, although not an active one of late, I'm ashamed to say. I used to be quite involved in my church but not now."

"May I ask why?"

Julie sighed, a look of exasperation on her face. "The members of the church I attended no longer wanted anything to do with me once I filed for divorce. Some of them knew the situation, but it didn't make any difference. Some even implied I'd committed the unforgiveable sin."

Colin's eyes snapped with anger. "You're not serious?"

"Afraid so."

"Of all the narrow-minded, hypocritical beliefs. Yes, God hates divorce, but it is *not* the unpardonable sin. Don't they understand God is merciful, forgiving, full of love and compassion, loving us in spite of our weaknesses and failures? My goodness, where would we be, *where would I be,* without those righteous qualities in our Savior? Although I gave my heart to Christ as a child, I didn't follow his examples as I grew older. Just recently, though, I rededicated my life to serving Him, experiencing his forgiveness and grace firsthand. Besides, didn't God say, he looks on the heart of an individual and, according to Scripture no one else has the right to judge except God?"

A smile flickered in Julie's eyes. "Are you sure you haven't missed your calling as a minister?"

Colin laughed. "Sorry, yet again. No, I don't think a pulpit is what God intended for me, nevertheless, I do find myself a frequent advocate for justice in our unfair world." He paused. "But, I must admit, it's difficult for me on occasion to stand back and let God work things out in his way and time."

Julie studied Colin. After a moment she took a deep breath. "Colin, I can't explain it, but I feel like we've been friends a long time. I believe I can trust you." She hesitated as she blotted her lips against her napkin. "What I'm about to say, I'd like to keep between us. There are a few at the paper who know my circumstances, but like you, I abhor the thought of my private life becoming a source of office gossip."

He placed his fork beside his plate. Giving her his full attention, he sensed this to be a profound moment for her, afraid if he uttered a sound it would break her confidence in him. He caught a glimpse of shame in her eyes before she looked away.

"As I told you the other night, I married a man I met at college ... one of my professors. I thought I'd made the match of the century. He bestowed on me all the affection any woman could ever desire. To his peers, the fellow members of his church and the community, he appeared a model professional, Christian, and outstanding citizen. But within a few months behind the closed doors of our home, I discovered he wasn't all he'd appeared to be in public.

"He was insanely jealous. I had to give up my friends, couldn't speak to anyone in a social setting unless he was at my side, and wasn't allowed to communicate with my family unless he could overhear the conversation. I discovered later he'd had someone wire my office phone so he could monitor all my phone calls. He even managed by his political influence to plant a receptionist in Classified who told him my every move at work. During the divorce proceedings, one of the witnesses for his case turned out to be that receptionist. Of course, every negative statement she made in court about me proved to be a lie. Thank God for that. Afterward, I discovered she and my husband were having an affair."

Colin rejected the impulse to reach out his hand to stroke her cheek. "You've had it rough. I'm sorry."

She nodded a look of gratitude in her eyes. "One day my brother, Clay, phoned the office to see how I was doing. My family had realized something was wrong by the personality change in me. I'd always been outgoing, liked to joke around, enjoyed playing with my nieces and nephews, but I became distant and withdrawn. When I heard Clay's voice that morning, I broke, sharing with him all the sordid details of life with my husband.

"That night when I came home from work, Jeff was waiting for me." She paused as tears formed in her eyes and scudded down her cheeks. "He beat me unconscious with a lead pipe, breaking several of my ribs, my arm, and my pelvic bone, then left me for dead. If Clay hadn't found me a few minutes after Jeff left the house, I wouldn't be alive today."

The sensation Colin knew so well torched his soul and flamed into a blazing fire. How could a man in his right mind do such an ungodly act? "Oh, Julie. Dear God in heaven. I knew something in your life was amiss, but I had no idea it was that bad. Please tell me he got what he deserved in court."

"It took almost two years, but yes, he did. He's now serving a long sentence for attempted murder. He denied the crime of course, saying an intruder had committed the act against me. An unknown in the town where we lived, I didn't have his weapons of prestige and money to adequately fight him, but thank God for my family's prayers. Jeff countersued in the divorce, but a friend introduced me to her attorney, who waged war against him and won each battle for me."

Colin could resist no longer. He reached out and took her hand in his. "I can't imagine the agony you've been through, but I know God knows and cares. And, although we can't understand why these things happen, He's there to give us comfort, peace and love. He said all we have to do is 'call on him and He will answer.' I'll be praying for you."

"Thanks, Colin. I appreciate it." She glanced down at her watch. "We'd better hurry if we are to take in that movie."

Colin smiled. "Would it really matter that much if we skipped it?"

She returned his smile pulling her fingers from his clasp. "Well, I've heard it's one we don't want to miss."

Colin relented with a bow of his head, taking her cue to drop the subject. "Whatever the lady desires, so shall it be."

She laughed, turning her attention to the meal.

· · · · ·

Later, following the end of the movie, Colin walked Julie to his car, the two still laughing from the comedic antics on the screen. Whoever had recommended the film to Julie had been accurate in their assessment. But, more important, he couldn't remember the last time he'd enjoyed an evening with such a likeable companion. Opting to forego his offer to extend their evening with a trip to Starbucks, Julie smiled at Colin.

"Could I take a rain check, please? I want to look over the documents of your father's case and the notes I took while listening to the recordings you brought to our first meeting before I go to sleep. Like Jack, I know there's something we're missing. And I told Mrs. Sharpton I would phone her brother around nine in the morning."

Colin smiled as he placed his hand over hers. "I had a great time tonight, Julie. I hope you're serious about the rain check. I'd like to see you again."

Julie moistened her lips. "I'd like that too." She reached inside her purse and drew a pen and notepad from it, scribbled a moment then handed the paper to Colin. "This is my cell number. Call me or text me when you want to get together again. Maybe I'll be free."

"Thanks. I'll be phoning you soon." Smiling, he drove onto the street, turning toward her address.

Once they arrived at her house, Colin walked her to the door and started to kiss her good night, but she drew back at his touch. Turning away from him, he watched her fumble in her purse for her keys. At a loss of what to say, he lifted his hand to stroke her cheek. "Good night, Julie. Thank you for a wonderful evening."

"Good night, Colin. I'll see you Sunday."

Late that night, he climbed to the second floor, making sure the women of his household were safe before he made his way to his rooms. Lying in bed a few moments later, Colin smiled. She might have refused his embrace, but she hadn't refused another date. *Not a bad start*, he thought.

The next morning Colin arose early, deciding to take in the dawn of day from the sunroom, his visit with his grandmother Kirby on his mind. Observing the charcoal sky as it turned varying colors of grey then hues of blue when the sun burst into full view above the horizon, he contemplated the incredible life she must have led married to his cruel, controlling grandfather. He couldn't begin to understand the physical and emotional pain his mother and aunt Mary had suffered.

Colin recalled the statement his grandmother had made regarding Nicholas Girard. Had his mother noticed similar tendencies of her father in the young lawyer, deciding to break her engagement to him when she realized Stuart Lambert's interest in her? If it were true, who could blame her? Did fear drive her to marry a man she didn't love? Then later, did Girard force her into an affair with him? Had terror been the motive for their sudden exodus from Oklahoma after the trial rather than Eileen's assumption the Lamberts would attempt to take her son as she'd suggested? *If I were a betting man*, Colin decided, *the blame would lie with Girard in a heartbeat.* The trepidation in her voice when she'd spoke of his phone calls hadn't escaped his notice, not once. What was Girard's hold on his mother after all these years?

Colin felt for his cell phone, withdrawing it from his pocket, glancing at his watch as he pressed the appropriate key. He pulled a deep breath. Yes, it was early. However, the dawn of the day might find Eileen more receptive to news of his grandmother. At least he could hope so. Colin drummed his fingers on the cushioned, wicker sofa while he waited for his mother to answer her phone.

"Good morning, Mother." He heard her sharp intake of breath.

BITTERSWEET JUSTICE

"Colin! What's wrong? Are you okay?"

"I'm fine. Sorry to wake you, but I thought this a good time to share something with you." He sensed her sudden alertness.

"Well, what is it?"

"I had a visit with Grandmother Kirby a couple days ago."

"W-What? My mother? You called her?"

"No. She lives in Haven now. In the same house she lived in when I was a boy. Mrs. Frakes informed me of her presence in town, and I decided to pay her a visit."

The other end of the line grew silent, the length of time so long Colin thought his mother might have disconnected the call. "Mother?"

"Yes, I'm still here. And Father? Did you speak with my father too?"

"No. I'm sorry to have to tell you this, but your father died. He passed away in California from a heart attack. Your mother, having nowhere else to go, moved back to your old home."

Colin heard his mother's sigh of relief. "How is she?"

"She seems to be well. Said she would give anything to see you and Aunt Mary." Colin paused, unsure of how to continue. "She told me about your life with Grandfather. Why didn't you tell me? I can understand why you didn't discuss it with me when I was a child, but I'm grown now."

"I guess an appropriate moment never presented itself."

"Mother, she lives in poverty. I'm sure you remember the house. Don't you think we ought to do something about it?"

"Why should I? She chose to stay with my father, knowing what he did to us girls. She turned her back on us, even went back to him after we had a chance to be free. Why would I want to help her now?"

"Did she tell you the reason she stopped the divorce?"

"No. Just thought she cared more for him than us."

"Your father threatened both your sister and you with worse than beatings if she didn't end the divorce proceedings. She didn't say so, but I felt she feared for each of your lives. The Bible says no love is greater than when one is willing to lay down his life for another. From all she told me, I believe the words apropos in your case—she chose life for you, such as it was, in place of freedom from his abusive nature." Colin waited while his mother pondered his words.

"She never said a word to us."

"Could have been her way of protecting you. Mother, she needs her daughters. Why don't you phone Aunt Mary? She might want to hear about Grandmother. You know it's not that far from St. Louis to Haven. Or maybe, I could arrange for her to come to you."

"I don't know about Mary, but I'm not sure I can forgive and forget quite that easy."

"God would help you if you'd let Him." Colin flinched at her snort of disgust.

"You sound just like Stuart. He told me the same thing years ago. But where was this God of yours when my father beat me just short of hospitalization at least three times a week. Do you know how often I entered school with black eyes and bruises covering my body, how awful it was to be a spectacle in the sight of the students and teachers and how I wondered every day why no one would do anything about it? So don't speak to me about a loving God."

"I'm sorry, Mother. I don't know how anyone could ignore something like that. But at least you can be thankful that things aren't that way in this day and time."

"In Haven, Oklahoma? Don't make me laugh."

Colin closed his eyes. *Father, God, only you can take the bitterness from Mother's heart. Please, in some way let her perceive your goodness.* "Please, Mother, think about Grandmother's life now. Try to forget the past and do right by her."

"I won't promise anything, but I will give Mary a call."

Colin turned toward the sounds of meal preparation in the kitchen. "Thanks, Mother, I'm sure you won't regret it. I'll ring off now so you can phone right away. Let me know what you decide. I-I love you, Mother." A sound of smothered shock soared across the line. He smiled. It had been a long time since he'd said those words to her. Could his heart be softening toward her after all this time?

Colin lifted his eyebrows. But did that discount the fact she'd been hiding something about Grandfather Braxton's murder? If it came to light she'd been involved like suspicion indicated, could he repeat his affectionate words then? Colin brushed the back of his hair with his hand, gritting his teeth. Should he just forget his endeavor and go back home? But how could he? Didn't his integrity toward his father count for anything? *Oh, God, help me do the right thing, no matter what may come of it.*

"Well, I love you, too, Son. Please be careful and come home soon."

"When I can, I promise. Have a good day."

Colin ended the call, before she could utter a condescending comment about his plans. A moment later, he strode toward the kitchen to await the fresh pot of coffee he knew would be brewing on his behalf, his thoughts on his advice to his mother. Would the sisters set the grievances of the past aside and shoulder their responsibility toward his grandmother, or would her care fall on him?

CHAPTER 13

His mind stormed by a tsunami of questions that seemed to have no answers, he uttered his frustration. "What was that Bible verse again about 'bearing one another's burdens'?" *Let me just say, God, I'm a bit overloaded right now, don't you think?*

Remember the eagle's wings, Son. Colin nodded at the Father's gentle reply.

Mrs. Frakes turned a startled gaze on Colin when he entered the kitchen. "Oh, Master Colin, I did not know you awake. How you like your eggs this morning?"

He sat down at the table, his expression thoughtful. "Scrambled, I think. Is the Duchess still asleep?"

"Yes, when I come downstairs. Probably for another hour or so."

Colin nodded. "What are the prospects of you two accompanying me to Bartlesville today?"

Mrs. Frakes's eyes dimmed with sadness. "I not know. Miss Beatrice still not know me last night. Too, she breathe heavy while sleeping. I thought to call her doctor, but she soon rest." All of a sudden, the housekeeper convulsed with sobs. "I-so-afraid-she-die." Mrs. Frakes drew a shaky breath. "She like sister to me."

Colin stood and embraced the housekeeper, keeping his arms about her until her tears were spent. She turned away to wipe her face with the tissue she extracted from a pocket on her kimono. "I so sorry. I fix your breakfast now."

"No need to apologize, Mrs. Frakes. We both will suffer great loss when it's my aunt's time to leave us. But I've purposed to enjoy her as much as possible for as long as I can."

"Yes. You are right. That is what we must do."

Colin returned to his place at the table. I hope she'll be in our world today. If a day trip is out, maybe I could bring her down to the sunroom or let her get fresh air from the patio before the temperature gets too high."

Mrs. Frakes smiled. "She would like that."

Following his meal, Colin retired to the office to catch up on his electronic correspondence while Mrs. Frakes tended to the Duchess. He sat down behind the desk, the housekeeper's words on his mind. Did Mrs. Frakes wonder what she would do once she no longer had to care for his aunt? As far as he was concerned she could remain at Briarwood. He still wanted to renovate the house but could only do it on weekends. It would be nice to have her there to prepare his meals while he was in residence. But would she consider it an option? Would she be afraid to stay here alone? With a deep sigh, Colin switched on his laptop. Thank God he didn't have to solve *that* problem today.

A half hour or so later, he glanced at his watch. The Duchess should be ready for a chat about now, he thought. Hopefully she would be able to clarify the identity of Tipper. A moment later, he climbed the back stairs to his aunt's suite. As he approached the door to her sitting room, Mrs. Frakes stepped into the hall. She smiled at Colin. "Miss Beatrice have good start on day."

Colin exhaled slowly to aid the release of the tension in his neck and shoulders. He took a cautious step into the room, eyeing his aunt's demeanor. "Good morning, Duchess."

She turned from the television program she was viewing to smile at him. "Same to you, dear boy." She picked up the remote from the table and pushed the off button. "Come in." She glanced out the window. "It looks to be the beginning of a beautiful day. The rain helped green things up a mite."

"Yes. Say, Duchess, are you up to an outing today? I thought the three of us might drive into Bartlesville. Mrs. Frakes said you haven't been away from Briarwood in a while. What do you think?"

"Why, Colin, what a nice surprise. I would love to go with you."

"Good. I have an errand to do while I'm there, but it won't take long. I've already phoned ahead for what I need, and it will be waiting for me." He grew quiet. "Duchess, do you happen to know anyone Grandfather referred to as 'Tipper'?"

Beatrice laughed. "Why, certainly. That was the affectionate title Braxton bestowed on your uncle Max because of his knowledge in the stock market. The man practically breathed the subject. But that was part of his job—to keep Braxton up-to-date on Lambert Oil worth and their investments." She threw him a look of curiosity. "You seem disappointed. May I ask why?"

Colin forced a smile. "Just trying to satisfy my curiosity. I read the name on an old memo Grandfather had written to remind him of an appointment and wondered who it might be."

"I see. Max was the risk taker of my two brothers, Braxton the more conservative. Often the boys would grapple over how to invest company profits, Braxton usually winning." Beatrice grew thoughtful. "It seems they were always at odds with one another, even as boys."

Colin groaned inside. Back-to-square-one, he thought, the purpose of his grandfather's discussion with Uncle Max most likely the findings in the company accounts. Colin leaned forward to hug his aunt. "I'll go now so Mrs. Frakes can help you get ready for our trip." "Duchess, I love you."

Beatrice took his face in her hands. "I love you too, Colin, more than you may ever know."

He laughed. "Now, what's that supposed to mean?"

She laughed with him. "That's my secret."

He slowly descended the front stairs a moment later, thinking of his aunt's playful declaration. Had she been serious or facetious? He shrugged his shoulders knowing it wouldn't do any good to pry. If she wanted to reveal something to him, it would be in her own time and way.

Mulling over the discovery of Tipper's identity, Colin frowned. Who was the company embezzler his grandfather reprimanded and threatened to expose that morning? Unless information unfolded that another individual had been at Briarwood that morning, his suspicion of Nicholas Girard as the killer had now accelerated from possibility to probability. Colin frowned. But again, proof, the obstacle.

Stopping in the foyer, his eye caught a glimpse of a pickup truck pulling to a stop on the driveway. Colin stepped onto the front porch to wait until Mr. Baker emerged from his truck. "Well, hello, Mr. Baker. What brings you to Briarwood this morning?"

"Well, to be honest, Mr. Lambert, I just couldn't bear the thought of the estate grounds looking so unkempt. With nothing better to do, I thought I'd mosey over here and start to put them in shape, if you don't mind. Just call it a good neighbor act."

Colin eyed the lawn care tools in the back of his truck. "I'm glad you're here. I intended to call you about the situation, but I've been tied up of late. And please, I want to pay you for your trouble. Let's see. Don't the Scriptures say something about a man's hire is worthy of pay?"

Mr. Baker laughed. "I guess you got me there." He looked around. "It may take several days to complete the work."

"That's fine. Take as long as you need."

Mr. Baker nodded then grew serious. "Any luck in locating your grandfather's killer?"

Colin shook his head. "Not so far. But I'm not giving up the search. Sorry, Mr. Baker, I'd like to visit longer, but I'm taking my aunt and Mrs. Frakes for a drive."

As Colin turned away, Mr. Baker called out from the back of his truck. "Give my regards to the ladies." With an affirming nod, Colin reentered the house and made his way to the kitchen, glad at last he could do something to give his aunt a fragment of pleasure before the life she knew ceased to exist forever.

· · · · ·

Early that afternoon, the three having enjoyed both a tour of Bartlesville and a hearty meal at a bakery that served lunch on the west side of town, Colin drove them toward Briarwood. He glanced at his companions in the rearview mirror. Mrs. Frakes caught his gaze and smiled before she adjusted the pillow behind Beatrice's head. He grinned back at her, secure in the knowledge the day had been a success. He glimpsed the package beside him. *In more ways than one*, he decided, the gun inside the box reassuring him of better protection for the two women.

Nearing the turnoff to the estate, all of a sudden his nerves stood at attention. A cloud hovered above the house. A moment later, his heart pulsed with fear as he realized the black haze was smoke. He looked over his shoulder at his passengers. They appeared to be asleep. Turning off the main road to drive into Briarwood Valley, his eyes widened as he took in the flames that leapt from the roof at the far end of the barn.

He yanked his cell phone from his pocket and hit the number for the sheriff's office. He heard a sharp intake of breath from the back seat. "Mr. Colin, the barn... Colin nodded his phone still to his ear. The officer assured Colin the rural fire department would be notified right away. The moment the car rolled to a stop Beatrice awoke. Colin lifted her from the car, praying she wouldn't see the smoke rolling into the sky. But to his dismay he saw terror leap into her eyes. "Colin, look! The barn is on fire."

"Yes, Duchess, I know. I've already called the fire department. Mrs. Frakes will look after you while I see if there's anything I can do to put out the fire." However, once he reached the back yard, he knew his words to be just that—words. Eying the crescendo of flames that shot out from the roof, he knew any hope of saving the barn had been shattered. If the fire truck made it to the estate before the barn and stables were a total loss, it would be a miracle.

Colin turned toward the road at the sound of sirens approaching the vicinity. Soon a fire truck, the sheriff's car, and another county car skidded to a stop on the south side of the house.

As though awakening from a trance, Colin hurried to open the gate leading to the stables, a fireman jumping off the truck to help him. The driver pulled through the entrance, firemen running in all directions to tackle the blazing inferno.

Sheriff Kinney walked up beside Colin, shaking his head. "Sorry we couldn't get here sooner. Don't worry, though. They'll do their best to keep the fire from spreading to the house."

Colin nodded, watching two of the men water the vegetation surrounding the barn as others kept a steady spray of water moving back and forth across the roof. "I wonder what caused it. We were returning from Bartlesville and near the valley turnoff when I noticed the smoke. From the ridge it looked as though the fire started at the rear of the barn. By the time we reached the house, the whole barn was in flames."

A couple hours later, while Colin, the firemen, the sheriff, and his deputies poked around the smoldering embers in hopes of discovering a cause for the fire, a shout was heard from one of the deputies several hundred feet from where the barn once stood. All looked toward the officer, eyeing the red gas can he held above his head. When the officer walked up beside them, Sheriff Kinney reached for the handkerchief-covered handle and held the container up for Colin to see.

"Well, it looks like we might have an arsonist in the neighborhood. Although an outdated type of gas container, it's not faded or rusted from exposure to the elements, which means it hasn't been lying in the field too long." The sheriff glanced toward the charred ground then at his watch. "About three hours would be my guess."

Colin looked stunned. "Are you telling me someone deliberately set the barn on fire?"

The sheriff nodded. "It looks like your adversary might have carved another notch in his plan to get you out of town. Could be his nervousness has reached the panic stage. Have you discovered something you haven't had a chance to tell me yet?"

"Not that the murderer would know. I did learn this morning from my aunt the identity of the individual known as Tipper. It seems Uncle Max had been given that nickname by Grandfather because of his brother's knowledge of Wall Street. What I concluded about the memo was that Grandfather wanted to confer with Uncle Max about the embezzlement. I remember my aunt mentioning something about Uncle Max's role in the company but never acquainted her statement with the name found in the memo. I still believe the murderer was the embezzler. And to me, Girard is the number one suspect."

Sheriff Kinney rubbed his chin with his free hand. "Too bad we don't have any evidence to close the gap between suspicion and conviction."

Colin sighed. "I agree. But we can hope tomorrow or the next day or the next will turn up something. Problem is... my father may not have many tomorrows left. I plan to visit him in the morning and bring him up to date on what we've accomplished thus far. Then Ms. Lonetree, Jack and I will meet in the afternoon to discuss our findings."

The sheriff placed his hand on Colin's arm. "We'll just have to work harder. Have your assistants come up with anything else since last we talked?"

"Yes. When I spoke with Ms. Lonetree last evening, she had discovered through a coworker the name of an individual who worked at Lambert Oil as a young accountant in the early eighties. She was to speak with him earlier today. We're hoping he might know of or heard something about a scandal or infraction in the company accounts. It was my intention to phone her just as soon as we returned from Bartlesville, but..." Colin grimaced, throwing a look toward the smoking field. "I've been a little busy."

The sheriff again held up the can. "We'll try to find some fingerprints on this, but I don't hold a positive note about it. Oh, by the way, we pulled in Girard's nephew for questioning. Denies all our allegations, claims he hit a deer on some country road and damaged his car. However, he couldn't seem to remember where he struck the animal. Said he'd been with friends that evening, and they'd taken a drive to have something to do. His memory failed him also about who he'd associated with that night.

"If the kid is telling the truth, which I doubt, the friends would have been Rudy and Samuel James, the family a bad lot, most of them anyway. Their claim to fame is their ancestry to the notorious outlaws, Frank and Jessie James. But no one seems to know if it's true.

"The boys' father is in prison serving his sentence for murder after beating his wife to death. Following his arrest, Rudy and

Samuel, barely old enough to attend school, became the wards of their grandmother, Daphne James. In her younger years she was a prostitute on Tulsa's infamous Third Street before the city fathers rid the area of its bars and human vermin in the seventies. She thinks the sun rises and sets in those boys, would do anything, say anything to protect Rudy and Sam, whether true or not.

"Their sister, Natalie, several years older than her brothers, joined the air force after she graduated from high school and became a nurse. When she retired from the service, she came back to Oklahoma and now lives in Bartlesville. She drives every day to Haven to work for Dr. Wexley as a physician's assistant. But she doesn't seem to have much to do with her family."

The sheriff took a moment to eye the movements of the firemen then turned back to Colin. "And, since you couldn't find any black paint on your car with which we could make a positive match, I have to drop it for now."

"I understand. Did you find your cattle thieves?"

"Still working on it. I think I know the culprits, but again, like in your case, it's that burden of proof that matters so much." With a glance toward the retreating fire truck, the sheriff held out his hand toward Colin. "Better be on my way. I'll let you know if I come up with any information about the fire. It could be a neighbor driving by the area saw someone near Briarwood around the time it started."

"Thanks, I appreciate it." Colin shook the sheriff's hand then threw a wave over his shoulder when he turned toward the house. As he approached the manor, he noticed Mrs. Frakes in the doorway, shaking her head.

"I assure Miss Beatrice the house is in no danger from fire. She's waiting to speak with you."

"Thanks. Just as soon as I wash this soot and sweat off me, I'll go to her."

Later, showered and feeling human again, Colin entered his aunt's sitting room. Noting the questions in her eyes, he sat down across from her hoping to answer them all. "I'm sorry, Duchess. The barn and corral is a total loss. Only ashes left of Dad's favorite place on the estate."

She nodded. "I thought that might be the case, since you were gone so long. So much of our former life has passed away and now this." She grew thoughtful, sadness filling her eyes. "Other than for you, Stuart lived to paint and care for his thoroughbreds. Max sold them and all the tack soon after Braxton died and your father was taken to prison. The sale surprised me, considering Max's love for horses as well." She sighed. "But I guess he couldn't care for them and Agatha too."

"I suppose not." He studied her countenance. "Duchess, are you okay? Should I call the doctor?"

A vague smile touched her lips. "No. He can do nothing to prevent heartache. It's a wonder something hasn't happened to the barn before now. The building hasn't been maintained since your father was taken away. Probably some faulty wiring caused the fire."

Should I tell her about the possibility of an arsonist? Colin thought. Beholding the sadness in her eyes, he decided against it. She didn't need her health jeopardized any further.

"You might be right."

She lifted her hand to her face to stroke her brow with her fingers. "If you don't mind, would you help me to the daybed? I think a nap before dinner is what this old woman requires. Thank you for the outing. I've lived a secluded life since your grandfather died. After Stuart had to go away and you moved to Missouri, I lost reason to exist for a while. Then Maxwell moved back here after poor Agatha passed away, his presence sparking hope in me. But, he too became lost to me. With God's help, I rallied for a few years, becoming more involved in our church and community, but when I had the heart attack, the doctor no longer allowed many outings." She looked up at him, winking. "But we won't tell him about today, will we?"

Colin laughed the teasing gleam in her eyes a memory he would always treasure. "Not a word, I promise." Once she'd fallen asleep, he tiptoed from the room, entering his office a couple minutes later. He keyed in the number he desired to reach then smiled when he heard Julie's voice.

"Hello, Julie, this is Colin."

"Oh, hi, Colin."

"I hope I'm not interrupting you from something, but I wanted to let you know I drove to Bartlesville this morning and purchased a gun. I feel more at ease now."

"That's good. I hope you never need to use it."

"Same here. But, after today, who knows what the future might hold."

"What do you mean?"

Colin relayed the incident of the fire, Julie, not at all taken aback, explaining she'd been concerned something else might happen to deter Colin from his goal.

"Colin, you be careful. It's obvious a killer is worried. You must realize if he's murdered once, he may not be afraid to do it again."

"Don't worry. I'll watch my back. Did you speak to that accountant this morning?"

"Yes. I've been waiting for your call. Mr. Donovan related an incident that occurred a few weeks before your grandfather died. The event, I believe, explains the memo found in the pocket of his suit."

"Now we're getting somewhere. What happened?"

"It seems Mr. Lambert had been in New York City attending a dinner hosted by influential Wall Street brokers, their motive—to incite speculators toward liberal investments in the stock market, the return rate on dividends at an all time high during that era of our economy. At some point in the evening your grandfather had a conversation with a gentleman inquiring when Braxton thought the man's investment in one of Lambert Oil's subsidiary projects known as White Eagle Basin might yield a return."

Colin frowned. "That doesn't seem out of the ordinary. I'm sure the company had numerous investors in their varying entities."

"After further discussion with the man, Mr. Lambert concurred that a top executive in the company had used his clout to initiate a scam involving investments in dry holes, the wells at that particular oil field having been capped several years prior to that night. Desiring to begin an investigation into the matter ASAP, Braxton cancelled his other appointments in the city and returned home the next day."

"And how did Mr. Donovan obtain all this information?"

"He said he happened to be in the office of his supervisor, the chief auditor in the firm, when his boss received the phone call from Mr. Lambert about the situation. As soon as their conversation ended, Mr. Donovan received instructions to begin research on White Eagle Basin, the accountant giving what information he'd collected to his supervisor a few days later, an audit into the affair beginning that day."

"I assume the auditor revealed his findings to his associate."

"The what, where, when and how but not the who. After the report had been relinquished to Mr. Lambert, he'd stated he wanted the name of the offender kept confidential, saying he would deal with the individual in his own time and way, planning to make immediate restitution plus interest to the duped investors."

"Did the accountant explain how the swindle took place?"

"The executive created a subsidiary on the company books into which the White Eagle Basin investments were funneled, authorizing an order to make him the only drawer on that entity. Once the funds hit the account, most of the money was expended to a fictitious drilling company which had only a post office box as its address."

"I see. It's too bad Grandfather kept the name of the swindler to himself. I don't suppose there's any hope that auditor is alive or a possibility the report still exists."

"Of course, I can't say about the report, but we can begin a search on the internet for the auditor. It may take some time, his name is fairly common."

He pulled a deep breath. "Today seems to be full of dead ends."

"What do you mean?"

Colin told of his own discovery regarding "Tipper." "Since no one else has yet to be found who was at Briarwood that morning, I have to assume, like my aunt, that Girard is the crooked executive and killer as well."

"Jack's well educated in crime reporting. When we share everything we've learned this week, maybe he'll give us more pointers in how to glean evidence for your theory. Uh, oh, my doorbell just rang. I'm expecting a visit from my parents. I'll see you tomorrow afternoon."

"Yes. See you then."

Driving to McAlister the next morning, Colin wrestled with his feelings about his visit to the prison. Would his father be pleased about the progress of the investigation to date or would he try to discourage his son's involvement in the case once he heard about the danger that now surrounded his family? Close to three hours later Colin parked his rental car in the visitor parking lot. He glanced at his watch. The entrance to the prison would be unlocked in ten minutes. He had just enough time to reach the outside waiting area to join the throng of individuals who waited to spend the day with their incarcerated family members. Colin frowned. He hated to cut short his visit with his father today, but the meeting with Julie and Jack was too important to miss.

Colin sat at a corner visitor's table waiting for his father to be allowed into the room, his heart pounding. Other than a few times due to unavoidable circumstances, he had made this trip to see his father every other weekend for eighteen years. And each time he experienced the same mixed feelings—sadness and frustration over his powerlessness to change his father's situation, yet excited about the opportunity to spend a few hours enjoying his company. But today would be different. He had never been able to bring his father gifts due to prison regulations, but this visit would be the exception. Colin had with him a gift that no one could deny his father—a gift of hope—the hope of freedom.

Colin and Stuart clung to one another, each blinking back tears. Noticing the additional weight loss in his father, Colin choked back his words of concern, aware that Stuart would not want to discuss his illness. Colin forced cheerfulness into his voice. "Dad, it's good to see you. How's it going?"

"You too, Son. Not much different here except for the fact another prisoner in my block gave his heart to the Lord Friday night at our church service. Things can't get much better than that."

Colin nodded. "I agree." He studied his father's features. "How did the visit go with your doctor this week?"

Stuart glanced out the window. "Nothing has changed. How is your aunt? The last letter I received from Mrs. Frakes stated that Aunt Beatrice had improved."

Colin sighed. His father could be a bit stubborn at times, his refusal to be blunt about his illness unnerving. "Yes, a new medication has been prescribed that seems to help her. But we never know what each day will bring. I spoke with Dr. Wexley a couple days ago and he confirmed what Mrs. Frakes relayed to me earlier—that the medicine will not cure the disease only postpone the inevitable." Colin inched forward to the edge of his chair. "Say, Dad, I have some news."

Stuart lifted his eyebrows. "Oh?"

Stuart listened without interruption as Colin shared all the developments of his probe into Braxton's murder. When Colin revealed all that had happened to frighten him away from Haven, Stuart ran his hand through his gray-streaked hair, his features molding into a look of unease.

"Colin, I know this is something you've wanted to do for years, but I can't sanction you putting yourself in danger, not to mention the harm that could come to your aunt and Mrs. Frakes." Stuart looked away. "In a few weeks it won't matter anyway. I'll be gone."

Colin smoothed the back of his hair. "Dad, I know you've tried to discourage me about my goal all along, but don't you see"—Colin reached out to lay his hand on Stuart's shoulder—"if there's any chance at all that you could walk out of here a free man, don't you think it would be worth it? Think what it would mean to the Duchess to see you living at Briarwood again"—Colin lowered his eyes—"and to me. I need you to be there as well. It would almost be as if the last twenty-five years had never happened."

Stuart sighed. "You can't change the past, Son."

"I realize that. But how many times have you told me that I should live my life doing all I can to better the future of others? That's the objective of my determination to find grandfather's killer—to bring happiness in the near future to those I love. Yes, I know it's dangerous, but I have this peace and awareness inside me that God is directing my every step and is pleased with my efforts."

Stuart mulled over Colin's words. After a moment he shrugged and smiled. "I guess I can't argue with my own advice. And who am I to debate the scripture, "If God be for you, then who can be against you." Stuart grew serious. "Please be careful, Son. Just remember *your* future is ahead of you. Your mother would be heartbroken should anything happen to you. As would I."

Colin nodded. "I will, Dad. And please, keep heaven bombarded with prayers for us. I have a feeling we're going to need them."

"You can count on that, along with intercession from the prayer team here."

"Thanks. Tell them I appreciate it." Knowing his father liked nothing better than to discuss God's Word, Colin changed the subject. "Now I'd like to hear about the happenings in your Bible study group and what you've been teaching them."

A few hours later following an early lunch with Stuart taken from the vending machines located in the visitors' room, Colin announced he had to leave, explaining about his meeting with the *Tulsa World* reporters.

"Again, Son, watch your steps," Stuart said, standing from the table to hug Colin. "I'll be looking forward to our next visit."

"Me too, Dad. Maybe I'll have even better news by then. Take care. I love you."

"Same here. Good-bye and God be with you."

While Colin waited for the door to be unlocked, he turned and waved to Stuart, smiling to hide the sadness that overwhelmed him. *God, please let us find the killer before it's too late.*

· · · · ·

Two hours later, Colin parked near the curb on the street outside Jack Granger's house, observing Julie as she slid from her car. The sun shining on her head revealed red highlights in her long, straight dark hair stylishly tied at the back of her neck with a black bow. He eyed her petite frame wrapped neatly in a becoming black pantsuit with white trim edging the jacket. A silver necklace and matching earrings dangled from her neck and ears. The word elegant came to mind as he returned her smile while she waited for him to alight from his car. Together they walked toward the door, Colin's finger on the doorbell a few seconds later. As Jack greeted them with a hearty hello, Colin couldn't erase, nor did he want to, the idea of how good and right it felt to have her at his side.

Although from his experience with her on Friday night, he knew he couldn't push their relationship; he'd have to take it slow with her. And who could fault her hesitancy to become involved with him after what she'd been through? But, oh, what he'd give to hold her in his arms. With God on his side, maybe he could help right all the wrong life had inflicted on her. Deep inside, he heard the familiar still small voice. *Delight yourself in me, and I will give you the desires of your heart.*

Seated at the Grangers' dining room table, Julie and Colin reported to Jack all that had happened since their last meeting. Studying his notes for a few minutes, Jack soon lifted his eyes to take in his friends. "Let's take a moment to look at what we've got.

"Thus far, we've the note found in the pocket of Braxton's coat revealing a meeting with both Braddock and someone known as 'Tipper' the morning of the murder, the man's identity we now know was Maxwell Lambert. Further, we assume Braxton wanted to confer with his brother regarding the company scam. Two, Nicholas Girard's nephew is a suspect in the hit and run, also the person who may have been following Colin at different times and the one who pelted the office at Briarwood with bullets a few nights past. However, when questioned by Sheriff Kinney, Keith denied the charges, claiming the repairs on his car were made because he hit a deer on a country road."

Jack looked up at Colin a hint of sadness in his eyes. "Three, both your mother and Girard seem to be untruthful and evasive about things connected with the murder; plus we have Jonathan Baker's info about the waitress at the diner who overheard your mother threaten to kill Braxton. Four, large amounts of cash were withdrawn from Maxwell's checking account with no explanation, which may or may not have anything to do with the murder. Five, Braxton discovered some type of embezzlement from the company, which we are now aware of, thanks to Julie." He smiled at her. "Six, someone seems to have deliberately torched the barn at Briarwood, no suspects to date. Seven, the three of us believe we've missed some clue in the reports or interviews that may tell us who the killer is. And eight, we have the suit that Braxton wore when he was killed, proving the bullet that killed him wasn't fired at close range because no powder burns exist on the coat, and the speculation that the gun was fired from either outside or inside the windows, this information substantiated by the coroner's report."

Colin held up his hand. "Don't forget Alfred Baker may have witnessed the murder. And that the killer may have threatened to harm him and his parents should he disclose the identity of the murderer."

Jack snapped his fingers. "That's right. What I'd give to see in his mind. If I could, our case would probably be solved."

Julie and Colin nodded.

Jack grew quiet, tapping his pen against the tablet as he looked over his notes. After a few moments, he drew a steady gaze on Colin. "So far we've no record of anyone else having been at Briarwood the morning your grandfather was killed other than your family; Mrs. Frakes; Mr. Baker and his son, Alfred; and Girard. At present, the most suspicious of all those listed is the lawyer. But I wonder, Colin, have you considered at all the possibility that any one of the other people on that list could have committed the crime?"

Colin frowned as a look of disbelief stole over his features. "No. Well... I... surely you don't believe any of my family capable of killing Grandfather. What would have been their motive? Besides, my aunt believes it was Girard and Grandfather who argued that day about the stock scam."

"I don't mean to upset you, Colin. I just think we should look at every angle of the crime, not taking everything at face value as did Sheriff Tucker at that time. You stated none of the others had a motive, but when you think about it we don't have a conclusive MO for Girard either."

Colin looked down at the papers in front of him. "I realize that. I'm sorry. I just can't conceive the idea that any of my family or friends would have reason to kill Grandfather."

"That's understandable. I'm sorry if I offended you."

Colin waved away his apology. "I know you're right. What's our next step?"

"Keep studying Sheriff Tucker's report on the statements given by each person on the property at the time of the murder to see if something doesn't add up or seems suspicious. Keep listening to your recordings from Mrs. Frakes and the Bakers. Listen for something, anything that might expose a murderer. Try to read between the lines for a motive, such as anger, profit or revenge. All we have at present is circumstantial evidence and a couple possible motives—hatred of the man and company fraud. Although the two MOs are our best shot so far, people have killed for far less reasons than these. We just have to keep going over the information until something we failed to notice before clicks in our brains..."

Jack paused at the sound of the doorbell. A moment later, the three companions looked up in surprise as Clay Walsh rushed into the dining room waving the paper clutched in his hand, his eyes flashing with excitement.

CHAPTER 14

Julie stood from her chair. "Clay, what is it? What's wrong?"

Deputy Clay Walsh looked from one of the occupants in the room to the other, Mrs. Granger looking on from behind him. "Nothing. In fact, it may be the break we've needed."

Julie walked around the table to stand beside her brother. "Break with the suspense, Clay. Tell us."

Holding the paper out of Julie's reach, he grinned. "Needing a ream of paper for my office copier, I stepped into the dispatcher's office to retrieve the keys to the supply closet. Opening the drawer on Sergeant Brown's desk where she kept them, I noticed a letter from OSBI on top a stack of mail she hadn't yet processed. Since this is the sheriff's day off, I called him at home to ask permission to open it. When I relayed the contents of the letter to him, he told me to bring it here right away."

Julie grabbed the letter from his hand. Scanning the details, she lifted her eyes, which sparkled with surprise and delight. Her lips curving into a wide smile, she looked at Jack then Colin, a moment later relinquishing the letter to Clay.

Clay fastened his gaze on Colin. "This is a report regarding your father's gun and the bullet taken from your grandfather's body that we sent to the lab a few days ago. According to this letter, the bullet that killed your grandfather did not, I repeat, *did not* come from the gun found in your father's hand."

Colin started to rise from the chair then sank down again, unashamed of the tears that spiraled down his cheeks. Julie placed her hand on his arm, her eyes bright with unshed tears.

"Colin, this is wonderful news. Do you know what this means?"

Reaching into the back pocket of his trousers for a handkerchief, he nodded. "My father's case can be reopened."

"Yes. However, it may be weeks before a new trial can be placed on the docket. We need to continue our search for the killer. An arrest of the true perpetrator would speed things up for your father's release."

Jack nodded his agreement then motioned for Clay to take a seat at the end of the table. He glanced at his wife, who stood motionless in the doorway. A grin playing at the corners of his mouth, he spoke to her. "Michele, I'm sure Deputy Walsh would like a cold drink."

She threw Clay an apologetic look. "Oh, I'm sorry. Elated at hearing Mr. Lambert's good news, I forgot my manners."

For the next few moments, they quietly sipped their tea, each lost in their own thoughts. Soon Colin glanced around the table at his friends. "I can't begin to express to you the gratefulness I feel in my heart for what you all have done for Dad and me."

Julie leaned forward, her face a portrait of understanding. "No need to try. All of us desire justice for one and all." Dismissing the matter with a smile, she focused on her brother. "So, Clay, where do we go from here?"

"I recommend a meeting with the county prosecutor to let him know about the evidence we've uncovered. This will officially reopen your father's case. He'll notify Sheriff Kinney to start an investigation."

Jack nodded. "Also, your father's attorney needs to file an appeal for a new trial right away." Jack paused to thumb through the court documents. "Ah, here's the name, Gerald Craig, attorney for the defendant. However, it's been over twenty-five years since he defended your father, and as I recall, Attorney Craig wasn't a young lawyer. I'm sure he's retired by now. If so, you'll need to find a good attorney as soon as possible. Once a brief has been filed with the court clerk, the judge, after reviewing the new evidence, can order an emergency hearing in which he has the option to grant a bond that would release your father from prison until the new trial or, should the killer be found in the meantime, permanent liberation. Stuart Lambert could be a free man within a couple of weeks."

Colin sucked in his breath. "I can hardly believe this is happening." Jack smiled. "Shall we get back to work?"

Lifting his hands in surrender, Colin shrugged. "You don't have to coax me. I'm in for the full ride. I'll phone first thing tomorrow for an appointment with the prosecutor in Pawhuska. Then I'll see if I can locate Dad's former attorney." He gazed momentarily at each of his companions. "All of you have walked the extra mile for me. Believe me, I'll never forget it." A short time later, they ended the meeting, the good report from OSBI spurring their determination to locate Braxton's slayer.

Colin hesitated outside the Granger home, desiring to spend time alone with Julie. Much to his disappointment, she seemed intent on a visit with her brother. Waving a reluctant good-bye to them, he walked to his car, his joy regarding the good news Clay had brought them superseding his displeasure. Besides, he could phone her later. Maybe they could arrange a get-together in a day or two.

As he drove toward home, Colin whistled a song of praise. Soon his father would be free. Nonetheless, once he'd navigated the car onto Highway 75 and set the cruise, the anger he'd held for so many years stabbed at his jubilation. Why hadn't Sheriff Tucker had the weapon and bullet analyzed in the first place—the furrow in Colin's brow deepened—or his father's attorney for that matter? Colin rubbed his forehead, attempting to ease his frustration. So many questions, so few answers.

Pulling his cell phone from his shirt pocket, Colin pushed number one on the key pad. Soon his mother answered the call. "Mother, I have great news. If everything goes as it should, Dad may be out of prison in a couple of weeks."

He heard her sharp intake of breath then nothing.

"Mother, didn't you hear what I said?"

"Yes, I heard you. Did the governor finally respond to your plea for a medical release?"

"No, better than that. We've discovered the bullet that killed Grandfather didn't come from Dad's gun."

Eileen gasped. "Really?"

"Yes. Osage County Deputy, Clay Walsh, found the items in their evidence storage room and mailed them to the Oklahoma State Bureau of Investigation to be analyzed. He just received the report yesterday. And it's conclusive, proving Dad didn't kill grandfather."

A few minutes passed while she seemed to absorb her son's words. "Well, I suppose you deserve to be applauded. You've accomplished your goal. When can I expect to see you?"

"Not for a while. I have to meet with the county prosecutor to make him aware of the new evidence. Once he has the report in his hands, he should reopen the investigation into Grandfather's death. I can't leave Briarwood until I know who's responsible for Dad's imprisonment."

"What difference does it make now? Your father will be free. Isn't that what you wanted?"

"Of course. But, he deserves to know who framed him."

"Colin, I don't understand why you insist on putting yourself in jeopardy. No. I won't allow it. You must leave there at once." The urgency in her tone swelled with her pitch. "Please, Son, before it's too late."

Colin closed his eyes, gritting his teeth to hold back the angry retort lodged on his tongue. Taking a deep breath, he forced calmness into his next words. "Too late for what?" Colin waited, but she didn't respond. "Mother, what are you not divulging about the murder? Don't bother to contradict me. Remember, I'm your son. I know you." Colin sensed his mother's refusal to be forthcoming before she spoke.

"How could I know anything? I was in Bartlesville shopping when it happened."

He sighed. "Yes, I know, Mother. We'll skip it for now. But I must warn you, if the sheriff discovers you haven't been candid about information that could lead to a killer, it won't be pleasant for you." *Not to mention what it would do to me*, he thought. At her silence, he rubbed his chest, the pain he felt in his heart seeming physical. "Good-bye, Mother, I'll talk to you soon." Colin pushed the end button, realizing she'd expressed no joy concerning his announcement. What would it take to soften her heart toward his father?

When Colin arrived at the estate, he searched out the housekeeper, locating her in the kitchen. He informed Mrs. Frakes about the ballistics report, the smile on her face a sight to behold.

"I so happy for you, Master Colin. Your father too. We must celebrate big time when he come home. I cook all his favorite meals. Maybe invite whole town."

Laughing, Colin held up his hand. "Whoa there, Mrs. Frakes. Let's get him to Briarwood first." He threw a glance over his shoulder toward the back stairs, the excitement in his eyes dimming. "Should I tell the Duchess now or wait? Do you think the news would be too much for her to hear? I don't want to risk her health."

Mrs. Frakes grew thoughtful. "Perhaps you should speak to doctor first. Maybe he suggest you tell her when we know for sure when Mr. Stuart come home."

Colin nodded. "I'll phone him in the morning and see what he says."

"Would you like me make dinner for you?"

"No, but thanks, anyway. I grabbed a burger in Bartlesville on my way home." Turning toward the rear hall of the house, he broke his stride when Mrs. Frakes reached out her hand to stop him.

"Miss Beatrice fine this morning, but when she awake from afternoon nap, she not think straight, believes she young lady again."

Colin lugged his body up the stairs, slowing his steps before he reached his aunt's suite. He battled against his sense of love and duty, the temptation to visit his aunt another time strong. He flinched at the taste of guilt in his soul. *But, God, it's so hard to see her that way.*

All at once a scripture he'd read in 2 Corinthians a few mornings previous came to mind. Something about "the God of all comfort who comforts us in our troubles so that we can comfort others in their troubles, which produces in us patient endurance." He quickened his steps, a smile tugging at his lips.

Okay, God, I guess I could use a little more patient endurance. But seriously, Father, as much as I'd miss her, I don't want her to live like this. Wouldn't it be better if you'd take her on home to be with you? You know it's what she desires. Colin stopped outside her door, tuning his inward ear to the still small voice in his heart. *In my time, Son, in my time.*

Entering the room, Colin stood inside the door, his eyes widening as he watched his aunt do a slow twirl in the center of the room. When she saw Colin, she paused, holding out her hands toward him. "Ethan, you're early, but I'm glad. We can take our time driving to the country club. Braxton won't be back until tomorrow night." She giggled. "He'll never know you escorted me to the dance."

Colin stepped forward, taking her by the hand. "Duchess, why don't you sit a while? You seem out of breath."

She smiled. "Maybe a little. It was that last dance. I just love to rock and roll." She tilted her hand then held out her arms. "Ethan, listen, they're playing our favorite song. We can't sit out this one."

Colin drew his aunt into his arms. Humming the first slow tune that came to mind, he waltzed her about the room for a moment or two then led her to the chair near the window. "I don't want you to tire yourself," he said at her questioning look.

She laughed. "I guess you're right. I'd hate to fall asleep on the drive home and miss an interesting conversation." She lifted her hand to his cheek. "We never seem at a loss for a subject to discuss."

Colin looked up as Mrs. Frakes entered the room, shaking his head, the sadness in the housekeeper's eyes mirroring his own desolation. "She thinks I'm Ethan."

Colin's brow furrowed as he studied the look of fear that appeared in Mrs. Frakes's eyes then vanished behind impassiveness that scampered across her features once she glimpsed his scrutiny. Why had the name of his aunt's friend upset the housekeeper? Requesting that Mrs. Frakes come to the office once the Duchess had been settled for the night, he left the room. Soon seated at his desk, he searched for the paper on which he'd jotted the name of his father's lawyer among the other notes he'd taken during the meeting at Jack's house.

Locating the page on which he'd written the name Gerald Craig, he flipped through the phonebook for Haven and the surrounding towns, soon afterward discovering a listing for Gerald Craig, Jr., attorney at law in the Yellow Pages. Jotting down the number along with his Bartlesville office address, Colin prayed he'd be able to speak with the man the next day, wondering if the attorney was his father's defense attorney or if the Jr. written at the end of the name signified his son.

At the sound of tapping on the door, he looked up, inviting Mrs. Frakes into the room. When she stepped around the door, he smiled to set her at ease. "Mrs. Frakes, I couldn't help but notice the look on your face when I mentioned Ethan. On another occasion she mistook me for the same person. In both incidences I gathered my grandfather didn't approve of the gentleman. The other evening my aunt told me she'd been engaged in her younger years. Was Ethan her fiancé, and if so, why didn't they marry? Recalling the Duchess's independent nature and her relationship with Grandfather, I can't imagine him preventing my aunt from marrying the man she loved."

Mrs. Frakes lowered her gaze. "Nothing Mr. Braxton say or do could convince Miss Beatrice to stop seeing Ethan Tritt. She love him. It hurt her much that her brother not approve of Ethan. But she determine to marry Mr. Tritt anyway. However, her dream of wedding come to end when he die in accident."

Colin straightened. "An accident?" he asked as recollection of an earlier conversation with his aunt staggered into his mind. Was this the accident the Duchess had referred to that day?

"Yes. He die when he try to put out fire at burning well in Lambert Oil Field."

"The accident must have crushed her heart."

Mrs. Frakes nodded. "She cry and cry. A couple months after funeral, Mrs. Lambert take Miss Beatrice on long trip to Europe. But, as you know, that end in tragedy, too."

Colin ran his hand down the back of his hair. "Yes, my grandmother died after the birth of my father."

Mrs. Frakes stood. "Please excuse. I need to make sure Miss Beatrice okay."

Colin nodded. "If you need me for anything, I plan to work here awhile before I go upstairs."

When she'd gone from the room, Colin pulled the file of court papers toward him, disturbed by another of his aunt's statements on the day she mentioned the accident. *Why had she declared Dad's father to be both Braxton and Ethan?* After a moment Colin brushed aside the notion that Ethan could be Stuart's father, recalling the Duchess's state of confusion at that time. Turning his attention to the file, he began to read, recalling Jack's instruction to let his mind concentrate on the reports instead of his heart. For the next few hours, he poured over the statements Sheriff Tucker had taken from those who had been in residence at Briarwood at the time of the murder. Close to midnight, Colin laid the documents aside, no longer able to focus on the material. Something at the back of his mind told him he'd failed to note something important. He rubbed his eyes, thinking he should go through the paperwork again, but decided against it, choosing to turn in for the night instead.

· · · · ·

Late the next morning, Colin stood outside Attorney Craig's building, thankful the lawyer could squeeze in an extra appointment between clients. Soon ushered into Mr. Craig's office, Colin hid his disappointment behind a smile of greeting. The man behind the desk, his age the younger side of fifty couldn't have been his father's attorney.

"Mr. Craig, now that we've met, I understand your father must have been the lawyer who represented my dad, Stuart Lambert at his trial twenty-five years ago. Does your father still practice law?"

"No, I'm sorry to say he's deceased, passed away about ten years ago."

Colin's shoulders slumped. Forcing his spine to straighten, he spoke. "I'm sorry."

"Thank you," the attorney said, his smile waning.

"I appreciate you seeing me. However, I don't want to waste your time. Since you're not familiar with my father's case…"

"On the contrary, Mr. Lambert, I know all about your grandfather's murder. A new junior partner in our firm at the time, I did a lot of the legwork for my father. I watched him agonize over the case. He felt the evidence stacked against his client overwhelming, even making the remark later that Mr. Lambert's insistence that he take the stand in his own behalf had proved futile due to his inability to explain the gun in his hand at the murder scene. The only reason the jury deliberated over the verdict so long was because no gun powder residue had been found on your father's hand. Armed with that fact and if the butler… what was his name?"

"Grayson, Eric Grayson."

"If Mr. Grayson hadn't seen the gun in Stuart's hand, my father could have easily won the case on reasonable doubt."

Colin leaned forward slightly. "That's what I came here to discuss with your father—the gun. I plan to speak to the Osage County prosecutor about it this afternoon."

When the attorney had finished reading the information about the weapon and the bullet, he sat stunned. A moment later, he picked up his phone, notifying his secretary to reschedule the next appointment.

Replacing the phone, he turned to Colin. "If you desire, I'll be glad to take your father's case." He smiled. "In fact, I couldn't live with myself if I didn't." At Colin's nod of assent, Mr. Craig continued. "Let me know after you speak with Terrill Logan. In the meantime, I'll prepare a brief to file in the appellate court."

The lawyer made a copy of the OSBI report then returned the original to Colin. "I can't begin to say how much my father would have enjoyed this moment."

Colin looked down and then directed his gaze toward the attorney. "Sir, why do you think neither your father nor the county prosecutor asked for a comparison between the bullet and gun?"

Attorney Craig shook his head. "I don't know. I can only assume that all concerned believed the bullet taken from your grandfather's body had been fired from your father's gun since both the bullet and the weapon were of the same caliber and your father had been seen standing over Braxton's body with a fired gun in his hand. If I recall correctly, the question of whether the bullet came from your father's gun was never mentioned at the trial, only that another individual could have fired the gun from the window." The lawyer leaned forward. "In spite of any mistakes made then, it's important we concentrate on the here and now."

"You're right."

"I must be on my way. I don't want to be late for my appointment with Prosecutor Logan. I'll phone you with the outcome later."

"Thanks. Tell Terry I'll be in touch."

"I appreciate your willingness to take on my father's defense." Colin walked out of the office, the spring in his step much higher than when he'd arrived for his appointment.

· · · · ·

Once inside the prosecutor's office and greetings conveyed, Colin got right to the point. "Mr. Logan, I asked to see you today in order to request your cooperation in reopening a murder case that took place about twenty-five years ago."

The attorney stood and moved forward to perch his tall, lanky frame on the corner of his desk, his dark brown eyes seeming darker against his wheat-colored hair. As Colin observed the man, an image of a sunflower stalk stirred by a summer breeze materialized in his mind.

Mr. Logan smiled. "Mr. Lambert, I'm aware of your grandfather's murder and your quest. Sheriff Kinney dropped by my office this morning, informing me of the new evidence found in the case.

"He also informed me of the criminal activity that has occurred since your return to the area. I assure you we'll do everything in our power to find the person responsible as well as the individual who murdered your grandfather. I must warn you, the possibility of finding the killer in a twenty-five-year-old cold case is near to impossible. But should my opinion prove false, I hope I have the chance to apologize to Mr. Lambert for the lack of a proper investigation into the murder by my former peer. I … ah … the sheriff told me about your father's prognosis."

"That's why it's imperative my father is cleared of this crime ASAP. I appreciate your confidence in his innocence."

He laughed. "I don't often express this sentiment in my job. However, I was born near Haven and lived there several years. Your father taught one of my Sunday school classes when my family attended Grace Missionary Church. Although my family had moved from the area and I was in college at the time of your grandfather's death, my parents kept me abreast of the situation by sending me newspaper clippings." Mr. Logan paused. "I never believed Stuart Lambert capable of the crime. I'm sure Sheriff Kinney will keep you posted about the investigation."

Colin nodded. "By the way, I spoke with Attorney Gerald Craig, the son of my father's lawyer. He told me to tell you he'd contact you about the case."

The prosecutor grinned. "If I know Gerald, he'll have a brief ready to file in the appellate court first thing tomorrow morning asking for an emergency hearing."

Colin returned the smile. "I believe that's his intention. Well, good-bye, Mr. Logan. Thank you for your help." As Colin turned to exit the room, his cell phone vibrated against his chest. Pulling it from his pocket, he noted the phone number, his heartbeat quickening. "Hello?"

He felt his skin grow cold then clammy at the sound of Mrs. Frakes' tearful urgency for him to return home. "What's wrong?"

Mrs. Frakes' answer hammering in his ears, Colin stood, darting his gaze toward the prosecutor.

"Mr. Logan, please phone the sheriff and tell him he's needed at Briarwood immediately."

Feeling the blood drain from his face, Colin pocketed his phone and rushed from the room.

CHAPTER 15

Once inside Briarwood, Colin raced up the stairs, pausing momentarily to scrutinize the scene in his aunt's sitting room before he dropped to the floor beside Mrs. Johnson's collapsed body. Feeling helpless, he observed Mrs. Frakes' silent weeping as she attempted to revive the woman, the sight tearing at Colin's heart. A few minutes later, he felt a sense of relief when Mrs. Johnson started to rouse. Her eyelids fluttered as she muttered something the housekeeper seemed to understand.

Without a word, Mrs. Frakes rose from the floor and rushed from the room, soon returning with a glass of water in her hand. Using his arm to steady Mrs. Johnson's head so she could drink, he waited while the housekeeper only allowed the woman a few sips before a nod let him know he could ease her head back onto the carpet.

Colin waited until the woman seemed coherent enough to speak then bent forward, subduing the terror he felt before he uttered the question on his lips. "Mrs. Johnson, can you tell me what happened and where my aunt is?"

Beatrice's friend turned her head toward Colin, seeming to find it difficult to focus her gaze on him. She moistened her lips. "Two men … shot …"

Colin gasped. He glanced at his housekeeper, who paled. Colin looked around the room but didn't see any sign of blood, only a jumbled blanket on the daybed. He slid his gaze back to Mrs. Johnson, but she still seemed too addled to give coherent information.

They heard the doorbell. "I'm sure it Doctor Wexley. I phone his office before I speak with you," Mrs. Frakes said as she hurried from the room.

Within minutes she ushered the doctor into the suite. Taking a moment to look over the situation, he asked Colin to assist him in lifting Mrs. Johnson's hefty form onto the daybed, the woman becoming more alert. The sound of a siren signaling the approach of the sheriff, Colin released Mrs. Johnson into the doctor's care and then sprinted down the stairs to greet the officer.

"Follow me," Colin said, motioning the sheriff up the stairs.

Upon entering Beatrice's suite, he nodded a greeting to the doctor then glanced around. "Mr. Lambert, Prosecutor Logan phoned to tell me about an emergency. What's going on here?"

Colin straightened. "My aunt is missing, but I don't know any details yet. He nodded toward his housekeeper. We've been trying to revive Mrs. Johnson. He glanced at the doctor who busy with his patient didn't seem to need their assistance at the moment. "Mrs. Frakes, will you please tell us what happened?"

She nodded then took a seat in Beatrice's chair. She brushed aside fresh tears with her trembling fingers.

"After lunch I phone Mrs. Johnson to see if she can stay with Miss Beatrice while I pick up her medicine at drugstore." Mrs. Frakes turned to Colin. "Your aunt napping when I leave. I knew I would be gone about an hour, arriving home before she wake. When I come upstairs, I notice it quiet. I think maybe both your aunt and Mrs. Johnson asleep. But, when I enter room, I find Mrs. Johnson passed out on floor and Miss Beatrice not in sight. I try to rouse Mrs. Johnson but can't wake her, so I phone for

230 VICTORIA BURKS

doctor and you then hurry to each room to look for my friend. When I not find her, I return to Miss Beatrice's rooms. Again I try to wake Mrs. Johnson. That when you arrive home."

"A couple of men came out of nowhere, grabbed me, and stuck a needle in my arm." Everyone turned to Mrs. Johnson, the slur in her voice making it difficult to understand her words. "Next thing I know Hanako and Mr. Lambert are at my side calling my name. I tried to wake up, but my head kept spinning."

Sheriff Kinney pulled a small notebook and pen from his shirt pocket. "Can you give me a description of the men?"

Mrs. Johnson moved her head back and forth. "Things happened so fast, I didn't see much except the masks on their faces, those hooded kind like skiers on TV wear. Just before I blacked out, I heard one of the men say to his partner, 'Let's put the old lady in the car and get out of here.'"

"Do you think you could recognize the voice if you heard it again?"

Mrs. Johnson scrunched up her face. "I'm not sure."

Observing the woman's difficulty at catching her breath, Dr. Wexley held up his hand to stall any more questions from the sheriff, urging his patient to take it easy.

Meanwhile, Colin crumpled into a chair, thinking his legs would never hold him upright again. *Oh, God, what have I done? If she's still alive, please protect her and help us find her.* Colin gazed up at the sheriff, tried to speak but couldn't find words to say. He turned toward the window, the landscape a blur, tears clouding his vision.

The sheriff remained silent a few minutes then stepped forward to stand near Colin. "I know it's not much comfort, but we must be getting close to the killer for him to pull something like this. I won't tell you not to worry. I'm concerned myself, but we'll do our best to locate her as soon as possible. All we can do now is hope the kidnappers send us some kind of message right away as to the purpose for all this."

Still unable to comment, Colin lifted his eyes to the sheriff and nodded to let him know his words hadn't fallen on deaf ears.

"Notify me immediately when you hear from them." The sheriff eyed Colin's skeptical look. "Oh, they'll contact you. I'd bet money on it. It's my prediction the killer knows your adoration for your aunt and believes you'll do anything to have her back in safekeeping, specifically a demand for the discontinuance of your search for him."

Colin swung himself upward, his body trembling. His jaw tight, he clenched his fists. "Just let me get sight of him, just one glimpse, that's all I ask." Sympathy filled the sheriff's eyes.

"Your feelings are understandable. But don't ponder those thoughts too long. You must let the law handle this, no matter how tempted you are to settle it your own way."

Colin stared at the sheriff for several minutes then lowered his eyelashes, settling his gaze on the floor. "I know you're right. I think I'm angrier at myself. How can I live with myself if she suffers … or … dies at the hands of those thugs?"

The sheriff put his arm around Colin's shoulders. "We have to hope for the best, son, and put faith in prayer." He scrunched his hat closer to his head. "In my opinion we're on the verge of exposing a killer. Your belief in your father's innocence is to be commended.

"Not sure I can agree with you. But thanks for your encouragement, anyway, Sheriff."

The doctor turned to Colin. "Mr. Lambert, it's my professional opinion Mrs. Johnson was given a sedative that produces temporary oblivion, the dose strong enough to put her out while they took your aunt from the premises. It's not unusual for a person to feel wooziness or like symptoms of intoxication when they first begin to regain consciousness from the drug." He smiled at his patient. "Her pride is probably more damaged than anything else."

Mrs. Johnson gave the doctor and the sheriff a wobbly smile. "You might say that. But I'm starting to feel near my old self again." She frowned. "I feel terrible I wasn't able to stop those brutes. They sure took me by surprise. I didn't hear a thing until they came blasting into the room." She lifted her eyes toward Colin. "I'm so sorry. Your aunt is a special lady, a dear friend. I'll be praying mighty hard for her safe return."

"Thank you, Mrs. Johnson. I appreciate your thoughtfulness."

The sheriff finished with recording Mrs. Johnson's statement, tipped his hat to the ladies. "If either of you remember anything else about the incident, give the office a call." He shook his head at Colin's offer to see him out. "I'll talk to you soon."

Following Sheriff Kinney's departure, Colin turned to Dr. Wexley. "I'll be downstairs, should you need me. And, Doctor, I'd like to talk with you when you're finished here."

At the doctor's nod of affirmation, Colin withdrew from the room, deciding to wait for the doctor in the living room. He couldn't make himself stay in his aunt's suite any longer. Colin rubbed his hand across his chest, the gesture becoming habitual of late. He plopped onto the sofa.

He jumped at the sound of Mrs. Frakes's voice, unaware she'd followed him. "Master Colin, can I get you anything, something to eat, drink maybe?"

He shook his head. "No. Nothing. Please, Mrs. Frakes, go to your room and rest. Maybe the doctor should examine you too. You don't look well."

"I be fine once Miss Beatrice home again." She grew thoughtful. "Yes, I believe I will lie down. Thank you for your kind offer. If you need me, just knock on my door." In spite of the pain registered on her own countenance, she came to stand beside her employer, bowing slightly. "Remember, Master Colin, like God say to Joshua in Bible, 'Do not be afraid, do not be discouraged, but be strong and courageous, for the Lord your God is with you and will deliver the enemy into your hands.' I will pray much for you and Miss Beatrice."

Colin refused to look up. He wanted to express his gratitude for her attentiveness, but the words just wouldn't rise past the lump in his throat. Instead, he just nodded. The familiar "swoosh" of her sandals fading, his thoughts like the sound of drums beating a deafening rhythm in his ears.

Lambert, you've done some foolish things in your lifetime, but this is the dumbest. You just had to be the heroic knight charging in to rescue your father from prison in spite of all the warnings, jetting right along, not counting the cost of your decision. Colin slammed his fist against the back of the couch.

God in heaven, please not at this price, not the Duchess's life. Colin blinked to ward off the tears. He had to keep some sense of control.

Within a few minutes, the doctor emerged from the foyer to stand near Colin. "You needn't worry about Mrs. Johnson. I'll see that she gets home. She'll be fine once she's slept off the effects of the sedative. However, I'll make sure her husband understands he must call me should any complications occur, as I don't know whether the syringe and needle used on her were sterile." He watched Colin slide his hand down the length of his head his fingers coming to rest at the nape of his neck. "What can I do for you, Mr. Lambert?"

"Doctor Wexley, this is my fault. You see, my father was convicted for a crime he didn't commit, and I'm here in Haven to search for the true killer, and, thanks to some friends aiding the investigation, we've come up with new evidence in my father's favor. I'm afraid I didn't realize the desperate measures the murderer would take to prevent us from discovering his identity.

Should he not intend to…to…kill my aunt, I need to know if you think she will survive under the duress of this ordeal."

The doctor shook his head. "I have to be honest and say I didn't think she would live this long. I'm sure you're aware of her heart condition." At Colin's nod, the doctor continued. "Miss Lambert is a strong-willed individual. She loves life, which I believe, along with her faith in God has sustained her thus far. I can only hope those two strengths will carry her through this situation and that she'll be given her medication. How the intruders would know the prescriptions and the amounts of dosage, I can't imagine."

Colin extended his hand. "Thank you, Doctor, for your promptness today. I won't keep you any longer."

Doctor Wexley shook Colin's hand. "Son, you can't fault yourself for desiring your father's freedom. The whole town is behind you one hundred percent. I've only been in the area a few years, but I've often heard the Lamberts' and your father's good reputation discussed. In fact, in Haven you all are quite the legend." The doctor turned toward the entryway then paused. "Although a man of science, I've seen a few miracles in my time that could only be attributed to faith in God. So don't give up, young man."

Colin straightened, a half smile touching his countenance. "No, giving in or giving up has never been one of my faults."

The doctor smiled. "Oh, by the way, I looked in on Mrs. Frakes before I came downstairs. Keeping her busy with looking after you will be her salvation. She's as healthy as an ox, but her heart is with your aunt. If you see her becoming depressed, give her an errand, not too strenuous, of course. Like others of us, she's up there in years."

"Sure thing, Doctor, I'll keep a close eye on her. And thanks. Not many physicians make house calls in this day and time."

"I'm what my colleagues refer to as a concierge doctor, this type of practice becoming more popular these days, especially in rural areas. Now if you don't mind, I'd like your assistance in helping Mrs. Johnson down the stairs and into my car."

Colin stood with his back to the door for several minutes after the sound of Doctor Wexley's car could no longer be heard, assessing his options of where he could start the search for his aunt. He whipped out his phone, punching in the sheriff's code.

"Hello, Sheriff, Colin Lambert. I want to help look for my aunt. What do you need me to do? I have this gut-wrenching feeling that Girard is in this up to his eyeballs."

"Colin, I know you're worried about Miss Lambert, as are we, but we're doing all we can to locate her. I have a couple of deputies combing the area, talking to the farmers and ranchers, hoping someone saw something suspicious."

"But, Sheriff, if Girard's involved, you can bet his nephew, Keith, is at his beck and call. Have you talked with them?"

"Colin, I can't just go barging into a respectable lawyer's office and start asking questions based on a theory. I have to have some type of proof of their involvement. You know that. And yes, I have a tail on Keith already."

Colin drew a deep sigh, his free hand pressing the back of his hair into place. "I can't just sit around and do nothing."

"I understand. But you're needed at Briarwood right now. As I said earlier, the intruders won't let too much time pass before they phone, giving you an ultimatum—the immobilization of the investigation in return for your aunt's life is my guess. Once the call comes in, the case will be an official kidnapping. I'll issue an all points bulletin after that, and we'll go from there. If she is found in another state, the FBI will get involved too. Please be patient and let us handle it. "Clay should arrive at your place any minute to wait for the call with you. In the meantime, think of something to say that will convince them you plan to give up your search. The information about the new evidence hasn't had time to spread, so the killer may not know about the reopening of the case. And the caller might be nervous enough to let something slip that will lead to his identification or the whereabouts of Miss Lambert."

"Okay, Sheriff, you're the expert. In the meantime, I'll inform Ms. Lonetree and Granger about my aunt's disappearance."

"Good idea. Don't worry, Colin, we'll keep you posted on the developments of the case."

Colin turned at the sound of the doorbell. "Sheriff, I think Clay just arrived. I appreciate all your help. Good-bye."

Clay checked out Beatrice's suite once again. Once below stairs, he shook his head at Colin's questioning glance. "Nothing. I'm sorry. If the kidnappers were amateurs, they were well informed as to how they should pull off the crime."

When he finished sending his messages, Colin escorted Clay to the family room, where he eyed Colin's appearance. "Say, friend, you look beat. A shower and shave might get your mind off things for a while. At least it works for me sometimes."

Colin darted a glance toward the phone. "But the call could come any minute."

They both turned toward the sound at the doorway. The housekeeper entered the room, the haunted look in her eyes and her pale features rekindling Colin's anger afresh. He stepped toward the woman, placing his hands on her shoulders. "Mrs. Frakes, the sheriff and his officers are doing everything possible…"

All three jumped at the sound of the phone. Colin lifted the receiver, his stance becoming rigid.

"Hello. Yes, this is Colin Lambert. Who is this?" Colin held the phone out a ways from his ear so that Clay could listen to the man's words.

The voice on the other end of the line gave a short laugh. "Like I'm really going to tell you. But you'd better listen good to what I do have to say though. If you want to see your aunt again, I suggest you pack your bags and get on the road toward St. Louis immediately. You've outstayed your welcome in Haven. We don't need the likes of you and those nosey reporters stirring up the past."

Colin closed his eyes as panic seized him. Had he put his friends in danger as well? "What about my aunt? How do I know she's safe now?"

The caller snorted. "I guess you'll just have to take my word for it."

"She has to have her medicine, or she might die."

"Just as soon as you get on that plane, she'll have all the medicine she needs."

"Okay, okay. Look, please don't hurt her. She doesn't know anything."

"You follow the rules in my game, and everything will get back to normal. You've got twenty-four hours. Savvy?"

Before Colin could respond, a loud click resounded in his ear. He watched Clay remove the small recording device he'd placed in the phone receiver earlier.

"Too bad your phone doesn't have caller ID. It would have saved us a lot of time."

Colin glanced at the retro device, a grim smile pulling at the corners of his mouth. "I'm afraid much at Briarwood is still in the Dark Ages." He glanced toward Mrs. Frakes who clasped the doorframe as though the house might collapse any moment. Crossing the room, Colin took her hands into his own. "Mrs. Frakes, I'm starving. I hope you've got dinner started."

"Wh…what? Oh, Master Colin, I so sorry. I forget about dinner. Yes, I cook right away." With that she turned toward the kitchen.

238   VICTORIA BURKS

Colin faced the deputy, the agony in his heart shadowed in his eyes. "Dr. Wexley told me to keep Mrs. Frakes busy for the sake of her mental health. She cares much for my aunt." At his nod of understanding, Colin continued. "Should I pack and run as I'm been ordered?"

"Not just yet. I'm sure Sheriff Kinney has already notified the National Crime Information Center that Miss Lambert is missing." Clay gave Colin a solid clap on his shoulder. "The most important thing right now is that you don't give up hope."

Colin nodded. "Much easier said than done. But I do know prayer changes circumstances; that's the base of my hope at the moment."

Clay gave Colin a thumbs-up and then extended his arm for a handshake. "I need to get this recording to Sheriff Kinney right away. We'll be in touch."

Keeping pace with the deputy in order to show him out, they both broke their stride at the sound of a car on the graveled driveway. Colin rushed forward to open the door, throwing a surprised look toward the deputy when he saw Julie and Jack emerge from the vehicle.

Julie smiled at Colin, her face an image of empathy. "I hope you don't mind us showing up without phoning first, but we just couldn't stay away after we received your message."

"I couldn't be more pleased. Come on inside." After all three bid Clay good-bye, Colin waved his friends inside showing them to the family room. "Have a seat while I let Mrs. Frakes know there'll be two more for dinner."

"Thank you," Julie said. "I hope we won't be an imposition. We didn't take time to grab anything to eat, just wanted to get here as quick as possible.

"Not at all. Mrs. Frakes can throw a delicious meal together faster than anyone I know."

When Colin reentered the den, Jack stood from the sofa. "Colin, we're truly sorry about your aunt. We know how devoted you are to her. We want to help in any way we can."

"Thanks, Jack. That means a lot to me. I just wish I could do something to assist the law in locating her."

Julie settled back in the armchair. "That's what we're here for—to help with the investigation." She pointed to the sofa. "Sit down and tell us all you know. Then we'll look at our options."

Obeying, Colin sat beside Jack, relaying all that had happened since he'd received the call from Mrs. Frakes stating that his aunt had disappeared, informing his friends about his visits with Attorney Gregg and Prosecutor Williams as well.

Julie smiled. "Just think, Colin, ten days ago, you had no idea how you might free your father from prison, and now his liberty is only days away."

Colin stood and paced back and forth, halting in midstride to face his friends. "Please tell me how I can ever justify trading one life for another? For all I know, the Duchess may be lying dead in some wooded area or buried in a shallow, unmarked grave..." The lump that had formed several times in his throat that afternoon refused to be held back any longer. His voice full of tears, he choked out his next words. "There's no way anyone can validate that." Sitting down again, Colin hunched forward, ashamed he'd been unable to hold his emotions in check.

Julie and Jack gazed at Colin, their expressions mirrors of compassion.

Mrs. Frakes entered the room and sat next to him. "Master Colin, I hear what you say, but you must be strong. Bad men not win. God keep Miss Beatrice safe. You must have faith. God say, not let your heart be troubled, but trust in him and in Jesus, His Son. Ask anything in his Name and he will do it. He will bring Miss Beatrice home again; you wait and see. He's good God, loves her, loves you, loves me. He will answer our prayers. But

240 VICTORIA BURKS

we must believe he will do what we ask and doubt not. Besides, what would Miss Beatrice say if she see you like this?"

Not a sound could be heard in the room while they waited for Colin's response. He lifted his head. A jagged smile appeared on his face. "Probably something similar to what I heard the day Bernie Hawkins bloodied my nose in a fight on the school bus.

"Just starting the first grade, I didn't want to go back to school because he'd threatened to do worse when he got the chance. But she insisted that I return to my classes, informing me I had nothing to fear. The next morning she drove me to the bus stop and walked onto the bus with me. Leaning over Bernie, she whispered something in his ear and then smiled at him as she tousled his hair. I never knew what the Duchess said to him, but he never bothered me again." He squeezed Mrs. Frakes's hand. "Thanks for getting me back on the right track."

Jack leaned forward. "Colin, we've all been in similar states of mind at one time or another in our lives."

The housekeeper stood and bowed. "I need to hear it too. Dinner will be ready in fifteen minutes. Now excuse, please. Meal will be served in dining room." Colin started to protest then smothered his retort at the look in her eyes.

"Thank you, Mrs. Frakes," he said returning her bow as she left the room.

Colin showed his guests where they could refresh themselves then raced up the back stairs to his suite. One look in his bathroom mirror and he winced. Glimpsing the time, he decided he could just fit in a quick shower and shave as Clay had suggested earlier. Feeling more like a human a few minutes later, he escorted his companions to the dining room.

Later, the three assembled once again in the den, Julie taking a large notepad and pen from her totebag. "Colin, you mentioned before dinner the possibility that Girard's nephew, Keith, and two of his friends might be involved in the kidnapping. What can you tell me about his buddies?"

"Their names are Rudy and Samuel James, troublemakers with several petty crimes to their credit, the family history similar in nature. However, the boys have an older sister who broke with family tradition, earning respectability in the armed forces as a medical professional. In fact, she's an assistant to my aunt's doctor here in Haven."

"Small world," Jack muttered.

Colin grinned. "Sometimes."

All of a sudden Julie straightened, her eyes lighting up like a firefly at night. "Do you suppose Mrs. Frakes knows where they live?"

Jack leaned forward. "Okay, Julie, I know that look. What do you have in mind?"

"Oh, just a little reporter snooping. What do you say?"

Colin brightened then stood to his feet. "I'll be back shortly."

A few minutes later, he returned with a hastily drawn map in his hands. "Their home is pretty far out in the sticks, as they say around here but doesn't seem too difficult a location. Your car or mine?"

Soon the three were in Jack's Suburban traveling south toward Haven. They turned onto a country road just outside of town, which twisted along a creek bed, the map directing them to a one-lane road that led to the Jameses' home about a mile off the country road. Crossing a low-water bridge, they arrived at their destination within minutes. The three eyed the rundown house that stood in a clearing surrounded by dense woods on three sides. A few old rusty cars sat near the weather-beaten dilapidated picket fence that bordered the unkempt yard. A large black Rottweiler stood on the unstable-looking porch barking and baring his teeth.

Julie looked at Jack and then over her shoulder at Colin. "Which one of you guys is brave enough to face the puppy?"

Colin threw up his hand. "Not me. That dog looks hungry. I'd like to make it back to Briarwood in one piece, if you don't mind."

A grimace overshadowed Jack's otherwise pleasant looks. "Not this bloke. I faint at the sight of my own blood. Besides you're the animal lover and the adventurous soul. Wasn't this your idea in the first place?"

Julie laughed. "Just what I need on my investigative team. A pair of teddy bears."

Still undecided as to who would be the first to venture from the Suburban, the three stared wide-eyed a moment later at the person who stepped from the house onto the porch, a volley of fear slicing the banter from their lips.

CHAPTER 16

An older woman, her face wrinkled and deeply tanned, stepped toward the edge of the porch, the dog close at her heels. Her long, gray-streaked hair had been plaited into one braid, which draped her left shoulder. She held a double-barrel shotgun in her hands, her stance readied to take aim and fire.

"My kind of dame," Jack muttered.

Julie rolled her eyes toward the headliner of the vehicle. "Got any suggestions, Mr. Investigative Reporter?"

He grinned. "Collect facts." With considerable caution, Jack opened the car door and stepped onto the dirt driveway littered with clumps of stubby weeds, his height towering above his car. "Hello, ma'am."

The woman strode closer to the fence. "You folks lost? We don't get many visitors out this way."

Colin eased into the seat behind Julie, lowering the window a few inches. "Not hard to understand why," he muttered. The dog began to growl. "Quiet, Killer," the woman said, keeping her eyes pinned to Jack.

Julie turned to face Colin. "Killer?" she gasped. "Did she say Killer?" She stared at Colin. "Are you going to let Jack face those two alone?"

The next instant Colin piled out the other side of the vehicle to stand alongside the older man. Jack glanced at Colin then focused his gaze on the woman amidst the nineteenth century milieu.

"Uh... no, ma'am. I'm Jack Granger, and this is..." He waved his hand toward Colin. "This is..."

Colin moved to the front of the vehicle, taking in the gun, the snarling dog, and the less than scale height of the fence. "Delaney, ma'am. The name is Delaney."

Not a hint of a smile crossed her features. "What can I do fer ya?"

"My friends and I are looking for a certain piece of property. However, it's possible we may have gotten our directions confused. May I ask with whom I have the pleasure of speaking?"

"You can ask, but it don't mean you'll be told." She raised the gun a little higher. "Ain't heard of no property 'round here for sale. So I'll just be sayin' good day to you." She pushed at her hairline with her forearm. "Ain't got time to stand in the heat jawin' with strangers." With that she turned and walked toward the house, Killer inching toward the car instead of following his master.

Colin and Jack exchanged a look then retreated slowly, not taking their eyes off the dog until they were inside the car and the doors shut. Just as the motor came to life, the woman did an about-face, studying her visitors momentarily before the dusty screen door slammed behind her.

Without another moment of hesitation, Jack stepped on the gas pedal, not one of the three companions looking backward or uttering a word until they reached the county road.

Taking a deep breath, Julie turned to Colin. "Delaney?"

Colin grinned. "That's right, ma'am. Colin *Delaney* Lambert."

Julie laughed. "Of course. Named after your great-grandfather, Walter Delaney Lambert, I presume."

"That would be correct."

Jack glanced over at the young reporter. "Got any more bright ideas, Julie?"

She smiled. "Not yet, but just pulled my thinking cap onto my brain. By the way I didn't see you taking any notes. Just what facts did you collect back there?"

Jack's expression grew grim. "One, to stay away from modern-day pioneer women that regard strangers as enemies and, two, to remind myself the next time we take a trip together to bring along that bottle of blood pressure pills my wife is determined I take every day."

Julie's laugh blended with Colin's. "Seriously though, do you think the woman knew who we were?"

Colin shrugged his shoulders, answering for both he and Jack. "I don't think so, but she sure seemed suspicious of us. Man, what I'd give to see inside that house. But I don't think she'll be inviting us to tea and crumpets anytime soon."

Julie laughed. "No, I don't believe I'll find an invitation in my mailbox, engraved or otherwise." A moment passed before she spoke again. "If she's holding your aunt prisoner in there, she's either the coolest cucumber I've ever met, or Miss Lambert isn't anywhere near the place."

"Yeah, I agree. What do you think, Jack?"

"I'd say her wariness of us was due to the fact we were strangers, not her fear a hostage might be discovered. Since Sheriff Kinney mentioned her grandsons' possible involvement with your aunt's disappearance, I wonder if he intends to get a warrant to search the premises."

Colin pulled out his phone. "I'll check it out." He settled back into his seat at the officer's greeting.

"Hello, Sheriff. Sorry to bother you again. I assume you've talked with Clay about the phone call from the kidnappers. Good. Uh... earlier you said the James brothers might be suspects in my aunt's kidnapping. Well, Mrs. Frakes gave us the directions to their home, and we just left the place. Not much of a welcome there. No, we didn't see the brothers, only the grandmother. No, sir, I feel certain she doesn't have a clue about our identity.

"Do you plan to check out the place…maybe obtain a search warrant? Yes, I know you need probable cause…I just thought…well…you know."

Colin adjusted his Blackberry to better hear the sheriff. "Yes, I understand your concern," Colin said sighing. "Much as I appreciate your interest, I won't promise, but I'll think about it. Thanks, again. Good-bye."

Colin pocketed his phone, the landscape outside the side window seeming to draw his attention. Soon, he switched his gaze to Julie's questioning eyes. "Sheriff Kinney thinks I should do as the kidnappers have ordered. Says it might speed up the return of my aunt. But I can't leave. It might jeopardize Dad's case. His attorney said I would need to testify at the hearing." Colin grew silent momentarily then spoke as though alone. "How can I possibly choose between my father and my aunt?"

Julie's eyes filled with compassion. "What if we made it seem like you had left the vicinity?"

Colin frowned. "What do you mean?"

Jack looked over at his shoulder at Colin. "Uh oh. Are you sure you want to listen to her?"

Smiling, Julie tapped Jack's arm with her fist. "Come on, Jack, it wasn't that bad."

"No. At least not for those of us who stayed in the car with the door locked and the window cracked just low enough to hear the conversation outside the car. No way was she concerned about when that black demon might go for her throat."

In spite of his own dilemma, Colin had to grin at the wounded look she tried to portray. "So I'm a coward. Get over it, guys. Let's get serious, okay?" She rested her elbow on the arm of the divided seat, her fist supporting her chin. "We need to come up with a plan to make the kidnappers think Colin has left Briarwood and returned to St. Louis."

"Julie, you know they'll be watching his every move. Just how do you think we can dupe them?"

Colin leaned forward as far as the seatbelt allowed. "Thanks for the thought, but I can't leave Mrs. Frakes alone."

Julie tapped her forefinger against her chin. "Give me a few hours. I'll come up with a foolproof plan that will work, you'll see. And don't worry. We'll see that Mrs. Frakes will be safe as well."

Jack tossed a skeptical look toward her. "Whatever scheme you come up with under that mop of black hair, just leave me out of it."

"Jack Granger, you wouldn't miss the action for anything. Sorry, sir. Your reputation precedes you."

A grin pricked the corners of his mouth. "And what is that supposed to mean, Miss Classified?"

"That you'll do whatever it takes to play out a hunch, taking advantage of every opportunity in order to make sure the good guy wins and the story is ready for press on time."

He shrugged his shoulder. "Sounds like somebody knows a lot about me."

Julie grinned. "Yeah, Michele is well acquainted with her husband." At his questioning look, she explained, "Your wife brought an ad to me a couple days ago about her garage sale this coming weekend, and we had lunch."

He lifted his eyebrows in understanding. "I see. I guess I should thank her for the vote of confidence."

Julie grinned. "She'd appreciate it, I'm sure. Diamonds are always a sure hit."

Jack rolled his eyes toward the sky. "Thanks for the tip."

When they arrived back at Briarwood, the housekeeper met them at the door. "Master Colin, your mother phone. She try your cell phone, but you not answer. So she call house. Say it important."

"Yes, I know. She left me a voice mail. But thanks for reminding me."

A short time later, enjoying lemonade and cookies Mrs. Frakes set before them, the three sat at the library table in the family room, each attempting to come up with the perfect camouflaged plan to trick the abductors. But nothing seemed viable.

Darkness beginning to settle over the landscape, Jack pushed back his chair. "Sorry, friends, I need to get home. Colin, as soon as you hear something..."

All of a sudden, Julie's eyes brightened. "I've got it."

Jack winced. "Something tells me we're not going to like this."

She frowned. "Come on, fellows, at least hear me out."

Colin grinned. "Okay. Spill it."

"I have this friend who's an airline stewardess for Southwest Airlines. I know she flies in to Tulsa from Phoenix tomorrow and has a day off before her next scheduled flight. With her help, I think we can get you inside a plane then right back off it again without the kidnappers' knowledge."

Jack frowned. "But if Colin is followed, the person will probably hang around the airport until the plane is in flight. He might see Colin when he steps back into the gate area."

"Not if we can smuggle him through the door at the end of the Jetway onto the tarmac."

Colin weighed her idea momentarily. "What if they see me walk down those portable steps through the airport window?"

"I thought of that. However, I'm sure Leigh Ann knows someone who could get you an outfit worn by those guys who drive the luggage carts and galley supplies to the plane. You could slip the uniform over your own clothes just before you exit the tunnel. With one of their caps on your head, you'd blend right in with them. Then you could ride the cart back to the luggage holding area where Leigh Ann or someone she knows would be waiting to get you away from the airport. It will take some organizing, but I think we can accomplish the goal."

Jack thought over her words then smiled. "I have to hand it to you, Julie. The idea is better than anything we've come up with so far. It might work at that."

"Thanks. The only other thing is how to get Colin back to Briarwood unseen."

"Jack smiled. I can handle that part of the plan. A repairman's clothes and truck would be the perfect disguise. Thieves get by with it often when robbing houses. And I know just the guy who can orchestrate it. He owes me a favor. Besides, if the intruders think Colin has left the area, it's unlikely they'll be watching the house."

Colin held up his hand. "All I'll have is a carry-on and my briefcase, but what about a ticket?"

Julie's expression grew smug then she smiled. "Got that covered as well. I think you will be eligible to fly on standby, receiving a dummy standby authorization from the ground attendant at the gate counter just before the flight leaves the terminal. Don't worry about your luggage. We'll have the attendant stow your things; then either Jack or I can pick them up for you later. Once you arrive at the gate, all you'll have to do is step up to the courtesy desk and show them ID once you're paged."

Julie stood, grinning. "You know what they say, 'Men are headliners; women are detail.'" She sobered. "Like Jack said, we need to get on the road. I'll phone you after I speak with Leigh Ann and things are worked out. Don't hesitate to contact us if you receive any news about Miss Beatrice." Julie placed her hand on Colin's arm. "We just have to believe your aunt will be home soon, and if our plan works as intended, we'll have you back to Briarwood in time to welcome her home with open arms."

He gave a slow nod. "Yes. That's what I'm counting on to happen." Colin turned to Jack, his eyes full of gratitude. "As I declared earlier, your visit this evening… well… it's hard to put into words…"

Jack threw his arm around Colin's shoulders. "No need to. You'd do the same for us."

"In a heartbeat." Colin said his gaze softening when he turned to Julie. He felt a sense of joy, the sparkle in her eyes a delight to see after the sadness he'd become accustomed to in her presence since they'd met. He'd seen a side of her today he hadn't witnessed to date but hoped would continue. What had brought on the change? Wondering when he might have the chance to satisfy his curiosity, he grinned to hide the despondency that hung over his head like a black cloud. "Thanks for being here for me, Julie."

"You're welcome, Colin. And try not to worry."

Colin escorted his friends to the porch, leaning against a colonnade until the Suburban reached the ridge road. He took a seat in one of the wicker chairs, stretching out his legs to prop his feet on the edge of the patio table. Pondering his options and the consequences that could follow his choice, he rubbed his fingers across his brow, his body growing limp with the sudden heaviness that overwhelmed him. Should he tell Julie to forget it and get an authentic reservation for St. Louis as the sheriff encouraged, leaving behind all they'd accomplished in his father's behalf until a future time?

Problem is, Colin thought, *Dad's future and today could be one and the same, ending at any moment.* And what guarantee did he have the Duchess would be released if he left the area? What if he stayed and… No, he couldn't and wouldn't think about that.

At the sound of the door opening, Colin looked up. Switching on the outside light, Mrs. Frakes stepped onto the porch to stand near him. "Master Colin, if you not need anything else, I think I retire for night."

Colin glanced toward the southwest, a flash of lightning catching his eye. "No. I'm fine. It looks like we might get a rain shower before daylight."

"That would be nice."

He lifted his chin, allowing himself to enjoy the breeze drifting across his face, the first coolness they'd felt in days, at the same time taking in the housekeeper's features in the dim light. Compassion drenched his soul. Another ten years had seemed to creep upon her countenance in the last few hours. He cringed inside. How many others of those he loved and cherished would suffer before truth prevailed? "Thank you for that great meal this evening, Mrs. Frakes. I'm sorry about the extra work. I wish I could have given you sufficient notice about our guests."

"Please, not worry. It help to stay busy." When Colin failed to respond, the housekeeper reached out to pat his arm. "Good night, Master Colin. Things look better in morning."

"Yes, maybe so. Try to get some sleep." She bowed then turned away, the touch of her kimono grazing his hand. A small comfort, a subtle hint that perhaps stability did exist beneath all the chaos he'd experienced since his arrival at Briarwood.

He picked up his cell phone he'd placed on the table prior to sitting. Maybe a conversation with his mother would take his mind off the decision that would mark his immediate future. He frowned. Then again, maybe not, but at least it would be a deterrent from his thoughts.

"Good evening, Mother. Sorry I wasn't able to return your call earlier. Been tied up with several things today."

"So I hear."

Colin removed his feet from the table to sit upright. "What's that?"

"Nicholas phoned to tell me about Beatrice's disappearance. Colin, this has gone far enough. The situation is becoming too dangerous. I-I'm afraid something might happen to you. I want you home."

Colin sighed. "News seems to travel at a rapid rate in Osage County."

"Don't be sarcastic, Son. Nicholas heard it on his police scanner. I beg you, Colin, you must return home quickly."

"Forgive me, but you're starting to sound like a broken record. How can I leave Briarwood until I know the Duchess is in safe hands? I don't mean to sound disrespectful, but you're not making sense. By the way, what seems to be Girard's interest in the case?"

"Well, he *is* a friend of the family. He's concerned about your well-being."

Colin repressed the mirthless laugh rising to his lips. *Sure he is. About as concerned as a hungry wolf munching his prey in a secluded forest.* "He's your friend, not mine. To be honest, I find nothing about the man that appeals to me."

"Colin, why are you so hateful to me?"

He drew a long breath gritting his teeth. "I really don't want to be, but sometimes…sometimes…" *Lord, I really don't want to discuss this with her now.* "Mother, I'm sorry. I know I sound cross. It's just that I'm under a lot of duress at the moment."

She sighed. "Yes, I suppose you are. Colin, the reason I called is…I need to know the number of George's safe deposit box at the bank and where you put the key to it. Our attorney said I should update my will and life insurance policy since George is gone."

His body grew taut as he pulled the business card on which he'd recorded the number from his billfold. "The key is in the right hand drawer of George's desk. Mother, you are okay, right?"

BITTERSWEET JUSTICE   253

"Certainly. I just need to get my papers in order." Eileen laughed. "I'm not so young anymore, you know."

"You're not that ancient. Haven't even reached sixty yet."

She paused momentarily. "Neither had George."

Colin stood and began to pace back and forth. Was there something she wasn't telling him, or had she thought of this as a ploy to get him back to St. Louis?

"Mother, have you been to the doctor lately?"

"Yes, a few weeks ago for my yearly checkup."

"And how did that go?"

"Colin, stop reading something into this conversation that isn't there. Don't you think I'd tell you if I wasn't in good health?"

Not if you could use the medical report as a manipulative tool to get me back behind my desk at Hemphill Marketing. Colin felt his face grow warm as guilt washed over him. "Yes, of course. And John is right. I'm glad you're taking his advice. Tell him I'll be in to see him when I return. I need to add Briarwood to my living trust."

Colin heard his mother draw a deep breath, taking the time to exhale before she spoke. "How is your grandmother?"

"Fine, as far as I know. I only visited with her that one time. But I intend to see her again before I depart for home. Did you and Aunt Mary decide what to do about her deplorable living conditions?"

"No, but we've discussed the matter, just haven't reached a decision yet."

Colin felt anger grip his chest. How could the two of them be so detached from their mother? He pulled his lips into a thin line. What would it take to get them to realize their obligation? He resisted the urge to vent his ire, forcing a measure of calmness into his voice.

"I hope you decide something soon. She needs you both. Look, Mother, do you mind if we talk about this another time? I really should ring off now. The sheriff could phone any moment with word about the Duchess. I'll keep you informed about the situation."

"Please do. She was the only Lambert who treated me decent. I wish I'd been more appreciative of her kindness back then. And, Colin, I really am sorry about her circumstances. I know how dear she is to you. In fact, it would be nice if you felt... oh never mind."

Colin pulled his phone away from his ear to read the number on the screen. Yes, he'd dialed the right number and the person on the other end of the line did sound like his mother. Had that been true regret he'd heard regarding the Duchess? Was this an answer to his prayers? Was God turning Eileen's heart of stone into flesh at last?

Eileen's words broke into his thoughts. "Well, obviously I'm not going to persuade you to leave Briarwood. Be careful, Colin, for my sake, *please?* I wish I could tell..."

Colin felt his stomach tighten at the tremor in his mother's voice. "What did you start to say?"

"Oh, nothing. Just thinking out loud."

What was on her mind? Colin sighed, deciding to let it go. The attempt to pull a healthy tooth would be easier than an endeavor to extract information from her. He breathed deep, not daring to tell her about the ultimatum he'd been given that afternoon. She wouldn't stop trying to persuade him to comply with her wishes. "Very well, Mother. We'll talk soon. Good-bye for now."

Colin stared at his phone watching the light fade into darkness. Had his mother been truthful about her checkup? *Oh, God, no more surprises of bad news, please.* All of a sudden, he relaxed. His aunt Mary would let him know if there was a problem. His mother told her sister everything, and his aunt kept him informed about important issues in a timely manner.

Just as he ended the call to Eileen, his phone jingled with its distinct ringtone. His heartbeat quickened. "Did you make it home, okay, Julie?"

"Yes…Colin," she said her voice laced with excitement. "I just got off the phone with Leigh Ann. She thinks we can pull this caper off without a problem. Said she'd work it all out. She'll call me early in the morning with the details when her flight lands in Tulsa."

"Sounds good, Julie."

"Colin, what's wrong. You sound pretty vague. Is it your aunt?"

"No. Not a word about her as yet. I'm just having second thoughts about this scheme of ours. Maybe it would be better if we forget the whole thing, don't want it to be a waste of everyone's time and efforts."

"Stop thinking like that. You can't let them win, Colin. We're so close. You can't desert the investigation now. And how do we know for sure the kidnappers will release your aunt? I'm sorry. I don't mean to sound cruel, but I think you'd never forgive yourself if you gave in to their demands and let your dream for your father fall by the wayside."

"You're right. She might not return to Briarwood at all. I can't see how she can remain alive without her medication. However, Doctor Wexley did say her strength of character and faith in God may sustain her." Colin moistened his lips. "I would like to tell her good-bye before she dies. But I guess that's the ideal in life, not the reality in most deaths."

"We must pray, Colin." Julie grew silent momentarily. "I've not had a chance to tell you, but I tagged along with Clay and his family to church last Sunday night. At the end of the service, I rededicated my life to God. I've not experienced this much joy in a long time, and it is wonderful."

Colin brightened. "I'm glad, Julie, really glad. I knew you were different this evening. Thank you for sharing the news with me."

"Thanks for your Christian witness. Watching your courage and love for Christ these last couple of weeks caused me to re-evaluate the direction my experiences had taken me. You made me realize that God still loved me and cared about every part of my life and would mend all my broken fences."

"Yes, that's why Christ came to this earth—to bring good news to the poor, give freedom to prisoners, give sight to the blind, liberate the oppressed and grant the Lord's favor to all who trust in him. As Jack intimated earlier, we've all experienced circumstances beyond our control, needed insight and wisdom to solve problems, been oppressed to the point of uselessness to ourselves and others or needed grace in our weakest moments. Thank God, he made provision through the death and resurrection of his Son whereby we can be free, ruled by peace instead of doubt and fear." Colin laughed. "I'm not sure I'm preaching to you or myself."

"It's true for all who wish to hear it. Colin, whatever you decide to do, go or stay, I'm behind you one hundred percent."

Colin closed his eyes. "Julie, I keep praying for guidance, but it seems like communication from heaven has been disconnected. All I can say is, 'Not mine, but Thy will be done.' Look, it's late. You should get some sleep. Until morning, Julie. Thanks again. Good night."

"Yes, I'll phone just as soon as I hear from Leigh Ann. Try to get some sleep yourself. Good-bye."

Later, unsure what time he climbed the stairs, Colin sat in his aunt's favorite chair, holding her Bible in his hands, the pages falling open to the Psalms. Thumbing through the pages he paused at Psalm 91, verses 14–15 snaring his attention. "'Because he loves me,' says the Lord, 'I will rescue him; I will protect him, for he acknowledges my name. He will call upon me, and I will answer him; I will be with him in trouble, I will deliver him and honor him.'" Colin stared at the words. Other than his father, Colin couldn't think of anyone who loved the heavenly Father more than Beatrice Lambert. As he read the same scriptures a second time, peace settled over him like balm soothing a wound. *Thank you, Father.* Colin now knew what he must do.

CHAPTER 17

Sliding between the cool sheets a few minutes after leaving the Duchess's suite, Colin felt assured that his aunt was in the protection of angels, God overlooking her care with his watchful eyes. He plumped his pillow to the perfect shape for a restful night. Reaching for his cell phone on the bedside table, he glanced at the time. No, he wouldn't disturb Julie's sleep; he'd wait and give her his decision when she phoned in the morning.

"Father, thank you for your faithfulness. Help us find the Duchess soon." He closed his eyes, the hooting owl in the distance lulling him into peaceful slumber.

The following morning, the musical chime of Colin's cell phone blazed a trail of wakefulness. Groping for the phone, he glanced at the caller ID and then lifted the cell phone to his ear. "Good morning, Julie."

"Hi, Colin. Just wanted to let you know Leigh Ann will arrange everything at the airport—"

"Julie, wait."

"She ... What?"

"Please phone your friend again and tell her thanks but no thanks. I appreciate all the help, but I'm not going anywhere. I can't and won't desert the Duchess or Dad."

Julie laughed. "Even as I spoke with Leigh Ann, somehow I knew good-byes between you and me wouldn't occur today. I'll give her a call back to tell her she can abort the plan. You're a brave soul, Colin."

He gave a slight shake to his head. "None too sure about that. I'm surprised you can't hear the tune my knees are playing."

She giggled. "I wondered about that background noise. Seriously, what's your plan?"

"I wish I knew. Just take each day as it comes, I guess. I hope Sheriff Kinney will understand why I have to stay. The decree of injustice against Dad is about to be overturned, and I can't miss that."

"Jack told me on the way home last night nothing would keep you from that hearing. No matter what happens, you know we're here for you."

"Yes."

"Gotta cut this short, Colin. Classified is waiting for me. If anything new develops, phone me at the paper."

"Will do. Have a good day."

"You, too. See ya."

Ending the call, Colin rubbed away a smudge on the cover, his stomach tightening at what the day might hold for the Duchess. Should he phone Julie and tell her he'd changed his mind—that she and her friend could follow through with their arrangements? He glanced toward the closet, moistening his lips. He could be packed and ready to go in fifteen minutes.

"Lambert, get hold of yourself. You've made your decision. What was all that talk about confidence in God you were reciting to Julie last evening?" Colin whipped the bedcovers aside and stood to the floor. *No turning back now*, he decided.

Dressed and hungry, Colin dashed down the back stairs hoping Mrs. Frakes had his breakfast prepared. Entering the kitchen, she stood at the stove gripping a pan of biscuits with a hot pad about to transfer them onto a plate.

"Mm... smells good, Mrs. Frakes. I'm hungry enough to eat the whole pan."

"I not surprised. You hardly touch your dinner last evening." She threw him a look of compassion.

"True, but after a lot of thoughtful prayer before retiring, I'm convinced God has everything under control and it's just a matter of time until all this will work out for our good because we love the Lord."

"Amen, Master Colin. Although it hard not to be afraid for Miss Beatrice, we must keep our focus on God and his will."

About to take his first bite, Colin put down the fork to answer his phone. Glancing at the name and number highlighted on the screen of the Blackberry, he held his breath. "Good morning, Sheriff."

"Morning, Mr. Lambert. Thought you might like to know I've issued that all points bulletin regarding the disappearance of Miss Lambert. If the amount of tips we usually receive don't pan out, you might think about offering a cash reward for information that will lead to her location."

Colin sucked in a breath as he brushed the back of his hair with his hand. A reward? He hadn't considered that. What amount did the sheriff have in mind? Of course he still had the money he'd intended to use as payment for the new air system thanks to the Duchess's generosity.

The sheriff didn't give a chance for Colin to comment on his suggestion, but continued to speak. "Also, I've asked OSBI to help with the investigation. When I told Investigator Donaldson what has happened since your arrival in Haven, he decided to run a check on Girard and his nephew, calling them people of interest in the matter. The bureau has more sophisticated ways of obtaining information than county officials. Donaldson has promised to send me a report on their findings. When I receive it, I'll let you know."

"Thanks, Sheriff."

"I suppose you'll be leaving for St. Louis today."

"Actually, no. Sorry, sir, I can't run out on my aunt or my father."

"I'm sure you're aware of the possible repercussions once the perpetrator gains knowledge of this."

"Yes. But I have to take the chance."

"As to your remaining at Briarwood, I can't blame you. I would have done the same thing had it been me in similar circumstances. Oh, sorry, got another call. I'll phone should I hear anything at all regarding your aunt. Take care."

"That I'll do. Good-bye, Sheriff."

Following breakfast, Colin phoned Tom Thorpe to check on things at the agency. Assured that he had everything in order, Colin ended the conversation and pulled his laptop toward him. About to open his messages, the sound of the doorbell interrupted his task. He stood quickly. Had the Duchess been found? He opened the office door and almost collided with Mrs. Frakes.

Startled, she stepped back. "Sorry to intrude, Master Colin, but Mr. Baker would like word with you on front lawn."

Colin's face a shadow of both disappointment and relief, he nodded. "Sure. Tell him I'll be right there."

Once outside, Colin greeted both Mr. Baker and Alfie with a hearty handshake. Eyeing the drops of perspiration drizzling down Mr. Baker's face, he grew concerned.

"You're not overdoing it in this heat, are you?"

Mr. Baker smiled. "No. I'm about through for the day."

Colin nodded. "Good. Mrs. Frakes said you needed to see me."

"Yes. I've trimmed away all those unruly vines. To be honest I don't think I'll be able to save the greenery along the front of the porch. Some kind of plant disease has about killed them. If you want me to try and resurrect them, I will, but I think it's a lost cause. In my opinion they need to be pulled up from the root, discarded and new plants established there. But I didn't want to do anything without your approval."

Colin took in the spindly almost leafless bushes. "I see what you mean. With those heavy vines covering them, I never noticed their condition before now. Mr. Baker, I'm sorry to say I have little knowledge when it comes to landscaping. I hope in the future to restore Briarwood to its original beauty. You draw me up a plan of your ideas, along with an estimate of the cost involved, and then we'll make a decision."

"I assume you want to include all the landscaping in general."

"Yes, the whole outside of the house."

Mr. Baker grinned. "You sound just like your grandfather. All or nothing. I hear tell he was like that about everything."

Colin laughed. "You're probably right."

He placed his arm around Alfie's shoulder. About to converse with the Bakers' son, they all three turned toward the road at the sound of an approaching car. They watched as the vehicle turned into the estate. Recognizing the car, Colin frowned.

"What's he doing here?" Colin said, ignoring the look of curiosity in Mr. Baker's eyes as he glanced Colin's way.

A moment later, Nicholas Girard emerged from his car and walked toward them, his arm outstretched. Colin felt rather than saw Alfie back toward his father's truck, muttering beneath his breath.

Following a handshake with each of the men, Girard looked at Colin, his face ruddier than usual. "A couple of OSBI investigators stopped by the house early this morning. It seems they'd been misinformed as to what knowledge I might have about the disappearance of Miss Beatrice." Girard's eyes filled with scorn. "How absurd the thought!" The attorney gazed off into the distance for a moment then lifted his chin. "Perhaps I misjudged their intention—their inquiry based on my former status as counsel to the Lamberts, the agents hoping I could aid their investigation. Now that I think if it, I'm sure that accounted for their visit."

Colin looked at his watch to hide his irritation, the stench of alcohol on Girard's breath a little too much to take at ten o'clock in the morning. "Anything is possible, right, Girard? Nonetheless, I'm glad to know the investigators aren't wasting precious time in their search for my aunt. She's been without her medicine close to twenty-four hours."

Moving a step sideways to dislodge himself from the odor of whiskey, Colin caught a glimpse of Alfie out of the corner of his eyes. Colin frowned, turning to catch a better glimpse of his friend. His complexion was pallid like chalk, his mutterings growing louder as Colin started toward him. Mr. Baker, noticing the concern in Colin's expression turned and closed the distance between father and son within seconds.

"What's wrong, Alfred?" he said, gently squeezing his son's shoulder, the trembling becoming more conspicuous.

"Bad man shoot Mr. Braxton, not Stuart," Alfie said, his lips quivering. "Bad man h-urt Mama, h-u-rt Daddy." Covering his ears with both hands, large tears cascaded down his cheeks. "Bad man sh-oot Mr. Brax-ton."

The color of Girard's skin deepened to a shade of purple. "What is that idiot babbling about?"

Colin's face reddened, but he chose to ignore the remark at the moment, Alfie needing his attention. "Why don't you go inside, Alfie. Are you hungry? I'm sure Mrs. Frakes can fix you a good snack or maybe even breakfast. What do you say?"

Alfie looked up at his friend, groping for Colin's hand, squeezing it hard when he glanced over at Girard who stood near the car, his eyes darting back and forth between Colin and the Bakers.

Taking him by the arm, Colin directed Alfie toward the house. "Mrs. Frakes might even come up with a cookie or two."

One last tear escaping down the side of his face, Alfie smiled as his body grew still. "Cookies? I like cookies."

Colin threw a glance toward Mr. Baker, who seemed to relax. "Alfie, your father will take you to Mrs. Frakes. Tell her to save a cookie for me, okay?"

Alfie raised his hand to Colin's face. "Yes. Save cookie for my friend, Colin."

"Thanks, Alfie. Now you go with your dad. I'll come inside momentarily."

Once the two had closed the front door behind them, Colin walked toward Girard, his fists doubled at his sides. "Just so you won't make the same mistake twice, Girard. My friend is not an idiot—a person who's had the misfortune of being born with Down syndrome, yes, but the most loving, kind, gentle human being I've had the chance to know. Now, if you'll excuse me, I have to be about the business of locating my aunt. And I can tell you this, once I discover the person who put her in harm's way, he will regret the day he was born."

It took Girard a moment to realize he'd stepped back a few spaces from Colin's glaring gaze. Girard pulled himself to his full height, his eyes narrowing. "Yes, well, I have a client waiting for me." Opening the car door, he turned back to Colin, a smug look dominating his expression. "If I can be of assistance, let me know. The Lamberts have always been important to me."

"Good day, Girard."

By the time Colin reached the kitchen, he'd subdued most of his wrath, his thoughts on Alfie's reaction to Girard. The scene hadn't been coincidental, Colin was positive. If any doubt remained in Colin's mind that Girard had been his grandfather's

BITTERSWEET JUSTICE   265

murderer, the skepticism had been washed away. As sure as the breath in his lungs, Colin believed that Alfie had seen Girard pull the trigger on the gun that killed Braxton Lambert. Colin sighed. Would Alfie be considered a reliable witness in a court of law?

Colin forced a smile. "Now, what did I tell you?" he said, eyeing the plate of cookies and glass of milk in front of Alfie. "Mrs. Frakes is the best, isn't she?"

"Yes. She cook good like Mama."

The three adults laughed, Alfie's grin a joyous sight.

Mr. Baker stood to his feet, wiping cookie crumbs from his lips with a napkin. "Son, we must be on our way. These nice people have things to do. We shouldn't bother them any longer. Also, your mother will be worried if we prolong our stay."

Alfie stood to the floor and pushed his chair close to the table, turning his gaze toward Mrs. Frakes. "Thank you for cookies and milk. Very good."

Mrs. Frakes bowed. "You very welcome, Alfred. I like to give you cookies because you enjoy them so much. You come back soon."

Accompanying the Bakers to their pickup, Colin pulled Mr. Baker aside once his son was settled inside the truck. "Mr. Baker, I'd like to talk to you later about Alfie's reaction to Girard."

Mr. Baker held up his hand. "I know just what you're going to say. Girard could be your grandfather's murderer. Lord, a livin,' who would have thought it? I suppose you need to speak with the sheriff about the matter. I'm concerned about Alfie, though. He's suffered much over the situation all these years, and I don't want to cause any additional harm to him."

"I agree. What about his doctor? Do you think he might have some suggestions how we might get Alfie to open up more about what he saw and heard that day?"

"That's a good idea. I'll have Nellie make an appointment as soon as possible."

"Good. Let me know how it goes."

"Sure thing. Now I best run along, before Nellie calls in the troops from Tinker Air Force Base to search for us. And I'll get those gardening plans to you in a few days."

"No hurry. Take your time." Colin waited until the truck drove onto the road before he hurried to his office, not wanting to delay the call to the sheriff any longer.

"So, what do you think," Colin said after informing Sheriff Kinney about Alfie's response to Girard's visit to Briarwood.

"Although we can't officially regard Alfred's actions today as evidence in the case, it does increase Girard's odds as a suspect in Braxton's murder. It will be interesting to hear Agent Donaldson's report regarding his talk with the man."

"Yeah, I'd like to know what you find out."

"Good as done, Mr. Lambert. We'll talk soon."

Colin had no more than ended the call to the sheriff when his cell phone rang. Glimpsing the identity of the caller, Colin smiled. "Hey, Julie, how's it going?"

"That's my question to you. Heard anything yet about Miss Lambert?"

"Not a word. But OSBI is involved now. Hopefully, they'll discover a lead soon."

"Yes… oh, the other reason I phoned is to tell you that Jack was in the chief's office bright and early discussing your father's case and its new developments. After listening to Jack's convincing words, the chief decided to assign Jack the story. So he's off to Osage County to collect information. The brief for the emergency hearing should be filed in the county clerk's office by now. He said he'd be in touch with you this afternoon."

"Hey, that's good news."

"Yes, it is. Like you, he's waited a long time to see his belief in your father's innocence confirmed."

"Sorry, Julie. I have another call. Might be about the Duchess. Talk to you later."

Please let it be good news, he thought.

"Colin Lambert speaking. Oh, hello, Mr. Craig."

He listened intently as his father's new attorney spoke the words Colin had longed to hear since his youth. "That's wonderful news, sir. You bet I'll be there. Yes, I'm sure your father would be pleased as well. Thanks, again. I'll see you at nine o'clock sharp Thursday morning."

Colin let his phone slide inside his pocket without a thought. His face bathed with delight, he left his office to search for Mrs. Frakes. He wanted her to be the first to hear that his father would leave Big Mac, the unofficial name for the prison at McAlester, Oklahoma. It didn't take long to find the housekeeper.

"There you are," she said, turning to give him a smile. "I just about ready to come tell you lunch is ready."

Colin sniffed the air. "Hm, lasagna, right?"

She nodded. "You still like it as when you a boy?"

"Yes, along with just about every other pasta dish you can name. I never grow tired of Italian food… uh, Mrs. Frakes, I just got off the phone with Dad's new attorney, Mr. Craig in Bartlesville. Judge Bentley in Pawhuska has ordered an emergency hearing scheduled this coming Thursday morning based on the new evidence in Grandfather's murder. Sheriff Kinney will personally pick up Dad at the prison and escort him to the Osage County Courthouse."

Mrs. Frakes almost dropped the table settings she held in her hands. "Master Colin, that is great news. I be so happy to see your father again." She glanced toward the window. "He will be sad to see stables gone."

Colin dished up a large serving of lasagna and salad onto his plate, sorrow filling his eyes. "I know. I'd like to rebuild them for him, the barn too, but it's impossible for me to accomplish the feat at this time. Besides..." He looked off into space.

The housekeeper placed her hand on his arm. "Don't think about cancer. Just enjoy what time you have with him."

Colin nodded. "I'm just thinking how hard it's going to be to tell him about the Duchess. He loves her as much as I do."

"Maybe she home by then." The housekeeper looked toward the ceiling. "My Father, I pray you grant this request. Should it not happen as we desire, help us to accept Your will."

Colin's mouth turned downward, his elation moments before drowned in the thought of the Duchess's plight. *God, help me to be strong should the outcome of this nightmare be less than what I expect from you—her safe return. And, yes, Father, in agreement with Mrs. Frakes, I pray your will be done. Amen*

His peace restored for the time being, Colin decided to take a walk along the old trail to the top of the hill behind the house where his father had spent hours doing his upmost to reproduce nature on canvas in at least three seasons out of each year before his incarceration. When not painting, he would sketch scenes to be painted later in his winter hideaway, an area of the attic he'd renovated into a fine art studio. Colin had spent many hours in that room reading while his father concentrated on the flow of paint from his choice of brushes among his large collection.

For Colin, it was enough just to be in the same room with his father, the two often never uttering a word to each other. Colin liked to think those moments had been special to Stuart as well. Since his return to Briarwood, Colin hadn't gathered enough reserve to climb the narrow staircase to the alcove that had nurtured the bond between father and son.

Once he topped the hill, Colin observed his boyhood home with a critical eye, his excitement ebbing at the sight of the rundown estate. How he hated for his father to see it in this condition.

Colon knew he owned a prospering enterprise, but his salary would never be enough to restore the mansion to its former grandeur. Maybe it would be best to sell the estate to someone who could afford the renovation. Colin shook his head. Out of the question. He couldn't renege on his promise to let the Duchess live out her last days in the home she'd lived in all her life.

Drops of perspiration trickling down his shirt collar, Colin descended the hill, wiping beads of moisture from his forehead with the back of his arm. The brisk breeze the only relief from the glare of the sun, he put the problem of Briarwood on hold until a future time. Standing near the back door, he glanced backward gazing toward the spot he'd stood moments ago. The beauty of the colorful wildflowers interwoven among the blades of prairie grass brought a welcome touch of comfort to his soul. The strains of a hymn waltzed into his heart and ascended to his lips.

> When peace like a river attendeth my way,
> When sorrows like sea billows roll,
> Whatever my lot, Thou hast taught me to say,
> "It is well; it is well with my soul."

At the sound of his phone, Colin entered the house, retrieving the instrument from his trousers pocket. "Hello," he said. Jack Granger's voice brought a smile to his lips as he recalled their trip to the Jameses' home.

"Hello, Colin. Any word on your aunt?"

"No. However, Julie informed me of your new assignment; that you were in Pawhuska looking for something to report in the *Tulsa World*. I suppose the prosecutor told you about the emergency hearing Judge Bentley set for Thursday morning."

"Yes, in fact, I just left Logan's office. From his viewpoint, this will be the biggest news the county has heard in years. Speaking of news, your aunt's disappearance is the top story of the day. A full alert with her description has been issued throughout the country. Personally, I think she's still in the area."

"I agree. I just hope and pray someone will see or hear something that will lead to her whereabouts."

"Let's count on it. Look, I won't keep you any longer, in case the authorities need to phone you. Logan informed me that OSBI is involved too. I think I'll stop by the sheriff's office. Maybe someone from the bureau will be there with an update from their side of the investigation. Don't lose heart, Colin."

"Thanks. Good luck with your story. Maybe it will make first page."

Jack laughed. "I hope so. Catch you later."

Helping himself to a cold glass of iced tea from the refrigerator, Colin started toward the back stairs, thinking a cool shower the next order of business for the day. He glanced at his watch. Just enough time to complete the task before the five o'clock news broadcast would begin. About to climb the first step, the doorbell caught his attention. "I'll get it," he called to Mrs. Frakes. Glancing out the side window beside the front door, he stopped in midstride, staring at the person reaching once again to push the doorbell, the harsh peal grating on his nerves. Or maybe it was the sight of the caller setting him on edge. He took a deep breath, exhaling as slow as possible. Tightening his lips, he opened the door, squashing the harsh words that assaulted the tip of his tongue.

CHAPTER 18

Colin stepped onto the porch, observing the visitor with wary eyes. He glanced toward the sky, taking in the surrounding horizon, a wry smile curving his lips. *Not a raincloud in the sky, he thought. Only the sweltering, July sun. No worry of an ice storm for months, nor did he believe Haven, Oklahoma, to be a suburb of Hades.*" He sighed. "What are you doing here, Mother?"

Eileen pushed past him and stepped into the corridor. "Nice of you to invite me in."

Colin following her, stood patiently while she looked around the entryway, her eyes narrowing when she took in the living room a moment later. She turned, her face paling. "Nothing has changed since the day I left—it's as if the world stopped breathing the day Braxton died."

Experiencing a touch of compassion for his mother, Colin nodded. "I had similar thoughts the day I arrived at Briarwood."

Mrs. Frakes walked into the entryway. She glanced at Colin and then his mother. "Mrs. Lambert...uh...Mrs. Hemphill, you surprise us. How nice."

Eileen eyed the housekeeper momentarily. "Surprise yes"—she glowered at her son—"whether nice, time will tell." "Colin, I've come to take you back to St. Louis. I expect you to be packed and ready to leave bright and early tomorrow morning." Eileen raised her eyes, taking in the top floor, her next words directed to Mrs. Frakes. "I assume my old suite is ready for occupancy, unless you've changed your habit of housekeeping in the years I've been away?"

Mrs. Frakes bowed. "No, ma'am, I not change. All rooms clean and aired for guests." She turned to Colin. "Will the two of you be dining at Briarwood this evening? I have plenty of food."

"Yes, unless Mother desires to dine at Chloe's Diner." The corners of Colin's mouth turned upward as a wave of irritation skittered across Eileen's face. He held up his hand, cutting off her next words. "On second thought, I believe it's your fine cuisine we'll enjoy tonight, Mrs. Frakes."

Eileen did an about-face and strode toward the stairs. "Colin, see to my bag, *if you don't mind*," she snipped, glancing briefly at him over her shoulder before she reached the top landing.

Colin eyed the swish of her fashionable summer frock as she climbed to the second floor, the anger he'd felt earlier crushing his insides. Would she never allow him to grow up, let him shoulder his own responsibilities? Later, after dinner, once he'd swallowed the last bite of his dessert, he would demand an audience with her in his office. He had to make her understand he was quite capable of making his own decisions.

• • • • •

A few hours later, Colin sat at his grandfather's desk, eyeing Eileen's conflicted expressions as she studied the room, her gaze lingering on the newly repaired window several moments before she took a seat on the sofa beneath the gleaming panes. Lifting her eyes above his head, she gasped. Colin turned to focus on the wall behind him, a constant reminder of Briarwood's moonlight visitor a few nights past. He shuddered at the memory of the frightening experience—one he wished he and Mrs. Frakes would never have to recall again.

"Colin, are you listening to me?"

His mother's voice broke the reverie. "I'm sorry, Mother. What did you say?"

"I asked if those holes were made by bullets from a gun."

Sighing deeply, Colin nodded.

She drew an exasperated breath, pointing above his head. "That's the very reason I'm here. Nicholas thinks..."

Colin stood from his chair, the black look on his face startling Eileen. "I could care less what Girard thinks. Did he persuade you to come to Haven or was this your own idea?"

"Well, I... I've been afraid for you, you know that. I kept hoping you'd come to your senses. And yes, Nicholas did inform me of the happenings at Briarwood of late—those incidents you've refused to take seriously or share with your own mother, I might add. From what I understand the news is not a secret. It seems the Lamberts are once again the center of attention in Osage County. Colin, what's it going to take for you to realize you're playing a dangerous game—the possible loss of your life, the winning prize?" Eileen searched his face, his stern countenance softening as he regarded the plea in her eyes.

"Mother, I haven't discounted the seriousness of the incidences. But I have to do what I feel is right in my heart. I can't leave Haven until Dad is free once again. I am less than two days away from seeing that happen. And I can't desert the Duchess, no matter what the outcome might be for us both." He rubbed the deep lines in his brow. "Mother, I don't mean to hurt you, but I'm not a little boy any longer. You can't make me leave my home and family this time."

Her eyes narrowed. "I take it you don't have any qualms about deserting me, permanently if you refuse to listen to me."

Colin gazed at Eileen for several moments, his face hardening. "I guess one could say that trend runs in the family. Since you plan to leave early in the morning, am I to assume you don't intend to visit Grandmother? Maybe you should reconsider your plans and go see her, now that it's not necessary for you to leave so soon."

Eileen's face reddened. "I-I just want to get you away from here—to protect you. I was told"—Eileen clamped her lips together, lowering her lashes as Colin's eyes darkened." A tear streaked down the side of her face. "Colin, what would I do if I lost you?"

Determined not to let emotion, hers or his, sway his decision, he sighed. "Mother, you won't lose me, I promise. Nonetheless, I'm not going anywhere for a while. And you're welcome to pass that information on to your friend, Girard, with my blessing."

Eileen stood and moved toward the door. "Colin, I do hope you know what you're doing. As for my mother, I'll think about it." She turned to face him before she exited the room, a half smile on her lips. "I might need to stay another night or two."

Colin relaxed, returning her smile. "I'd like that, Mother, on one condition."

She frowned. "One condition?"

"Yes…that we don't have any more arguments about my leaving."

"Okay, Colin. We'll do it your way."

Watching the door close behind her, Colin sighed. He'd have to see it to believe it.

• • • • •

The following morning, while waiting for Eileen to join him downstairs, Colin lingered over coffee and his daily scrutinizing of Mrs. Frakes's copy of the *Tulsa World*—"her touch with the outside world," she'd commented one morning when he had asked to borrow her daily edition. The sound of the doorbell interrupted his perusal of the front-page story about his father's upcoming release from prison on behalf of the new evidence pointing to his innocence. Noting Julie's name beneath Jack Granger's byline at the end of the article, Colin smiled. She'd made the front page after all. He'd give Julie a call later to congratulate her on her first break into reporting.

Mrs. Frakes deserted the task of clearing away the breakfast dishes to answer the door. She returned a moment later to announce Mr. Baker's presence in the foyer.

Colin glanced at his watch. "I'll see him in the office, Mrs. Frakes," Colin said, refilling his cup before leaving the kitchen. "Perhaps Mr. Baker would like a cup of coffee as well."

"I'll bring a tray of cinnamon rolls and coffee to office."

"Thanks."

"Mm. Delicious," Mr. Baker said once he was seated in the chair near the desk and sampling Mrs. Frakes's pastry.

When Mr. Baker had scraped the last crumb from the plate, Colin refreshed both their coffees. In the meantime, Mr. Baker pulled a piece of paper from one of the bib pockets of his overalls.

"I finished the landscape plans last evening and thought I'd drop them by this morning so we could go over them. Also, I've itemized everything I'll need and estimated the cost for the job."

"Colin took the papers from Mr. Baker, smiling as he perused each page. "You're quite the artist, Mr. Baker." These are good drawings of the estate."

Mr. Baker lowered his head, his lined cheeks turning pink. "Just a hobby I've enjoyed since I was a youngster. It's nothing compared to your father's work, though."

"Yes, Dad is gifted." Colin's expression turned sad. "Had Dad been able to pursue his career in the manner he desired, he'd probably be well-known in artist circles today." Colin brightened. "I suppose you've heard about the hearing tomorrow."

Mr. Baker laughed. "Yes. It's the talk of Haven and probably half the county. I expect the courtroom will be packed with folks from the area hoping the best for your father."

"You think there are that many people who remember the first trial?"

"Sure do. Have you heard any news about Miss Lambert?"

Colin shook his head, his eyes revealing his desolation. "Not so far. Maybe today."

"Well, if it's any consolation to you; a lot of people are praying for her safe return."

Colin nodded. "So I've been told."

The two men grew quiet, each harboring their own thoughts. Mr. Baker stood a moment later. "Well, I guess I'd better mosey along. Let me know what you decide about the plants." Mr. Baker snapped his fingers. "Almost forgot. Did you hear about the break-in at the medical clinic and Taylor Drug last night?"

Colin eyes widened. "No. I didn't. How did you hear about it?"

"One of Nellie's friends phoned her around eight this morning. Said she was walking her dog across the street from the drugstore when the sheriff and a deputy arrived to investigate a robbery at the place. It seems Mr. Taylor discovered the theft of several prescription drugs from the pharmacy when he arrived at work this morning. Also, while at the drugstore the sheriff received a call from the clinic which reported a break-in last night as well, but Nellie's friend didn't know what the thieves had stolen from there."

"Interesting. Any suspects?"

Mr. Baker shook his head. "Don't know of anyone as yet."

"Let's hope they catch the thieves soon." Dismissing the issue from his thoughts, Colin picked up the landscape plans from his desk. "Thanks for these. I'll get back with you after I've had time to look over them."

BITTERSWEET JUSTICE

Mr. Baker nodded and then smiled. "I'll see you in court tomorrow."

Eileen peeked around the half-closed door. "May I come in? Mrs. Frakes said Mr. Baker was here and I didn't want to miss saying hello to him."

Colin looked stunned. He couldn't remember his mother ever being cordial to the former caretaker of Briarwood. His eyes narrowed. Should he suspect her sudden friendliness?

"Come in, Mother. Mr. Baker was just leaving."

Eileen ignored her son's remark, stepping close to Mr. Baker with her hand extended. "Mr. Baker, how nice to see you again. I couldn't help overhearing about the robberies as I came down the hall. Was anyone hurt?"

"Hello, Mrs. Lambert," Mr. Baker said, taking her hand. "It's my understanding no one was at either place when the break-ins occurred. I didn't realize you had come to Briarwood with Colin."

She smiled sweetly. "The name is Mrs. Hemphill now, Mr. Baker. And I didn't arrive at Briarwood until yesterday afternoon. I assume you've heard about the terrible things that have happened since Colin came to Briarwood. And now, these robberies. I'm concerned about his safety, so I came to persuade him to come home, although I haven't yet convinced him to leave." She gave Mr. Baker an engaging smile. "Maybe you could help me with my task."

Mr. Baker glimpsed the set of Colin's jaw. "We might have a bit of a problem, Mrs. Lam...I mean...Hemphill, with the hearing just a day away and his aunt nowhere to be seen. It's my opinion Mr. Lambert won't budge from this place. He's determined to see his father free and his kin home again. Afraid I'd feel the same way, if I were in his shoes."

Eileen opened her mouth to speak, but a knock on the door held her tongue. All three occupants of the room turned toward the door eyeing the entrance of Mrs. Frakes and Sheriff Kinney. The sheriff touched his fingers to his hat when he spied Eileen's presence in the room.

"Sorry to intrude," the sheriff said before the housekeeper could announce his arrival. "But I knew you'd want to hear what I came to tell you as soon as possible."

Colin stood. "By all means, Sheriff, come in. Your expression reveals that it's good news."

"Well, yes and no. We haven't located Miss Lambert, but we have evidence she's still alive."

Colin's eyes widened. "Thank God."

"Mr. Lambert, last night a person or persons unknown broke into the medical clinic and Taylor Drug, taking items we believe verifies our theory."

"Mr. Baker informed me a few minutes ago about the events."

The sheriff balanced his weight onto his opposite foot, a patient look on his face.

"Forgive the interruption, Sheriff, please continue," Colin said.

"When Dr. Wexley discovered that his clinical records had been vandalized, he found the only medical file taken from the clinic was Miss Lambert's. And, once Mr. Taylor finishes the inventory of stolen pharmaceutical drugs, it's my guess among the missing medications will be those the doctor had prescribed for Miss Lambert. Mr. Taylor said he should be through with his inventory by noon. We'll know for sure by then."

Colin took his chin in hand, frowning. "But if what you say is true, it still doesn't give us a lead to her location."

The sheriff placed his arm around Colin's shoulders. "This is true at the moment, Mr. Lambert, but within a few hours, that situation might change."

Colin stared at the sheriff. "What do you mean?"

Sheriff Kinney grinned. "Girard's nephew, Keith, and the James boys are at this moment occupying cells at the jail for cattle rustling. Just past dawn this morning, Clay caught them red-handed about to drive away from the Walker Ranch with a couple of steers in the back of a farm truck owned by Mrs. James, the boys' grandmother.

"Seems Walker had gotten up early to ride fence, hoping to locate the place where some of his cattle, which had recently disappeared, had broken through the fence. At least that's what he assumed had happened to them until he spotted three men from a distance herding his steers into a lit truck parked alongside the road leading to his ranch. Hiding in a ravine nearby, he phoned me on his cell phone to report the crime. I notified Clay and another deputy who lives not far from the ranch, and my deputies arrived in time to make an immediate arrest." The sheriff laughed. "Just like in the movies."

Colin ignored the officer's humor. "I'm sorry, Sheriff, but I don't understand how cattle rustling ties in with my aunt's disappearance." Colin studied the officer's features and then smiled. "However, something tells me the three might have been involved in the robberies also."

Sheriff Kinney lifted an eyebrow. "Let me put it this way. When Clay searched the truck, he found several bottles of prescription painkillers, the ones most sold on the streets, some drug paraphernalia, and a concealed weapon in their possession. I'd say the boys are going to grow older in prison unless the prosecutor agrees to a plea bargain—information in exchange for a possible lighter sentence. But so far none of the three are talking."

"So, am I right to believe the three are definite suspects in the kidnapping?"

Sheriff Kinney nodded. "It's looking more probable with each passing moment."

Colin paced back and forth across the floor of the office, pausing momentarily, his expression taut with conviction. "Say, what about the James boys' sister? Didn't you say she worked at the clinic? Maybe she stole the records and made it look like someone else broke into the place and took them."

Sheriff Kinney shook his head. "Dr. Wexley said she's on vacation, Hawaii, he thought."

"Well, if those three are my aunt's kidnappers, you can rest assured Girard is the one who handed out their orders."

Eileen gasped. The others turned their eyes on her, the sheriff stepping forward his hand outstretched. "I don't believe I've had the pleasure of making your acquaintance, ma'am."

"Forgive my lack of manners, Sheriff," Colin said, taking Eileen's arm. "This is my mother, Eileen Hemphill. She arrived last evening for a visit. Mother, this is Sheriff Kinney of Osage County."

Eileen allowed the sheriff to take her hand for a quick handshake. "I do hope you can clear up this whole situation right away so Colin can return to St. Louis, where he belongs."

"Yes, ma'am. I will do my best."

Eileen lifted her chin, a chilly smile on her lips. "I suppose all we can do is hope your best is good enough to keep my son alive." She faced Colin. "If you need me for anything, I'll be upstairs." With a nod to Mr. Baker and Mrs. Frakes, Eileen hurried from the room.

With an apologetic expression on his face, Colin turned to the sheriff. "My mother is not at all pleased about my stay in Haven."

Sheriff Kinney nodded, a grin lighting up his leathery complexion. "Wasn't hard to detect that at all." His look sobered. "When I get back to the office, I intend to interrogate Samuel, the younger James. He's just seventeen and was mighty scared when I locked that cell door, his face white as a sheet. I'll make

BITTERSWEET JUSTICE   281

sure he understands the punishment allowed for the crime he's alleged to have committed. Maybe that will frighten him enough to talk about their escapades last night."

"Has Agent Donaldson reported any of OSBI's findings?"

The sheriff shook his head and took a step toward the door. "Not yet. But I'll be speaking with him later today. Who knows, I might have some vital information for him before the day ends." Sheriff Kinney tipped his hat to Mrs. Frakes then turned back to Colin. "Don't give up hope, Mr. Lambert. With the lead this morning, time is on our side."

"Thanks," Colin said. "I appreciate all your efforts in our behalf."

"Just goes along with the job, son. Good day, Mr. Baker."

Mr. Baker followed the sheriff. "I'll walk out with you, Sheriff, if you don't mind the company."

Colin escorted his visitors to the door and stood in the doorway watching until the men drove their respective vehicles out of sight. All of a sudden, weariness overcame him. Along with everything else, he now had to contend with his mother's presence at Briarwood.

Praying for an extra measure of grace, Colin reached toward the pocket on his shirt, his cell phone showing an e-mail from Tom Thorpe. Colin hoped problems at the agency were minimal. Guilt ate at him. He'd been away from his responsibilities in St. Louis almost a month. True, the technological supervision had worked thus far, but his stepfather had expected Colin to run the business in house, not from Briarwood.

Once seated at his desk, he toyed with the paperweight shaped like the head of a horse, the piece of paper found in his great-uncle's billfold tucked safely beneath the object. Wondering anew at the reason for the number written on the note and why he felt it to be of great significance, he glanced up at the knock on the doorframe, his mother standing in the open doorway.

"May I come in?"

"Of course, Mother." He motioned toward the sofa. "Is everything okay?"

"Yes. Once in my room I realized my earlier rudeness." Eileen lowered her gaze at his raised eyebrows. "No, please don't say what you're thinking. I don't want us to quarrel." She hesitated and then straightened. "I-I thought over your suggestion about seeing your grandmother and decided I would pay her a visit." Colin eyed the graceful fold of her hands as she clasped them in front of her. "I thought you might like to accompany me."

Colin sat upright, perplexed at the softening in his mother's expression, a look he rarely saw unless she was especially pleased with him about something. *Another answer to his prayers?* He sighed, realizing his actions of late were quite the opposite of her pleasure.

Eyeing his scrutiny, Eileen raised her chin, her lips set. "Well, after all, I'm here. I'm sure Mary would like to know if Mother is well."

His mother's reserve back in place, Colin closed his laptop, sighing. Any construction of a bridge over the troubled waters between them would have to be shelved for now. "I need to take care of some things this morning, but I'll be glad to go with you later. After lunch, okay?" At her nod, he motioned for her to sit down. "By the way, I assume you found the keys to the bank deposit box and were able to get everything updated as you desired?"

"Yes, I—" Eileen's eyes widened at the look on her son's face. "Colin, what is it?" She stood beside Colin within seconds.

His features dotted first with shock and then understanding, he lifted the image of the thoroughbred and extracted the scrap of paper from beneath it. "I found this number in Uncle Max's wallet. I think I now know what it represents.

"A few days before Uncle Max died, he asked Mrs. Frakes to drive him to Bank of Oklahoma in Bartlesville, requesting that she remain in the car while he attended to business inside the bank. Armed with his briefcase, he entered the establishment, returning a few minutes later exhausted from the excursion, according to Mrs. Frakes. The thought just occurred to me he might have stored something in a safe deposit box."

Colin opened the desk drawers one at a time and hurriedly rummaged through their contents, a moment later looking confused. "Now what did I do with them?"

Eileen sighed. "Colin, what are you talking about?"

Colin looked at his mother as though he just realized she stood before him. "Uncle Max's keys. Mrs. Frakes gave them to me the night we discovered someone had vandalized the office. I removed the front door key from his set and added it to my key ring." Colin snapped his fingers. "I threw the rest of Uncle Max's keys in the drawer of the nightstand in my room. I'll be right back."

A moment later, Colin withdrew his hand from the doorknob to answer his cell phone. He glanced at his mother, who had resumed her position on the sofa. "Hi, Julie. Glad you called. We might have a lead in locating the Duchess." Noting Eileen's raised eyebrows when he mentioned Julie's name, Colin stepped out into the hall and closed the office door. "Oh, so you know about the robberies. Did Clay inform Jack as well? Good. I suppose we'll read about it in tomorrow's edition. By the way, congratulations on your first news story. Yes, I know you collaborated with Jack on it, but it's a great start to a new career."

"Thanks, Julie, I appreciate the prayers. Hey, that's great. I'll see you and Jack at the courthouse in the morning. Talk to you guys then. Good-bye."

"Do I know this Julie?" Eileen asked when Colin returned. She pulled herself forward to the edge of the couch.

Colin eyed his mother, his facial expression turning bland. No way would he share his feelings for Julie, not yet anyway. They were too new, her feelings for him not reaching beyond friendship at this point. He refused to allow their friendship to be subjected to Eileen's sometimes cruel assessment of his relationships, especially since she believed Allison to be the perfect match for him. He picked up the scrap of paper he'd forgotten earlier and strode toward the door, pausing to face Eileen. "I think I mentioned in one of our earlier phone conversations the two reporters who were aiding my endeavors to prove Dad's innocence. Julie Lonetree is one of them; Jack Granger the other."

"I see," Eileen said, her eyes revealing she knew there was more to the story than he intended to disclose.

"Now, Mother, if you'll excuse me, I need to check Uncle Max's keys to see if I'm right about the safe deposit box. And don't forget our afternoon visit with Grandmother Kirby. She doesn't have a phone, so we'll have to go unannounced. I hope we find her at home. I know how much the visit will mean to her."

Eileen seemed reluctant to leave the office but did so seeming to realize Colin would say nothing more to quench her curiosity about Julie.

When his mother had exited the room, Colin took the back stairs two at a time, hardly taking a breath until he reached his suite and held his uncle's keys in his hand. One by one he moved them along the ring, smiling a moment later as he gazed at the number 685 stamped on a key similar to the one in his stepfather's desk in St. Louis.

Had his uncle rented a deposit box that day? If so, what had he deemed important enough to store at the bank knowing his death was close at hand? Suddenly a new thought struck Colin. Perhaps Uncle Max hadn't been storing anything at all but removing items from the box instead, closing out his rental.

Colin shook his head. But that didn't make sense. The key to the box was still on the key ring.

Colin tugged on his wallet in his back pocket, a moment later pulling the business card the courtesy clerk at Bank of Oklahoma had given him the day he'd closed out his uncle's account. Colin frowned. He still hadn't discovered the reason for all those monthly cash withdrawals Uncle Max had made. And it was possible the why would never be known, the mystery buried with his uncle.

Colin reached for his phone and dialed the bank's number. "Cara Williams, please." Colin ended the phone call a moment later, the clerk's voice mail giving him the message that she was on vacation and would be back in the bank on Monday of the following week. He drew a long sigh, disappointed he wouldn't be able to inquire about the safe deposit box today. He thought about dialing the bank again and talking to another individual but decided to forget it. Besides, his calendar for the next few days would be filled if the court hearing went as expected for his father.

He returned downstairs, the growl in his stomach growing louder. He headed for the kitchen to check out Mrs. Frakes' menu for lunch. Stepping into the room a moment later, his eyes grew wide, the scene hard to grasp.

CHAPTER 19

Colin stared at his mother, who stood at the stove stirring what he detected was the sauce for one of his favorite entrees, chicken fettuccine alfredo. The apron tied around her waist reminded him of June Cleaver.

"Close your mouth, Colin, before you trap the fly that's been doing cartwheels in the kitchen the last few minutes. You look as though you've just seen an alien."

Colin laughed and then strode over to the stove to give his mother a hug. "Well, you have to admit observing you like this is a little foreign to me. We ate out most of the time after you married George."

"Well, I never claimed to be a cook." She glanced at Mrs. Frakes, who was busy setting the table for their meal. "There wasn't a need for me to learn when I married your father." Besides, I would never have been able to do it as well as Mrs. Frakes."

Mrs. Frakes bowed low. "Thank you for compliment, Mrs. Hemphill."

Colin took his place at the table. "Well, I hope lunch is about ready. I'm starved."

Colin ignored the lift of his mother's eyebrows when he insisted the housekeeper join them for lunch after noticing she'd only set the table for two. Offering a prayer of thankfulness beneath his breath when Eileen chose to keep her thoughts to herself, Colin said grace, helping himself to a generous portion of food a moment later. If she mentioned it later, he would make sure she realized that he considered Mrs. Frakes more a family friend than a mere servant and had insisted she take her meals with him soon after his arrival at Briarwood.

"Wonderful," Colin said in between bites, the two women exchanging a smile. Maybe his mother's visit would turn out okay after all, he thought, puzzled by her unusual friendliness.

· · · · ·

An hour later, Colin killed the motor to Eileen's car outside his grandmother's house. After taking in the shabbiness of the bungalow, he turned to Eileen. Although she said nothing, he could see the sight bothered his mother as well, her eyes reflecting both anger and sadness. Compassion filled his heart. How difficult it must be for her to recall her young life with her parents. He hoped her pain wouldn't override her concern for his grandmother's welfare.

He gave Eileen a smile of encouragement then helped her out of the car. "No need to be afraid, Mother. Grandmother told me she's been praying for this moment for years."

Once at the door of the house, Eileen's spine grew rigid when Colin knocked on the door. Within seconds Mrs. Kirby stood eyeing the two of them, her hand over her heart. "Eileen, is it really you? Oh, please, do come in," she said, taking hold of her daughter's hand and pulling her into a hug before she had a chance to protest. A tearful smile of gratitude on the woman's lips, she embraced Colin, a moment later beckoning them inside. Eying his mother's inspection of the room, he felt reassured the visit hadn't been a mistake when he saw tears fill her eyes.

Mrs. Kirby removed a magazine from the sofa to make it easier for her visitors to occupy the small couch, seating herself in the chair opposite them.

Silence hung in the air like intense humidity just before a downpour. "How are you, Grandmother?" Colin said, giving Eileen time to regain her composure. Sorry I haven't been able to come back before now. I've been quite busy."

"No need to apologize," she said, not taking her eyes off Eileen. "The news about Stuart and Miss Beatrice is the main topic of conversation in town. Is there anything I can do to help?"

Colin shook his head. "Sheriff Kinney has assured me that law enforcement is doing all they can to find my aunt. Waiting to hear something is hardest of all. But I believe God has assured me he's in control of the situation."

Mrs. Kirby nodded. "All we can do in times like these is trust God." She took in Eileen once again. "How have you been, Daughter? Colin told me about your recent widowhood. I'm so sorry... and how is Mary?"

Eileen cleared her throat. "I'm doing fine. Thank you for asking. Mary is well also, busy with her family and various charities." All at once tears formed in Eileen's eyes and spilled down her cheeks. She stood from the sofa and dropped to her knees in front of her mother. "I'm so sorry. I blamed you for so many things, but Colin told me what really happened. I...I hated Daddy and resented you for not stopping him from abusing us. But now I understand. You stayed with him to save us. How can you ever forgive me?"

Colin gaped at his mother. He'd never known her to ask forgiveness from anyone. He blinked back the dewiness in his own eyes. *Father, could this be the beginning of her journey toward accepting your gift of salvation? I pray that it would be so.*

Mrs. Kirby leaned forward and threw her arms around Eileen. "It's okay, Daughter. I have my own grief of the past to bear. I should have tried harder to find help for our domestic problems, but fear is a mighty force. Only later did I discover that my source of strength depended on faith in God. But I didn't know how to get in touch with either of you girls to try to mend the strife between us. Please forgive me, Eileen, for not being the mother you needed at the time."

Eileen raised her head from her mother's lap. "You did the best you could, Mother, given the circumstances." Eileen took hold of her mother's hands and pulled them both to their feet. "I suppose I could spend the rest of the day apologizing for all the things I've done wrong"—Eileen glanced around the room—"such as your horrible living conditions." She smiled, darting a glimpse toward Colin. "But that's about to change." She took in her surroundings again. "Shouldn't take too long to get you packed and ready to go home with me in a day or two…"

Eileen paused momentarily, frowning at her mother's perplexed look. "You really don't want to live the rest of your life like this, do you?" she said, sweeping the contents of the room with her outstretched arm. "Not when I have a beautiful home with plenty of room for the both of us. And Mary lives close by also. You could see her as often as you desire."

Mrs. Kirby's countenance took on a look of skepticism shadowed by sadness. "Perhaps Mary doesn't wish to see me."

Eileen shook her head. "Not true. We've discussed the matter several times in the last few days." Eileen laughed. "She's concerned you don't want to see her after she ran away from home and never attempted to get in touch with you."

Colin observed his grandmother's stanch expression. He smiled, wondering who would win in this war of wills.

"But, Eileen, this is my home. My church and friends are here. True, I don't have a lot of possessions, but I'm content and happy, at least now that I've seen you and have been able to make things right with you."

"Colin, please help me convince her," Eileen said, taking a seat next to him.

Colin smiled at his grandmother. "Mother just wants the best for you. After all, you're not getting any younger and all your family lives in St. Louis. Wouldn't you like to get to know your other grandchildren?" Colin glanced at his mother narrowing his eyes. "We would never force you to do something you didn't want to do, but please consider the offer. Or at least come for an extended visit. You might decide you like the area and want to settle there." He grinned. "If living with Mother becomes impossible, we could always look into buying you a home nearby."

Eileen rolled her eyes. "Mother, I would really like to get close to you again. Besides, with Colin in his own apartment now and making his own decisions"—Eileen directed a gaze full of meaning toward her son—"it would be nice to have you with me."

Mrs. Kirby looked from one to the other. "I promise I'll give it some thought and pray for God's perfect will in the matter too." She looked down, smoothing the wrinkles in her apron. "It would be nice to be near you and Mary. What were the names of her children again?"

Later, after Eileen and Colin had done their best to bring Mrs. Kirby up to date on their respective lives, the two journeyed toward Briarwood, Eileen's silence growing since they'd gotten into the car. She fidgeted with the wedding ring she still wore.

Colin glanced at her. "Mother, what's bothering you? Are you reconsidering your offer to Grandmother?"

"No. There's something I need to tell you, but part of it will be difficult."

Colin grew alarmed. "Is something wrong?"

She smiled at him. "No. No. Quite the contrary. In fact, I think you'll be pleased when you hear it... at least some of it."

BITTERSWEET JUSTICE

He grinned. "Are you going to keep me in suspense the rest of the way home?" The look in her eyes wiped the smile from Colin's lips.

"Do you remember that church at the end of my street, the one you attended when you were in high school?"

"Yes..." Colin slowed the car and drove onto a wide, shady spot beside the road, feeling he needed to give Eileen time to reveal what she had on her mind.

"Well, I was taking a walk the other evening, and as I approached the church, I could hear singing. I've strolled by the church numerous times but never paid attention to the goings on there. However, that evening, something caused me to stop and listen. A few minutes later, I found myself inside, seated on a pew near the back of the sanctuary. It was as though some unknown force had placed me there and captured my thoughts, causing me to listen to the minister who spoke in a gentle but authoritative way, his message like solace to my tortured soul.

"He talked about the love of God in a way I'd never heard, how that He loved mankind so much he sent his Son to pay the penalty for the vilest sinner—his death on the cross cleansing us from all the wrong we've ever done, even... mur-murder..."

Colin gasped, the image surfacing in his mind too horrible to conceive. "Mother?"

She held up her hand to silence him. "Please let me finish. When the preacher asked for those who wanted to accept this free gift of salvation to raise their hands and come for prayer, I just couldn't go forward right then. But later in my bedroom while thinking over his message, I knelt beside my bed and asked God's Son to cleanse me from all my sins, at first not understanding how he could save a rotten person like me, but somehow he did..."

Eileen lifted her eyes to gaze at her son. "I-I guess what I'm trying to say is... I've been born again, and a peace I've never known entered my heart that night. I know I still have issues, but I'm meeting weekly with the pastor and I'm learning to overcome them by God's grace. Also, I'm studying my Bible every day, desiring to become the Christian I should be."

Colin felt like he was dying on the inside, the joy he should have felt at her words swallowed by the thoughts rolling in his mind. "That's wonderful," he said, trying to muster some kind of gladness in his tone. "I've been praying for that to happen for a long time." He paused, running his tongue over his lips to moisten them, the dryness like the parched recesses of his heart. "Mother, there's something else you want to tell me isn't there?"

Eileen gazed at her son for several minutes. "I don't want to, but I have to. In fact, I've wanted to for years, but I couldn't bring myself to do it; I was afraid you'd hate me."

Colin closed his eyes. "I could never hate you. You're my mother."

She shook her head. "Hating a parent isn't all that difficult. Believe me, I know. It's the forgiving that's the problem. But I'm working on that too. Pastor says we can do all things through Christ who strengthens us. And believe me; I need His strength now more than I ever have in my life." Eileen drew a deep breath.

"Colin, do you remember asking me about my conversation with Nicholas in the garden at Briarwood on the morning your grandfather was murdered and about the package I gave him?"

Heartsick, Colin nodded. "Yes. What about it?" he asked, believing he knew the answer already.

She frowned. "Colin, you're looking at me like you believe I killed Braxton."

Sadness overwhelmed Colin. "Isn't that what you're trying to tell me?"

She looked shocked. "Good heavens, no!"

Colin brightened and then exhaled slowly. "Please continue."

"I felt I couldn't tell you this because Nicholas threatened to harm you if I told anyone what I'm about to relate. And now, he's threatened to kill you if I don't stop your probe into your grandfather's murder. My past experience with Nicholas assures me he means what he says. That's why I want you to leave Haven."

Colin rolled down the window, taking a deep breath as though his next breath depended on the fresh country air. The window back to its original position a moment later, he turned to Eileen. "What was in the sack you gave to Girard that morning?"

She looked down, wincing at the look in his eyes. Nicholas caught me as I was about to leave for my shopping trip that morning, saying he'd seen Braxton's murder through the window to the office and wanted me to hurry and get your father's gun from our bedroom, so he could toss it into the office through the open window, hoping your father would be blamed for the crime. It seems when he'd arrived for his appointment with Braxton that morning, Nicholas overheard an argument between Stuart and your grandfather and said the prosecutor would use the confrontation between them as your father's motive for murder.

"Nicholas said we'd be able to marry once your father was executed, and I would receive his inheritance from Braxton. When I protested, we argued. That's when he threatened to harm you. I felt I had no choice but to do as he said—give him Stuart's gun and hold my tongue."

She looked up, a plea for understanding in her eyes. "Colin, I couldn't let anything happen to you. You were all I had. Nicholas has always hated your father for taking me away from him. He's an evil man and is capable of anything. In fact, all these years since, I've believed he lied to me about some other person committing the murder, instead, Nicholas himself, using your father's gun to kill Braxton in order to satisfy his thirst for revenge."

For a moment Colin couldn't say a word. So many things added up now—Alfie's reaction to Girard yesterday morning and now his mother's confession. The attorney's guilt had moved from possible to plausible. He looked up at the sound of her voice.

"Colin, be angry with me, yell at me, don't talk to me, but please, I beg you, don't hate me."

"How could you let my father rot in prison all these years?"

She spread her hands. "I can't tell you how much guilt I've suffered over that. My only excuse is fear for your life. I hope someday you and Stuart will be able to forgive me."

Colin sighed. "If I'm to follow God's commandments, I don't really have a choice, do I?"

Colin opened the car door and walked a short distance away. *I can't do it, God. To forgive her for taking me away from all I had loved as a child is one thing, but to forgive her deliberate silence that has kept Dad in prison all this time for a crime she knew he didn't commit ... oh, God, how can I do it?*

Maybe you should take her pastor's advice as well? You know the part about relying on my Son's strength to do all things.

You're asking a lot of me, God.

Nothing more than I asked of my firstborn—he was willing to die for you. Remember, he said, "Not my will, Father, but Yours be done." He denied himself, took up the cross and followed my plan. Do you love me enough to do the same?

All I can say is I hope so.

Think about what it took for my daughter to disclose this to you. She risked all she loved—you.

Colin walked slowly back to the car, the sight of his mother's face enclosed in her hands and her hunched shoulders stirring Colin to tears, his anger ebbing away. At the sound of the door opening, she looked up at him her tear-stained face more than Colin could bear. He slipped inside the car, taking his mother into his arms.

"Colin, I'm so sorry for so many things."

"It's going to be okay, Mother. The scripture says there's no one who hasn't committed sins, no not one. But I guess you realize we'll have to talk to the sheriff. What you've stated may be enough to arrest Girard for murder."

She nodded. "Do you think they will arrest me for withholding evidence?"

"I don't know. I'm sure protection of a child will be a consideration in the matter. I can't say how, but I believe God will work everything out if we will trust in him."

Back at the estate a short later, Colin phoned Attorney Craig to apprise him of the situation, seeking his advice in the matter, Eileen agreeing to take the witness stand at tomorrow's hearing to further validate Stuart's plea of innocence. Furthermore, Mr. Craig suggested they meet within the hour at the sheriff's office in Pawhuska in order for Eileen to give an official statement. Only then would Sheriff Kinney be able to bring Girard in for questioning. In the meantime, their attorney would speak to the prosecutor, Eileen's arrest unlikely because she willingly disclosed her knowledge of Girard's part in Braxton's demise.

Following a late dinner, Colin and his mother sat on the porch watching a gorgeous sunset, the orange and purple hues striking the hilltops rising above Briarwood Valley with vibrant color. About to comment on the beauty before them, Colin's cell phone vibrated in his pocket. His breath caught and held at the name poised on the screen. Had the Duchess been found at last?

"Hello, Sheriff."

"Howdy, Mr. Lambert. Just wanted you to know I spoke with Samuel again after you left the office this afternoon and still no response. Right now, he's mimicking his older brother, playing tough and tight-lipped. His face did pale a mite when the public defender mentioned Samuel's upcoming eighteenth birthday next month and that Samuel could be tried as an adult in the case. And the prison term usually given for involvement in cattle rustling and kidnapping. I think once he chews on that information for a spell, he'll reconsider the silent treatment we've endured from him.

"Of course, it didn't help matters earlier in the day when Mrs. James came storming into the office demanding to see her grandsons right away. The kid seemed to gain some confidence after his grandmother's visit though, buttoning his speech even tighter. And too, still no word from Donaldson. Hopefully, we'll hear something from the bureau soon."

"Thanks for updating me."

"You're welcome. Just as soon as the paperwork is processed on Keith and his buddies, and Logan gives me the word, I'll be paying Mr. Girard a visit with a formal invitation to the office for questioning."

"That's good. He's the killer as far as I'm concerned."

"Well, circumstantial evidence is piling up against him, that's for sure. But as you well know, a person is innocent until proven guilty beyond a shadow of doubt. See you in court, tomorrow."

Colin bit his lip, holding back the retort on his lips. Too bad the shadow of doubt had been forgotten in his father's case. "Okay, Sheriff, see you then."

· · · · ·

The next morning, Colin and his mother waited on a bench outside the courtroom waiting to be called in to take the witness stand on behalf of his father's defense. Gazing at his mother from the corners of his eyes, he wondered what her feelings were at the moment.

She caught his gaze. "I suppose you're questioning how I can face Stuart after all these years."

He smiled. "Something like that."

"Well, it won't be easy, I can tell you that. I was a fool. Afraid of my father and Nicholas all those years, I turned my fear and hatred of them toward your father, who loved me in spite of me. At least I can repay him a little for loving me enough to endure Braxton's wrath for marrying me. I wonder what he saw in me, the awful creature I'd become?"

"You didn't have a lot going for you then. You were a victim of both your father and a controlling lover."

"I wish I would have realized that back then. Perhaps I could have found help for our marriage. Stuart suggested marriage counseling once, but I laughed at him, blaming all my troubles on him and his lack of interest in Lambert Oil. I thought money would solve all my problems, even up to a few weeks ago." She smiled. "Until I realized God is my source for all things."

"Mother, it's so good that we see eye to eye on spiritual matters now." He reached to give her a hug, but before he could carry out his intent, the courtroom door opened and a bailiff motioned him into the courtroom. A moment later, his name was called and he made his way to the witness stand, lifting his hand to place it on the Bible held out to him, swearing to tell the truth, the whole truth, and nothing but the truth.

Once seated, the judge explained to him this wasn't a trial but a hearing to focus on the new evidence found in his father's case. Nodding to show he understood the proceedings, Colin settled back in the chair, marveling at the crowded courtroom. He glanced around, searching for the man he wanted most to see his father set free, but Nicholas Girard was nowhere in sight.

Dismissing his disappointment, he bent his head slightly to acknowledge Jack's and Julie's smiles and then turned to take in his father, who sat less than ten feet from him, the look of hope and gratefulness on his face causing Colin's eyes to smart with tears. Blinking, he set his gaze on Mr. Craig, who'd stepped up to the witness box, Colin ready to answer any question put before him.

His mother entered the courtroom to take her place on the stand as Colin exited through the doorway. He gave her a thumbs-up and whispered, "You'll do great, Mother. I promise."

Following each of their testimonies, the judge had instructed Colin and his mother to wait outside the courtroom until all testimony in the case had been given, the judge cautioning them not to discuss their statements given under oath.

Glancing at his watch a short time later, Colin looked up to see the door opening and several people exiting the room, including his friends from the *Tulsa World*. Introducing them to his mother, they stepped aside the others milling about the hall to stand some distance away to talk in private. Jack explained that the judge had announced a recess, retiring to his office with the two attorneys in tow to go over the findings of the hearing before he declared a ruling in the case. A few minutes into their conversation, Colin spotted Mr. and Mrs. Baker among the crowd. Stepping toward them, he motioned them aside, thanking them for their well wishes before introducing them to his friends.

Conversation grew still as the bailiff entered the hall to announce the end of the recess. All stood as the judge and the attorneys entered the front of the room, Colin's erratic heartbeat pounding in his ears as he watched Judge Bently take his seat. A moment later the judge gave the order for the spectators to be seated.

Colin ran his hand down the back of his head, ignoring the beads of sweat popping onto his forehead, his feelings very similar to those he'd experienced in this same room twenty-five years earlier. He glanced toward Sheriff Kinney, who caught the glance and smiled. Colin returned the gesture, turning his attention to his father who stood next to Mr. Craig to hear the judge's decision.

"Mr. Lambert, in all my years in law enforcement, I've never encountered a case such as yours. It is evident that your case wasn't handled properly at its onset. In most cases, I would order a new trial, but after the testimonies today and the new evidence presented by your attorney, it is my judgment that you were convicted wrongly for the murder of your father, Braxton Lambert. I sincerely apologize for any wrongdoing on your behalf by any law enforcement officers formally employed by Osage County in said case.

"Also, I waive the official procedure regarding this case. You will not have to return to the prison to await the filing of my findings. Once I declare this case dismissed, you will be formally released. Do you have anything you would like to say?" Not a sound could be heard in the courtroom as the audience waited to hear the reply.

Stuart pulled himself to his full height and then turned to face his son, who showed no remorse or embarrassment as tears cascaded down his cheeks unchecked. Stuart smiled at Colin and then faced the judge once again. "All is forgiven, sir. All is forgiven."

The judge held his gaze on Stuart for a long moment and then raised his gavel, his voice resonating in the crowded room. "Case dismissed!"

Once outside the courtroom, congratulations came from all sides, Stuart not having shook that many hands in decades. Meanwhile, Colin thanked Mr. Craig, Prosecutor Logan, and Sheriff Kinney for all they'd done to secure his father's freedom while Eileen waited off to one side until her son could claim her for their return trip to Briarwood. Waving good-bye to Julie and Jack, who had accepted Colin's impromptu invitation to come to Briarwood on Saturday evening to celebrate Stuart's freedom, soon Colin, his mother and father stood alone outside the courthouse.

Stuart turned to his ex-wife. "Hello, Eileen. You're looking well."

"Yes, well…" She reached out to touch his arm. "Stuart, I-I don't know how to begin to express my sorrow for how I treated you and our marriage. Will you please forgive me?"

Stuart bent forward to place a kiss on her cheek. "Eileen, it's just as I said in the courtroom a few minutes ago. All is forgiven. I wasn't perfect either." His eyes grew sad at the self-incriminating look on her face. "It's best we try to forget the past and concentrate on the future." Perhaps we should focus our interest on doing all we can to aid Colin and the authorities in their search for Aunt Beatrice and for Father's killer."

Colin and Eileen passed a look between them. Stuart's future looked bleak unless God had a miracle in mind. Colin herded his parents toward Eileen's car. "The murderer… Dad, that's just what I want to discuss with you."

Close to an hour later, Mrs. Frakes stood in the kitchen with widened eyes, both hands on her cheeks, observing the man she hadn't seen in more than a quarter of a century. When Stuart crossed the room to greet her, she bowed low then allowed him to take her hands in his. "Mr. Stuart, welcome home. So good to see you. I pray very hard that judge let you come home soon.

Stuart's face lit up with a smile He blinked away the sheen of moisture in his eyes then glanced around the room taking in Eileen and his son. "It seems God's favor rests on all of us today. It's wonderful to see you as well, Mrs. Frakes. You haven't changed a bit," Stuart said, facing the housekeeper once again.

She laughed. "Oh, Mr. Stuart, you always such a teaser." The three family members chuckled.

The sights and smells in the kitchen letting them know that lunch was ready to be served, Colin guided his family toward the dining room where Mrs. Frakes and his mother finished the task of setting the table with the finest Briarwood china. At Colin's raised eyebrows, the housekeeper motioned Colin aside, speaking to him in a low voice.

"I have faith Mr. Stuart be here. We do things my way today, Master Colin." With that she bowed, giving him a smile before she exited the room.

Grinning at her unusual impertinence, Colin reached for his vibrating cell phone, growing more alert when he read the name of the caller. Could it be news about the Duchess? Stepping into the foyer, he punched the green arrow on his phone.

"Hello, Sheriff, what's up?"

Colin's eyes grew wide. He felt fury boil inside him as he listened to Sheriff Kinney's words.

CHAPTER 20

Colin's knuckles grew pale from his grip on the phone. "The rotten scoundrel! Do you think Girard's wife lied about his disappearance?"

Sheriff Kinney paused a moment. "No, I don't believe so. After leaving the courthouse, I stopped by his office to see if he'd come in willingly for questioning, but his secretary said he'd canceled his appointments for the day because of urgent business at home. I drove straight to his house. Mrs. Girard was in tears when she answered the door. She said her husband had emptied both their savings and checking account and couldn't be reached at his office or on his mobile phone."

"How did she learn about it?"

"The clerk, who'd handled the transactions at the bank, a friend of the family, phoned Mrs. Girard to question her about their sudden plans to relocate to another city, the story Girard had told the employee."

"I see. I assume you've checked the airlines."

"Yes. Neither Tulsa, Oklahoma City, nor Wichita have any record of a ticket purchased by him. My guess is his sudden *relocation* is the result of the visit Agent Donaldson paid Girard this morning at his office, not his wife's belief he ran off with his mistress. She told me she's suspected his involvement with another woman for months. Whether that's true or not, he has a huge problem with the U.S. Government. Donaldson dropped a copy of the IRS report by my office a few minutes ago, stating he hoped the 'lawyer had a good tax attorney.' As far as any proof he engineered Miss Lambert's disappearance, they couldn't find a thing to associate him with the crime."

"That's too bad. I assume the tax evasion amounts to a large sum of money."

"More than I'll ever see in my lifetime. Donaldson believes Girard is out of the vicinity by now. Our theory is that he'll ditch his car soon. If so, maybe someone will notice the abandoned car and report it to their local police. Now that an all points bulletin for his arrest has been issued by the FBI, every police department in the U. S. will have wind of it. But of course it may be days before we know which direction he's headed."

Colin sighed. I thought by now we'd have proof he murdered my grandfather."

"We have no motive, Son, just suspicion, speculation, and circumstantial evidence."

"Of which I'm all too aware. Thanks for the information, though." Colin glanced at his watch. "It looks like Girard has got a good start on you guys. Hope you get a lead soon."

By the time Colin ended the call and returned to the dining room, the rest of the family was seated at the table, Mrs. Frakes serving the first course.

Eileen glanced at her son, her eyes widening. "Is something wrong, Colin?"

His face riddled with disappointment, he related his phone conversation with Sheriff Kinney.

Mrs. Frakes placed Colin's entrée in front of him and then patted his shoulder, glancing toward Stuart. "But you can still rejoice, Master Colin. Mr. Stuart free man now."

Colin nodded. "Yes, I am very grateful for that," he said, smiling at his father.

· · · · ·

The next morning, after Eileen drove off to visit her mother, Colin and Stuart took a walk around the estate grounds and then settled inside the sunroom for a long chat, enjoying a glass of iced tea from a pitcher perched on the silver tray they found waiting for them upon their return to the house. *Mrs. Frakes must have a sixth sense,* Colin thought, smiling as he refilled their glasses.

Colin's grin faded when he noted the yellow hue of Stuart's complexion, a sure sign his father's disease had progressed. "Dad, it's so good to see you at Briarwood again. I'm sorry, though, you had to see it in this condition. My plan is to renovate the estate as finances permit. In fact, Mr. Baker has already outlined the plan and cost for a complete redo of the landscape. But I think I want to do some work on the inside of the house first. Do you remember Jonathan Baker?"

"Of course, his wife and Alfred too."

"You'll get to visit with them tomorrow evening at our little get-together. I know it's hard to be festive with the Duchess still missing, but at least we have hope she's still alive. I did so want to celebrate your homecoming. And who knows, maybe God will see that she's here to join us. If so, I just pray she recognizes you."

Stuart smiled. "I can't think of anything more wonderful. When you called to tell me about the kidnapping, the prison had never felt so confining. I could do nothing but pray."

Colin winced. "I know the feeling. I keep thinking there must be something I can do."

Stuart gazed at his son for several minutes, so long that Colin wanted to squirm like a child under scrutiny for a misdeed.

"Is everything okay, Dad?"

Stuart's smile deepened. "Yes, Son. I just can't get over what a fine young man you are. And how you've accepted responsibility for Aunt Beatrice's care..."

"Which I should have done several years ago." Colin lowered his lashes. "Perhaps I could have helped Uncle Max with his problems too."

Stuart shook his head. "You had to get an education and learn the advertising business. Had you not done so, how else could you have stepped in and filled your stepfather's place in the agency. Son, no one can fault you for that. You've been wonderful to me—faithful to visit me in prison, to make sure I had everything I needed and..." Stuart's voice grew husky. "And so much more it's hard to find the words to adequately thank you. I couldn't have asked for a better son. It's too bad your grandfather didn't live to see the man of integrity you've become."

Colin forced words past the lump in his throat. "Thank you, Dad. You've always been there for me, if not in person, in your spirit and in your prayers. I've always known it, even when I was much younger. It was as though you were at my side guiding my steps at every turn in my life. I love you, Dad, more than you'll ever know."

"I love you too, Colin, and so proud of you." A look of sadness shrouded his expression. "Always remember that, Son. That is the only bequest I have to leave you." Stuart held out his empty glass and smiled as if to rid the room of the melancholy that had drifted into their conversation. "Mrs. Frakes still makes the best peach tea this side of heaven."

Caught up in his thoughts while they drank their tea, Colin failed to notice his father had fallen asleep. Hearing a snore, he glanced toward Stuart, his eyes narrowing with concern. Had their trek about the estate been too taxing for his father? Should he cancel the plans he'd made for the next evening? Not yet, Colin thought. Best to wait and see how his father fared tomorrow.

A few minutes later, Colin held his finger to his lips to silence his mother when she stepped into the room. Easing from his chair, he tiptoed from the sunroom, taking his mother's arm to guide her toward the office. They could talk there.

"How is Grandmother?" Colin asked, spreading the *Tulsa World* across his desk. "Has she decided to go with you when you return to St. Louis?"

"Yes, even though it took a while to convince her. I think the persuading factor was the thought that she might not see Mary again."

"Good … Mother, I'm glad you decided to help Grandmother. I hope she remains near us so we can see to her needs."

Eileen nodded. "I agree, although it might be stressful at first. We haven't had a relationship for many years."

"Give it time along with some prayer. Love responds to love in most cases."

"I hope you don't mind that I invited her to Briarwood tomorrow night. She always liked your father. I told her I'd pick her up late tomorrow afternoon."

"Not at all. However, I think it best if we don't ask anyone else to the party. Have you noticed how thin Dad is? Earlier, watching him sleep, the thought struck me he hasn't many days left. But, thank God, he won't die in prison. I hope the murderer is found before I lose Dad. He deserves to know whose cell he occupied all these years."

Her glance fell on the newspaper. "Be sure to read Jack Granger's account of your father's release."

"Okay. Mrs. Frakes told me about it at breakfast. You know Dad's victory is closure for Jack. He was one of the reporters covering Dad's original trial and has believed in his innocence."

"I see." Eileen smiled. "And how does Ms. Lonetree fit in all this? I heard you on the phone with her when I came downstairs."

Colin eyed the impish look in his mother's eyes. "Miss Lonetree said the editor in chief was all smiles when he came to work this morning, which means…Jack will probably receive a promotion and a raise in pay."

"You seem to care a great deal for your new friends."

Oh, no, Mother, we're not going there. The anger he often felt toward his mother rekindled. With God's help he'd been able, since her arrival at Briarwood, to curb his reaction to her interfering ways. Pushing the feeling aside, he met her gaze, his lips curving into a knowing smile.

"Ms. Lonetree and Jack are great people. Their help and support for my mission in Haven have meant a lot to me. I hope we'll be friends for years to come."

Before Eileen could respond, the sound of Colin's phone startled them both. A movement from the doorway caught his eye as he put the phone to his ear. He motioned his father into the room, his alertness sharpening at the urgent tone in Sheriff Kinney's greeting.

"Mornin,' Mr. Lambert. Wanted to let you know Clay and I are on our way to Bartlesville. We know where Miss Lambert is being held. Thought you might want to meet us at the police station there."

Colin's shoulders caved in, his sigh of relief crashing into the phone. "Is she okay? When, how did you learn of her location?"

"Feel pretty sure she's alive and in good care. Just get on the road, son. I'll share the details when I see you."

Colin stared at the silent phone before he slipped it into his shirt pocket. Mrs. Frakes entered the office. She bowed. "Lunch is ready to be served, Mr. Stuart," she said bewilderment overtaking her expression as she glanced at their faces.

"Sorry, Mrs. Frakes, we'll have to put lunch on hold. The Duchess has been found. I have to leave for Bartlesville right away."

When Mrs. Frakes swayed, Eileen reached out to steady the housekeeper. Colin moved to her side answering the question in her eyes. "Mrs. Frakes, the sheriff didn't give much information about the discovery, but did think the Duchess was okay. Sorry, I have to leave now. I'll phone when I can."

"I'll go with you, Son," Stuart said, following Colin out the door.

Colin turned to observe his father's features. "Are you sure you're up to it, Dad? I don't know what we'll find when we get there."

"No time to think about that. Let's get going." Stuart looked back at Eileen and then rested his gaze on the housekeeper, frowning at her pale complexion. "Do you mind staying with Mrs. Frakes? I think she could use the company right now."

Eileen glanced at the housekeeper and then took her arm. "Mrs. Frakes, come sit beside me on the sofa. We can say a prayer together. Can I get you something?"

Less than a half hour later, Colin and Stuart entered the police station. Sheriff Kinney introduced the Bartlesville police detective, Captain Russell Nash, who stood next to Deputy Clay Walsh just inside the entryway. "You're just in time. Officers with search warrant in hand have already been dispersed to the home of Natalie James, where we believe Miss Lambert is a hostage. We're on our way there now."

Colin looked aghast. "The James brothers' older sister?"

The sheriff nodded, glancing at Clay. "Yeah, a shock to us too."

"Shall we proceed?" the captain asked, moving forward to usher them out the glass door. "The woman's condo is just a short distance from here."

Once the five of them entered the condo, the city officer's were already inside, Miss James seated on her living room sofa, sobbing into her hands. She looked up at their entrance into the room, speaking to Sheriff Kinney whom she seemed to recognize. "I'm so sorry. They threatened to kill Miss Beatrice if I didn't keep her here. And I just couldn't let that happen. She's such a dear person. I've known her since she became Dr. Wexley's patient."

Stuart stepped forward. "Then she's alive. Is she well? And, who is the *they* you spoke of earlier?" he said, his eyes filled with scorn.

The detective placed his hand on Stuart's shoulder. "Sir, we'll handle the questioning. Why don't you and your son follow this officer"—Nash pointed to a policeman across the room—"down the hall to the bedroom, where Miss Lambert is being examined by a physician at this moment. He can better relay her condition."

Stuart and Colin didn't hesitate. A moment later they stood at the foot of a bed in a roomy, well-lit, well-kept bedroom, the doctor just finishing his examination. Colin breathed easier when he saw that she was awake and aware they were near her. But would she know them? Stuart sat down on the edge of one side of the bed while Colin claimed a similar position opposite his father.

"Hello, Mother," Stuart said, picking up Beatrice's hand and holding it against his cheek.

Colin glanced at Stuart, his eyes widening, his mouth gaped in surprise. Had he heard correctly? Did his father just call the Duchess, Mother?

Stuart glanced at Colin. "That's right, Son. She's my mother. I'll explain later," he said quickly as they both set their gaze on Beatrice when a sound escaped from her throat. They watched as recognition filled her eyes.

Lifting her other arm, she extended it toward Stuart. He clasped both her hands in his, scrutinizing her long knobby fingers before he enclosed them in his palms. "Are you okay, Mother?"

"Oh, Stuart, is it really you? Or is it that we are both in heaven?" she said her voice raspy. She glanced over at Colin. "Both my babies with me again." She sighed, a faint smile appearing on her face. "At least a part of heaven, that's for sure. How did you find me?"

"Sheriff Kinney gets the credit for that. He hasn't had time to give us the details, but the important thing is you are safe," Colin said, kissing her on the cheek.

The doctor stepped forward as the sound of an ambulance beckoned their attention. "You can visit with Miss Lambert later at the hospital. Dr. Wexley wants to run some tests on her to make sure she's physically sound. I notified him that she'd been located a few minutes ago. He's on his way to Jane Phillips Medical Center now."

"By all means," Stuart said, nodding. Two paramedics entered the room. "Son, why don't we step outside and give these gentlemen space to work?" He gave Beatrice a hug and kiss. "We'll see you shortly, Mother. Don't worry. You're in good hands now."

"I believe I have been all along. Miss James is an excellent nurse. And God is always with me."

When Colin and his father returned to the living room, they were surprised to see Julie and Jack quickly taking notes as they listened to the conversation between Miss James and Detective Nash. Colin left Stuart's side momentarily to greet his friends.

At the questioning look in Colin's eyes, Julie grinned. "It helps to have a brother on the inside track," she whispered in Colin's ear.

Returning her smile and nodding, he turned his attention to Jack, gripping his outstretched hand. Stuart, nodding a greeting as he moved to their side, the four focused on the captain's interaction with Miss James. Reading her the Miranda rights, he helped her from the sofa, an officer nearby pulling a set of handcuffs from his belt. His intent to take her to the waiting patrol car was interrupted as the medics entered the foyer carefully toting the gurney on which Beatrice lay. Colin left his friends to escort the Duchess to the ambulance, his father at his heels. Assisted by the policeman guarding the front exit of the condo, Beatrice was soon ready for transport.

"Colin, please follow in the car. I'm riding with Mother," Stuart said, climbing into the back of the vehicle.

"Sure thing, Dad. I'll meet you at the hospital." As he stared after the ambulance, Colin recalled some of the Duchess's puzzling actions and words since his arrival at Briarwood. What he'd believed to be Alzheimer's, now seemed to be hidden truth revealed. He shook his head. He hoped his father would soon clear the remaining confusion.

Looking back at the entrance to the condo, he watched the exit of the policemen and Miss James, Jack, and Julie bringing up the rear. Colin paused beside his car, waiting to speak with his friends. They watched as an officer placed a crime seal on the outside of the door.

Julie gave Colin a friendly hug. "I'm so glad your aunt is safe. What did the doctor say about her condition?"

Colin, noting the pen she held poised above the pad in her other hand, grinned. "Off the record or on it?"

Julie laughed. "Both, if you don't mind."

He smiled and then grew serious. "The doctor didn't elaborate. Just said Dr. Wexley would meet them at the hospital and run some tests. However, she seemed pretty much okay considering her health issues, even recognizing both Dad and me." Colin held out his hand to Jack for a handshake. "Sorry to rush off like this, but I need to get to the hospital. Dad seems to be handling everything well, but I'm concerned about him."

Jack nodded. "We understand. We'll catch up tomorrow night." He paused. "I assume the celebration is still as planned."

"I'll let you know if we have to postpone it."

· · · · ·

On the drive to the hospital, Colin phoned Eileen to apprise her of the situation, asking his mother to reassure Mrs. Frakes that her mistress was doing well. "Also, I don't know when Dad and I will be home. Depends on the results of the tests. Yes, I'll phone you just as soon as we hear." Shortly thereafter, Colin found his father seated in the emergency waiting room.

"No word yet," he said at Colin's questioning look. "The nurse said she'd let us know when the tests are finished and Mother has been placed in a room."

Stuart frowned. "Why are you staring at me like that, Son?"

"Sorry Dad. It's a little unnerving to hear you refer to the Duchess as Mother. Would you mind explaining all that?" All of a sudden Colin grew still, his eyes widening. "The Duchess isn't my great-aunt... she's my grandmother."

Stuart smiled. "That she is, Son; that she is."

Colin's eyes filled with anger. "Why was I not allowed this information as a child?"

"Would it have made any difference in your love for her?"

Colin calmed his soul. "No. But didn't I have the right to know she's my grandmother?"

"Probably. But your grandfather insisted his world know otherwise."

"What do you mean?"

Stuart propped his elbow on the arm of the chair, resting his chin in his hand. "I suppose I should start at the beginning," he said, his brow knitted in concentration.

"As good a place as any," Colin quipped, a grin tugging at the corners of his mouth.

Stuart settled deeper into the chair. "The knowledge came to me by accident one afternoon. I was on my way to pick up your mother for a date, realizing a few miles down the road I had forgotten my wallet.

"Returning to Briarwood, I'd reached the landing near Mother's suite when I heard my name mentioned. Pausing outside the door to listen, I overheard her tell Mrs. Frakes how proud my father would have been of me. Curious at the statement, since your grandfather, who I believed was my father at the time, had, not a half hour past, given me the riot act about dating Eileen. Entering Mother's suite, I told her what I'd overheard and asked for an explanation, your grandmother informing me I needed to discuss the matter with Father. Which I did without delay." Stuart grinned. "I forgot my date with Eileen that night, and she didn't speak to me for several days."

"Obviously Grandfather was cooperative, since you're aware of it now."

"Not at first, but he gave in once he realized I wouldn't be put off."

Colin thought back to the day he'd arrived at Briarwood and had stood admiring the family portraits on the wall above the front staircase. "So...were you adopted by the Duchess and Grandfather?"

"By Braxton, but not Mother. I was born to her in Naples while she was on an extended trip abroad with Braxton's wife, my deceased mother." Stuart lifted his shoulders. "Or so I'd been told. As the story goes, your grandfather had forbidden Mother to marry the man she loved, Ethan Tritt, a wildcatter for Lambert Oil. By the time she discovered she was pregnant with his child, he'd been killed in an accident at Lambert Field. Of course, Mother had to tell Braxton. Still in mourning for her

314 VICTORIA BURKS

fiancé, Dad suggested she travel to Europe with Erin, his wife, who was also pregnant with their first child, her due date a few weeks prior to my expected arrival.

"But, as you know, tragedy struck Erin before they could return home. She contacted a fatal virus in Italy and died, the child along with her. It was then that your grandfather decided to adopt his coming niece or nephew as his child incognito to save his sister's reputation. He told everyone I had been born premature and was in a Naples hospital, Mother staying in Europe with me until I was strong enough to travel to Oklahoma, his tale even more convincing when I came out of the womb just under five pounds, although a full term pregnancy."

"Did anyone else in the family know about this?"

"No one except Mrs. Frakes, Mother's friend and confidante."

"Dad, you've had plenty of opportunity to tell me about this. Why didn't you?"

"Well, Son, the Bible instructs us to honor our parents. Each of them had asked me not to tell you. They felt it might discredit them in your sight. Father loved you a great deal as does Mother."

"Yes. I don't doubt that for a second."

"Due to my earlier concern over Mother, I forgot to call her Aunt Beatrice in your presence. To be honest, I'm glad, for your sake, it's out in the open. You were right. You deserve to know that someone you've adored since babyhood is your grandmother." A nurse entered the waiting room and smiled at Stuart.

"I can take you to your mother now, Mr. Lambert. She's all settled and looking forward to your visit."

"Thank you, ma'am. Did Dr. Wexley say when he'd have the results of the tests?"

"He's with Miss Lambert now. I'm sure he'll discuss that with you. Now, just follow me."

A few moments later, they entered Beatrice's hospital room, Dr. Wexley standing at the foot of her bed making notations in her chart.

Noticing that the doctor had finished penciling in his instructions, Colin left Beatrice's side to speak to Dr. Wexley in the hallway outside the room. "Doctor, when will you know the results of the tests?"

"Early this evening or in the morning. But looking at the readings of her vital signs, I'd say she's doing good considering her heart condition. Miss James did an excellent job caring for her."

Colin took a deep breath. "That's wonderful news. When do you think she can come home?"

"Not for a couple of days at least. I don't want to rush things. Let's see how she responds to treatment and talk about it again on Monday when I make my rounds."

Colin nodded. "I'll pass the word along to Dad." Colin glanced up to see Sheriff Kinney, Detective Nash, and another gentleman strolling toward them.

The sheriff nodded a greeting. "Afternoon, Mr. Lambert, Doctor. Colin, you've met Detective Nash." Sheriff Kinney turned to the other man accompanying him. "And this is Agent Donaldson from the OSBI. Donaldson, meet Colin Lambert and Dr. Wexley, Miss Lambert's physician." The men shook hands. The sheriff continued, "We would like to have a word with your patient." At Dr. Wexley's frown, Sheriff Kinney held up his hand. "No more than five minutes. We just need to clarify if she remembers who brought her to Miss James's home, also Girard's visit to the condo. According to Miss James, he came to her home intending to extort money from Miss Lambert. However, she seemed incoherent of him and his purpose. Miss James said he left the condo seething, warning her to contact him when she appeared rational."

VICTORIA BURKS

Stroking his chin, Dr. Wexley glanced away momentarily then centered his gaze on the officers. "She's awake now, but no more than five minutes. His expression hardened. "I mean it. We don't want to put any more strain on her heart than necessary."

"Understood. We'll be as easy with our questioning as possible," Detective Nash said, moving to enter the room, Colin and the other officers following suit.

• • • • •

The next morning Colin, having slept in after a long night at the hospital, awakened at the sound of his cell phone. He noted the time, frowning. It was almost noon. He grabbed the phone from the nightstand.

"Good morning, Sheriff."

"Thought you might be interested in the fact we have a singing canary at the jail."

Colin blinked the sleep from his eyes. "Excuse me?"

"I told you yesterday, I'd get back with about the details of our locating your aunt. It's just as I predicted. Our young jailbird, Samuel James, couldn't chirp a tune fast enough when his attorney informed him his arraignment had been set for tomorrow and he would be bound over for trial since he had no money or means for bail. Samuel asked to see me right away, stating he wanted to sign a confession. The young man spared no details about the kidnapping, hoping that by turning states evidence against Keith and Rudy, it would gain him a reduced sentence for aiding and abetting the kidnapping and possibly a suspended one for the rustling.

"I have to give you credit, Mr. Lambert. You've been right all along about Girard. Samuel stated the lawyer was the instigator of Miss Lambert's kidnapping and each attempt against you to steer you away from Haven."

"And how does Miss James figure in all this?"

"According to Detective Nash, she was romantically involved with the lawyer for several months, breaking off the relationship when she discovered a violent streak in him. A few days ago, he dropped by her house unexpectedly, threatening her with physical harm and your aunt's murder, if she didn't allow him to use her home to hide Miss Lambert."

"Such a man of integrity, this notable attorney," Colin said with disgust in his tone. "Fear tactics seem to be his calling cards. Any news on his location?"

"No. No word yet."

Colin stood from his sitting position on the bed and walked toward the bathroom. "That creep needs to be put away for a long time."

"I agree. I'll be in touch and soon, I hope."

Turning the knob to start the water for his shower, Colin contemplated his daily conversations with the sheriff. To some of his colleagues back home, he might seem nothing more than an Oklahoma redneck, but the man knew his job, Colin surmised, and if he handled other cases as he'd dealt with this one, the people of Osage County would be doing themselves a great injustice should they not re-elect him at the end of his term.

Once dressed, Colin took a peek at the date on his Blackberry, disillusionment forming in his mind. He'd had such high expectations when he'd arrived on Oklahoma soil. Had too many years passed? Evidence grown too stale—the answers he'd desired from age twelve never to unfold? Had the killer won against truth after all?

· · · · ·

Late Saturday afternoon, Colin returned home from spending several hours at his grandmother Lambert's bedside to find Eileen, his grandmother Kirby, and Mrs. Frakes hard at work preparing hors d'oeuvres for the small get-together that evening in honor of Stuart's release from prison. Once he'd given them the update on Beatrice's promising progress, he glanced at his watch, realizing it was just short of an hour before the festivity would begin. Giving each of the women a quick kiss on their cheeks, he dashed up the back stairs for a quick change before the arrival of his guests.

Later, seated on the porch in the wicker lounge, enjoying the feel of an unexpected cool breeze from the south, he watched the approach of two cars, recognizing the vehicles as soon as they left the ridge road to head into the valley. A few minutes later, he stood to welcome the Grangers, Julie, their passenger, and the Bakers. Colin smiled. It would be interesting to see Alfie's reaction at the sight of his dad. As though on cue, Stuart stepped onto the porch from the foyer to greet their guests alongside his son.

The Bakers were the first to emerge from their car. Colin moved forward to shake their hands and then frowned. "Is Alfie ill? I so wanted him to see Dad."

"I'm sorry, Mr. Lambert," said Mrs. Baker. "I considered bringing him along but decided against it, my sister agreeing to stay with him this evening. After seeing Mr. Girard the other day, Alfie has started having nightmares again, and I was concerned the sight of Mr. Stuart might make them worse. We tried with his doctor's help to get the information of what he saw the day your grandfather died, but to no avail." She placed her hand on Colin's arm when she glimpsed the stricken look on his face. "It's not your fault. I'm sorry we disappointed you this evening."

"No, no. It's quite all right. You know what's best for Alfie." Colin smiled. "Please don't worry about it."

Stuart moved forward to shake the Baker's hands. "Please come in. Welcome to my home."

Colin blinked to stay the moisture gathering in his eyes. His father's pride and love for Briarwood had never ceased to exist. *Thank you, God, for allowing Dad to spend his last days here.*

Colin turned to greet Julie, Jack, and his wife, Michele. "Welcome to Briarwood, Mrs. Granger. Come right in. The rest of the family is on the patio looking forward to everyone's arrival."

Colin guided his friends through the house and out the back door, encouraging them to partake of the attractive array of appetizers, pointing out the other table topped with assorted summer drinks stationed nearby. Soon, after greetings all around, they took his advice and were enjoying both the fare and pleasant conversation.

Colin felt a tug of sadness as he glanced about the gathering, the absence of the Duchess on his mind. Her presence would have made the event complete. But at least she was safe. Soon she'd be in Mrs. Frakes's loving care. He smiled within, unable to decide which of the two would be the most joyful at Beatrice's homecoming.

He turned to Julie seated in the lawn chair next to his. "I'm sorry Julie. I was thinking about the Duchess. Did you say something?"

Julie's eyes filled with compassion. "She'll be home soon, Colin."

"Yes, the first of the week, if all goes well." He smiled, taking in Julie's loveliness. "You look fantastic tonight. That shade of blue was made for you. Now what were you saying?"

Julie's cheeks heightened with color. "Thank you. I-I started to tell you that I am now an official rookie reporter. After Jack told our editor in chief about my help on your father's story, he called me in to his office yesterday to ask if I'd be interested in becoming Jack's assistant, pay raise and additional benefits included."

Colin grinned. "I suppose you told him you'd think about it."

Julie laughed. "Yeah. For about two seconds."

Colin's insides grew weak at the sound of her deep chuckle. He would love to spend the rest of his life making her laugh. "That's great, Julie. The career you've wanted all along."

"Yes. I feel like my degree in journalism is starting to pay for itself." She smiled. "Maybe now I won't groan as loud every month when my college loan payment comes due."

Colin laughed. "I know that feeling."

He glanced up to see Jack strolling toward them from the other side of the patio where he'd been in conversation with Stuart. "Colin, your father is remarkable. All those years in prison and not an ounce of anger spoken against society for their mistake against him … I'm not sure I could be so forgiving."

Colin nodded. "But he learned the art of forgiveness from the greatest teacher who ever lived, as we all should."

Jack grew more attentive. "Oh? And who might that be?"

"Jesus Christ, of course. He had no trouble forgiving those who hung him on a cross to die, his only crime loving us enough to give his life so that we might live eternally with him."

Jack nodded slowly. "My folks were good moral people, but they never took us kids to church. Each summer, though, one of our neighbors would conduct a back yard vacation Bible school. The teacher would tell stories about Christ's death and resurrection, illustrating with pictures, citing the rewards for those who accept his gift of salvation. But when I became an adult I never considered such matters. Other things were too important to me."

Inside his heart Colin prayed for wisdom. "Are you saying you've had recent thoughts about God, maybe … what it would be like for you if He had a major part in your life?"

Jack nodded. "Yes, I suppose I have, especially since meeting you. My wife suggested not long ago the possibility of our attending a church on Sundays, but we haven't done so." He glanced toward the sky. "Maybe her thoughts of late have been similar to mine."

"A good Bible-based church is an asset to one's life." Colin grinned. "As the saying goes, 'Try it, you might like it.'"

Jack smiled. "You know, we might do just that."

Julie leaned forward. "Why not visit my church. I think you'd be pleased—the people friendly, good teachers of God's Word and a great youth group, Cassie, your daughter, might like. I've been going there a few weeks now and enjoy every part of the services."

"I'll talk to Michele about it and get back with you."

"Anytime."

Darkness closing in on them, the guests helped move the party inside to the spacious den where Colin and Stuart shared several humorous tidbits about their growing up years at Briarwood.

After a while, the hour growing late, the Bakers took a few minutes to thank Colin and Stuart for the enjoyable evening, offering to escort Mrs. Kirby home when she expressed her desire to call it a night as well. Colin excused himself from his other guests to see his grandmother and the Bakers to the door.

Returning to the den, Colin took in the occupants of the room, the Grangers and Julie preparing to take their leave. She crossed the room to speak to Colin.

"Thanks, Colin, for the great time tonight."

"And thanks to you for accepting my invitation. I know Dad appreciated your kindness."

"Your father is a special man." She grinned. "But I suppose I don't have to tell you that."

Colin threw a glance toward Stuart. "Very special, indeed," he said, taking her hand in his. "Would you like to go to dinner, say on Tuesday night? I've missed you."

She smiled. "That would be great. Pick me up about six thirty?"

"Six thirty it is."

Upon his return to the den after biding his friends good-bye, Colin helped himself to a second slice of strawberry pie. About to take his first bite, the sound of the doorbell drew everyone's attention, the ladies pausing in their task of clearing the room so Mrs. Frakes could answer the door.

Colin glanced at his father. "Someone must have forgotten something."

A commotion in the hallway drew their attention. Eileen moved close to Colin's side. Stuart and his son about to check out the disturbance, a familiar face and voice stopped them cold.

CHAPTER 21

"Good evening," Nicholas Girard said from the doorway, his hand gripping Mrs. Frakes's arm. "A perfect evening for a party, so I thought I'd join you. I hope you don't mind. I'm sorry I arrived too late to meet your other guests." He shoved the housekeeper forward, the unexpected thrust causing her to fall to the floor.

Seething, Colin helped Mrs. Frakes to her feet, all the time eyeing the gun in Girard's other hand. He thought of his own handgun lying in the drawer of his nightstand. A lot of good the weapon would do him now. But he did have something that would aid the sheriff once the lawyer was caught and arrested.

Mrs. Frakes's body shielding his actions, Colin reached inside his shirt pocket and pushed the record button on his Dictaphone. Stepping sideways, he glared at Girard. "What do you want? You're not welcome here."

The attorney weaved slightly. "I'm on my way out of town, but I need to take care of some unfinished business before I leave."

"I doubt you get far since you're wanted in every state for kidnapping my aunt among other things."

The evil glint in Girard's eyes heightened. "So I heard." He turned to Stuart, the hatred in his eyes almost tangible. "I hoped you would rot in prison. Then when I discovered you had incurable cancer, it seemed like ice cream topping on a cake, so to speak, my taste of revenge sweeter."

Sadness filled Stuart's eyes. "I'm sorry you hate me so much, Nicholas. We were good friends once."

Girard seemed deaf to Stuart's words. "You had it all—money, prestige, respect, college education free and clear, a substantial inheritance waiting in the wings, any girl you wanted, everything a man could desire. You didn't have to work for anything or grovel at anyone's feet to better yourself or gain notoriety. You were a Lambert."

Holding his gun higher, he moved close to Stuart and spit in his face. Colin started toward Girard, but the man waved his gun in Colin's face. "Stay where you are, boy." Again he spoke to Stuart. "But you stole the only thing that had ever mattered to me." Girard turned his gaze toward Eileen and then back to Stuart. "For years, I fantasized about how I could get even with you. And when you were sent to prison, my only disappointment was you'd received life without parole, not execution. But here you are, a free man"—he turned to Colin—"thanks to your intrusive son. You just couldn't leave it alone, could you?"

Anger flared in Colin like a locomotive speeding down a mountain without brakes. "Nor will I stop searching until the proof that you killed my grandfather and framed Dad is in the palm of my hand."

A mirthless laugh spilled from the lawyer's lips. "That won't ever happen, Colin, my boy, because I'm not the murderer. You have your dear old uncle Maxwell to thank for that."

Several gasps sounded in the room. Colin moved a few inches forward, his fists clenched at his sides. "You're a liar, Girard. Uncle Max wasn't even on the property at the time of Grandfather's murder."

Girard shook his head. "Not true." His expression took on a faraway look as though in his mind he traveled back in time. "Once in my car that morning after my appointment with Braxton, I remembered a report I'd forgotten to give him. On my return to the office, I heard him shouting through the window he'd opened earlier during our conference. Curious as to who'd fallen from his grace, I paused to listen. A few seconds later, I saw Maxwell shoot Braxton, the silencer on the end of his gun deafening the noise from the gunshot. In Maxwell's rush to leave the office, he never saw me standing outside the window."

Girard again focused his attention on Stuart. Having heard your argument with Braxton when I arrived for my appointment with him, I realized my opportunity to financially secure my future and get my long awaited revenge on you at the same time." Girard set his gaze on Colin's mother. "Isn't that correct, Eileen?"

Stuart faced his ex-wife. "What nonsense is he sputtering?"

Eileen lost all color in her face. She turned away from Stuart's penetrating gaze.

Colin felt sick. He hadn't wanted his father to know about his mother's part in Girard's plan. Before Colin could utter a sound, Stuart spoke. "Nicholas, you're crazy. What possible reason would incite Uncle Max to kill his own brother? I believe after hearing the quarrel between Father and me, you devised a plan to murder him and frame me, using my gun as your weapon."

"Yeah, I used your gun all right, after I made Eileen get it for me. I stopped her before she reached the garage and told her what I planned to do, making sure she knew to remain quiet about it or her son wouldn't reach maturity. If that idiot kid of the Bakers hadn't seen me put on the gloves I found outside the window, fire your gun into the air, and then toss it in the window, no one would have ever known I was still at the estate. And later, discovering you'd been seen standing over Braxton's

326   VICTORIA BURKS

body holding your own gun"—Girard laughed—"I couldn't have planned it better myself. By the way that was my car you heard that morning. As for Maxwell's motive, he never enlightened me. I guess he thought the monthly installments he paid for my silence was payment enough when I voiced my curiosity about his reasons for the murder."

"Eileen was right about you. You're a monster, a murdering monster." Stuart moved forward but stopped when Girard pointed the gun straight at him.

Again, the attorney shook his head. "I'm not a murderer, at least not until now." His eyes took on the look of a madman. "I want you dead, friend...you and your son. I want it more than I've ever wanted anything—even your wife." Before anyone could move, Girard fired the gun toward Stuart, turning the gun on Colin.

"No!" Eileen shouted, stepping in front of her son. Another shot rang out, Eileen collapsing at Colin's feet.

For a moment, Colin couldn't move his face a mirror of shock. He looked at his father lying a few feet away and then at his mother, who'd fallen near his feet. Blood seemed to be everywhere. He felt as if the world around him had suddenly begun to revolve in slow motion. He heard someone yell, "Oh, God, no!" realizing seconds later, the words had come from his own lips. The sound of running feet down the hallway seemed to come from far away. He glanced up to see Sheriff Kinney and Deputy Walsh tackle Girard, pinning him to the floor.

Colin fell to his mother's side, reaching for her hand, his stomach lurching at the smell of her blood. "Mother, Mother, please don't die."

Mrs. Frakes was on the floor beside them within seconds. After checking Eileen's pulse and then her wound, Mrs. Frakes laid her hand on Colin's arm. "She not die, Master Colin, I promise."

He felt another touch, this time on his shoulder. He looked up to see Clay standing over him. "Colin, your father needs you."

Colin crawled to his father's side. He glanced up at the sheriff, who held Stuart's head far enough from the floor for him to see his son. At Colin's silent question, Sheriff Kinney slowly shook his head. Dear God, his father was going to die.

His breathing labored, Stuart reached out to Colin. "Better this way, Son," he gasped. "Take care of your mother." Stuart squeezed Colin's hand with the last of his strength. "I love you," he said as his breath left his body.

Tears streamed down Colin's face. "I love you too, Dad." However, Colin knew his father hadn't heard him. He watched as the sheriff lowered his father to the floor. Standing, Colin took the lap quilt spread across the back of the sofa and covered his father's body, the wail of a siren sounding in his ears.

Noticing that Colin had heard the approach of the ambulance, the sheriff put his arm around Colin's shoulders. "Clay phoned for an ambulance right after we arrested Girard."

Mrs. Frakes motioned to Colin. "Miss Eileen awake and calling for you." He hurried toward his mother and dropped to his knees beside her. "I'm here, Mother."

Eileen looked up at him, her eyes filled with questions. "Your father?"

Colin hung his head as fresh tears sprang to his eyes. "He-he's gone, Mother."

She reached out to touch his cheek. I'm sorry, Son, truly I am."

Colin nodded, unable to respond with words. Medics appeared in the room, Sheriff Kinney directing their movements.

Colin watched the medics place his father's body on a gurney, careful in their movements to keep his face covered. Pain ripped through Colin's heart like the rending of rotten cloth. His father had enjoyed less than three days of freedom—only a few hours to become reacquainted with his family and his beloved Briarwood. *Dear God, how will I ever tell the Duchess her son is dead?* Colin closed his eyes. He couldn't think about that now. His mother needed him. Walking toward the front door behind his mother's stretcher, he noticed two deputies he hadn't seen enter the house guarding their handcuffed prisoner in the living room. It took every ounce of self-control Colin had in him to keep from ripping the smirk from Girard's face.

Within moments he sat on the passenger side of his mother's car, Deputy Walsh maneuvering the sedan out of the driveway to follow the ambulance to the hospital in Bartlesville. Colin had tried to convince the deputy he was capable of driving, but Clay had just smiled, saying, "Sheriff's orders." Too emotionally drained to argue, Colin sat quietly, the numbness in his mind and body a blessing in disguise at the moment.

· · · · ·

A few days later, Colin once again sat in Grace Missionary Church staring at a casket, only this time he sat on the front pew, his mother on his left, his grandmother Kirby and Mrs. Frakes on his right. He wanted to listen to the minister's kind words about his father, but guilt overwhelmed him. How could he face the crowd of mourners that spilled into the foyer and onto the church lawn? How could he look them in the eye accepting their condolences knowing he'd killed his father just as if he'd pulled the trigger himself? *Oh, God, why didn't I listen to Mother? Even Dad thought my goal futile, knowing he would die soon anyway. Was it for his sake that I had to prove him innocent or mine? Had I been ashamed of my father and not realized it? Had that been the force that drove me? God, let it not be so!*

Colin started when the Duchess's name was mentioned from the pulpit, the minister reading the names of the surviving family. At least she wouldn't have to be told of Stuart's death right away. While the bullet was being removed from his mother's arm, he had slipped into the Duchess's hospital room, surprised she was awake at that late hour. He drew near her bedside, his heart heavy with his appointed task of relaying his father's death. However, she had elapsed into a world he could not enter and had remained thus since Dr. Wexley had allowed her to be transported to Briarwood. Thankful she'd been spared the agony for now, he'd kissed her, tiptoeing from the room seconds later.

∙ ∙ ∙ ∙ ∙

An entourage of people flooded Briarwood during the afternoon hours, stopping by the estate to pay their respects. Sheriff Kinney and Deputy Walsh arrived last, waiting until all others had left to speak to Colin alone.

Colin ushered them into his office. While he was sure they needed to ask him some questions about the night his father died, he had some questions he needed answered as well.

"I can't begin to thank you enough, Sheriff, Clay, for all you've done to help my family and me throughout this ordeal." Colin looked away. "There have been moments I wished I'd flown back St. Louis following my uncle's funeral."

The sheriff nodded. "We all have regrets from time to time, Son, but once you weigh the good you've accomplished the past month against all the bad that's happened, I believe you'll see the value of your stay in Haven."

A look of skepticism darted into Colin's eyes. "Food for thought anyway... Say, I'm glad you stopped by. I've been meaning to phone you to ask... How did you know Girard was at Briarwood Saturday night—in that you arrived almost in the nick of time?" Sadness carved a path across his features.

He watched the sheriff wince, Colin immediately sorry for the note of sarcasm that had infiltrated his words. He offered an apology with his eyes.

"We got an anonymous phone call at the office from someone believing they'd seen Girard's car on the county road near Briarwood, and the dispatcher notified me immediately at home. I left the house within minutes, phoning for backup on my way here." The sheriff lowered his head. "I'm so sorry we didn't make it in time."

Colin sighed. "As we all are, Sheriff. But it couldn't be helped." He eyed the sheriff's hesitation. "Was there something else you needed to know about that night?"

"Just a statement of all you remember in the moments before your father was killed, all Girard said, did, etc. I've already got a statement from your mother and Mrs. Frakes."

Colin drew a deep sigh, his face lighting up with recollection a moment later. "I think you'll have all the information you need when you listen to this."

Colin reached into the desk drawer and withdrew the pocket-sized recorder he'd placed there the morning after his father was murdered. He pushed the play button before handing it over to Sheriff Kinney, the sound of Girard's voice echoing in their ears within seconds. At the sound of the recorded gunfire, Colin closed his eyes. Shutting off the machine a few minutes later, he handed the recorder to the sheriff, aware that it would be needed for evidence against Girard. The officers took their leave soon afterwards, offering additional condolences before parting.

· · · · ·

Late that evening, Eileen entered the office with a tray of sandwiches and a cold drink. She sat it down among the papers spread atop the desk. "Colin, you have to eat. I haven't seen you put away more than a few bites of food in the last three days."

"I'm not hungry."

A look of exasperation alternated with a look of helplessness in her eyes. "Son, it's your head and heart telling you that, not your stomach."

He looked up from his perusal of the work in front of him, the first hint of a smile to appear on his face since his father had been murdered. He took in the food on the plate, his gaze lingering as an awareness of hunger overtook him. He set the plate on top of the open file, took one of the sandwiches in hand, savoring every bite until the plate sat empty.

Eileen smiled when he'd finished eating. "You should listen to me more often." She glanced at the paperwork scattered across his desk. "What are you doing anyway?"

"I want more than anything to believe that Girard lied about Uncle Max, but deep inside me something keeps urging me to search for the truth. I have to know if he killed Grandfather." Colin set the dishes aside.

"As many times as Julie, Jack, and I read Dad's case history, we kept feeling we'd missed something. Earlier, I was studying the statements given by Mrs. Frakes and Mr. Baker the day of the murder. Something Uncle Max said to Mr. Baker caught my attention for the first time. I think I've found the elusive clue."

Colin lifted a report from the file. "Mrs. Frakes stated that Uncle Max had his briefcase in his hand when he left for work that morning. However, Mr. Baker's statement reveals Uncle Max reentered the house, indicating to Mr. Baker he'd forgotten his briefcase. Both Mrs. Frakes and Grayson cleaning the north side of the upstairs during that time, Uncle Max could have taken the back stairs to his suite, grabbed his gun, slipped down to the office and killed Grandfather." Colin sat back in his chair and smoothed the back of his hair. "The Duchess thought she overheard Grandfather shout at Girard as she came down the hallway that morning, but if he told the truth, it was Uncle Max. He probably entered Grandfather's office right after Girard left

VICTORIA BURKS

the house, the Duchess and the lawyer hearing the confrontation about the same time, she from the hallway and he outside near the window.

"And when Mrs. Frakes phoned Lambert Oil to tell Uncle Max about Grandfather, Uncle Max hadn't as yet arrived at his office, which meant he had left Briarwood several minutes later than when Mrs. Frakes and Mr. Baker assumed. Rereading the sheriff's notes as to the time everyone returned to Briarwood, Uncle Max entered the house within a few minutes of your return from Bartlesville. According to my estimation, he would have been about ten miles the other side of Bartlesville when he got the call from Mrs. Frakes on his car phone."

Eileen frowned. "You know I do recall thinking something must have delayed Max's departure to Tulsa that morning when he entered the house shortly after me. Paying for my purchases just before I got the page from Mrs. Frakes, I phoned her from the dress shop, leaving for Briarwood within minutes of her phone call.

"I'd seen Max in his car that morning ready to leave for work when I returned from taking you to the bus stop. Later though, upset with Nicholas, I didn't pay any attention as to who might or might not still be at the estate when I left for Bartlesville."

Colin closed the file and picked up the soft-bound book beneath it, handing it to Eileen. "Another clue that indicates Uncle Max could be Grandfather's killer is that journal of letters he wrote to Aunt Agatha after she passed away. Read the one on the page I marked. I thought the major indiscretion he referred to in that letter was a mistress, but now I'm not so sure."

Eileen returned the journal to Colin a few minutes later. "So you think he might be referring to Braxton's murder in his statement of remorse?" She shook her head. "Sorry, I just can't fathom Maxwell Lambert a killer. What on earth would have been the motive for killing his brother?" Eileen shuddered.

"Well, I have a theory about that as well." Colin leaned forward and reopened the file, pulling a document from among the other reports. "This is a typed copy of a recorded phone session Julie had with an ex-employee of Lambert Oil, a young accountant in the firm at the time of the murder."

Eileen read the report and then gave it back to Colin. "I assume you believe Max the top executive, the accountant mentioned."

Colin folded his hands behind his head and leaned back in his chair. "It adds up. And too… according to Girard, he'd been receiving blackmail payments from Uncle Max. That would account for the monthly cash withdrawals from his bank account."

Eileen sighed. "Experiencing Nicholas's cruelty firsthand, his use of blackmail doesn't surprise me one bit. And, I'm sorry to say, at that time in my life, I might have gone along with that scheme. Nicholas always had an angle working for ways to get more money out of the Lamberts. Did you speak to Sheriff Kinney about your findings?"

"Yes, earlier this evening. It's getting late. What say we call it a night? Are you and Grandmother packed, ready to go?"

Eileen nodded. "We plan to leave in the morning, right after breakfast."

"That should put you in St. Louis before dark."

As Eileen turned, she caught a glimpse of Colin's keys. "Do you plan to check out Max's safe deposit box before you go to the airport?"

"Yes. I'll say my good-byes to you and Grandmother and then drive to Bartlesville. My plane doesn't leave until late tomorrow night." Colin opened the door to the office, turning to give his mother a hug, being careful not to touch her wounded arm held by a sling. Colin's eyes filled with remorse. "I'm sorry my stubbornness almost got you killed. I only hope someday you can forgive me."

She lifted her free hand and stroked his cheek. "Colin, there's nothing to forgive. You only wanted to show your father how much you loved him."

He reached to switch off the light, hoping the dim hallway shadowed the tears that threatened his composure. Laboring up the stairs behind his mother, he wondered how long it would be before he could forgive himself.

· · · · ·

Waving a final good-bye to Eileen and Mrs. Kirby the next morning, Colin escorted Mrs. Frakes back inside the house, thankful his mother and grandmother had helped tidy the house before they started on their journey to St. Louis. Eyeing the weariness in the housekeeper's stance, he took hold of her shoulders and turned her to face him. "Mrs. Frakes, as your employer, I order you to take it easy today. All you are to do is see to the Duchess's care."

She smiled. "Like I not do that anyway."

Colin grinned at her attempt to speak youthful lingo. He gave her a hug. "You won't even have to cook for me today. I have to go to Bartlesville and won't be back for lunch. Also, I have dinner plans with Ms. Lonetree before I go to the airport." Seeing her downcast expression, he lifted her chin. "Don't worry. I won't leave Haven without saying good-bye to you and the Duchess."

Less than an hour later, Colin sat in the foyer of Bank of Oklahoma, flipping through a sports magazine, Ms. Williams busy with another customer. Setting aside the magazine, he drummed his fingers on his briefcase that he'd placed on the seat beside him, all the while wondering if his uncle did indeed have a safe deposit box and what it contained. The receptionist directed Colin toward Cara Williams's office.

"Mr. Lambert, I believe," she said, moving a sheaf of papers to one side of her desk. "How can I help you today?"

Colin pulled his keys from one of his trousers' pockets, thumbing through them until he'd singled out the key he'd taken from his uncle's key ring. Removing it from the set of keys, he handed it to Ms. Williams.

"Ma'am, when I was in your office a few weeks ago, it never occurred to me my deceased uncle, Maxwell Lambert, might have a safe deposit box here at the bank. Looking through his keys a few days ago, I found that key. Since it is similar to my mother's key to her box, I realized my uncle may have one also. I have to return to St. Louis this evening, but I wanted to make sure all my uncle's affairs are in order before I leave."

She examined the key. "It certainly looks like one of our keys. But let me check it out for you." She stood from her chair, smiling. "I'll be right back."

True to her word, Ms. Williams soon returned to her office, a gentleman accompanying her. "Mr. Lambert, this is Mr. Stapleton. He will escort you into our safe deposit vault. Please feel free to take as much time as you need. When you're finished, I'll help you close out the rental."

"Thank you."

A few minutes later, Colin sat in a secured room, his fingers trembling slightly as he pulled the lid from the box, his eyes widening at what lay on top of the papers inside the steel container. He closed his eyes, swallowing hard, his glimmer of hope dashed to pieces as he stared at the weapon he felt sure had killed his grandfather, the silencer attached to the barrel, proof that Girard had told the truth. Taking his cell phone from his pocket, he punched in Sheriff Kinney's number.

"Hello, Mr. Lambert. What can I do for you?"

"Sheriff, I'm at the Bank of Oklahoma in Bartlesville and have just opened my Uncle Max's safe deposit box. I think you will find the bullet that killed my grandfather will be a perfect match to the gun I just discovered in this box."

"I guess Girard wasn't lying after all."

"If you'd like to meet me at Briarwood in say an hour, I'll turn this gun over to you."

"I'll see you there."

Checking to make sure the gun cartridge held no bullets, he wrapped his handkerchief around the gun then placed it in his briefcase, turning his attention to the rest of the contents. An envelope with his name scrawled on it caught his eye. Removing it from the box, he slit it open. Unfolding the single sheet, he noticed it was a correspondence addressed to him and written by his uncle a few days before his death according to the date at the top of the letter.

> Colin,
>
> It is with much sorrow and regret that I pen this letter to you. I had hoped I would never have to speak of the most horrible moment of my life—the day I killed my brother. But my conscience requires otherwise. Braxton discovered I had been embezzling money from Lambert Oil and our stockholders and insisted I return the stolen funds or he would prosecute. He was just that way. I'm sorry to say there wasn't much love between us. But to repay what I had taken would bankrupt me. I just couldn't do that to my wife. She'd suffered too many disappointments in me already—the horses, the drinking—and later, following Braxton's death, she just couldn't understand why I drank myself into oblivion every night. I could never tell her why. She would hate me too much.
>
> When your father was arrested for the murder, I truly believed he would be acquitted for the murder. But when the court found him guilty, I couldn't make

myself come forward with the truth. I just couldn't trade Aggie's trust in me for your father's freedom.

All these years I've believed no one would ever forgive me, especially God. But now I know different. His book is the only one I read now. I've come to understand that his definition of the word justification means "just as though it never happened." Having recently asked God to forgive me, I feel I must clear Stuart's name, although the thought of him knowing I killed his father is unbearable to me. Not only did I have to live with what I did, but I became victim to Nicholas Girard's greed—he, witnessing the murder. Yes, my cowardice destroyed me financially and as a man.

Mrs. Frakes told me a few minutes ago about the cancer that would soon take Stuart's life. Since it doesn't matter about me—I'll die soon, I've decided to spare him this additional agony he would endure should he learn I was responsible for his father's death. So it will be up to you to clear his name. I hope you can forgive me someday. I remember how much you loved Braxton and your father.

Your great-uncle,
Maxwell Lambert

Colin returned the letter to the envelope, the victory of his father's exoneration and the discovery of his grandfather's murderer bittersweet at their best. Too caught up in his feelings concerning his discovery, Colin stuffed the other documents into his briefcase to go over them later. He reached for the phone sitting beside him to let Mr. Stapleton know the empty box was ready to be returned to its place in the vault. Completing his business with Ms. Williams within moments, he soon drove toward Briarwood, still unable to comprehend the fact that his uncle could murder his own brother.

Maybe he never would. Colin wondered if Adam and Eve had experienced similar feelings when they discovered their son Cain had slain his brother Abel.

Following the departure of the sheriff from Briarwood later that day, Colin climbed the stairs for a final visit with the Duchess before he had to depart for Tulsa. Easing open the door, he tiptoed to her daybed, noticing once inside the room she appeared to be napping. He sat down in the chair close to her, gazing on her countenance. He was glad she'd never have to know about Max. She'd suffered enough loss in her lifetime.

Since she had arrived home from the hospital, it saddened Colin that she hadn't recognized him or Mrs. Frakes. Contemplating whether he should wake her to tell her good-bye, he decided against it, blowing her a kiss as he stood to leave her in peace. His back to her, he started to open the door when he heard her voice. He turned to see her beckoning him to her side.

"What did you say, Duchess?"

"I said I know about your father—Stuart. I had a dream. He's in heaven. Jesus came to me in the dream and told me. And then I saw your father. He was laughing at something Jesus said. He seemed so happy." Beatrice held up her hand. "Colin, don't mourn too long. Stuart wouldn't want that. Yes, we'll miss him and be sad at times. But don't throw away happiness in your own life for something you never could have changed or understood. Remember, Christ is the Author and Finisher of our faith, never circumstances."

"Duchess, I have to go back to St. Louis tonight, for a while anyway. But I'll be back as soon as I can. Mrs. Frakes and Dr. Wexley will take good care of you. They know I can be reached day or night. I'll phone you often, I promise. Now I must go." Colin took Beatrice in his arms. "Good-bye, Grandmother, we'll talk soon."

"Good-bye, Colin. I love you, dear boy. No grandmother could wish for a better grandson than you. Don't stay away too long please."

· · · · ·

Sitting at the airport with Julie just before he had to go through security, he turned and apologized to his friend. "I'm sorry, Julie. I was rotten company tonight."

She laid her hand on his arm. "That's understandable, considering what you discovered last night and today. Clay phoned me this afternoon and told me that the gun was registered to your uncle. He said he'd let us know when OSBI sends the sheriff the report on the gun and the bullet. But he feels sure the report will show the bullet was fired from that gun."

Colin glanced at his watch. "Looks like I'd better get to my gate." He stood, pulling Julie to her feet. They walked a short distance away for a more private good-bye. Not caring whether she protested or not, Colin drew her into his arms, kissing her thoroughly. Startled that she'd responded in kind, he pulled back, his eyes full of questions. "I'll miss you, Julie. I wish I didn't have to leave, but I need to help Mother settle my grandmother and start managing the agency. I've been away long enough. Perhaps we could see each other every few weekends."

She put her fingers to his lips. "Colin, you have a lot of things to work through in your mind right now. To be honest, we both need to establish our faith in Christ before we pursue a relationship with each other outside friendship. Personally, I need a lot of healing from the past before I'm ready for another romance. I know we each desire God's best for our lives. Maybe we should do as the Bible suggests—allow perseverance to work in us so we can be mature and complete not lacking anything in our lives and then see what happens." Julie stood on her tiptoes to kiss him lightly. "When you decide the time is right for you to return to Oklahoma, I'll be waiting."

Colin pulled her to him for another kiss, reluctantly letting her go a moment later, keeping her in sight until he cleared security, at last lifting his arm for a final wave. She was right. It was too soon for a romantic relationship between them. But in the deepest part of his soul, he knew in time their friendship would grow into a lasting relationship of trust and love in and for one another.

EPILOGUE

Colin stared at his father's gravestone, the caption above his name that read, *All Is Forgiven*, holding him spellbound. It had been a year and one month, almost to the day since his father had been murdered by Nicholas Girard. His guilty plea at the arraignment without a sign of remorse had been grueling for Colin to bear as he'd sat in the courtroom that day. Within a few months, the ex-attorney had been convicted and sentenced to death, the man now on death row at McAlester State Prison. His nephew, Keith, and the James boys were now serving back-to-back sentences for kidnapping and a string of other crimes. Colin was glad to learn Natalie James had received a suspended sentence since Girard had coerced her into hiding the Duchess.

Colin recalled how hard it had been in the weeks after his father's death. He had busied himself at work, in the evenings helping his grandmother Kirby adjust to her new home with her daughter, Eileen, and the ongoing reunion with his aunt Mary and her family. But he hadn't been able to shake the despondency and self-loathing that had flooded his mind when his father had been killed and his mother wounded in the attempt to protect her son. Only after he had sought counsel from the pastor of the church he now attended with his mother and grandmother and had poured God's Word into his heart and soul had he been able to overcome his depression and shame. And now, eyeing his father's statement to the court the day he was released from prison, Colin realized his victory had become reality when he had chosen to follow the same path—all is forgiven.

It hadn't been easy. It had taken months before he felt he could walk the road of forgiveness. He'd read in *The Art of Forgiving* by Lewis B. Smedes, "Forgiving is a journey; the deeper the wound, the longer the journey."

He'd had to deal with his bitterness against his mother, acknowledging finally he'd never forgiven her for uprooting him from his home, nor her lack of love for his father. Also, the weight of anger and hurt he'd carried from childhood for the injustice against his dad, Colin had at last cast the burden into the hands of his Savior.

The integrity of his family bashed and bruised, he'd had to face his sin of false pride, coming to grips with the fact that all have sinned and come short of the glory of God no matter their station in life, even a Lambert. It had been simple to forgive Uncle Max for the loss of Lambert Oil, grief for his wife's illness and death the excuse, but to tarnish the Lambert name with the murder of his own brother—that mountain had been rocky and steep. But God had forgiven Uncle Max, and so must his nephew.

The crowning moment had come when he'd read 1 Corinthians 14:5, the scripture verse declaring that love "keeps no record of wrongs." It had taken a while, he recalled, to apprehend the fact that true forgiveness releases the person responsible for the wrong from their accountability to make the matter right. Returning to Oklahoma for Girard's sentencing, Colin had gone to the Osage County Jail to pay a visit to the ex-attorney. When Girard had refused to see him, Colin had sent a message to the prisoner, stating that all was forgiven. Colin had sensed that Jesus and his father had stood side by side nodding their approval for his actions by the overwhelming peace he'd experienced upon leaving the sheriff's office that day.

The most difficult climb had been self-forgiveness, but as he'd begin the trek one step at a time, God had taken over at the point of impossibility for Colin and carried him to the top of the cliff, setting his feet on the solid rock of his Word. Romans 8:1–2 had been his release from his guilt of self-incrimination—"Therefore, there is no condemnation for those who are in Christ Jesus, because through Christ Jesus the law of the Spirit of life set me free from the law of sin and death."

Colin glanced over at the freshly covered grave next to his father's, the dozens of wreaths mounding the sight still looking fresh in spite of the late August temperatures. It had been difficult to say good-bye to the Duchess at her funeral the previous day, but he knew it was what she'd desired the past year, the vision she'd seen of Stuart in heaven her main topic of conversation in her lucid moments.

Reverend Smith had related when he'd stopped by Briarwood the morning of her peaceful passing that once a person who's lived a full life on earth and is shown a true glimpse of heaven, he or she is never satisfied with his earthly existence again but yearns for his eternal reward. Colin smiled. But at least he'd been able to give her one last gift—Briarwood magnificence as she'd known it in its former days.

On his flight home to St. Louis a few days following his father's funeral, Colin remembered the contents of his uncle's safe deposit box he'd stuffed into his briefcase. Devastated by the discovery of the gun and his uncle's written confession stating he'd killed his brother, Colin hadn't wanted to explore the rest of the items.

Taking his briefcase from the overhead compartment, Colin had opened the case, removing the two thick brown envelopes inside. The first one contained his uncle's missing checkbook and reduced photocopies of his bank statements for almost twenty-five years. Nicholas Girard's name and a date had been written beside each monthly cash withdrawal, the notation representing, Colin believed, the days on which Girard had received the blackmail payments. The next day, Colin had mailed the items to Sheriff Kinney to be used as evidence in Girard's trial. When the sheriff had received them, he'd phoned Colin to thank him, stating that the attorney had confessed that Keith had been the intruder that had vandalized the office the night of Colin's arrival at Briarwood. Girard had sent him there to search for any record uncle Max might have kept regarding the blackmail transactions.

Colin drew a long sigh, exhaling slowly. He still could hardly believe a person could harbor that much hate toward his father, especially someone he'd considered his best friend in youth and young adulthood. But somewhere along Girard's journey in life jealousy and insatiable greed had captured his heart.

However, Colin had been taken aback for several minutes when he'd opened the other envelope. Once his shock had abated, he'd had difficulty restraining his anger. Extracting the folder from its wrapper a few minutes prior, he'd discovered a prospectus for thousands of shares of stock in S&P 500 A-rated companies, the dividends paid quarterly from a brokerage firm in New York City, Stuart Lambert, owner of said shares.

Realizing the name of the brokerage firm had been the one listed each quarter on his uncle's bank statements, Colin had been infuriated, aware that his uncle as Stuart's power of attorney, had stolen his father's dividends to pay for blackmail, telling Stuart his inheritance from Braxton had been lost in high risk stock trading.

Colin shook his head. Someone once stated to him that "greed has no conscience," Maxwell Lambert's and Nicholas Girard's criminal deeds proof of the fact.

The only bright spot in that moment inside the plane had been the discovery of Stuart's last will and testament inside the folder, the document dated soon after he'd been convicted for murder, the will bequeathing the stock to Colin. Once home, he'd taken his findings to his attorney, the stock and its dividends soon in Colin's own name.

Finances now available to renovate Briarwood and his mother agreeing to help, he and Eileen, along with his grandmother Kirby had returned to Haven Labor Day weekend of last year to employ Jonathan Baker as overseer to the complete restoration of Colin's beloved childhood home. They had returned every weekend possible to choreograph the project. He'd saved his grandmother's suite until last, desiring to supervise the renovation himself. Arriving at Briarwood a week ago to begin his three-week vacation from the agency, he had entered the Duchess's sitting room the next day to see if her morning was "good" or "bad." He'd wanted to get her opinion for the décor of the suite and share the news about his engagement to Julie the night before. At first thinking she was napping, he drew nearer to her daybed, realizing a moment later his grandmother need no longer yearn for Stuart. She was now with him.

Colin turned as a shadow of a person fell across his father's headstone, smiling at Julie as she walked up beside him. "Mrs. Frakes said I would find you here," she said, smiling. She stood on her tiptoes to receive his kiss. "Are you okay?"

He smiled wanly. "Yes. Just seeking closure."

"Did your appointment today with your aunt's attorney go well?"

Colin laughed. "I'd say so. I thought Mr. Jordan would to have to carry me out of his office on a stretcher by the time he finished reading the Duchess's last will and testament. It seems Uncle Max wasn't the only Lambert savvy about Wall Street. She'd more than tripled her inheritance from my great-grandfather, Walter Delaney. And she'd deeded everything over in my name with the exception of the generous endowment to Mrs. Frakes and Grace Missionary Church. It will take some time before I can grasp it all."

Colin grinned. "The best way I can describe my meeting with Mr. Jordan is leaving an inheritance for our children and grandchildren won't likely be a problem for us. I've already started praying for extra wisdom in finances."

Colin pulled his fiancée to him, kissing her long and deep. Although their wedding was only three months away—Julie had insisted on a Christmas wedding in the living room at Briarwood—the wait seemed endless. The renovation of Briarwood almost complete and the closing for the purchase of a sister marketing agency in Tulsa only a few weeks away, Colin breathed a prayer of thankfulness for God's goodness. Colin would manage the new business while his assistant Tom Thorpe would oversee the agency in St. Louis. After their honeymoon over the holidays, Colin and his bride would return to Briarwood to make their home, he and Julie commuting to Tulsa each day to their respective employment.

"How were things at the paper today?" he asked, unlocking her car door.

"You know how Fridays tend to be rush, rush, rush to meet the deadline for both the Saturday and Sunday editions. But okay in every other aspect." Julie glanced at her watch. "I made good time today. Mrs. Frakes is holding dinner, waiting for your return to the house."

Colin took her arm. "Well, we best be on our way. If we're too late she might insist I wash every dish."

Julie laughed. "That'll be the day. It's my guess she won't let you near her new kitchen."

When the family had gathered in the den following dinner, Eileen's mother stood up from the sofa. "Family, I'd like to make an announcement." The four other occupants in the room gave her their full attention.

Mrs. Kirby set her gaze on Colin. "I won't be returning to St. Louis with you when you go home. I've decided if it's okay with you, I will make my home at Briarwood. Mrs. Frakes and I have talked this over, and she doesn't mind at all." She turned to Eileen. "You've been very gracious opening your home to me, but my heart is in Haven. I'll still visit you often. St. Louis is only an hour flight away." She glanced around the room, focusing on her grandson. "I think I could be of some use to Mrs. Frakes. Neither of us are spring chickens anymore, but we believe between the two of us, we can make Briarwood comfortable for you and your soon bride-to-be."

Colin scooted toward the edge of the sofa. "Well, Grandmother, I have no objection at all." He glanced at Julie, grinning. "It's not like we don't have enough room in the place."

Julie stood giving Mrs. Kirby a hug. "I'm sure you'll be great company for Mrs. Frakes."

The housekeeper nodded. "We get along fine."

Eileen stood as well. "I have an announcement of my own. Nothing is official, mind you, but I've been seeing a gentleman who attends our church for the past few months and I think he's on the verge of asking me to marry him. I had intended to turn him down, not wanting to disrupt Mother's life again, but the Lord seems to be working things out for all of us."

A few minutes later Colin and Julie took their leave to watch the sunset from the wicker loveseat on the front porch. "You know Julie, I miss the Duchess so much already, but I am grateful she's no longer in the clutches of Alzheimer's disease. At times it seemed intolerable when she didn't recognize me. A part of me aches and will for a long time, but in my heart I rejoice because she doesn't have to suffer anymore."

Julie snuggled closer to him. "Colin, that's understandable. No one desires to see their loved ones in pain."

"She gave me some good advice right after my father died—I'm so glad she never knew how he died—but it took a few months before I felt able to apply her words to my life. She said I shouldn't discard my happiness for something I could never change or understand, but allow Christ to be the Author and Finisher of my faith." He kissed Julie on the tip of her nose. "I'm so glad I finally followed her instruction."

Julie grew thoughtful. "Since we are writing our own wedding vows, what do you think about inserting into them that part about Christ as the Author and Finisher of our faith?"

The sun sinking below the horizon, Colin pulled Julie close. "I think the idea perfect—Christ, the Author and the Finisher, Christ, the Alpha and the Omega, Christ, the Beginning and the End of our lifetime together."